STRANGERS AND PILGRIMS SERIES

Book Three

Farmer and Emile's Granddaughter

JANEE

Written By

John and Patty Probst

XULON
PRESS

Copyright © 2007 by John and Patty Probst

Janee
By John and Patty Probst

Printed in the United States of America

ISBN 978-1-60477-217-3

Unless otherwise indicated, Bible quotations are taken from the King James Version.

Cover illustration by Yakovetic

www.xulonpress.com

For Rich & Cindy

Janee's story will
reach deep inside
and the Lord will
touch you. Be
Blessed dear ones!

Love in Christ,
Johnny & Patty
Mar. 2009

Dedicated with love to our dear Britney, who has given us a taste of the celebrity life. Her strong faith encouraged us to press on in our writing.

With a great sense of pride to daughters Marla and Jessica, who have proven themselves able and courageous fighters in the arena of life.

To daughters Missy and Sandy, though living far away are always near to our hearts.

To special friends Joe and Samii, whose prayers and input were invaluable to the outcome of Janee.

FOREWORD

🌹

Jesus told his followers;

For the kingdom of heaven is like unto a man that is an householder, which went out early in the morning to hire labourers into his vineyard.

And when he had agreed with the labourers for a penny a day, he sent them into his vineyard.

And he went out about the third hour, and saw others standing idle in the marketplace,

And said unto them; Go ye also into the vineyard, and whatsoever is right I will give you. And they went their way.

Again he went out about the sixth and ninth hour, and did likewise.

And about the eleventh hour he went out, and found others standing idle, and saith unto them, Why stand ye here all the day idle?

They say unto him, Because no man hath hired us. He saith unto them, Go ye also into the vineyard, and whatsoever is right, that shall ye receive.

So when evening was come, the lord of the vineyard saith unto his steward, Call the labourers, and give them their hire, beginning from the last unto the first.

And when they came that were hired about the eleventh hour, they received every man a penny.

But when the first came, they supposed that they should have received more; and they likewise received every man a penny.

And when they had received it, they murmured against the goodman of the house,

Saying, These last have wrought but one hour, and thou hast made them equal unto us, which have borne the burden and heat of the day.

But he answered one of them, and said, Friend, I do thee no wrong: didst not thou agree with me for a penny?

Take that thine is, and go thy way: I will give unto this last, even as unto thee.

Matthew 20:1-14 KJV

To God be the glory, great things He hath done; so loved He the world that he gave us His Son, Who yielded His life and atonement for sin, And opened the life-gate that all may go in.

O perfect redemption, the purchase of blood, To every believer the promise of God; The vilest offender who truly believes, That moment from Jesus a pardon receives.

Great things He hath taught us, great things He hath done, And great our rejoicing thro' Jesus the Son; But purer, and higher, and greater will be Our wonder, our transport, when Jesus we see.

Fanny J. Crosby

CONTENTS

Chapter 1

Tragic Words

🌹

The news hit Janee with a blow so hard it was impossible for her little nine-year old mind to comprehend. All she knew was that the pleasant memories of a laugh filled dinner outing to Hollywood earlier that evening were ripped to pieces with the ringing of the telephone and shocking news.

She ran to her bedroom and huddled on the bed, frightened and alone. She was confused and did not understand. She had watched in eager anticipation when her father Harold announced it was Uncle Clifton on the phone. She wondered in curiosity when she saw her mother Leah take the phone and her happy smile go straight. Tears filled her eyes as she dropped the phone grabbing for Janee's daddy.

The stabbing words kept filling Janee's mind, "Grandpa Farmer has been killed". What did that mean? She just talked to him three nights before! Where was grandpa, in Heaven? She didn't want him to be there – she wanted him home where she could visit him and grandma next summer.

Her heart cried out now to call him on the telephone – just to hear him say, "Well, Janee, I be plumb surprised but reckon mighty pleased to get your call, even ifen it be late. Oh, I forgot its Saturday and ya get to stay up late. Grandma an I be powerful pleased about yer acting in the movies an we been pacen the floor here waiten for yer new one ta get up here ta our theatre." Then Janee would laugh, then grow serious and close with, "I miss you grandpa, and grandma too, and Dusty. I love you."

"We love ya too with hearts as big as these Oregon Mountains. Goodbye Janee…"

Janee hid her face in her arms and cried in frightened sobs. She could hear her mother's loud grieving wails and her father's low consoling voice in the other room. The only image Janee had in her mind now was that of a bird which once frequented their back yard. Janee kept feed and water out for it. She slowly had gained the bird's trust. She was thrilled the day she got it to eat out of her hand, but devastated some weeks later when she found it dead amongst the flowers. She never told her parents, but placed the dead bird on a bed of leaves. She believed with all the faith she could gather that her friend was only sleeping and would wake the next morning. She arose with the sun and ran out the back door into the yard fully expecting her little bird to greet her with a song. Instead, to her horror, it was covered in ants and bugs. It was disgusting!

This image transformed into a shocking picture of her grandfather lying somewhere on the cold ground covered with ants, bugs, and worms. She shook, her sobs turned into gulps of air.

Her bedroom door opened and her mother and daddy quietly sat down on the bed beside her and all three of them held each other closely without anyone speaking. Janee felt safe in her parents loving arms, and although she had a hundred questions, she wanted to ask – needed desperately to ask- she lacked the will or courage.

It was finally her daddy who spoke.

"Janee, your Grandfather Farmer was killed in a hunting accident this morning. They just found – his - him – not long ago."

Her mother began crying again, while a strange feeling began surging through Janee, refusing to accept those tragic words.

Chapter 2

Questions with no Answers

🌹

Janee was not a child who hid from her problems in sleep. That night was the longest of her life. She prayed to God that it was all a mistake and that her grandfather would be alive in the morning. She begged for a miracle, yet a dread settled upon her prayers that it was just as her little bird remained dead – so would grandpa. She finally cried herself into a restless and fitful sleep even though she was nestled in her mother's arms.

The times she awoke, and they were often, she could hear the low voices of her mother and daddy. Those pieces of her parent's conversations were the only thing that gave her some sort of clue to what was going to happen over the next few days.

The phone rang several times in the night waking Janee. Other times Janee was conscious of her mother or daddy calling out and talking to different people. She heard her mother on the phone to Grandma Emile and knew they were crying.

"How could someone be so careless and mistake Daddy for a deer?" Leah declared loudly. "He should be hung!"

Leah's exasperation and pain broke in to more crying. Janee felt an anger and hate for the man who shot her grandpa began to pulse through her veins.

"Mom! What in the hell was daddy doing out on the ranch? He hasn't been out there since we moved off the place," Leah was loud again!

"What do you mean you don't know? Didn't he tell you? I can't believe this – What?"

Janee could hear her mother mutter words that didn't make sense, and then she was shouting into the phone.

"What! The coward ran away and didn't tell anyone until dark? Oh God, what if daddy was alive and – and – oh – oh!"

"Leah – Leah – shh- shh it's all right." Janee could hear her father trying to calm her mother.

Janee got out of bed and went to her parents. They had hung up the phone and her daddy was holding her mother.

"I want to talk to grandma," Janee whimpered.

Leah held out her hand.

"Oh, Janee, I don't think this is a good time."

"Please, let me call her," Janee was insistent.

"Janee, it's in the middle of the night and your grandma is so tired."

"Please, I need her," Janee cried.

Leah started to protest again and Harold touched her lips with his hand. She looked at him and there were unspoken words of agreement.

"Only for a – little," her mother nodded the ok.

Janee took the receiver off the hook and dialed the number. There was the long static pause, then the signal it was ringing grandma's house.

"Hello," Grandma Emile's voice sounded weak.

"Grandma."

"Janee?"

"Grandma, I wish to speak to grandfather please." She used the acting voice she had learned for the movies.

There was a long pause before her grandma spoke.

"Oh Janee, I wish with all my heart you could!"

Suddenly, a grief so deep it threatened drowning her flooded Janee's heart. She broke down in pleading sobs.

"Please, let me talk to Papa, Grandma, let me talk to Papa!"

"I can't Janee; he's not here – now."

"Where is he? I want Papa!"

"Jesus took him home to be with Him."

"No! Why would Jesus want to hurt us? Papa's home is here! I want Papa here – in your house – with you!"

"Oh, Janee, my heart is breaking and I know yours is too, but we must be brave."

"I don't want to be brave, I want Papa!"

Janee was crying uncontrollably as her mother gently took the phone from her hands.

Chapter 3

Understanding Gained

The next morning was a flurry of preparations to leave for Oregon. Janee heard her daddy talking about taking a train and calling in the night to check on tickets. She caught parts of conversation that they would go into Springfield and they would need to get someone from Douglas Landing to pick them up.

Uncle Walter called around the time the sun was beginning to rise, waking Janee from sleep. He was telling her daddy something that he was agreeing with, but Janee had no idea what it was all about so she went back to sleep.

Her mother was packing bags when Janee came out of her bedroom.

"Are we riding the train?" Janee asked stretching with a long yawn.

"No," her mother replied not looking up from folding clothes for the suitcase.

"I heard Daddy-"

"I know, but the train left too early this morning for us to get tickets. The next one isn't until tomorrow. Daddy says that if we leave soon we can be there late tonight. So hurry and get dressed. We are leaving as soon as we have breakfast."

"Where's Daddy?"

"Asleep. He's been up all night and needs some rest if he is to drive."

"What did Uncle Walter say?"

"He is taking Uncle Clifton, Aunt Rachel, and your cousin David Lee in his plane to Douglas Landing. They will get there before we do and can help your grandma. Now hurry along, so we can get on the road."

The trip to Douglas Landing was gloomy. Any other time, Janee would have been so excited she couldn't wait to get there. This time held no joy, and for once she welcomed the seemingly endless hours of highway.

The question of why would a God who loved her let such an awful tragedy occur kept bombarding her thoughts. Once she asked her parents the question.

"It was an accident," was their response.

Janee was smart enough to rationalize that there were no accidents with God, so that answer was unacceptable to her. The longer she pondered this, the more turbulent her mind became.

She hoped that seeing her grandma and the rest of the family would relieve her distress, but that was not to be.

She and David Lee became lost in all the preparations for their grandpa's funeral and the constant shuffle in and out the house of well - wishers. One in particular had a profound effect on the family, and it occurred the day after Janee's family arrived.

"Isn't that Rollin Graves, the banker, getting out of that car?" Aunt Rachel asked, curious.

Grandma Emile peered out the window with Rachel.

"I declare, it is."

Janee ran to the window to see a white haired, distinguished gentleman approaching the front door. Walter greeted him.

"Please come in Mr. Graves," Walter spoke quietly.

The old man went immediately to Emile, taking her hand.

"Emile, I am stunned at this tragic news."

The family made a place for him to sit.

"It is kind of you to come Rollin. I know Farmer always carried a quiet respect for you."

"And I for him – for your family. I grieved when you lost the ranch. I told him that the morning he was shot."

"You talked to him?" Everyone jumped with the same question.

"Yes, I must confess with sadness I was part of the reason he was on the ranch. I never dreamed he would go right then for God's sake."

"I don't understand." Tears blinded Emile.

Janee ran and sat next to her. Who was this man who claimed responsibility for her grandpa's death? Her mind was racing!

"Yes, I came to town to make an offer – to your family and the Brooks. I was surprised to see Farmer come in the café. We had coffee."

"You didn't know this, Mom?" Leah blurted.

"No," Emile shook her head, "Farmer left early before I woke up."

"Let Mr. Graves tell his story," Walter spoke impatiently.

"I told Farmer I had worked a deal with Cascade Mountains to buy the ranch back at a very reasonable price. I would make the loan."

"O dear Lord!" Emile cried out. "Farmer said he would never go back unless he – he –." She couldn't go on.

"He was reliving his dream," Walter concluded.

"Yes, I believe so," Rolling Graves stood up to take leave.

"I am so sorry, Emile, and to the rest of you. I know it isn't the time or place right now, but my offer still stands for your family."

Chapter 4

A Happy Thought

The morning of Janee's grandpa's funeral had dawned to a grey, dismal sky. Janee always loved going to church, but not today. The last few days were more than Janee could bear. She had witnessed and experienced so much grief and heartache, she couldn't stand it. She wanted no more.

Her mother and daddy were already up, letting Janee sleep. She could hear voices in the living room, and sounds of the preparation of breakfast came from the kitchen. Absent was laughter! For two days Uncle Walter and Uncle Clifton attempted to make light the conversations to lessen the pain; however, their jokes went flat on everyone else. Even David Lee, who laughed at anything, had sensed the darkness over the family, and remained solemn.

Janee just wanted to be happy! She had learned from acting, when doing a happy scene go somewhere in your memory that will generate the mood you wish to be in. The sounds from the kitchen directed her thoughts to a very joyous time when she was seven. She was staying with her grandparents for the summer and had just awakened from her first night there.

Her grandparents were talking in the kitchen. Smells and sounds of sizzling bacon made her hungry. Grandmother was cooking breakfast. She heard her grandfather's hearty low laugh. He was no doubt teasing grandmother. He liked to do that!

Janee couldn't wait to see them! She bounded out of bed and ran to the kitchen.

"Grandmother! Grandfather! I'm awake!" she announced.

"Good morning, Janee!" Emile greeted her and scooped her into her arms for a morning hug.

"Well, I reckon ya ta be a pretty sight this mornin'. Do tell, ya remind me shore nuff o' yer ma," Farmer exclaimed.

"Go wash. Breakfast is ready," Emile instructed.

Fresh air and the mountains gave Janee a ferocious appetite - and everything looked so yummy.

After Farmer said "Grace," Janee had a strong desire to pray.

"May I also say a prayer?" she asked.

"Yes, of course," Emile acted surprised, yet pleased.

"Dear Father, thank you for letting me come stay with grandfather and grandmother and have such a wonderful time. I hope I don't get fat because I think I'm gonna eat a lot!"

Everyone laughed and dug in. It was one of the happiest times of Janee's life!

"I read me a story in the Bible this mornin' I reckon is right hard to imagine," Farmer paused as he took a swig of coffee. "This fella was tryin' to run away from his Father an' got his self swallered up by a whale."

"Oh, I know that story, grandfather, but you didn't get it right," Janee piped up.

"What?" Farmer was shocked and puzzled.

"Yes! It was Pinocchio, grandfather, but he was trying to find his father, not run away from him. That's when the monster whale swallowed him up. And don't forget Pinocchio had Jiminy with him."

"Who?" Farmer was lost. Emile giggled.

"The cricket! Jiminy Cricket!"

Farmer scratched his head as he eyed his granddaughter.

"An' where did ya hear this tall tale, Miss Janee?" he inquired.

"I saw it in the movie, silly," she laughed.

Farmer started to speak, but Emile reached over and stopped him.

"You better stop while you're ahead," she said playfully.

"Don't reckon one ever gets ahead o' this young'n," Farmer smiled as he watched Janee devour her breakfast.

Later Farmer took Janee out back to greet Dusty.

Dusty was as anxious to see Janee and stood at the fence pawing the ground. Janee ran to the horse!

"Oh, Farmer, is Dusty safe for her?" Emile asked. She stood on the back porch.

"Reckon he's gettin' too old ta go fast, but the mustang is still sure on his feet," Farmer replied pulling the bridle over the horse's ears.

"Ya remember all I taught ya thet time ya was here with yer Ma and Pa?" Farmer asked Janee.

"Oh, yes, grandfather! I'm a good learner, and I used what you taught me in a movie I played in last winter."

"So's I won't hev ta tell ya all again?" Farmer growled with a sly smile. He threw blanket and saddle on Dusty's back.

"Oh, no, sir! I'm ready!" She was excited and eager to ride.

Farmer lifted her up onto the saddle and handed her the reins. Janee turned Dusty around toward the open field. With a "Yaah!" Janee sent the horse into a gallop.

Janee felt free and alive with the wind rushing in her face and through her hair.

"Faster, Dusty! Faster!" and the mustang flew across the grass to the trees.

"Fly, Dusty, like a shooting star," Janee whispered, "take me over the mountains to where you are. Take me away from here!"

The sound of the bedroom door opening broke her daydream.

"Janee," she heard her mother call. "Get dressed. Breakfast will be ready soon. Guess who arrived in the night? It's Auntie Susan and Uncle Andrew, and grandpa's brothers and their families. They are anxious to see you. We must hurry, Janee, the service is at 10:00."

Chapter 5

Farmer's Funeral

Janee desperately tried to hold on to her happy thought and enjoy the family, but the magnitude of all the sadness around her made happiness keep slipping away. She could only see the grey sky and think about how everything she truly cared for was taken away. First it was her little bird friend – then Dusty – now Papa. When Janee got in the car she buried her face in her arms. She felt her mother slip her arm around her and hold her tight. They both wept. The procession to the church did not take long enough.

"We're here," her father spoke softly.

Janee looked out to see they had arrived at the Church in the Woods. There were cars and people everywhere. She knew she must go inside, but didn't want to. She lacked the will – she felt lifeless.

Donald and Beth Parrigan came to the car and opened the doors. They held Janee's mother and daddy for a long time without any words spoken.

Janee saw her Uncle Clifton and Aunt Rachel and little David Lee walking towards the church with the Baltman's. The Brook's car just pulled up with her Uncle Walter, the cars from Texas were last.

"Take my hand," her mother spoke sadly.

Janee began to whimper like a little baby.

Outside the church they were escorted through a wall of faces. The inside was packed, standing room only. The family was seated in the front. Janee gasped! She caught sight of her Papa's face in the open casket. Her heart sank in hopelessness – she was beside herself!

Some women sang several hymns, one she remembered from going to church. Today, Janee refused to sing.

The preacher who had been to the house several times ministering to the family, stepped to the pulpit to speak, but his words fell on deaf ears. Janee's mind was draped in gloom. She refused to look at her grandpa, to be brave for him and not cry, but when she glanced at her mother and grandma and understanding their grief that also filled her heart – she suddenly felt so small and alone. She couldn't help herself and began sobbing.

When the pastor concluded his message, he made an announcement.

"I have had so many people ask to say a few words and the family has given their consent, but I must ask that statements be brief and only a few. Who will be first?"

"Farmer was my best friend," Joe Baltman spoke up.

"And mine," Donald Parrigan added.

"Farmer and Emile were the first to our house when we got word of our son. . ." Gordon Brooks choked, putting his hand on his wife's shoulder.

"They took me in," Beth Parrigan said, remembering the day Farmer found her on the side of the road.

"He tol me bout Jesus," a man by the wall shouted.

"He kept our family from starving during the depression," a woman on the back pew shared from a grateful heart.

When it appeared no one else was going to speak, a man who was standing in the corner stepped forward to the isle. He talked haltingly and shuffled around nervously.

"You don't know me – but you know of me. I am the man – who – who – shot Farmer Trevor. I am so sorry. I can't function – sleep – I've been in turmoil. I came to ask – no – beg - your forgiveness. I know I – can't..."

By now Walter and Clifton were on their feet.

"Get him out of here before I kill him!" Clifton screamed.

Emile and Rachel grabbed his arm. The erupting confusion in the church scared Janee. She wanted to run, but sat paralyzed.

"No Clifton!" Emile was firm. "What would your father want you to do?"

"I'm leaving," the man spoke in sorrow. "I didn't mean to disrupt. What I said was from a broken heart that seeks..."

"Shut yer mouth!" Walter snapped. "Ya could a picked a better time an place!"

Janee got the courage to look back to see some men roughly helping her grandpa's killer out the door. She only saw the back of his head, but knew she hated him.

The preacher led in prayer hoping to defuse the tension.

The service concluded, a large number of people filed by the casket to pay their last respects to a man they had known and loved. In a few moments, only the family remained, and they gathered around the casket.

Shock and fear hit Janee when she looked on her grandpa. He was so pale and still. No familiar smile upon his lips. No sound of that deep voice – no hearty laughter – only silence.

Then the preacher who stayed with the family made a statement meant to be consoling.

"Jesus has taken Farmer home."

At that Grandma Emile went to pieces. She fell onto the casket clutching a handle and patting her husband's face.

"Oh, Farmer, don't leave me!"

Janee heard her grandma's pleas and sobs. This became more than Janee could stand! She flew to her grandma's side and clung to the handle of her grandpa's casket as though her life depended on it.

"Papa! Papa!" she cried out in her little shrill voice. "Don't go! Don't leave us!"

The words the preacher spoke kept ringing in her head. 'Jesus took him home, Jesus took him home.'

This Jesus who would hurt her so was not the Jesus she knew in church back home. This Jesus was a selfish monster!

"I don't want you to go with Jesus! She yelled. Her mother and daddy were trying to loosen her grip on the handle. She fought! Others were assisting and consoling her wailing grandma who had nearly collapsed.

"Your home is here Papa! Please don't go with Jesus! I want you here!"

Then a rage Janee had never experienced rose inside of her until it burst into a furious flame.

"I hate you! I hate you! I hate you, Jesus. I never want to hear of you again! Go away!"

Janee fell into her mother's arms.

Chapter 6

The When and Why of Change
🙊

After Farmer's funeral and burial, before the families went their separate ways, a decision needed to be made on the ranch. Janee remembered heated words of disagreement between her mother and uncles over whether to purchase the land back. Some of them blamed the ranch for Farmer's death.

"Why should we want it?" her mother blazed.

"You were born there!" Walter retaliated.

The arguing went on long after Janee fell asleep. The last words Janee heard was her grandma stating resolutely, "I can never live there again."

However, because the deal Roland Graves offered was so undeniably attractive, the decision was made next morning to purchase the old homestead and keep it in the family. Grandma Emile would remain in her house on Peppertree and Breach Road.

Another change was with Janee.

Before her grandpa's death Janee loved going to church. She attended often with her mother and dad, liked Sunday school and the music. Janee had a good singing voice and on occasion was invited to sing a solo in the morning service. Going to church was invigorating to her young mind, and she was known to get into heavy and often heated discussions with teachers over Bible stories or concepts. She seemed to thrive on ideas that were fresh to her and was unafraid to take on anybody, even the pastor, in a lively debate. Leah or Harold usually had to rescue any unfortunate soul who picked an argument with their daughter.

Going to church with her grandparents was a treat. The church was in a beautiful setting, and it was so peaceful there. Janee laughed at some of the member's speech and way of doing things, but inside her heart she loved their simple and uncomplicated ways. When any Sunday arrived, she was always eager and anxious to go – that was *before* her grandpa's funeral.

Something happened to her that day which changed the course of the path she was walking.

The instant Janee screamed, 'I hate you, Jesus. I never want to hear of you again! Go away!' something as cold as ice settled in her young heart. It was as if something bright and lovely vacated and the dark icy chill of winter took its place.

At first it frightened her, but after some time she would learn to embrace it and foster its growth, because it afforded her a sense of power.

On the drive to the cemetery, Harold and Leah had attempted to calm their distraught daughter.

"We know you are hurt and upset, but you couldn't mean what you said to Jesus, you love Him so."

"No I don't! I meant every word! If Jesus loves me how could he take my grandpa? I can't love Him anymore – I won't! He doesn't care about me or what happens to me! I think He likes seeing us hurt and cry! I hate Him!"

From that point on in her life she no longer had any interest in church. She loathed going, and every Sunday became a knockdown drag out fight between her and her parents. She refused to sing in church anymore and caused major disruptions in classes and eventually in the worship service itself.

Harold and Leah were frustrated and heartsick over the change in their daughter. Janee had gone forward when she was seven to receive Christ as her Savior and was baptized two weeks later, so they held desperately to the hope at least their daughter was saved.

"That was a big act!" Janee sneered. "I went through the baloney because it looked like fun."

After her grandpa had been laid to rest and Janee had time to think, she made a vow.

"I'll never allow myself to hurt that much ever again," she mouthed the words out loud into the quietness of the dark of night.

The determined nine-year old, was true to her word. She shielded herself from hurt so much she succeeded in killing any love she had for anyone, starting with God Himself. The last ounce of love and semblance of compassion that held on in Janee Stemper was for her Grandma Emile. Janee began to resent more and more Emile's constant speaking about religious matters and viewed it as preaching to her. Eventually, this last ounce of love, too, would evaporate, and Janee's visits, phone calls and letters cease. The absence of love in Janee's life dried her up like a desert – even taking her tears!

This girl who could express love or turn on the tears in a scene she was shooting for a movie was equally able to turn off those feelings and tears, submerging them so deeply inside they would never be heard from again.

Chapter 7

Some Good Advice

It was now fall of 1959. Janee was just a few months' shy of her eighteenth birthday. She had just arrived home from a shopping spree with some of her friends. Her best friend, Paige Wenger, was still with her.

"Your agent just called Janee," her mother announced as the two teens walked into the kitchen.

"What did old pimple face want?" Janee laughed sarcastically. Paige thought Janee's remark funny and snickered.

"Don't say that, Janee!" Leah scolded, "He has gotten you some good work."

"He's an embarrassment! He's old, and his face is – full – of those acne craters, and when he laughs – it's like – this." Janee mimicked her agent's facial expressions and laugh, to the delight of Paige. Even her mom had to laugh!

"You are so goofy," Leah playfully shoved her daughter. "You are so busy poking fun, you have no idea what your agent wanted."

"Okay – Mother! What – did – my – agent – want – of me?" Janee got close to her mother's face snapping her teeth as if to bite Leah's nose.

Leah went on about preparing supper as though she weren't paying attention to Janee's antics, but a sly smile curled the corners of her lips.

"Only that he was able to get a director to watch some clips of your roles. The man liked what he saw and wants you to come to his house tomorrow evening to talk about a part in a new movie."

"Who is – the director?" Janee asked cautiously.

"Someone named Aaron Mocknour," Leah replied casually without even looking at her daughter.

Janee felt her heart stop.

"Aaron Mocknour!" she screamed.

"Is he good?" Paige asked, searching her friend's face.

"Is he good? He's about the hottest new talent to hit Hollywood. He did 'Raging Jealousy'!"

Janee and Paige started screaming and jumping up and down. Leah, who had hidden her excitement, joined in.

Janee couldn't sleep that night. Her head was in a spin! She was excited and frightened all at the same time. She picked up her phone and dialed Grandmother Emile. She got a sleepy response.

"Hello."

"Grandma, it's me. I'm so excited and nervous I can't sleep."

"What is it, Janee?"

"Would you believe Aaron Mocknour wants to talk to me – me! About a part in a new movie."

"Who is Aaron Mocknour, dear?"

"What! You don't know who Mocknour is?"

"Is he a movie star?"

"Nooo. He's the greatest movie director to hit Hollywood. He wants me in his movie!"

There was a long silence. So long Janee inquired, "Grandma?"

"I'm thinking – and praying…"

"I don't need you praying, I need you excited with me!"

"Janee, you know I am. My hearts is pounding and I'm thrilled for you!"

Another pause.

"But?" Janee sought to search her grandma's thoughts.

"We make so many of our decisions based on experience, child, you are so young and even though you have tasted many things you still lack experience."

"Grandma, I'm not a child," Janee bristled. "I'm almost eighteen."

"So young and beautiful and I worry so. I read and hear of the evil surrounding the movies."

"Well, I'm not blind or stupid."

"I'm not saying you are. May I read the words of a very wise man?"

"Grandpa's?"

"No, but I know he would agree with them."

A long breath – a sigh – and Janee consented.

"Just a minute, dear, while I look this up."

Janee drummed her fingernails on her nightstand as she waited.

"I take it that Mr. Mocknour is very wealthy?" Emile asked when she came back to the phone.

"You have no idea."

"These are words from Proverbs 23. 'When thou sittest to eat with a ruler, consider diligently what is before thee: and put a knife to thy throat, if thou be a person given to appetite. Be not desirous of his dainties; for they are deceitful meat. Labor not to be rich: cease from thine own wisdom. Wilt thou set thine eyes upon that which is not? For riches certainly make themselves wings; they fly away as an eagle toward heaven. Eat not the bread of him that hath an evil eye, neither desire thou his dainty meats; for as he thinketh in his heart, so is he. Eat and drink, saith he to thee; but his heart is not with thee-"

"Are you implying that Aaron Mocknour is evil?" Janee cut her grandma short. "How can you say that when you don't even know him?"

"Janee, I'm not. I'm just wanting you to be - "

"Fine grandma! I just needed you to be excited with me, not give me a lecture."

"You know I love you so very much, and worry about you, Janee. I am excited for you! I'm not lecturing you. It's just that I don't want anything to ruin you."

"I've had roles in twenty-two movies since I was little. Am I ruined?"

"No dear, but – somehow – this sounds different."

"It is Grandma! This could be my chance at a very big role."

"I'll ask God to give you protection and guidance."

"Keep God out of it! Damn, grandma, give me some credit for brains."

With that Janee slammed the phone down on the receiver.

Chapter 8

Meeting Mocknour

A aron Mocknour sent his driver and limo to bring Janee, her parents, and her agent to his house. Situated atop the mountain above Beverly Hills, the night view of the Los Angeles basin was spectacular. They had visited some pretty fancy places but Mocknour's house was beyond compare.

"Wow!" Janee exclaimed breathlessly as they climbed out of the limo to look around.

The driver, who had introduced himself as Chickey, announced their arrival at the security gate. A man who was obviously an employee of Mr. Mocknours stood near the drive ready to greet them.

"Greetings. My name is Paltow. Please follow me." His manner was not warm – polite, but curt. He led them through a garden like walk to the front door.

Janee was taken aback when she walked into a house full of noisy people. She was bewildered, although she knew better. Hollywood moguls always had parties going on.

An extremely good-looking man turned when he saw their entrance. Janee caught her breath. She recognized the director.

He held out his hands to her.

"You grace my home with your beauty, Miss Janee Stemper." He spoke in a deep voice that flowed as smooth and rich as creamy chocolate. He gently kissed her hand.

Janee felt her face flush hot as she glanced around the room. A few of the guests eyed her curiously. Mocknour sensed her discomfort in the crowded room.

"Don't mind them," he smiled. "They are left over from last night – or was it the night before. Some of them believe they live here. Most I only tolerate as long as they are interesting. When they become boorish, I dismiss them."

He stopped to look deep into Janee's eyes to make sure he had driven his point home.

Janee broke away from his penetrating gaze.

"These are my parents, Harold and Leah Stemper. You know my agent."

Mocknour firmly shook Harold's hand and gently taking Leah's hand he lingered with the kiss. Leah's neck reddened. He released her hand and spun on his heels.

"Come! Business first, then when the deal is done we celebrate."

Mr. Mocknour led them though a crowd that seemed programmed like robots, smiling, jabbering, but nothing else – except for one. He tugged on Janee's dress.

"Janee Stemper!"

Immediately Aaron Mocknour stood between Janee and the stranger. No introductions were made, and the man disappeared.

Mocknour took them to a remote place in the house. Janee was awestruck with the expansive size of his home. She could easily get lost in it.

They came to a set of beautifully finished mahogany doors, which swung open wide to a very plush study. A cozy fire crackled in a rock fireplace, filling the room with dreamy warmth. The rich finished mantel above displayed pictures and awards. Bookcases were lined across two walls boasting a respectable library. Directly in front of the doors and to the side of the fireplace sat a large desk with matching wood to the doors – all, custom made, no doubt. Over-stuffed couches and chairs surrounded the desk. Coffee and end tables were accessible. The study provoked an atmosphere for work that aggressively pushed away any dreamy mood. Janee surmised that many a creative idea was born here.

"What a lovely – office," Leah hesitantly complimented.

Janee could tell her parents were intimidated.

"Thank you," Mocknour smiled and motioned for them to be seated. He sat facing Janee, staring at her for some time before he spoke.

"I viewed some of your work, Miss Stemper, and I was impressed."

"Thank you Mr. Mocknour," Janee stammered.

Her tongue felt thick, sticking to the roof of her mouth. She imagined it made a popping sound inside with each word she spoke.

Mocknour had the uncanny ability to read her mind.

"I'm forgetting my hospitality. Let me fix us all a drink."

"She's not old enough to drink – alcohol," her agent spoke up.

"Dummy rot!" Mocknour replied. "If Miss Stemper is going to make it in Hollywood, she'll need to learn, a drink won't hurt, and I'll make it mild."

"Only one," her parents spoke up.

Janee burned with embarrassment. She hated feeling inadequate, not in control, and made to appear like a child. She flashed a look at her agent that made it clear to shut-up!

Mocknour saw that look also and smiled triumphantly as he passed out the drinks.

Janee took a sip of hers. It burned all the way to her stomach making her choke. Then her throat cooled. The drink tasted of an unfamiliar fruit flavor – she liked it.

"After I viewed your clips, Miss Stemper, I said to myself, 'I must have this young woman for a part in my upcoming movie'."

"Oh! That would be wonderful Mr. Mocknour! I can do the role – I know I can! What is it?"

Mocknour laughed at her girlish exuberance.

"It's the story of some hip high school kids, their music, their lives, loves, competitions, including a drag race."

"I love it!" Janee screamed. She could hardly sit still.

"What's the title of the film?" her agent asked.

"The script is nearing completion, but we don't even have a working title yet. Janee, this movie will be a musical."

"I sing like – well – let me show you."

"She sang in church when she was little, even solos," Harold added.

Janee went into a song she had done in an earlier movie along with the choreography.

Mocknour watched her carefully.

"The film will have dance sequences as well."

"I can dance too!" Janee transitioned into another song, kicking her heels off into the deep carpet, and commenced a lively dance routine in rhythm to her singing.

"Bravo – bravo!" her agent exclaimed, clapping enthusiastically. "I told you her talent was extraordinary, Mr. Mocknour."

"Yes…Yes," he spoke thoughtfully, lost in thought. Then suddenly it was like something energized him. He stood up to address them.

"What I tell you is confidential – you must tell no one. Agreed? No one!"

They all nodded their heads. All eyes were focused intently on the director.

"In this business, ideas are money. Timing can mean gain or loss. I have spies out with their ears to the ground. They are very good – and very expensive. They have picked up that

Ross Hunter's people over at Universal are kicking an idea around about a college campus and town. It will come out in '61 sometime. They don't have a director signed on yet, but have talked to a lead actor – and a blond actress who we don't know her identity – yet. We have the jump on them – ha! Already have a script – almost – and the director is tops. With rock and roll busting all over the charts, the country is prime for a high school setting. Universal is targeting the college crowd. Hell, they are too busy to go to movies – but teenagers will flock to see my movie, and drag their parents. Right?"

Harold and Leah smiled in agreement.

"Well, I have a lead actress in mind. I just have to get her signed up."

"Oh my!" Leah exclaimed. The agent and her daddy looked pleased. Janee's heart was racing.

"Janee, stand up," Mocknour motioned for her to come closer. "Let me look at you – a camera's view." He formed his fingers to the shape of a camera lens. "Walk towards me."

Janee walked, stopped, posed, threw her head and hair back with a laugh.

"Perfect!" the director viewed her from several different angles.

"You will look marvelous on the big screen," Aaron spoke in a flattering voice. He circled around Janee; he dropped his hands, his eyes covering every part of her body.

Janee instantly felt the change in Mocknour's stares. His eyes were now undressing her, one article of clothing at a time. He was no longer viewing her as through a camera, but was admiring with lust.

She stopped, lost her smile and cleared her throat.

Mocknour again resumed the camera stance for one last look, talking as he proceeded.

"Janee, your role and your male counterpart are the two supporting characters."

"Supporting role?" her agent coughed.

"Yes," Mocknour now addressed her agent to finalize a deal with Janee. "She will be shot in approximately one-third of the scenes."

Janee's anticipation and excitement dropped with a thud. Her mind raced. How could she influence this man and her future? Then the thought of how Mocknour looked at her refocused for an instant and an idea hit her.

"I want the lead role." Janee spoke bluntly.

Mocknour stared at her blankly.

"I already have another actress in mind. Besides, what makes you think you are ready for this big a part?"

"I can sing and dance just as good as her, and you damn well know I can out act her."

Mocknour was flabbergasted. "You don't even know who she is."

"I don't have to. I know who I am and what I can do."

"Excuse me," her agent interrupted. "Mr. Mocknour, I need to speak with my client, somewhere private."

"Yes you do," the director sounded annoyed. "Stay here, I need a short break." He left briskly out of the study. The agent turned to Janee.

"Are you crazy, young lady? You can't talk to Aaron Mocknour like that."

"I just did," Janee shot back.

"He's offering you a great role."

"It does sound very generous Janee, and better than any part you've played so far."

"But, it's not THE role. Listen, I have a hunch. Let me play it out."

"Janee, you are going to blow this!" her agent was angry.

"Well if I do, we can drop back to a supporting role."

"Believe me, if we get Mocknour riled you won't be able to get work as an extra! Let me handle this."

"No, let me!"

"Janee, I don't know," her dad tried to reason.

"Mother, Daddy – let me do this. I realize what's at stake, but I'm willing to gamble."

Her agent shook his head in despair. He turned his head. Her parents looked horrified.

About that time, Mocknour threw the study door open expecting to find the problem solved. One look at the four revealed it wasn't.

"What have you decided?"

"I want the lead role," Janee stated her wishes firmly.

Mocknour shook his head.

"Come now, you know I can do the part – and do it – better. Exactly as you envision – just as you want it – to be."

She drew close to him acting coy. She touched his sleeve playfully. She spoke softly.

"You know that I'm ready. Come now, Mr. Mocknour. Make me a star – and I'll make you a whole lot of money."

She could hear Mocknour take a deep breath. He turned to the others.

"I'll have to think about this. It will take some doing to change my mind. I'll be in touch."

"Mr. Mocknour, I" the agent was cut short by the director.

"I'll be in touch. I would rather you didn't mingle on your way out."

The agent and Janee's mother and daddy filed out heavy-hearted. Mocknour grabbed Janee's arm and drew her close to him. He spoke low so the rest did not hear.

"You were very brazen tonight and you excite me. I am fascinated by your unpredictability, and ravished with your beauty. May I kiss you – good night?"

Janee stiffened and pulled away.

"No, Mr. Mocknour, I'm sorry, but I hardly know you. I'm not that kind of a girl."

Then she leaned up close to whisper in his ear, "I know what you want, Aaron, but you can't - have it."

Chapter 9

Her Big Break

🌹

To the amazement of everyone close to her and the inner circles of Hollywood as well, Janee was cast in the lead role of Mocknour's movie, which was billed "Rock-A-Baby High".

Aaron Mocknour avoided Janee except for time on the set or location. She was treated the same as the other actors. Some days he was soft spoken and caring; others, he infuriated her with his raging tirades. It was fascinating to watch him work, but mostly she was afraid of him.

The shooting was going well. The crew laughed and played with the story. They were having fun doing the film, spurred on with exceptional music and skilled choreographers. Cast and crew sensed down deep that they had a hit on their hands, but an incident occurred on location one day that changed it from a hit to a blockbuster.

They were shooting a scene on the High School set. It revolved around two students, Janee and her leading man whose stage name was Cincinnati Cole. The story was of these two who opposed each other in fierce competition, but something was changing with Janee's character. She had slowly secretly, began to fall in love with Cincinnati. She wanted to tell him, but couldn't find the words. They rehearsed the scene several times but Janee didn't like her part. She asked Mocknour to change the script; however, after a brief conference with the writer they decided to leave it as is.

"You can do this Janee," he encouraged.

They shot three takes on the scene and the director called a short break. He was not getting what he wanted, and Janee was frustrated.

She sought a secluded place. The problem was with her and she knew it. She didn't know how to love. She had suppressed love so long, how should it feel. This was a pivotal scene and she realized that if she were ever to be a star – it would be proven here.

They were called back on the set, and soon Mocknour's, "Action," began the shoot.

Janee started into her rehearsed act when something happened inside her. She went back to days past. Happy days at home and visits with her beloved Grandpa Farmer and Grandma Emile – then, to the shock and pain of her grandpa's death and funeral. Tears welled up in her eyes and trickled down her cheeks. She locked eyes with her startled leading man.

"Cincinnati, I must tell you something. It's hard and I have been so afraid – of you, my feelings. Not knowing how or when to say it. I'm digging up a lot of pain to tell you this. When I was little I lost someone very close to me that I loved with a strong love. I vowed then that I would never hurt like that again, love again- ever. I buried love so deep so I couldn't feel it! But Cincinnati, you have awakened something in me I thought was – gone forever. I just had to tell you..."

Janee reaches up and softly kisses him on the lips, then runs away crying.

"Cut – Cut – Cut!" Mocknour yells.

"Wasn't in the script," a supervisor remarked.

Not a sound. Janee walks quietly back on the set.

"Hey boss, I vote we keep that one," Cincinnati commented, wiping his eyes, "Janee's energy was all over me."

Mocknour rubbed his chin in thought.

"Janee, that was an incredible scene. Yes, people, we will keep that and rewrite some of the story around it."

Loud cheers of applause burst forth, and Janee did a little bow.

Chapter 10

Possible Suitor

I n making a film, there can be a scene so powerful that will move the hearts of moviegoers everywhere. Mocknour knew they had such a scene because it was not just an act, but life as Janee was living it. That's what made it so tender and real.

The Producer saw it, and with out a word spoken, cast and crew knew they were working on a story that would capture millions of people. This quiet awareness generated an excitement that bred an atmosphere of celebration. Fine champagne and catering was ordered in from Bartinis.

During the meal, Janee had just concluded a conversation with the supporting actress and was heading to the bar table for another glass of champagne when Les Dennison, the young man who was playing Cincinnati Cole, came alongside her.

"Janee, I can't tell you how dramatic that scene was we did today. You took a bold turn, but it sure paid off. You are such a gifted actress, you pull the best out of me."

"Why, thank you, Les. I couldn't have wished for a better leading man, well, maybe Rock Hudson."

"Too old, too old!" Dennison threw up his hands slopping some of his drink.

"Sorry," he was embarrassed and they both laughed. Then he grew serious.

"Janee, I can't get over how you looked today – at me – I'm having trouble, gosh, this is hard!"

"What Les?"

"I'm having trouble separating myself from the character… It seems so, so real, and I find I do like you a lot."

Janee was shocked. She searched his eyes with a penetrating gaze, wanting to understand what he was saying, feeling.

Les gulped like a shy little boy, totally opposite of his Cincinnati character, which was loud and boisterous.

"After we finish – I mean the film – could, would you go out with me? Gosh Janee, why is it so hard for me to talk to you?"

Janee laughed out loud then covered her mouth still laughing.

"Of course, I'll go out with you, Les, silly."

"I don't think it would take much for me to – umm – fall for you," he replied.

That statement abruptly ended Janee's laughter.

"Yes, I'll go out with you, Les Dennison, but remember, a few more weeks and we will be finished shooting. There will no doubt be plenty of interviews and promo shots during Post Production. Some we will do together, then there will be the Premier. After that, we go different directions, and who knows if we will ever work together again. The truth is Les; I don't have any feelings for you."

"Ouch!" Dennison clutched his heart.

"The scene we shot today was real – for me. I don't love anyone, I'm not sure I ever can again. I am touched, however by your compliment."

Les conveyed in looks and actions that he had been deeply wounded. Janee detected his tears and regretted her honest but cruel words. As she watched him walk away, she admitted to herself she had not been completely honest with him. Secretly, she had her sights set on a bigger prize. True to the part she played earlier in the day, something slowly, powerfully was awakening in her heart.

Chapter 11

Surprise Move

Aaron Mocknour's flashy Jaguar was parked behind Janee's car. He had disappeared near the end of the party but Janee didn't think much about it because he did that sort of thing all the time. She was surprised and curious to find him there in the studio lot. His car was rumbling at a slow idle. Janee approached cautiously.

"Ride with me, Janee," his voice was low and husky.

"Where to?" she was hesitant.

"Some place I want you to see. Don't worry I won't harm you. My driving may scare you, but I'll return you unhurt – I promise. Get in."

Janee complied and they screeched off and roared past the guard shack.

Mocknour headed west toward the Pacific. He spoke of the film shoot and how they were pressing on ahead of schedule. He elaborated on different scenes in the movie, but never touched on the one done in the afternoon. Janee sat quietly, listening, the wind from the open top blowing in her face and hair. She felt the exhilaration of feeling wild and free. She was conscious only of the wind and Aaron's low soothing voice. She paid little mind when the car turned off the Pacific Coast Highway and wound up a road in the

Malibu Mountains. He pulled into an open area that over looked the ocean.

"Oh my gosh!" Janee exclaimed.

A crescent moon sent a million sparkles across the water dancing in rhythm with the waves. The mood was mystic and romantic. Suddenly, Janee felt unsure, afraid, and unsafe.

"Aaron, I know what you want, but you can't -"

Aaron silenced her by softly placing his finger against her lips. He gently caressed them as he spoke.

"I didn't realize how much you have affected me until that scene today; your independence, spontaneity, freshness, energy, your beauty. You captivate me."

Janee took his hand in hers, "Aaron, please."

"No Janee, I mean every word. I speak from my heart, to your heart."

"Aaron, it was just a scene – in your movie."

"I don't want to talk about movies. I want to talk about us – and our future together."

Janee gasped! Her heart was pounding madly!

"Ye-yes," she stammered weakly.

Chapter 12

Rock-A-Baby High

During the final weeks of shooting Rock-A-Baby High, Janee had several secret, intimate encounters with Aaron Mocknour. Her growing love was like a storm surge, it enveloped her in a hypnotic flood. The night they confessed their love for each other was the happiest of her life. Aaron sternly warned her that they must be most discreet and no one – no one should know, until they were ready to make their big announcement.

When they were filming, Janee had to hide her feelings. She dare not embarrass her love by acting like a giddy teenager in front of the cast and crew.

But she did feel like a giggly, goofy girl in love. A smile was perpetually glued to her face, offering no small problem when she had to play a sad or serious role in a particular scene. She was on guard every time she looked at Aaron, afraid she would give her feelings away. There were times of doubts when Janee thought everyone must be aware she was in love.

He only had to smile at her, that damnable smile that held such power over her. The one she knew was meant only for her, the one that could melt her into a glob in her shoes.

His smile that easily made her blush, threatening to expose her love to the whole world.

Aaron could just touch her! Maybe he was giving direction for doing a scene – or just making a point, but his touch sent chills racing across her whole body – dang; she could even feel them in her hair. Her hair! When he brushed across her hair with his hand, she felt light headed and thought she would go mad with desire. How could the rest not notice? She dreamed of the day she could tell everyone and become Mrs. Janee Mocknour making her fairy tale romance complete.

Janee's parents and agent were also in the dark. If her mother had any inkling, she never questioned. They just seemed caught up in Janee's successful career and figured this strange and happy behavior was an out-pouring of the same – or maybe it was her youthful exuberance!

After the filming was finished Janee didn't see much of Aaron, but she thought that would happen because the director was so heavily involved in postproduction.

The night Rock-A-Baby High premiered, Janee was in her prime. Cheering crowds, many of them teenagers, screamed when she stepped out of her limo and reached out hoping for a smile or nod as she was escorted into the theatre on the arm of Les Dennison. Spotlights beamed high into the sky tracking back and forth, while on the ground bright lights of news crews illuminated celebrities and faces of shouting, noisy spectators hoping for a glimpse of one of the stars. Some girls went crazy when they saw Les, trying to bolt past security just to touch him.

"You made a hit," Janee remarked to Les, keeping her smile and never losing eye contact with the crowd.

"You're the hit, Janee, and you know it," Les responded under his breath.

Once inside the theatre, she sat next to her escort with her mother and father on the other side. Next to them sat her Grandma Emile and her Uncle Walter, who had flown in.

"I'm so excited and proud for you Janee," Emile reached over and took her hand.

"That means so much grandma!"

"I love you more than I can say. Grandpa would be so proud and happy."

Janee turned her head to Paige who sat down on the other side of Les.

"Hey girl," Paige smiled and reached for her.

"Hey yourself. This is my leading man, Les Dennison, but don't make eyes at him tonight. He only has eyes for me," Janee teased. The trio laughed.

As the movie was about to start, Aaron stood up from his seat in the aisle ahead of Janee to greet her family. She was pleased and thrilled at how graciously he spoke to them, making each one feel at ease and welcome. When he acknowledged her, he smiled that smile and gave a sly wink. Janee felt her face warm and a growing, overpowering desire to be next to him. Was she losing her mind? Was she going mad from lovesickness? Just to sit with him, hold his arm, and lay her head against his shoulder as she had seen her mother do with her father, and remembered her grandma doing the same to grandpa – that's all she asked!

Just to let the world around her know, he's mine! That was all she wanted – not fame or wealth, just Aaron. She knew it was a lot, and not possible, at least not now, but their time would come.

Janee Stemper's lead role in the Aaron Mocknour movie, 'Rock-A-Baby High' and working with the director enlarged two things in her life.

Her career skyrocketed, establishing her without question in Hollywood Stardom. The movie was a huge box office moneymaker. Crowds lined up across the country totally hooked on the story and the music. Reports were published of teens and even families going back to see it over and over again. Word of mouth created a groundswell that placed Janee on magazine covers, and made her enough money that she never needed work again. She contemplated that possibility, but fear of losing her place in the spotlight would drive her on to accept new and varied projects over the years.

Coming out of the movie's soundtrack, two of Janee's songs were instant hits. They quickly climbed the charts, and record outlets couldn't keep enough 45's in stock to meet demands. Janee's musical debut exposed her also as a credible singer.

The second thing that was enlarged in Janee's life came from the director, himself. He developed not only a movie star, but caused a flaming love and devotion to grow in her.

Chapter 13

A Slap in the Face

Janee was so involved in a flurry of interviews and guest appearances she didn't have time to think. She treasured her retreats to bed where she could dream of the secret times spent with Aaron and her future life with him. In the face of her happiness was a troubling uneasiness she had not seen or talked with her love since the Premier. Days had blurred into weeks, now two months had rushed by and no calls from Aaron. She had attributed his silence to business – after all, Rock-A-Baby High was creating a giant change in both their lives. The media touted Mocknour as a genius, placing him in high demand. Still, he had confessed his love for her. How long does it take to pick up a phone and say, 'Hello, darling, I love you'?

Now Janee was worried. When she could stand no more, she called Aaron late one night. She held her breath as the phone rang – and rang – and rang. She slowly hung up the phone.

"Aaron where are you? Please call me my love!" she whispered.

Early the next morning she was startled with a thought. Aaron should have called by now to discuss their next movie together. She grabbed her bedside phone and called her agent.

"Have you been calling Aaron Mocknour to set up a meeting for our next movie?" she barely let him say hello.

"Miss Stemper, do you just call people when you feel like it?"

"Just you. The money you're making on this movie, you can afford to answer my calls, whenever I feel like calling!"

"It's still dark out and you know I'm not speedy until I have my coffee."

"You aren't speedy after your coffee either!"

There was silence.

"Well?"

"What?"

"Have you called Aaron?"

She could hear him take a deep breath.

"He won't return my calls."

"Is he out of town?"

"No, I heard he is talking deals with Paramount. I tell you Janee, you pissed him off."

"What! Are you crazy? This movie is the rage all over the country."

"You don't know Aaron Mocknour. He has a reputation around Hollywood. He is a powerful man that is both admired and adored, but one who is also feared and hated. Word is, that when crossed or put down, he waits his time – like a viper in the dark, poised to strike, when it's his time."

"That's a bunch of crap!" Janee exploded. "I don't believe that – I won't believe it! I got the lead role – Aaron got his blockbuster!"

"I hope you are right Janee. I'll keep calling him and I'll make a trip to his office."

A week of silent phone passed by. Even her agent didn't return her calls.

"What the hell is going on?" Janee cursed. She thought she was losing her mind.

After another week had passed, her agent finally called.

"Where have you been?" Janee yelled into the phone. "You better have been on a Melanesian tour or we are through!"

"Settle down Janee. I didn't want to call until I had something definite to tell you."

"Have you spoken to Aaron?"

"No, I have not. His secretary keeps telling me he is unavailable."

"I don't understand," Janee was fighting back tears.

"Janee, rumor has it Mocknour has signed a deal and already cast the leads."

Janee was devastated! She couldn't speak. She slammed the phone down, weeping uncontrollably.

The phone rang. Janee let it ring. It was persistent. She gathered herself together and answered. It was her agent.

"What's wrong with you Janee? Did you just hang up on me? Why?"

"I can't believe Aaron would do this me," Janee replied sadly.

"Yeah – well forget Mocknour. I'm working on another deal. MGM is interested in contracting you apart from Mocknour."

Janee couldn't think. It was raining in her mind . . .

"I – I – not now, need some time to – sort this, I'm tired."

"That's ok, Janee. Get some rest and call me back. Let me know what you think."

But Janee didn't rest. She called Aaron's home insistently at all hours. Sometimes, it just rang, and when she got an answer it was Paltow. His response was the same each time.

"Mr. Mocknour is not in."

"When will he be in?"

"I do not know."

"Paltow, why won't Aaron talk to me?"

"He has been very busy, Miss Stemper."

"I want you to cut this stupid game and go and get your master right now." Janee tried to keep calm.

"I cannot. He is not here. Perhaps you should try his office."

She shook her head and stared out the window.

"His secretary is as difficult as you Paltow," Janee spoke with disdain.

"I'm sorry Janee."

She sensed a note of sorrow in Paltow's voice.

Janee locked herself in her room and continued making calls to Aaron, but in vain. She experienced long sleepless nights interrupted by hours of weeping and beating her fists into her soaked pillows. Her life was falling apart and she was going insane. Eventually, she was driven to make an appointment with Doctor Davis. Perhaps, he could prescribe something to ease her pain and help her sleep.

He could tell something was terribly wrong the instant he entered the examination room.

"Have you been sick? You don't look well."

"No . . ."

"Then what is it?"

"Just – some – personal things, doctor. I haven't been sleeping. I hurt and . . ."

"Where?"

Janee buried her face in her hands.

"Do you have a pill to cure a – a – broken heart?"

"Ahh, I see. Only God can help with that."

Janee shook her heard. "He doesn't care. He sees no tears. He's nowhere!"

"Let me take a look, Janee." He made no comment to her remark. He did a thorough exam before he spoke again.

"So, my dear Janee, you met the love of your young life and he has jilted you."

Janee's lip began to quiver and her face squinted in pain. She had trouble getting the answer to come out.

"Yeeees."

"I want to speak to you in my office after you get dressed."

A few minutes later Janee slipped into a chair in front of a very serious Doctor Davis. He studied her for some time and shuffled papers on his desk. He appeared nervous.

"I have treated you and known your mama and daddy since you were born."

Janee nodded with a half smile.

"You are placing me in a very ticklish position, but I can't prescribe anything for pain or sleep."

"Because?" Janee sat up straight.

The doctor wasn't making sense.

"I'm not positive, but almost certain Janee, that you are pregnant."

Chapter 14

Taking Care of Business

ॐ

Two weeks passed, Janee was a nervous wreck! She had another appointment with her doctor. As she sat across from him she heard the words she was dreading.

"Janee, you are definitely pregnant. All your tests confirm your condition."

She wanted to cry, but fought off the tears.

Doctor Davis' expression grew solemn.

"Shall we start appointments for pre-natal care?" he asked.

Janee sat up trying to gain her composure.

"I will give that some thought. I must break - this - news - to the father. He may have a doctor – that" . . . her voice trailed off.

"That would be quite alright. Whomever you choose can call for your medical records, but don't put this off, young lady," Doctor Davis warned sternly.

As Janee rose from her chair, she gave him that angry scowl she was known for.

"What I do is my business!" she spoke with biting words, as she looked hard into her doctor's eyes.

"This information remains HERE in your office and no one else is to know! Do you understand?"

Janee was settled in her mind that she must tell Aaron of their child right away. There was no question he was the father - she had never known any other man.

She wasn't sure what his reaction would be to this news. She had two versions of it in her dreams.

She could picture him. She would arrive at his home and fall into his embrace. With carefully planned out words, she would tell him she is pregnant with his child. He would be happy and excited. He would hold her and assure her of his love and devotion, he would promise to take care of her - and their baby.

The second version was her favorite and the one she found herself obsessed with. She is getting ready for bed when her phone rings. It is Aaron!

"Darling, I miss you so much! I must see you - tonight! I have something most wonderful to tell you. I cannot contain myself. Please say you'll be ready, and I can pick you up in one hour."

"Yes - oh, yes! I'll be ready!"

Not soon enough for Janee, Aaron's limo pulls up in front of her house. She knocks quietly on her parents' bedroom door to inform them she is going out with Aaron Mocknour, and rushes outside into his waiting arms.

The limo drives along the Pacific Coast Highway. The moon shines brightly and shimmers on the ocean waves, the same way it did that first night. Janee is in heaven, and as the limo gently rolls along, Aaron drops to one knee and takes Janee's hand. She gulps, and her heart races!

"Darling, I want you to be my wife - forever! Please - say you will!"

"Yes! Yes! A thousand times - yes!" She throws her arms around his neck.

"Darling, we shan't wait! Let's get married - tonight!"

"Yes! Oh, yes!" Janee claps her hands in sheer excitement.

"Chickey," Aaron calls to the driver, "take us to Palm Springs. Find us a minister! By God, we will be married tonight!"

But Janee never got to Palm Springs. Something would always interrupt her dream at that point. And her phone didn't ring, even though Janee continued calling Aaron Mocknour's home and office.

In Hollywood, if you wanted to apply the ultimate hurt, you just ignored someone. How long would Aaron punish her, and for what? His silent treatment now frightened her! She felt panicky, making her phone calls more persistent! Finally, Aaron's secretary called.

"Mr. Mocknour will see you Tuesday morning at ten o'clock in his office. Will you be able to make that appointment?"

"Yes, I'll be there," Janee answered.

Tuesday took forever to arrive. Janee was very apprehensive! She had not seen Aaron since the Premier of, Rock-A-Baby High, and that was three months ago.

She arrived at the Mocknour Productions offices and was told to have a seat. Certainly not the greeting or treatment of a star she was accustomed to.

Ten o'clock arrived and passed. Ten fifteen, ten thirty, and ten forty - the minutes ticked slowly by, and Janee felt insult and anger.

The intercom buzzed on the receptionist's desk. Janee recognized Aaron's voice.

"Send Miss Stemper in, please."

The receptionist rose to escort Janee to Mr. Mocknour's office.

"I know my way around," Janee spoke curtly.

"Janee, darling, so good to see you," Aaron greeted her with a smile, as she entered his plush office.

"Aaron, I've missed you terribly! Why haven't you called?"

The smile evaporated from Aaron's face.

"I've been very busy," he said matter-of-factly as he motioned for her to have a seat. He sat on the edge of his desk with one leg up, the other on the floor, so he could face her. Aaron's absence of affection struck Janee with an immediate unsettled hurt. She had expected at least a kiss.

"Is that the reason for this appointment? So we could see each other?" Aaron's manner was abrasive to Janee. She wanted to slap him - then kiss him!

"Well, yes, sort of," Janee stammered. "I have something - I want - need to - tell you."

Aaron stared at Janee. She felt uneasy and unsure of how to proceed. Should she just tell him or ease into it? Without a second thought she heard herself speak words that were so natural for her.

"Aaron, I love you!"

"That's what you wanted to tell me?" he appeared annoyed.

"No, no! I mean, yes, I wanted to tell you that, but there is something else."

"I'm listening."

An awkward moment of silence followed as Janee struggled for the right words, but nothing fit together.

"Aaron, I'm pregnant!" she blurted out.

He studied her for a long time. His face was expressionless. He slowly stood up, walked around his desk to the other side, and sat noisily into his chair. The only sound in the room was the squeak of Aaron's chair as he rocked forward and backward.

He looked at his appointment calendar and wrote something before looking up at her.

"Come alone to my house tomorrow night around midnight. We will discuss this then."

"Why can't we discuss this now?" Janee was insistent.

"Miss Stemper, I'll thank you to not make this difficult! This is neither the time nor the place. I'm a very busy man! You can take it or leave it. Tomorrow evening at midnight, your choice." Aaron's eyes blazed with anger Janee had only ever seen directed toward others. He now turned on her! She felt whipped, like some animal.

"But, Aaron -"

"Good day!"

Janee knew she had been dismissed, and she left Mocknour's office troubled deep in her soul. This was not unfolding even close to how she had dreamed. This was more like a nightmare that she wanted desperately to wake up from.

Maybe he would be different in his home - away from business influences. She longed and wished the next day that her dreams would come true. That he would make everything all right! "He'll be much different tonight," she kept telling herself.

It was near midnight when she drove up to the Mocknour estate gate. She pressed the intercom button and heard Aaron's voice.

"It's me," she called into the box, and the gate slowly opened. She proceeded up the long drive. She was relieved to see no cars in the drive. That meant Aaron had no company. He swung the door open before she buzzed and motioned her in. She reached out to hug him, but he turned aside brushing her cheek with a slight kiss.

"Let me take your coat," he offered.

"I was expecting Paltow to answer the door," Janee remarked, removing her coat with Aaron's assistance. She watched his face - his hands - as he hung up her coat. She couldn't hold back! When he turned toward her, she threw her arms around his neck and kissed him deeply, but something was different. He didn't kiss her back as in past encounters. He had changed! Aaron broke their embrace and motioned her into the living room. She sat on one of his sofas while he stood at the fireplace staring into the crackling flames.

Aaron broke a long silence.

"You say you are pregnant?"

"Yes."

"Are you sure?"

"The tests are conclusive."

"Are you telling me this baby is mine?"

Janee was incensed!

"I don't sleep around, Aaron!" she shot back.

"Of course, I'm sorry. Who knows of this besides you and me?"

"My doctor."

"Will he - keep this to himself?"

"I told him to."

"Excellent! Now, I know of someone who can take care of this little problem."

"I don't see it as a problem!" Janee objected.

"What do you see it as? For God's sake, grow up, Janee!" Aaron began to walk around the room. "What would this do to our careers, our lives?"

"Other people have babies," Janee argued.

"Not us. You have a baby; they will forget you exist. You'll be a has-been! You bring my name into it; I'm ruined! Can you even get an inkling of what the tabloids and news-casters would do with a story like this? I can't believe you were so careless! Didn't you use any precautions?"

By now, Aaron was screaming at her!

"You careless, stupid broad! How could you do this to me?"

Janee could not hold back the tears, and she wept. She was hurt and afraid.

"Get hold of yourself, Janee. For God's sake, what do you want from me? Money? How much? I'll write you a check right now."

"I don't want - your - money," Janee choked out the words between sobs.

"Then what?"

Janee couldn't believe he was being so insensitive and cruel!

"What?" Aaron stood in front of her, his hands defiantly on his hips.

"What?" he yelled.

"I - I - want - to - to - marry - you," Janee wailed.

Aaron threw his hands up in the air and spun around, returning to the fireplace.

"Out of the question," he muttered.

"Wha - what?" Janee didn't understand what he'd said.

"Impossible! That will never happen!"

"But, Aaron, I love you. You said we had a future together!" Janee cried out - lifting her hand toward him.

Aaron shook his head and stood in thought as he stared again into the flames of the fireplace. He turned and walked toward her - stopping a few feet away. Janee looked up at him with wet face and eyes. He handed her a tissue as he stepped closer.

"Look, Janee, what we had was special. It was exciting and fun. We lived and loved with a passion few people experience while we were filming, and I'll never forget it. But the truth is, it's over! The movie is finished, and so is our affair. I thought you knew I fall out of love as quickly and intently as I love. It was a great roll in the sack," Aaron Mocknour chuckled in that deep voice of his.

Janee's mouth fell open. She was dumbfounded and speechless.

Aaron pulled a card out of his pocket. He had placed it there for just this moment.

"Now you listen carefully to me, Miss Stemper, as I'll not see you again. Take this card, and call this man for an appointment. When you call, tell him you need a growth removed.

He will understand and get rid of your little problem. He is most discreet, but I warn you, if you try to make trouble, I'll bury you so deep no one will ever find you. As a matter of fact, I will do the same to anyone else who speaks of our affair or your pregnancy. Do you understand that I mean what I say? You call this man tomorrow, and I'll do the rest. You know I'm the best at taking care of business!"

Chapter 15

On a Dark Night

The next few days were a literal hell for Janee. She was heartsick and crushed! She avoided contact with anyone, which was so uncharacteristic of her. It was obvious to the point the news media picked up on it, but couldn't find out anything, so little was printed. One tabloid hinted at disagreements between her and Mocknour.

The love Janee felt for Aaron was smoldering into hate. The child growing inside of her who at first was a precious wonder was becoming an object that reflected Aaron Mocknour. With each passing day, disgust mounted, for this man who had cruelly stabbed her with a flaming tongue. Love so strong and intense was replaced by a hatred of equal proportion. She wanted him dead! She wanted revenge - but how? Aaron was so powerful and well protected. He existed in a fortress.

Janee was torn over what to do! At first, the thought of having a baby was exciting, and the fulfilling of a deep longing she was unsure of - it just seemed - right. It was Aaron's baby! The man she was in love with!

But all that had changed. She loathed Aaron Mocknour, the pompous, egotistical blockhead of a director. The thought of having any part of him near her - and especially in her - filled her with rage!

By the end of the week she knew what she must do. She had no choice! With firm resolve, she parked her car in front of a phone booth. Janee got out of her car, looking around to make sure no one was spying. She had driven far enough, she felt secure no media was following her. Glancing at open windows to be certain there were no cameras, she entered the booth and pulled the door closed. She dialed the number given her by Mocknour. Someone picked up on the second ring.

"Hello," it was a woman.

Janee had an instant of panic. She started to hang up, but she resisted and gathered her wits. She had decided! She must rid herself of - this thing - of Aaron's - inside of her! She had to do it!

"Hello?" the woman questioned.

"Yes! Hello! I have -" Janee's mind went blank. She couldn't remember the words Aaron had told her to say!

"Yes, I'm here. You have what?"

The whole matter felt so confusing - so awful to Janee. What she was about to do appeared incredibly ugly all of a sudden. She couldn't believe she was talking to a live person about it - or soon would be. Janee was bewildered!

"I'm pregnant! I can't be pregnant! I mean I don't want to be - I don't want a baby!" she unloaded to the woman on the phone.

"Try to stay calm," the voice, instructed. "Who referred you to us?"

"Aaron Mocknour," Janee whimpered. Right then she felt like a little girl. Not the strong, resolved, tough woman she made out to be. She wanted to run to her daddy and be held.

"Are you Miss Stemper?"

"Yes," Janee sniffed.

"Mr. Mocknour told me you would be calling."

A flash of anger jolted Janee back to herself! How could he be so sure she would do exactly what he told her? That air of confidence he displayed now infuriated her, and she had a fleeting desire to keep this baby just to show Mocknour how wrong he was about her. Yet the thought of facing her parents, her family, Grandmother Emile, her friends, the whole world with an out-of-wedlock pregnancy was more than she could handle.

"Are you there?" the voice on the phone asked.

"I'm here. What do I do?"

"Listen carefully. Write this address down, and destroy it after this is over."

Janee dug in her purse for paper and pencil.

"Can you come on Friday evening at nine o'clock?"

"Yes," Janee answered.

"Bring clothes and items you will need to remain over-night. The doctor will not release you until the next day. You may want to go somewhere for the weekend where you can rest and be alone."

"A doctor does this?"

"Yes, and he will keep you here until you are well enough to leave."

"Will this - hurt - much?" Janee was suddenly apprehensive.

"You will have cramps and bleeding through the night, but it will all be over by the next morning."

"No one will - know of this?"

"No one. No information is given out, no records kept."

Janee wrote down the address, and the next day she told her parents she would be going out of town for the weekend.

"Where are you headed?" her dad asked.

"I'll be in Palm Springs," Janee answered. "I'll call you."

"Do be careful driving," her mother implored. "There seem more drunk drivers on the highways these days. You remember our neighbors' son who -"

"Yes, Mother," Janee cut her off. "That was two years ago."

Janee was nervous by the time Friday evening rolled around, but just as anxious to get on with it. It was on a dark night in February 1961 that Janee Stemper, the movie star, pulled up in the driveway of a large, custom-looking house. It was situated in one of the affluent bedroom communities of Los Angeles.

There was a cloud cover blocking any light from moon and stars, making it difficult to read the number on the house. Janee maneuvered her car's headlights onto the face of the house until she caught the reflections of the house address.

"Thirteen-ten," she muttered to herself, thankful she had pulled into the right drive.

She struggled with her coat. She could feel the chill of a winter's night coming off the glass of her car. The house stood before her tall and foreboding. It was dark, outside as well as in, except for one window that was lit up behind drawn curtains.

Janee felt her way to the front door, stumbling on a step as she reached the entrance. She knocked, and the door opened almost immediately. Janee made out a thin, attractive brown-haired woman in the dim light of the entrance hall. Her looks depicted the woman's expensive taste in clothing.

"We're expecting you, Miss Stemper. Please come. Follow me!"

"And you are...?" Janee inquired.

"We don't use names here," the woman turned to look at Janee with an accommodating smirk. The woman gave the impression she disliked or resented Janee.

"Use this room." The woman opened a door to a brightly lit room. The room had sink and cabinets lining two walls, a chair and an examining table in the center.

"Get completely undressed and put his on," the woman handed her a folded up gown. "If you will give me your car keys, I'll have your car parked out of sight."

Janee complied with the woman's demands. When she had donned her robe she walked curiously around the room. There were no framed degrees - nothing to suggest a name or address. Even the labels had been cut out of a couple of magazines she found on a countertop. She had the address; it would be a simple enough matter to find out who lived here. But what purpose would that serve? In the end, she would be glad not to know who was doing the extraction of her child. She just wanted to put it all behind her and get on with her life.

The abrupt, unannounced entrance of the doctor startled her. He was covered with a hospital-type gown, a middle-aged man with a handsome but expressionless face. He gave the notion of being in a hurry, and Janee sensed from his manner, she would get no kindness or sympathy from him. She hoped he would at least be gentle.

"I understand you have a little problem?"

"I'm pregnant," Janee blurted out.

"Lie on your back and spread your legs," the doctor ordered as he went to a cabinet and pulled surgical gloves out of a box.

"Don't you have a nurse?" Janee asked. She felt uncomfortable.

"No nurse."

The doctor gathered some instruments and approached the table.

"Why do - you - do this?" Janee ventured.

"To keep young women like you from some dark alley or a coat hanger."

Then an almost evil smile crossed his face.

"The money isn't bad either," he spoke with sarcastic humor.

A question crossed Janee's mind. She started not to ask, but the desire to know - the fear of the answer drove her to the point she couldn't hold back.

"Does -" she swallowed hard. "Does Aaron send - well - a lot - I mean a few women - or am I - the only one?"

"You know better than to ask a question like that!" the doctor snarled as he pushed Janee's gown back.

She stared up at the ceiling. What the doctor was doing to her felt similar to the exam Doctor Davis had performed on her a few days ago.

"You're about twelve to fourteen weeks along," the doctor spoke as he worked. "You are fortunate. Now, this won't take much longer."

Suddenly, a pain shot from Janee's stomach to all the way up her back. It was so intense she thought it would explode out the top of her head. She screamed! Her back arched and twisted!

"Don't move!" the doctor yelled. "You must be still. Only a moment more..."   Janee grabbed hold of the table edge and held on until her fingers cramped. She tried with all her might and will to remain motionless, but horrible pain was shooting from her stomach to every inch of her body. She screamed again!

"It's all over," the doctor announced. "Your little problem will soon be gone."

Janee wanted to slap his face. She wanted to bite him - kick him - she wanted him to go away!

The doctor placed some kind of a bedpan under her and instructed her to remain on it until he came back. Strong fierce cramps grabbed her insides. She desperately wanted to double up, but fought to remain rigid. Tears ran down both sides of her face, into her ears.

Over the next hour she had violent pains shoot through her insides. She could hear something dripping into the pan. She knew instinctively it was blood, and whatever else. Her back hurt unbearably now, and she struggled to keep from vomiting. She wondered if the doctor had forgotten about her, so she called out to him several times. Finally, he entered the room again to check on her.

Removing the bedpan, he examined its contents.

"Uh-huh," his utterance carried the tone that he was satisfied with what he saw.

The doctor commenced to clean her up. His touch was rough and clearly indicated the man's impatience. When he finished his hurried task, he stood up facing Janee and attempted a weak smile that came across more like a sneer.

"Your little problem is gone," he remarked. "We will move you to another room where you can rest. You will remain there until I'm certain no infection has set in. So far you are doing good."

'How can he say that when I hurt so bad?' Janee thought.

The doctor left and came back in a short time accompanied by the woman. They helped Janee off the table. As soon as she tried to stand up, her legs felt like jelly, and had the doctor and the woman not supported her weight, Janee would have collapsed on the floor. She was weak and dizzy. Each step she made aggravated the horrible pains and cramps. The room where they were taking her could have been a mile away for what it seemed to Janee. She just wanted to lie down, and the bed was certainly a welcome sight when they reached it.

The doctor changed her pad as she had already soaked the one she had on. He told her he would check on her through the night. Janee was relieved at least that he was somewhat professional.

After he left, the woman helped cover Janee with an extra blanket. It was dark in the room except for light coming from a small bathroom. Janee groaned in agony.

"You've had your play - now you must pay!" the woman said hatefully. She left the room closing the door behind her.

Janee hurt too much to rest or sleep. She spent a fitful night. There were times she needed to use the bathroom, but was too weak to get out of bed. She had no way to call the doctor - she tried yelling, but to no avail. He checked on her when he felt like it, and she had to wait on him to go to the restroom.

In the early morning about 4:00 a.m. a thunderstorm hit. Janee could hear the wind gust against the house, and the thunder clashing. Through a long wall of windows in her room, the lightning flashes illuminated trees and shrubs of what might have been a garden area. Next sheets of rain beat against the window glass. As Janee watched the storm she felt one raging inside her soul. She was frightened and alone. All her fame and money meant nothing! She was stripped of everything. She felt tired and vulnerable and longed to be home, a little girl again. She stared out into the dark, wondering what she had done.

Chapter 16

Bernard Swift

The doctor let Janee go the afternoon after her abortion. She made a hurried, painful trip to Palm Springs in her car.

Not the exciting, wondrous ride with Aaron Mocknour in his limo to be married, but sad and alone after aborting his baby.

On the way, she detected a photographer or news journalist following her, so she drove some diversionary routes to lose him. It was dark when she checked into a resort hotel. The first thing she did was call her parents. Leah answered.

"Hello, Mother, it's me."

"Janee, where are you?"

"In Palm Springs like I told you!"

"We thought you would call last night. We were worried! We called the hotel we usually stay at, and you weren't there."

"I'm at a different one. I needed a change."

"Janee, are you feeling okay? You sound tired."

"Mother, I'm doing fine. I just needed to unwind. What's Father doing?"

"He had some late work, a secret hush-hush new plane for the Air Force. You know your father, dear."

"I sure do! Listen, Mom - I ..."

"What is it, Janee?"

"I just wanted to tell you not to worry. I'll be home in a few days. I love you"

There were a couple of changes Janee determined to make during the weeks following her abortion.

The first was to find her an apartment and leave home. Her parents, of course, didn't understand and objected strongly, but Janee was dead set. They resigned to the fact their daughter was no longer a little girl, but grown up, and they couldn't hold on to her like that forever. Her father held out the longest, but finally gave in and assisted Janee in locating a luxury apartment. Leah called around inviting family and friends to a moving party. Some came thinking this to be a groovy party and got roped into helping Janee move.

Soon, Janee found herself in her own place, and discovered she didn't do well with the loneliness. She talked her best friend into moving in with her instead of staying at the college dorm.

""How will I make classes?" Paige objected, "I don't have a car, and taking the bus is too slow."

"Use my car. No! I'll buy you one! A brand new one! We'll go tomorrow!"

It was settled. Paige moved in the following week to share Janee's apartment.

The next item on the agenda was to fire her agent. She knew she must sever all ties with anyone who was a part of her time with Aaron Mocknour. She must bury her past along side her love. She got rid of old pimple face with no regret.

Numerous agencies approached her in the following months, hoping to sign her on as their client, but none of them suited Janee. True, some were top agents who many actors would have died to have. They just didn't seem right for Janee. She desired something - new. A fresh start, but time was slipping away. A year had passed since Janee had taken a movie, and she began to fear her public would forget all about her - and who she was! That's when she met Bernard Swift.

It was a blustering March evening in 1962 that Janee found herself at a celebrity party thrown by well-known actor Jason Finn at his Beverly Hills Estate.

Bernard Swift was there fresh from the east coast and green as a June bug on a brown leaf, and just as conspicuous.

Janee was shaken! She had just come face to face with Aaron Mocknour who earlier made his grand entrance to the Finn party. Mocknour was civil toward Janee, but cool.

As she gazed into his eyes she felt her heart soften, and she wanted to kiss him and be held by him. That made her angry! She suppressed the powerful urge to claw those beautiful eyes out. She stiffened up, turning away and fighting back tears that could so easily have flowed and betrayed her heart.

Aaron revealed no tender feelings, no concern or interest in how she was. It was life as usual for him, never caring about what she went through that horrible night at the doctor's house. She felt she was suffocating and quickly made her way into another part of Finn's house.

"Hello," came a pleasant salutation from somewhere in the crowded room. She looked around until she made eye contact with a young man who was looking directly at her.

"Hi! Do I know you?"

"I wish, but I don't think so. I arrived here just recently from back east."

"Are you an actor? Writer? What are you doing here - at this party?"

"My boss got the invitation and sent me. I'm a talent agent."

"Oh?"

"I work for the Rufus Englethorpe Agency."

"I've never heard of it."

"Just my style! A no-name agent working for an unknown agency," the man laughed.

"You are on an uphill trek," Janee couldn't help but like this boy. He was so stupidly honest.

"Yes, but I'll be beating the bushes all the way."

"Do you know who I am?"

"Yes. I see enough movies to recognize Miss Janee Stemper."

"You know more than I."

The young man caught her meaning and turned red of face.

"I'm sorry, Miss Stemper, I must have left my manners back home in Virginia. I'm Bernard Swift." He stuck out his hand, but Janee did not respond.

"I wasn't aware they grew agents in Virginia," Janee remarked sarcastically.

"They don't - I mean I studied in New York."

"And how many wonderful talents have you signed up, Mister Swift?"

Bernard dropped his head and his face again displayed red splotches. "None," he mumbled.

At that moment another guest tried to edge in and vie for Janee's attention. She motioned the woman to wait.

"I'll see you in a minute. I'm talking to my agent."

Bernard looked bewildered.

"Bernard, how quickly can you get me a movie deal?"

"I - I - er -" he shook his head. "I don't know," he sputtered.

"Well, do you want to represent me or not?" Janee demanded.

"But - but - Miss Stemper - I was - certain - I mean - I thought - well - surely you - already have an agent."

"That's no concern of yours. I'm asking you!"

"I - I -" Swift appeared close to fainting.

"Bernard, I don't believe I mumbled or stuttered."

"Yes - of course - I'll start first thing - right now - what do we do?"

Janee had to laugh!

Chapter 17

USO Tour

August 7, 1964, was the official entry date into the Viet Nam War for the United States following two attacks on our ships in the Gulf of Tonkin by North Viet Namese patrol boats.

March 8, 1965, marked the first penetration of our ground forces when Marines hit the landing zone or LZ at Da Nang. That began the extension of a war that would cost America the lives of over 50,000 men and last seven long years.

Janee was too busy making movies to give much thought or concern to a war she didn't fully understand being fought on the other side of the world.

Bernard had proven his weight in gold as he successfully landed Janee one lucrative role after another. He didn't take full credit and was the first to admit his client's beauty and talent made it easier to close contracts.

Janee was sought after by many studios, which afforded her the luxury of choosing only the best of offers. Her career shot into the sky and burst into a brilliant blaze of fireworks.

After "Rock-A-Baby High" she did two surfer movies. She had a blast acting those parts; she even did some of her own stunts. Finishing those, she starred in an epic western titled, "West From Waco," which was her first major upturn to more mature roles. She found herself again in a wagon train of settlers leaving Texas to travel west. The director even wrote in some of the stories Janee relayed about her grandparents' trip from Texas to Oregon.

As the shooting of, "West From Waco," was nearing its completion, Janee was offered a major role in a Biblical story. She turned it down!

"Why?" Bernard was baffled.

"Not interested!" Janee's voice projected a biting edge.

"Have you read the script? It's a darn good story."

"No, Bernard, I haven't."

"Then how can -."

"I don't believe in that crap so why be a hypocrite and play the part - like some do."

Bernard held up his hand.

"Hey, I don't pretend to be a Christian, so don't get upset with me. You do other parts about things -."

"Bernard, if you say another word - you're finished!"

Bernard threw up both hands, spun around and left, slamming the door behind him.

Janee starred in another very successful film, rolling in the money at the box office. It was a love story called, "Penny Auntie." She played an unmarried sister, unfortunate in love, living with the younger sister and her family. Janee got so deeply into her character it took weeks to come back to herself.

Then the role of a lifetime came in her next movie that drew rumors of an Oscar nod for the young star. It was the story of an Oklahoma farmer's wife, widowed and left with her two children on a dry farm that was blowing away. She struggles to survive and save the farm. She is rescued and romanced by none other than Jason Finn. Promotion on the film was huge, and Janee found herself in countless interviews and publicity shots with Jason even before the film's release.

It was early one morning just before their movie, "A Bowl of Dust," was to be premiered, that Janee arrived at a television studio for a promotional interview. The interview was going well, and Janee was really getting into it when she caught sight of Jason Finn standing amongst the crew behind the cameras. When the director saw him, he called cut, and asked Jason if he would be a surprise guest on the show.

"No, this is Janee's interview with you. I didn't come to jump into the show."

It was only after Janee's insistence that Jason agreed to step in and plug the movie.

After the taping was over, Janee was curious.

"What are you doing here today, Jason?"

"I needed to talk to you," he appeared very serious.

"Oh?"

"Yes. As you know, in a few months is Christmas and New Year's. Over the weekend, Huggie Newman called and invited me to help him put together a show for a USO Tour to Viet Nam. There would be several performances in and around Saigon, and a big one at the Marine base at Da Nang. Janee, I would like for you to go with us as a singer-performer."

Janee was floored! The war in Viet Nam had to be the most remote thing from her mind. She had heard of other performers doing USO shows for the troops but never entertained any probability of going there herself.

"Well - Jason - I - really - don't know... We are about to premier, "A Bowl of Dust," and we will be so busy!"

"What do you have planned for Christmas and New Year's more important than cheering up a bunch of GI's?"

As Janee looked into Jason's face she realized from his eyes - his look - this held far more meaning than just giving a performance to an audience of soldiers.

"We will arrive just before Christmas. The first show scheduled in Saigon will be on Christmas Eve. We will do several more performances in that area through New Year's. Then in January we will work our way across bases north of Saigon ending in Da Nang. We are scheduled to return January fifteenth. Think about it, Janee."

Something grabbed hold of Janee's adventurous spirit. A smoldering coal was being fanned into a flame.

"I'd be - honored - Mr. Finn - to accompany you on this USO Tour."

Chapter 18

Muddy Water

"You're going where?" Bernard thundered.

"Viet Nam."

"Are you nuts? People are getting shot and killed over there!"

"Come on, Bernard, where is your sense of adventure?" Janee spoke coyly.

"Adventure nothing. You have to be crazy!"

Janee laughed, "Don't you think the two go together - sometimes?"

"You can't go!" Bernard, face crimson and distorted, choked out the words. "I forbid it."

"You what?"

"I - forbid you to go! As your agent, I forbid you to go to Viet Nam. "A Bowl of Dust" is about to premier. You can't miss that."

"Bernard - calm down! I'm going from December 23rd until January 15th. The premier and publicity will mostly be past by then."

"Let's see," he flipped open his planner.

"You have four Christmas parties you're invited to. Lots of important contacts -."

"Go in my place."

"Not the same! You have three television shows to make guest appearances on and five radio programs between Christmas and January 15th, Janee. It can harm your -."

"Call them and reschedule."

"Janee, I don't want you to go!"

"Why? You afraid of all the handsome soldiers I'll be around - or Jason Finn?"

The pained look on Bernard's face told Janee she had clawed a raw spot.

"That's it, isn't it, Bernard? You're jealous!"

Bernard's face paled. He dropped his eyes but did not answer.

Janee regretted what she said but liked the feeling of power it gave her.

"Besides, Bernard, where did you get the notion that you can forbid me going anywhere? I'm going to Viet Nam whether you like it or not, and if I sleep with fifty guys - that's my business, not yours!"

"Don't talk like a slut!" Bernard yelled.

Janee soundly slapped his face.

Bernard recoiled in shock! He was wounded. He covered his smarting cheek with his hand.

"You are scaring me, Janee. What if you get hurt - or worse - killed?" His voice sounded more like that of a little boy than a man.

Janee knew she had deeply hurt her agent. She changed her tactic.

"You want to come with me to shield me from bullets and rescue me from hungry males?"

Bernard sadly shook his head no. Janee was surprised, Bernard's' refusal hurt her! He returned the pain to her heart without even knowing it. To Janee it meant that when the chips were down, Bernard wouldn't be there for her.

"Well, you needn't worry yourself," Janee said coldly. "I'll make it on my own just fine!"

She left a troubled Bernard. The conversation was spent, and neither one felt good about the course it had taken. Bernard was certain that danger awaited Janee, plus he could not bear to watch her acts of indiscretion around a mass of love-starved, homesick GI's. Janee was determined to follow out her plans, and viewed Bernard as a coward. Their communication was strained for days until Bernard showed up at her apartment late one night.

"I need to talk to you," Janee heard his voice crackle over the intercom.

She buzzed him in. She met him a few minutes later at her door.

"Couldn't you have come later?" Janee greeted him coolly.

"I apologize for the lateness of the hour. The truth is it took this long to get up my nerve."

"Couldn't it wait until morning?"

"No, I've got to settle this now. I can't stand hard feelings between us."

Janee studied the man's face. She could sense he was struggling to find the right words and put them in a reasonable order. She knew he must have played out this conversation over and over in his head. She determined to eradicate any preconceived rehearsal of what Bernard thought in his mind was about to take place.

"What's to settle? I'm going to Viet Nam on a USO Tour with Huggie Newman and Jason Finn, and I plan on going to bed with either one of them if they ask me."

"Huggie's married for cripe's sake!" Bernard shot back.

"So. We'll be on the other side of the world, and his wife is here." Janee enjoyed the reaction she got from Bernard. "Besides, there will be an unlimited supply of willing soldiers."

Bernard looked like he had been shot! He slumped down into her sofa and sat in silence for several minutes. Then the strained face of the agent dissolved into a tender look.

"I'm sorry for what I said to you that night, Janee. It's just that I worry - about you. I'm afraid for you. It's dangerous in Viet Nam."

"No, Bernard, the truth is, you're afraid for yourself. Afraid that if something happens to me, you are out of work, and you really aren't sure anyone else would take you in. That's what you really are afraid of, isn't it? Truth? That's the truth. And what about other men? You're afraid I'll like someone else better than you. That's the truth too, isn't it? The truth? I've never told you I'm in love with you - never even implied it! Well, put it out of your mind Bernard. I'll be safe! The United States military isn't going to place civilians in dangerous places, and mister, what I do around other men is no concern of yours."

Bernard buried his head in his hands under Janee's heavy verbal barrage. When he finally looked up his face was wet. It was then Janee knew her words had cut deep into the heart of this man. He spoke in a voice so low and subdued that she had to listen very carefully to make out what he said.

"What you say is right, Janee. I was out of bounds with you, and I forgot my place. I'm sorry! I do admire you for going. I'm happy - and proud for you."

"But you won't go with me?"

"You don't need me in Viet Nam. I can do more for you by staying here. I just don't want any muddy water between us, Janee."

"Nor do I, Bernard." She smiled sweetly and stepped closer to him. "You are the best agent I've had."

Bernard gave a half laugh and attempted a smile.

"Now, Janee, that isn't saying much seeing as I'm only the second one you've had and the first was pretty awful!"

"Really, I'll be safe and fine. I'll miss you, Bernard," she purred as she gently kissed his lips. "Promise that you'll see me off at the airport and be there when I come home."

Bernard sighed, "I promise."

"I think we have cleared the muddy water tonight, don't you?" she spoke softly as she opened the door for him to leave.

Chapter 19

Preparations

The next two months were a rush of activity that roared through like a speeding train. The premier of, "A Bowl of Dust," contained all the glitz and glamour Hollywood was famous for. Subsequent weeks at theatres produced long lines of people waiting to see the feature. It also garnered huge ticket returns netting the production company and all who had points in the film handsome profits. Janee and Jason had been paid outright for their roles. Both actors had signed contracts for record salaries.

As soon as the popularity of, "A Bowl of Dust," waned, the USO team had to begin preparations for their tour in Viet Nam. Janee never forgot the first time she met Huggie Newman. She was with Jason when they walked onto the sound stage. She spied a little rollie-pollie baldheaded man standing with five other men on a makeshift set. He laughed and waved enthusiastically when he saw Jason and Janee walk in. He approached them - arms open wide to embrace them in a hug.

"Well, I see we have beauty and charm here on this team. You are without a doubt - charm - Miss Stemper," he spoke warmly as he held her hand. "I'm beauty, but danged if I can figure what Jason is!"

"Hey, Huggie, I can be funny," Jason objected good-naturedly.

"Sure you can. First day of school was when you were funny, Mr. Straight Man."

Huggie let go of Janee's hand as he slapped Jason on the shoulder. He made faces and told Jason to loosen up. He kept on cracking jokes until Janee was laughing so hard tears rolled down her cheeks. She knew she was in store for a fun-filled trip.

Huggie called the other men over and introduced them.

"This be Compton Moore, our director. His duty be to direct us to the Officers' Club bar - then to the stage." A tall, solemn-faced man shook Janee's hand, then in turn, Jason's. All the while, he gave Huggie a stern scowl.

"I know, I know, no drinking on duty - sir!" He saluted Mr. Moore, who could no longer hold back a smile. Huggie whispered in Jason's ear but loud enough for all to hear.

"He's less funny than you."

Turning to a pale-faced pudgy man with a thick head of hair and long sideburns, Huggie giggled. The man tried to be straight-faced but burst into laughter when Huggie did a second quick high-pitched giggle.

"I tried to get a woman to take care of our sound but couldn't find one, so I got the next best thing - Phil - Phil Hanson, our sound man!"

Phil did a little wave of his left hand and took a sweeping bow. Everyone clapped.

Huggie pulled a pair of sunglasses from his pocket and put them on when he faced the next person. He was a dark-skinned man of medium build. He wore a T-shirt, shorts and low-cut leather boots. Janee made note he had a smooth face and beautiful eyes. Huggie cradled the man's face in his hand and got up close to the fellow cheek to cheek. Both grinned at the rest of the team.

"Juju be our lighting director. His duty be to always shine lights in our feeble eyes, and if he becomes derelict of duty, we'll ship him north!" While he was making the introduction he was moving Juju's mouth to mimic what he was saying. The whole team roared!

Suddenly Huggie grew very serious. He spoke low in a monotone. He cracked not even a hint of a smile. Everyone got quiet.

"These last two fine-looking, well-dressed gentlemen are very important, and you all must treat them nicely. You see, they carry things - heavy things - lots of things - very heavy things - and if they get upset they won't carry all - those - heavy things."

Janee giggled. Huggie held up his hand for silence.

"This is most serious business - that we treat these two fine-looking, well-dressed gentlemen with extreme nicety - because if they get upset and won't carry - carry all - those - heavy things - which means we will have to carry them ourselves - and I have a bad back - so that - means - you will have to carry - all the very heavy things."

One of the men being introduced, unable to hold back any longer, burst into a loud, "Hee haw," that rumbled up from his belly.

"Lady and gentlemen - I present our grips, Doc Martin and laughing boy, Buster. Now, Mr. Director, Compton, sir, I turn it over to you to make us work!"

Rehearsals had to be worked around eight persons' schedules, which proved a worthy challenge. Everyone was busy and coming into the Holiday Season compounded the schedule tightness. Then, getting a sound stage for rehearsal was another major hurdle. The team found they were rehearsing some days 'til four in the morning. Other times were after midnight.

Compton set four writers to develop and script three shows. The first to be presented on Christmas Eve, Christmas

Day and four more performances leading up to New Year's. They would switch to their second show for New Year's Eve and New Year's Day 1968 Special. Those eight performances would take place in Saigon and surrounding areas. After New Year's, the team would perform show three as they worked their way north to the other bases. The tour was to end in a grand finale on the huge Marine base of Da Nang. From there, they would fly out on January 15th, returning stateside.

In addition to memorizing parts and songs, routines and choreography had to be hammered out. Countless details in support of the actual shows must be covered. This meant permission for use of each copyright song had to be obtained. They would need a sound system compact enough to fit on the planes. Yet not so small as to compromise sound quality, but strong enough to fill large open air settings.

For Janee, a small orchestra was brought in to record background. In rehearsals, Janee practiced singing with the tapes; however, this required adjustment for the singer. She was familiar with live musicians accompanying her, affording a little flexibility, but singing to a tape was rigid. If she missed the intro or got out of rhythm, it was difficult to get back in sync. Sometimes she just had to start over, and Janee was uptight she might require that in a performance. She practiced long hours to get each piece down solid. She worked so hard that the rest of the team would throw in the towel and beg for mercy. Even Huggie, who appeared a bundle of energy, gave out.

"You got it, girl! You got it! Don't flog it to death, or the song will have no feeling when we get to Viet Nam," Huggie laughed.

Time passed in a blink, and now the USO team faced each other for a last rehearsal before their departure to a war-ravaged country on the far side of the world.

"That's a wrap," Compton Moore concluded the rehearsal. "We're ready! Are we ready to do this?"

Everyone began to shout and clap.

"Are we ready?" Compton shouted.

"Yes!" the team shouted back.

"Get some rest; we have a grueling schedule for the next three weeks. Be at the airport at 6 a.m. to check baggage and get boarding passes. Don't forget your tickets and passports," Moore instructed.

Jason caught Janee's arm as the group was leaving the sound stage. His face looked drawn - strained.

"Janee, can we talk? Just for a few minutes. Can we go somewhere and have a drink?"

"Sure, Jason."

"The LeFount is near. I'll meet you there."

"Ok," Janee agreed. She was curious. She had never seen that look on Jason's face before.

She hurried to her car and ripped out of the parking lot and through the gate. A few minutes later, she pulled up in front of the LeFount. An attendant took her car while Janee entered the lounge. Jason was waiting for her.

The pair was escorted to a quiet corner table. The hostess lit a candle and took their drink orders. Janee studied Jason's face and searched his eyes.

"Jason, are you alright?"

Before he answered, their drinks arrived. He toyed with his glass never looking up at Janee. She lost patience!

"Jason, what? This is not in character for you! What is it?"

Finally, he looked up and seemed to have obtained a grasp of what he was about to say. He took a drink.

"Janee, you know how important this trip is to me."

"I think so."

"Yet, I'm feeling so damn scared!"

"If you're scared, why are you going?" Janee snapped out the question before she took time to think.

Jason straightened up and took another drink. Janee followed, never losing eye contact.

"I've thought about that - a lot, the last few days. I have felt guilty about not joining the military, but to be honest, I was afraid – very afraid."

"What about the draft? They will get you eventually," Janee smirked.

"I have powerful and influential friends in the right places," Jason laughed as his eyes watered up.

"This tour is my service. The long hours of rehearsals and backbreaking preparation became my boot camp. My uniform is the costume I wear. My weapon -laughter and entertainment. I'm not in the trenches, but I can do a part. I can make a hard life a little more bearable - if only for a short time. This will be redemption from my guilt! I'll be able to come home and walk with my head held high and agree with myself that I'm not really a coward."

Janee was amused. She stifled a laugh. Jason had been serious and openly honest with her, but it struck her as funny. This man who played tough guy roles – a coward?

"Don't worry Jason," Janee smiled sweetly. "I'll be right there to protect you from all those bad boogie men."

Chapter 20

Flight to Viet Nam

The airport was alive with early morning travelers preparing to depart on international flights.

Janee was the last member of the team to arrive at the ticket counter. Compton Moore was on the verge of panic.

"I swear, Janee, you're gonna give me a heart attack."

"Mr. Moore, I knew you absolutely could not leave without me," Janee smiled charmingly, but inside she wanted to snap his head off. She had just come from emotional good-byes with Paige and her parents. She wasn't tearful, but they were, and she hated it! What was the big deal? People flew back and forth from Viet Nam everyday.

Doc Martin and Buster already had the equipment checked through. They helped Janee with her luggage. Phil and Juju greeted her - relieved that all the team was now present.

Crowds of adoring fans surrounded Huggie and Jason. Some young girls in what appeared a school or church group recognized Janee and screamed. Instantly, a sea of kids seeking to get close to her engulfed her. Hands held out scraps of paper, books, napkins, anything to hold an auto-graph. She was relieved and thankful when security rescued her and led her to the boarding gate.

The plane was large and comfortable, one contracted by the military to transport service personnel and military families who were allowed into Viet Nam.

The USO team was flying in first class. It wasn't long into the flight before Huggie was speaking to one of the stewardesses. After breakfast was served, Huggie addressed the tour team.

"Listen up, team. I see a lot of green recruits on this flight. This is their first time so far from home, and some won't be returning - least, not alive. So I figure, this as good a time as any to cheer up a bunch of scared kids and get our tour started. I got permission to spend time back there talkin', laughin' and buildin' up our service boys. I would count it as a personal favor, if you would go with me in this."

With the snap of his fingers, he drew the curtain aside that separated first class. He took a couple of steps down the aisle smiling into the faces of the travelers peering all the way to the rear of the plane. Some began to laugh and applaud. He held his arms open wide and shouted.

"I'm Huggie Newman and a part of a USO Tour. We want to be the first to welcome you to the tropical paradise of Viet Nam. You are going to love it here - the people are very friendly!" He paused for response. "Well, most of them," he continued as the laughter and applause grew.

"You will benefit from the R & R you receive here. Think of the tan you'll get. Great food - starts with CC for rations. But let me warn you 'bout the fireworks!"

"He's got them!" Jason remarked to Janee.

Huggie walked up and down the aisle holding the whole plane captive for forty minutes with his spontaneous jokes and stories bouncing off of conversations with the passengers. When he became spent, he introduced the rest of the team. Some of the crew were shy but made their way to the rear of the plane shaking hands and talking to ones who showed interest.

The plane came alive when Jason Finn appeared. They cheered and clapped for him. Some of the women squealed loudly. The stewardesses were hard pressed to keep order. Jason laughed and told everyone to behave or the team would go back to first class.

Janee's heart was beating madly when she slipped past the curtain. The GI's shouted and whistled in wild glee when she appeared.

She began walking the gauntlet of smiling, happy faces. She held hands, teased, patted faces of soldiers who appeared mere boys in uniform. As she laughed and joked, her heart ached with the awareness that some of them would never see family or loved ones again.

"Aren't you afraid to go to such a dangerous place, Miss Stemper?" someone tugged at her arm.

She turned to look into the frightened face of a soldier. She couldn't determine if his fear came from going to Viet Nam or meeting a celebrity.

"How old are you, soldier?" she asked.

"Barely eighteen. I enlisted soon as I could."

"Where's home?"

"The mountains of Kentucky. Never been anywhere - that is - 'til basic training."

Janee looked deep into this soldier, searching his soul.

"Are you afraid?" she asked.

"I don't want to be, but I trust the Lord and pray to Him more than ever before."

'Stupid, foolish boy,' she felt anger over his answer to her question, but covered it up. "Well, honey, how could I possibly be afraid when I have brave young men all around me with great big guns. When I see you brave, then I won't be afraid."

Janee took his hand and squeezed it. The soldier sat up with a new determination. His grip tightened on Janee's hand.

Tears came in his eyes.

"Thank you," he whispered, and he released her hand. She went to the next soldier.

When the team retreated to the quietness of their seats, Janee was exhausted. She fell into a dead sleep for hours only to be stirred by Juju. He was shaking her gently.

"We descending into Saigon," he pointed out the window.

She sat up and with squinting eyes saw the deepest, richest emerald-green-covered mountains offset by rice fields outside her window. Buildings began to appear underneath the plane.

"We made it!" exclaimed Doc Martin. "Viet Nam!"

Chapter 21

Christmas Eve in Saigon

Saigon was a crowded city of strange sights, smells, sounds and people. Military vehicles from the airfield transported the team to a nice downtown hotel. They had ample time on the way to get a feel for this city, which was to be their home for the next few days.

Although they had been warned that the enemy could be anywhere or anyone, Saigon as far as what the tour saw seemed peaceful enough. It was hard to imagine that fighting and killing was a daily occurrence in this beautiful place. Janee shuddered as she thought of it.

The people were in constant motion. Bicycles filled the streets. The voices and horns, the little bells on the bicycles all blended together becoming an irritating noise. Janee noticed that most of the people appeared friendly and were conscious of the Americans' presence. She saw many indications of western influence. There were Christmas trees in some windows and decorations along the way. She wondered if these people understood why they were celebrating Christmas. She smiled at their probable ignorance. 'How foolish,' she thought, 'celebrating the birth of a God that doesn't care.'

Pedestrians on the sidewalks would occasionally shout or wave. Every time the Air Force bus transporting the team stopped at an intersection, small children with dirt-splotched arms and faces would crowd alongside the bus holding up their little hands for whatever they could get.

'Where are their mothers?' Janee wondered. These children were far too young to be out on a busy street.

'Maybe the parents are working,' she surmised. Then her eyes locked with those of a little boy. He had a beautiful, dirty face and dark eyes. He held both hands up to her, and for an instant as their eyes met she felt he was holding his hands up to her, not for what he could get, but for her to pick him up. Janee had a strong compulsion to run off the bus and grab this little one up into her arms and hold him. She knew that is exactly what her Grandmother Emile would do. She shook off the urge!

"Where are these children's parents, for God's sake?" Janee shouted up to the Airmen in the front of the bus.

"Most of the children in this area have no family. They were killed in the war. The homes for orphans are full beyond capacity, so these are street children," came the answer.

Janee covered her mouth with her hand.

"How awful!" she softly cried out. She looked back at a sad little boy watching the bus pull away. Janee suddenly felt very small and totally helpless to remedy the situation. She rode in silence the rest of the way to the hotel, and late that night she finally got through to her own parents on the phone. She told her mother what she had seen and confessed what she felt for that child. Later she wept and then became incensed, refusing to tolerate such weakness in herself. Janee quickly smothered any affection she had for a people she did not know.

There was only time for one rehearsal before their first show, which would be on Christmas Eve. The base in Saigon was fortunate to have a large theatre where movies were shown, and the team was amazed at the seating capacity. There was a stage with a curtain covering the screen that afforded plenty of space for the performances. The theatre gave them an excellent sound system. Phil Hanson was excited over this unexpected turn of events and set about plugging in his equipment. Doc and Buster hurried to turn the stage into a Christmas set.

Compton confiscated a large decorated Christmas tree complete with a string of lights from a hushed source. Juju got the stage lighting in place. He would man the spotlight and lighting changes from a control panel in the projection room. The plan for the Christmas programs was for Huggie to come out first and do his routine. Then Jason and Janee would join him for their humorous three-act skit. Jason would be in an officer's uniform, and Janee was a "grunt" with her hair under a hat that's brim partially covered her face so she look like a boy.

Then Janee would finish the show with Christmas songs. When the team was putting the show together back in California, she had words with Compton over the selection of her Christmas songs.

"You have no Christmas carols, Janee," he sounded displeased looking up from the list of her songs he had just gone over.

"You know I don't believe in that junk, so why should I sing about it?"

"Do you believe in Santa Claus?"

"Humph!" Janee snarled her nose. "I left that when I was six."

"But still you sing about him."

"I'd believe in Santa before I would Christ!" she quipped.

"I'm sorry you think that way. If it wasn't for the baby Jesus, we wouldn't be celebrating Christmas."

Janee felt her blood begin to boil. She couldn't understand Compton. She had given him credit for more intelligence than this.

"So you are - one of those - Christians," she accused.

"If you mean, do I see the spirit of Christmas in the Christ Child, and do I believe that is why we have Christmas, then, yes, I am a Christian. Janee, we won't rob these GI's of Christmas music because you are mad at God for whatever your reason."

"How dare you!" she raised her hand to strike the director; then drew back.

"This is no longer a request. I want three Christmas carols in your song mix!"

For a week, Janee fumed. She ranted and raved - throwing and breaking things in her apartment. Reluctantly, she selected, "Away in a Manger," "Silent Night" and "Hark, the Herald Angels Sing." Even now as they neared their first show, Janee felt sick at the thought of singing these three carols. She finally smoothed her ruffled feathers with – 'they are just songs - like the rest.'

All too soon, it was show time! A colorful mixture of military personnel began filing into the theatre. There were Airmen in their blue uniforms, Navy in white, Marines were mostly in khaki, a few officers in their dress uniforms, while the Army greens were scattered throughout. Janee watched in fascination from off stage. The audience was almost exclusively male except for the few female faces that dotted the rows and rows of men. 'They must be in paradise,' she mused as she thought about the handful of women she could make out.

Jason Finn came up beside her.

"Jason, the theatre is overflowing!" she exclaimed. "The space in front of the stage is crammed; they line the walls and are seated in the aisles. Look at their faces! We've never performed before such an eager audience!"

"Unbelievable!" Jason agreed as he peeked out. "But we have a problem. No one has seen Huggie or knows where he is!"

"What? I thought he was in a dressing room."

"No. Compton is going crazy. He left the hotel early."

"Do you think he got drunk?" Janee asked, a sick feeling forming in the pit of her stomach. "Compton will kill him!"

Just then Compton came up behind them. Jason gave him a questioning look.

"He's nowhere! I can't believe he would do this to us!" Compton fumed.

"Nor can I," Janee wanted to defend their comrade in this venture. "It's just not like Huggie to be so - unprofessional."

"Just the same, I want you both to be ready to -" Compton was interrupted by a commotion out on the theatre floor. To their amazement they saw Santa Claus with his sack walking down the aisle.

"I swear - it's Huggie!" Compton breathed in amazement.

"I never knew he brought a Santa suit. He is so full of surprises!" Janee cried with glee.

Huggie was huffing and puffing as all out of breath. He began shouting - "Merry Christmas! Merrrry Christmas!"

The crowd came alive! Huggie bounded up onto the stage, plopped down his sack and took a microphone from its stand.

"Whew, so glad to be here. Had a narrow escape. You see, I made a turn over Hanoi."

The crowd booed and hissed.

"My elves made a special gift for me to drop off. You know what it was?"

Many responded with, "No."

"Me neither," Huggie laughed, "but it had 'Stink Bomb' written on the side. My wee helpers said it would brighten up Charlie's Christmas and was strong enough to melt the barrels of their triple A's - if you get the drift of what I'm saying. Speaking of drift, President Johnson asked me to give out fifty-two hundred special awards for bravery in latrine duty," Huggie paused for effect.

"Back to my narrow escape. The - 'Stink Bomb' musta worked 'cause I encountered no triple A fire, but let me tell you - the ground fire was somethin' else. Charlie was shootin' anything they could get their hands on. Makin' a final run on Hanoi, a spit wad hit me - right here on my face. Then a huge blob of bubble gum smacked Rudolph in the nose and put out our radar. We were flyin' blind 'til I spied all these truck headlights - or was it bicycles? I ain't for sure. 'Thank God,' I said, 'It's the Ho Chi Minh Trail!' On Dasher, on Comet, on Donner, on Blitzen - you too, Rudolph - follow those supply trucks! And Comet, quit complainin' I didn't name you first - gadzooks! These reindeer! Now where was I? - Oh, yes, following the Ho Chi Minh Trail!"

"That's were you should have dropped the bomb!" a Marine out in the audience shouted.

Huggie stood silent looking around. Then he wiggled his eyebrows up and down. He held his nose, and then with a laugh, "Actually, I think I dropped the bomb with that last joke!"

The crowd erupted into a roar!

"By golly, he's got them now," Jason exclaimed.

For the next forty minutes, Huggie dazzled the military audience with his brilliant hilarity. These were men and women who needed a release from the harsh brutality of the war, and for a very brief niche of their lives the USO Tour was giving an all-out dose of deliverance.

The service men and women were delighted with the clever, funny, three-act play performed by Huggie Newman, Jason Finn and Janee Stemper. Everyone was aware that Janee was one of the actors on the stage, especially the multi-tude of men, even though her feminine curves were covered up by the baggy uniform she wore and a cap pulled down covering her pretty face. But did she have a surprise for them when she came on stage later to sing!

After the play there was a brief intermission during which Janee changed. She let her hair down and combed it out. She put on a silky knee-length white dress. It was a modest cut at the top, but clung seductively as she walked in trim heels that flattered her feet - still firm enough to dance. And when she spun, the dress flared out showing off her shapely legs.

The thought of showing herself off before all these men didn't intimidate or embarrass her, it excited her! The affect she knew she would have on them gave her an overwhelming sense of power. An adrenaline rush was surging through her veins, and she felt pumped!

"Go get 'em, girl," Huggie laughed. "You already broke a leg!"

"Gentlemen," Janee smiled at Huggie, Jason and Compton. "We made them laugh, now I'm going to make them cry and beg for more."

She gave the high sign to Phil to start the music. She waited and then the big band sound of trumpets belted out an upbeat "Jingle Bells." Janee went running out onto the stage. The crowd came to their feet!

She picked up the song, "Dashing through the snow - in a one-horse open sleigh." In a few minutes, the whole theatre was rocking to the beat. She could make out servicemen snapping their fingers, some clapping in time, and many swaying back and forth to the music.

Next, she slowed down with, "Have Yourself a Merry Little Christmas." This song had a melancholy effect on the audience, but she picked them up when she put on a pouty little-girl face and sang, "You better watch out - you better not cry - better not pout - I'm tellin' you why - Santa is here - he's got his list."

From that song, Janee got the whole place thumping again with a fast, "Rudolph, the Red-Nosed Reindeer." That concluded the opening four-song melody.

"Hello, I'm Janee Stemper, and I'm so happy to be a part of this USO Tour in Viet Nam. Are you having a good time tonight?"

Everyone hooted, clapped, cheered and whistled. Shouts were directed at her, but she couldn't make out what was said, but their enthusiasm and looks said it all to this young performer. She sang several more songs, which had many of the GI's in the front aisles dancing to the music. She motioned for Phil to hold the music before she did the Christmas carols. Juju brought up the lights.

"I know there must be more women here than just me. I want all the women to please stand. Please, everyone be seated - except the women."

Janee saw some women hesitantly one-by-one stand up.

"Don't sit down - stay standing," Janee instructed. She counted them. Twenty-seven.

"Twenty-seven women here. I want all you big husky guys to take a look at these women who serve alongside you. I think they are truly special and very brave. You see, fellows, even though we - hate - to admit it, sometimes we gals get - well - you know - sorta frightened, so I want to be sure you take care of us and with respect."

Janee could tell she struck a chord. The men began to clap, and ones next to the standing women stood up and shook their hands, some gave hugs. Soon the entire audience was back on their feet, where they remained through the next three songs. Juju dimmed the lights and Janee began, "Silent Night, Holy Night."

She heard a low roar and thought it to be feedback from her microphone, until it grew stronger, and she could see the movement of people's lips. They were singing with her! She moved into, "Away In A Manger," and the voices followed.

By the time, "Hark The Herald Angels Sing," began, the sound rebounded off the ceiling! The men and women were singing their hearts out. The last chorus, Janee quit and just held out the microphone to them.

"Hey, you all are pretty darn good!" Janee shouted, and a cheer arose from the floor of the theatre.

Janee sang several more peppy Christmas songs, and then brought out Huggie and Jason, and the three finished with, "We Wish You A Merry Christmas." The trio took their bows to a standing ovation, and then made their exit.

The crowd refused to leave. They clapped and whistled and stomped their feet.

"Listen to that!" Compton was excited.

"Janee, Janee, Janee, Janee," the GI's shouted in unison. "Janee, Janee, Janee, Janee, Janee! More, more, more, more!"

"We used all the Christmas background. I could pull up something from one of the other shows," Phil offered.

Janee thought for a moment.

"I have something!" she shouted as she ran back on stage. The chants from the audience shifted to a huge cheer, and the men were wildly ecstatic. Janee took the mic with the long cord and sat down on the edge of the stage with her feet hanging down. She motioned for all to take their seats. A hush fell over the theatre.

Janee smiled and, in a lovely voice, began to sing, "I'm Dreaming Of A White Christmas." A miraculous transformation took place as she sang. Janee saw grown men cry. Some, embarrassed, brushed away the tears. Others, unashamed, let them flow freely. Others buried their faces in their hands. When she finished, there was no applause.

"I have one last song for you, and I am sad to go, but the hour is late, so I want you to be good boys and as you leave, know we are all very proud of you!"

Janee bowed her head, and then looked up.

"I'll be home - for Christmas. You can count on me," she began, and as she sang she saw a soldier stand up holding high a piece of paper.

'What is he doing?' she wondered. 'Does he want an autograph?'

"Please have snow - and mistletoe," she sang on.

Then another stood up. He held up a picture. Janee could see a woman and child. Another stood up - holding a letter. One after another they stood - holding high something precious to them - from home. It was their way of saying, 'I'll be home for Christmas.' Not physically, but in their hearts-in their dreams. They continued to stand as Janee sang. Even tough old Sergeants were moved by the glow of the Christmas spirit that stirred something deep inside from long ago.

Janee left the stage to applause that vibrated the building.

Jason hugged her as she went backstage.

"Well, my dear, you certainly stole the show!" he laughed good-naturedly.

And that was Christmas Eve in Saigon 1967 for Janee Stemper.

Chapter 22

Performance in Da Nang

ℒℰ

The tour team did several more Christmas shows in the theatre. They soon realized that there were so many troops in Saigon that the audiences were scheduled in rotation, so all the military could attend. They shifted to an Air Force Base on the outskirts of the city to do a New Year's Eve and New Year's Day special. This base afforded a large hangar they were able to use; however, this presented more of a challenge for good sound and lighting. The team agreed that the theatre definitely spoiled them.

The USO Tour had presented fifteen back-to-back shows upon completion of the New Year's Special. They were ready for a breather.

"I left two days open for a brief rest," Compton announced. "Let's take in Saigon before our next shows."

Janee relished the sights of the city and enjoyed some exhilarating shopping. The haunting thought would occasionally steal into her consciousness that a war was raging all around them. So far she had seen little evidence of any fighting. Saigon was a hustle of running people going about living their lives. She wondered if the military wasn't shielding the team from the terror - or perhaps the war truly was far north. She pondered this as she wondered if the smoke she saw in the distance from her hotel window was a bomb explosion or someone's house on fire. Had the peace she saw around her eluded to a false sense of security?

The next six days were scheduled shows at bases surrounding Saigon. They now shifted to their third production designed for after Christmas and New Year's. The team had a lot of fun with this one, and the GI's loved it, but something bothered Janee. There was little contact with the soldiers apart from the stage time. They were given military escorts responsible for their safety. As soon as a show was completed, they were whisked off to their hotel. Oh, yes, there were several evenings when the team was guests of base commanders at the Officers' Clubs, but this was formal and regimented. Something in Janee wanted to talk to and spend time with the common guys.

"Must be from my Grandfather Farmer," she mused. "Where else would that nonsense come from?" she scowled.

The USO Tour was driven back into Saigon to the hotel where they stayed before. They assembled in Compton's room.

"Listen up, team," Compton started the meeting. "We've given some great shows, and I'm proud of you. I know accommodations weren't quite so nice the last six days."

"Say that again!" Huggie laughed. "That room two nights ago had creatures crawling on the walls."

"And under my bed!" Buster added.

"The creatures on Huggie's wall is what we ate for breakfast," Doc commented without expression.

"Come on, man, just some harmless lizards," Juju poked at Doc Martin.

Janee shuddered.

"Come on, guys!" Compton attempted to restore some serious thinking.

"We fly out early in the morning day after tomorrow for Da Nang. There is no hotel so we will be staying on base -

probably in a barracks. Da Nang is a large Marine Base, so they have two performances scheduled the nights of the 12th and 13th."

"Do they have a theatre?" Phil asked.

"I understand the stage is open air."

"Sound will be crappy!" Phil grumbled.

"To match the lights," Juju chimed in.

"I know, I know, do the best you can! This will be the first show in months for these Marines, and our last. Let's go out with a bang!"

"Yeah!" Huggie agreed and began a slow clap. The others joined him.

Janee slept until noon the next day. By the following morning she was primed and excited to get to Da Nang. She was packed and ready an hour before the team was to depart.

They boarded a military bus that picked them up at the hotel. The bus wound through streets to an airfield where they were dropped off at a waiting transport. This plane was smaller than the one that had flown them from the states, but it was comfortable. Once in the air, the team was able to mingle with the other passengers, most of who were replacement recruits.

"Please take your seats, and fasten your seat belts. We are starting our approach to Da Nang," the pilot's voice squawked over the intercom.

The approach was not gradual but sudden, leaping Janee's stomach up into her throat. She gripped the armrests tightly!

"Whoa!" gasped Jason, who sat next to her.

When Janee finally braved looking out the window, she saw multitudes of planes, helicopters and equipment spread out around the airstrip which came into view as the plane banked. Beyond the runway she made out a vast array of tents and seemingly temporary buildings. All became a blur as the plane touched down.

A small detachment of Marines, and a Naval officer who stood out in her white uniform, waited for the team as they came down the steps. The female officer quickly singled out Janee and approached her.

"Welcome to Da Nang, Miss Stemper. I'm Ensign Tesoro Gonzalez. I've been assigned to you."

"Assigned to me?" Janee questioned.

"Yes. I'm responsible to make your stay in Da Nang as comfortable as possible. You will be bunking in the nurses' quarters."

"Any - men nurses?" Janee spoke with a sly smile.

"No," the nurse responded curtly.

The team climbed into a military truck after loading luggage and equipment. Men whistled at the sight of the two women on the truck as they passed down roads lined by tents and Quonset huts. Gonzalez kept her eyes straight ahead, while Janee smiled and waved at the Marines. Many hollered or waved back.

Janee could make out small talk between the rest of the team and the Marines. The trip from the airfield to where the men were staying took about fifteen minutes. Janee was amazed at how much the base was spread out. She saw signs that denoted a base exchange and mess hall. The bus passed a large open area with a platform on one end. Curtains had been hung to form a backdrop.

"Is that where we will - be?" Janee asked.

"Yes," Gonzalez answered.

"Where are the seats?"

"They will sit on the ground."

"That seems rather uncomfortable."

"Believe me; they would stand on their heads to see you. Word has come up how good your show has been."

The men unloaded at a barracks, and the bus drove on. Soon they came upon huts with the familiar Red Cross. The bus stopped in front of one of them, and Ensign Gonzalez helped Janee with her baggage.

"You don't believe in traveling light, do you?" the Navy nurse observed sarcastically.

Janee bristled!

"Have I offended you in some way?"

"Not in the least, Miss Stemper."

"Good. I'm a long way from home, and I want to make the best of this experience."

"As do I," the young woman replied calmly.

When Janee arrived back at the field later where the performances were scheduled, the crew was hard at work getting set up.

"Listen closely to your monitor," Phil instructed when they did a mic check. "All your sound will be lost out in space and feel hollow. You may get some feedback so don't get near the speakers. I'm having to run the system at max so the audience can hear, but we'll sacrifice quality."

The team did a rehearsal, ate a quick bite of a meal brought from a chow hall. By then Marines were flooding onto the field.

"You get A to K," Gonzalez informed without a smile.

"What does that mean?" Jason asked.

"Everyone whose last name starts with A to K comes tonight. The rest get to see your show tomorrow night."

Huggie opened the show with his routine, after that came the little three-act play, with Janee's songs to close out the evening. They used the same order as before, except Huggie's jokes were geared for after Christmas and New Year's. Some of his material was spur-of-the-moment, which gave it freshness from night to night. He was energetic and amazing with his ability to make people laugh.

The three-act play was different from the Christmas and New Year's plays. For this one, Janee wore a tiger suit. The Marine and Navy audience was noisy and rowdy, but really got into the show. The excitement and involvement of the crowd energized the cast on stage!

For her songs, Janee had selected some pop hits of the '60's.

She opened with two melodies, "Groovin" and "Lazy Days" to take their memories to a weekend park in the summer.

Next she wound the GI's up with "Higher and Higher," then got everyone rocking to "Bad Moon Rising." A roar went up as she began the Elvis' song, "Suspicious Minds," then she slid into "Midnight Special."

The audience quieted down when she sang, "Different Drum," but perked up with Janee's renditions of the Beatles' tunes, "Hello, Goodbye" and "Ticket to Ride." By now they were singing so loud that she had trouble hearing her monitor. The last chorus she gave up and clapped with them until they finished the song.

The music intro into the next song was softer and slower. She motioned for everybody to sit down. She saw the same transformation take place she had witnessed at every performance on the tour, when she went into her last song.

"Simon and Garfunkel made this hit. I hope you like it!" she shouted.

"Homeward Bound," she sang. As the song progressed she could see many a tough Marine break down. When she finished there was a pause, then an ovation that shook the stage. They refused to stop even after the trio took their bows. They wanted another song from Janee, and loudly made their demand known.

Finally, Janee ran back onto the stage, and belted out, "Young Girl," and "Hooked on a Feeling," to the delight of the Marines and Sailors.

"Some folks back home don't think we should be here. I say they are wrong! What do you say?" Janee shouted into the noisy crowd.

A cheer rose from the field as though the lot of them wanted to make their voices heard clear back to the states. Marines and a few Navy men crowded around Janee making her captive. She grew frightened and feared for her safety, but the men's warm smiles and gentle voices reassured her of their respect and admiration. Military Police tried to reach her, but the throng was too strong for them.

Men were shaking her hand, telling her how they loved her movies and songs. One Marine, when he took hold of her hand, dropped to one knee and looked up at her with pleading eyes.

"I love you - marry me!"

"Hush your mouth! Don't pay "Cherry Pit" no mind, 'cause he ain't got one," another Marine next to Janee laughed.

She patted "Cherry Pit's" face. "Honey, I'd marry all of you if I could!"

Laughter began around Janee, followed by the Marines shouting loud "Ooh –Rahs." Strong hands lifted her up on a shoulder, and she was paraded up and down the field of the GI's. She waved, laughed and blew kisses, amid cheers, howls, well wishes and thanks from her admiring court. She found herself immensely enjoying the performance in Da Nang.

Chapter 23

Eye Opener

Some of the Da Nang officers had cleared a large bunker for the USO Tour. They formed a welcoming party. A well-stocked bar stretched across one end. The bunker filled to "standing room only" by the time the team was escorted inside. A Major did a short introductory speech and "welcome" to the USO team. He invited everyone to the bar, and as soon as his speech concluded, music played over a makeshift sound system.

"That hurts my ears!" Phil complained.

Marines and Sailors pushed and crowded to get close to their guests. Women present were vastly outnumbered, and Janee was overwhelmed with offers of drinks or requests to dance, some just seemed anxious to hear her voice or hold her hand. She became aware that Nurse Gonzalez never left her side. Once she stepped in to rescue Janee from an overbearing lad who was obviously letting the liquor do his talking.

"Straighten up, Corporal, and mind your manners!" Gonzalez commanded.

By midnight the party was really rocking. Any women who showed up were ushered right in, but the men pressed hard at the doors trying to get through. The party lasted into the early morning, and Janee reveled in every moment. She was definitely in her element and hit her stride with these Marines and Sailors. This was the part that had been missing in the other bases, and now that she had it - she was lapping it up and loving it.

The rush she got from the party and the drinking had her high when she and Ensign Gonzalez returned to the nurses' quarters. Some of the women straggled in behind Janee and Gonzalez; others were already asleep. The barracks consisted of small rooms, each furnished with two single beds, two lockers, a table and two chairs. Bathroom was "community" down the hall. Janee bunked with Ensign Tesoro Gonzalez. The young Ensign tried to quiet the noisy and loud movie star who was talking and laughing nonsense as the pair stumbled down the hallway. She held a finger firmly against Janee's mouth.

"Quiet! Some of these nurses have morning shift!"

Janee tried a sloppy salute that broke off in laughter.

Inside their room, Janee was still feeling the effects of the party. She was talking incessantly about everything and anything. Gonzalez was silent and sullen. She left Janee talking to herself and returned a few minutes later with two coffees from a vending machine. She handed one to Janee.

"You're - no - fun," Janee complained. She took the coffee and sipped, making an ugly face. The coffee was bitter strong.

Gonzalez sat at the table and fingered her coffee cup. She never made eye contact with Janee. Janee stared at the young officer for a long time. Finally, it got to her!

"So-so or whatever your name is, you don't like me very much, do you?"

Gonzalez turned fiery eyes on Janee. "Not really."

"Why? You don't even know me!"

"I know you are a spoiled, rich, big shot white girl from Hollywood, and my name is Tesoro."

"So, Tesoro, I'm the rich white girl, and you are the poor Mexican kid who never got a break. Poor-poor pitiful you – give me a break! So you are jealous."

"Ha! Of what? You? Fat chance! My father and mother came to America for a new start. They settled in Tucson, and they worked hard! Hard for everything they have. I worked and put myself through college to be a nurse."

Janee rose off her bed, and Tesoro met her face to face.

"You don't think my parents worked? They worked hard living in a one-bedroom house when I was born. You think that making a movie isn't work? Four a.m. calls that go on until midnight and then up at four to do it again. Sometimes we do a scene fifty takes before we get it the way the director wants. There's never any private life; I don't even have time for a boyfriend."

"Humph! That's hard to believe the way you made hoo-hoo with the boys tonight."

"So that's it! Did I attract the attention of your boyfriend? Or do you even have one? Don't take it out on me just because you're "plain Jane" and no men pay you any mind!"

Tesoro's face contorted in rage from Janee's stinging barrage. She took a swing at this woman who had invaded her room and her life. Janee blocked the blow with one hand, and with the other sent Gonzalez careening off the table and crashing onto her bed. Tesoro bounced up ready to fight, but Janee popped her a hard punch in the mouth before she got her footing. She fell backwards onto her bed, groaned and rolled on her side. Janee could see she was crying, but wasn't about to give any mercy.

"I was shocked to arrive here and be given such a lousy reception. The Marines were excited to see us and made the team feel welcome. But you? Oh, no, you made me feel like a trespasser. I don't buy that rich bitch from Hollywood garbage, so what's your problem?"

Tesoro sat up. Her eyes blazed at Janee.

"You don't know anything about what's going on!"

"No, I don't! Tell me!"

"What do you think you did to those men when you were on stage?"

"I took their minds off the war a few minutes! Made them happy!"

"Can't you see you were tearing their hearts out?!"

"What?"

"When they saw you on stage in your sexy dress and heard you sing, they ached for their girlfriends and wives; they are homesick! Couldn't you see that?"

"I saw it on Christmas Eve in Saigon. I saw men hold up letters from home, and pictures of girlfriends and wives and family. I saw strong men cry!"

"Then why play with their emotions?"

"Don't you think that happens when they see you walk to the Base Exchange, or they hear a song, or watch a movie, Tesoro? Do you think they would be better for our not coming? We made them laugh, yes, we made them cry, and remember, but maybe - just maybe - we gave them hope."

Tesoro gazed intently at Janee. She seemed to soften over what was spoken.

"We hoped to cheer the troops up, to take minds off this dirty business of war. To lighten and lift their thoughts from fighting and killing."

Tesoro stood up. She held out her hand to Janee.

"I'm sorry, Miss Stemper," she said slowly.

Janee took her hand and held it. "I'm Janee," she corrected.

"Janee, you still don't understand, but if you truly want to help, come with me!"

Officer Gonzalez led Janee out into the night and entered one of the Quonset huts. A corpsman seated at a desk inside the door saluted Gonzalez. She returned the salute.

"I'm checking this ward. Miss Stemper will accompany me."

They walked through a set of doors into what appeared to be a hospital room lined with beds. In the dim light, Janee could make out that some of the men stirred from sleep, aware of the women's presence.

Tesoro stopped by one bed and peered closely at the man's face.

"Not sleeping, Ron?" she whispered.

"No, m'am," came a husky voice. "I don't sleep very well - sometimes."

"Ron, this is Janee Stemper. Do you know who she is?"

"No, m'am."

"She's a movie star."

"We never got to see a movie where I lived in Pittsburg. I can tell though, you're pretty enough for the movies."

"Janee, this is Lance Corporal Ron Everett from Pittsburg. Ron, tell Janee what happened to you."

"Rather not!"

"Ron, you don't have to be ashamed. It's war wounds."

"No! They ain't! Getting' mauled by a tiger ain't! I came to fight Charlie and got tore up by a damn tiger in the high-lands for my trouble!"

"You'll be back in the fight soon, Marine," sadness filled Tesoro's voice.

They moved to another bed. Janee could see the man's mouth move but couldn't hear what he said.

"This is our Indian Brave, Terry Longdime," Tesoro whispered.

"Oh! My grandparents met an Indian family out in the Arizona desert. They had walked from Montana. I think they were - Crow? Are you from that tribe?" Janee whispered, trying to be cheerful. She saw the man's mouth move.

"I didn't hear you," Janee replied as she put her ear near his mouth.

"Navajo," he choked, "from New Mexico."

"Have you been sleeping, Terry?" Tesoro injected into the conversation. She held her ear close to hear the man's response. Janee gave Tesoro a questioning look.

"He says his insides hurt something fierce." She looked at the man's chart.

"We can't increase your dose of morphine, Terry. Hang in, Marine!"

Janee again gave Tesoro that questioning look, and they walked farther into the room.

"Threw himself on a grenade to save his comrades. When he came in on a chopper, the corpsmen were holding his guts in their hands. The doctor stuffed them back inside and sewed him up."

"Will he make it?"

Tesoro shook her head. "I don't think so."

As they neared another bed, Janee could distinguish the sounds of a man sobbing.

"Wilson, what's wrong?" Tesoro spoke with a tenderness Janee had not heard in a woman's voice outside of her Grandma Emile.

"Nurse, my unit needs me! I just gotta get back in this war. I'm letting my buddies down."

"Now, Wilson McDonald, wouldn't you rather go visit your family in Maine and rest awhile?"

"No! Please nurse," Wilson struggled to get up. Tesoro restrained him and patted his face.

"Do you think I can ship back to my unit soon?"

Janee started to speak, but followed Tesoro's glance at Wilson's legs. She gasped and covered her mouth when she saw that Wilson's left leg ended at the knee. Janee turned her face!

Tesoro touched her shoulder and motioned for her to follow. They stopped at the bedside of a Viet Namese man.

"This is Sami. He is a Viet Namese regular. He was at an outpost near Khe Sanh. They were overrun by the V. C. and Sami was captured, but escaped. Sami, this is Janee Stemper from America."

A broad smile burst across the man's face. He held up two bandaged hands and took Janee's face in them.

A chill went up Janee's back when she discovered Sami had no hands.

"His captors cut them off, so he could never use a rifle again. Next would have been his feet, then tongue, finally they put out the eyes, if he would have lived that long. Luckily, Sami escaped."

Janee could take no more. She fled out the door, forcing back the tears.

Tesoro joined her outside.

"Tesoro, I - I think I - understand!"

Chapter 24

Unscheduled Stop

๖๏

"I have a proposal to make," Compton announced next morning at the team's breakfast meeting. Everyone was quiet and tired. Their attention was half-hearted.

"North of here is a sizable outpost near the DMZ. They built a base last summer and have steadily been increasing troop strength. It's called Khe Sanh, and the Soldiers and Marines there have no entertainment aside from their radios. Now, I was talking to some officers, and they offered to fly us up there and do one show. What ya think?"

Everyone sat in stunned silence. Jason was the first to speak.

"What would be our schedule?"

"Tonight is our last performance here, which is January 13th. We can't get out of here until tomorrow afternoon, but have to fly back to Saigon. The negative part is we will have to stay in Saigon until the next plane for Khe Sanh which is early the 16th. We can do a show that night, but will stay on base until the plane returns on the 19th. Or maybe we can do all three - one each night."

"I don't know," Jason scratched his head. "I have a mountain of work waiting for me when I get back."

"I'm scheduled for a gig the 18th," Buster noted.

"I really should get back," Jason reiterated his concern.

"I say we get the hell outa here!" Phil implored.

"What do you say, Huggie?" Compton turned to the comedian who had so far said nothing.

"Me thinks me funny bone got tangled up with me tonsil."

Everybody groaned.

"Now what the heck does that mean, Huggie?" Compton was exasperated.

"It means the team is tired and homesick," Doc Martin broke in.

"Wait a minute! Just hold on!" Janee couldn't believe this bunch of sissies.

"Jason, weren't you the one who told me this tour was your service? So when the battle extends, you tuck tail and light out for home?" Janee was incensed! "I say we go do the shows."

"My, oh, my, I say we have a little crusader in our midst," Huggie jabbed.

"What's the matter, Huggie, you missin' your bottle?" Janee jabbed him back with biting words.

"That's enough," Compton wanted to calm tempers.

"Listen," Janee wouldn't let go. "Something big happened to me last night that changed my perspective of what we are about. Tesoro took me into one of the hospital wards! I talked to an Indian man from New Mexico and a Marine from Pittsburg. He got chewed up by a stupid tiger - a tiger! Another guy was delivered with his insides hanging out. The doctor shoved 'em back in like soup. I heard another guy crying he wanted to get back to his unit. Only problem for Wilson that he hasn't figured out yet - he only has one and a half legs. A Viet Namese Soldier held my face in his hands 'cept he doesn't have any, 'cause the enemy chopped 'em off! I was touched deeper than I can express to you in words. Sure, we've had great shows with incredible audiences, but have any of you had that big something hit you? Huggie? Compton? Phil? Doc? Juju? Buster? Have you, Jason?"

Jason hung his head.

"Maybe it is something so profound it reaches down to the very depth of our souls and makes us - different."

Huggie began his slow clap. "Right as rain, Miss Stemper, you are. It's not about us - never has been - it's about them Soldiers - out there - up there."

"I'll need to get to the Mars Station and let them know to schedule someone in my place," Buster smiled.

"You all are nuts - but - okay!" Phil conceded.

One by one the others nodded in agreement.

"My work can wait," Jason admitted. "You sure are a spitfire to get your way, Janee."

"Got that right, Mister Actor," Janee grinned triumphantly.

"Then we are agreed," Compton seemed pleased. "We'll do a show in Khe Sanh!"

Chapter 25

Taking Khe Sanh by Storm

᠎᠎᠎

Janee found herself strapped in a small, unbending canvas seat aboard a military C-130 Transport. The plane afforded no windows to see out and was noisy to the level; any conversation meant screaming at one another. The USO team was seated along the sides of the aircraft, along with a company of Marines. In the center were crates of food, medical supplies, and what Janee found out were containers of ammunition. Near the rear she could see some kind of large gun and a Jeep.

The landing was jerky and rough. Janee waited for the engines to shut down, but to her surprise they remained running after the aircraft taxied to a stop. A large back door dropped open to form a ramp to the ground. Soldiers and equipment converged up the ramp to unload the cargo. They worked proficiently and quickly.

Marines on the plane disembarked without words, and the USO group retrieved luggage. A Captain came on the plane and told them to hurry. They were whisked aboard an armored vehicle and taken from the airstrip into the outpost.

Khe Sanh was unlike any of the other bases the team had performed on. It was much smaller, walled by dirt mounds and sandbag barricades. The airfield was on the perimeter of the base, and thick foliage had been cleared away on all sides. Janee could make out coiled rows of barbed wire in the clearings. Raised towers rose above the walls in various locations, but even these weren't very high although they were well fortified with machine guns.

Janee was shocked at first sight of the base; it appeared there were no buildings. She soon discovered that everything was underground with only the roofs showing.

"This outpost was built to withstand attack," the driver explained. He pointed out along the way that these were bunkers that protruded out of the ground no more than three to four feet.

"This will be home for the next few days," the driver motioned ahead. He stopped the vehicle near steps at one end of a bunker. "Welcome to Khe Sanh," he said with a wide smile.

The team gathered their baggage and equipment with the help of the Marine driver.

"Here's your welcoming committee," he nodded toward a fast-moving Jeep sliding around a nearby curve in the dirt road. It came to an abrupt halt while the cloud of dust that followed caught up, blowing in the faces of the team. Their driver spoke to the Marine in the Jeep as he stepped onto the ground. He turned to the USO team.

"Are we ever glad to see you! Welcome to Khe Sanh. I'm Master Gunney Wade Thomas. Most just call me Gunney. I'll be your host while you are here, and let me tell you, the whole post has been counting the days, all two of them. Ha! We've near gone crazy for something to do."

"You are saying there's been no fighting here?" Jason Finn sounded relieved.

"Intelligence keeps telling us there's an indication of enemy build-up, but we haven't heard or seen nothen'. Charlie musta turned tail and moved elsewhere. Anyway, it's been boring. We have to hunt for things to stay occupied, and sure are ready for some live entertainment."

Compton broke into the discussion.

"I'm the director of the team, Compton Moore. This is Huggie Newman, Jason Finn and Janee Stemper, the stars of our show. That's Juju behind me. He lights us up, and Phil Hanson there makes us heard. Doc Martin and Buster put us together."

Gunney greeted each team member with a comment. He lingered with Janee holding her hand.

"I saw one of your movies when you were a little girl. I was a lad with a crush!"

"I hope you didn't get over it, Wade Thomas," Janee flashed her charm with her words and smile.

"If I did, it all came tumbling back on me seeing you face to face and all grown up!"

Gunney led the team down into a trench to the opening of the bunker. The doorway had piles of sandbags all around it, reminding one of a mole hole.

"This isn't exactly the Hilton, but we did the best we could with what we got," Gunney motioned them through a door he held open.

"We cleared out a debriefing room - well - we haven't had all that much to debrief. Ha!"

It took a minute for their eyes to adjust to the dim lighting. The walls were lined with planks that resembled railroad ties. A bulletin board hung on a wall to the right. There were no windows and no pictures hung, a long table with chairs around it was the only furniture present, unless the eight cots lined up in two rows counted.

"We prepared the room through that door for you, Miss Stemper. You must know that you are the only female on this outpost."

"Wooo-wooo!" Buster teased Janee.

"Except for some hooch maids who come in to cook, or clean, and keep some of us company," Gunney continued with an impish grin.

"I know I'll be safe with all you big strong Marines to protect me," Janee spoke soft and low. Out of the corner of her eye she caught Jason shaking his head. She immediately sensed he did not approve, but decided to let it go. She opened the door to step into a small, bare room with a cot on one side and a chair next to it.

Doc set her luggage down beside the cot and retreated, closing the door behind him. Janee thought it odd that the men just assumed because she was a woman, she wanted to be alone. Or was it, they didn't want to deal with her? She looked around the dark, bleak room.

"I've been in strange places before," she spoke out loud to herself, "but this beats all!"

To the delight of the several thousand Marines at Khe Sanh, arrangements were made to do three shows - one each day, January 16, 17 and 18. They decided to do their Christmas show on the 16th.

"We'll just get a jump on Christmas this year," Huggie laughed. "In case there be some not here in December."

"That's not funny!" Phil snapped.

"Hey, loosen up, sound man, I mean DOERS, not DEAD!"

"What you mean, Huggie, this DOERS?" Juju asked - puzzled.

"If we're gonna live in Viet Nam, we best learn the lingo," Huggie's eyes danced. "It stands for, 'Date of Estimated Return Stateside.' You know, - fly into the sky in a Freedom Bird."

"I'm not living in this hell hole. I can't get on that Freedom Bird quick enough! I say let's get these shows done and get outa here," Phil wanted it known he was not happy about being in Khe Sanh. "Here we are in a place of outdoor toilets - we musta been crazy to come here!"

"Oh he's crying the blues! Give the man a snot rag," Huggie came back.

Gunney later explained their shows would have to be in the afternoons.

"Can't have lights at night. Makes us too good a target for the Viet Cong."

The Marines loved the Christmas show and were moved with memories. The New Year's special brought a more festive mood, and the team shifted to the show they did in Da Nang for the third and final performance.

Each showing proceeded without incident, which seemed a bit of a let down for Janee. What had she expected? What could possibly produce the changes she had spoken of?

Sure these GI's were supercharged which sent electric shocks of energy throughout cast and crew of the team. Janee was thrilled to see the men respond to their acts, especially when she danced and sang. She had no regrets they came.

During the day, the team was allowed to roam the post and mingle with the troops. Janee really liked that and, of course, was the center of attention wherever she went. Gunney followed close behind when she took her walks.

Armed Forces Radio filled the camp, belting out hits of the '50's and '60's over loud speakers. Every hour news bits from the states were broadcast. One morning there was news of an anti-war demonstration-taking place in Washington. That brought out angry responses in many Marines, dismay and confusion in others. GI's kept asking Janee what she thought.

"Blind cowards - every one of them!" she condemned the demonstrators' efforts with her own brand of anger.

The team talked to Marines as well as the South Viet Namese Rangers stationed there. Most of them spoke good English.

"Walk the trench - that side - one mile. Other side - half a mile." A Ranger laughed good-naturedly. "Good walk! Good exercise!"

The team did hike the trenches - talking to the Marines. Janee would sing along to a song on the radio with them - she might do some dance steps for an admiring audience - often she would just listen to them talk and tell their stories. Over and over the team members were told how much they were appreciated. The base was thrilled to have the USO come to such a remote outpost. Every Marine and Ranger there was able to take in at least one of the shows.

Contentment had settled in on Janee. The days were mild and lazy. The shows were wildly received, and Janee felt their presence instilled a little happiness into these G. I.'s uneventful lives. It was peaceful here; in fact, it was hard for Janee to think of this as a country embroiled in war. She had seen none of it. Now the sun was coming up on her last day in Khe Sanh. In three hours she and the rest of the tour would be on the plane back to Saigon, then off for home. Home.... She had come to Viet Nam, taken Khe Sanh by storm, and would return the "Conquering Hero!"

Chapter 26

Under Siege

🏵️

Morning news coming over the base loudspeakers from Armed Forces Radio filtered into Janee's brain. The Tokens were singing, "The Lion Sleeps Tonight." She stirred. Somewhere in the refrain - "the village, the peaceful village, the lion sleeps tonight," Janee grew aware of men yelling something in the distance. Rapid gunfire and lots of it followed. Janee sat up in her cot. Suddenly, an explosion shook the bunker throwing her over onto the floor. "Whole Lotta Shakin' Going On" was hammered out by Jerry Lee Lewis on the base speakers. Another explosion! This one knocked Janee to her knees followed by a blast of sound that hit her eardrums with bursting pain. Seconds later a third explosion filled her room with dust! The base radio crackled and then went out. Sounds of men yelling and screaming in mass confusion and hysteria could be heard. Heavy machine gun fire was growing in numbers and intensity.

Janee threw open her door to stare into the wide eyes of seven men.

"What was that?" she yelled. The commotion outside was deafening! "Where's Gunney?" she shouted.

Another blast hit near their bunker, throwing the team flat on their faces. Dirt from above dumped on their bodies and filled the air making breathing difficult.

"Cover your mouths!" It was Compton. He was tearing up a t-shirt and handing out strips of cloth to help them breathe.

"We're gonna die! We're all gonna die in this hellhole! Oh, God, I don't want to die!"

Janee looked up. The dust was thick, mixed with something so pungent it burned her nose and throat. The lights were out from the last explosion making it difficult to see in the room. Another succession of blasts violently shook the bunker. The noise jarred Janee's ears and head to the extent she feared her eyes would pop out, and she would perish right there! Whoever had cried out before was in hysterics. It sounded like Phil.

Compton found a flashlight. He and Huggie made their way to Phil who was on his knees and elbows. He was covering his head with his hands and screaming. He would not be quieted! His screams were wild, spawned by fright and panic. Compton and Huggie attempted to calm Phil, but fear had overcome him, and he was out of control. Janee crawled closer.

"Shut up, Phil - shut up! Don't be such a baby!" Janee screamed in volume to match Phil's. Abruptly, Phil stopped. It was then Janee saw that Phil's knees rested in his own urine.

"I hate you, Janee Stemper! You're the reason we are in this God-forsaken place. I didn't want to come! If it hadn't been for you, we wouldn't be in this mess. I hate you talking us into - I hate you! You're getting us all killed!"

"Listen!" Jason shushed them. "There haven't been more explosions, and the gunfire has subsided. Maybe it's over!"

The team slowly got to their feet and moved around.

"Look at me!" Phil felt foolish and ashamed as he looked down at his wet pants.

"Hey, man, don't sweat it!" Juju encouraged. About that time, Gunney bounded in through the door! He was breathing hard!

"One of our night patrols was jumped by some VC's," Gunney was winded from running. "Viet Cong chased our boys back onto the base and sprayed us with machine gun fire and mortar rounds. We drove them back into the trees."

The team clapped and cheered with relief.

"I was so scared - I lost it," Phil confessed.

Gunney eyed him a minute before he replied.

"You're not the first person to piss his pants in this war. You all get your gear ready. Charlie is still out there, but we got to try and get you safely on that 130 coming in."

The tour team scrambled, throwing clothes and personal effects into suitcases. No one took the time to be neat or clean up, nor was anyone interested in having breakfast. They just wanted to get off this outpost as soon as possible.

Gunney loaded them into an armored vehicle. Marines manned weapons mounted on top. Gunney climbed in beside the team with, "I'm seeing you to the airport. Ha!" He gave the go-ahead to the driver. The vehicle whipped the passengers back and forth weaving between bunkers and skidding around sandbagged trenches filled with helmets and rifles facing out toward an unseen enemy. Janee felt she was the heroine in an action movie running for her life. She giggled then wiped the laugh away with her hand when she caught Jason's annoyed glance.

The vehicle slammed to a bouncy stop in the shadow of a high earth mound. This mound afforded protection from V.C. sniper or machine gun fire. Just beyond the mound was the airfield. Gunney was on the radio.

"Your ticket home is five minutes out," he smiled as he pointed toward one end of the field. "The transport will approach from the other end and turn around down here. We'll time it to meet the plane as it turns positioning this armor between you and the enemy. If Charlie stays quiet, we'll do okay."

"And if he doesn't?" Compton asked.

"It could - get - pretty hairy," Gunney spoke with a severity that frightened Janee!

"I see it!" Doc shouted. Everyone began gathering their things - not that they didn't already have their luggage handy. It seemed a nervous response of doing anything to hurry up their exit.

Without any warning, flame and smoke bellowed up, blasting into the side of the vehicle. The concussion was so powerful it lifted the armored carrier off the ground. Janee screamed.

The Marines above them opened fire. Explosion after explosion erupted dirt and rocks into the air. Janee could hear objects that sounded like metal pieces hitting against the armor.

Gunney turned pale. "Charlie has us under a mortar attack!" he shouted in an attempt to be heard against the machine gun chatter.

Another blast hit nearby, almost rolling them over. The gun nearest Janee went silent. All she could see was the Marine's legs and feet.

"I think he's hurt!" Janee shouted to Gunney.

"The plane is getting closer!" Doc cried nervously.

"Oh, no" Janee covered her mouth. Blood was running down the Marine's boot. It dripped on Huggie's leg.

Gunney was already up in the gun hole by the Marine. "He's gone," he remarked solemnly as he slid back down into the vehicle. He barked an order to the driver and got back on the radio. The armored carrier roared out from behind the mound and raced to meet the approaching transport.

As the C-130 made its descent, enemy mortars began exploding on the runway. Gunney was talking furiously on the radio, but Janee could not hear above the noise. She felt her stomach come up in her throat. She fought off tears and waves of nausea!

"Merciful God, they're taking fire!" Gunney yelled. He was soaked with sweat. Buster began to cry, and Phil barfed into his hands. The dust and smoke was so thick it obscured the runway, and they were out in the open. Blast after blast hit all around them with terrible veracity. Janee found herself screaming. She hated it as a weakness, but was helpless to control herself. Once she started, she couldn't contain herself - until Jason pulled her down into his arms.

The roar of the transport grew loud, but it wasn't slowing to turn around - the plane was airborne.

"Oil or something's pouring off one engine," Janee heard Compton declare.

"Get us the hell outa here!" Gunney ordered the driver.

Back in the bunker, the team sat in silent shock. Phil fixed a hollow stare interrupted only by rare pauses when he glowered at Janee. She knew he blamed her for the danger they were in. She was afraid to stay in her little room alone. She asked to bring her cot out with the men. Compton seemed to understand.

"If my wife were here, she wouldn't sleep in there. She wouldn't leave my side." Janee saw his eyes water up.

"Out there - this morning - I wasn't - sure - I would see - her - and my children again," Compton choked. "I sure - miss them - right now!"

"By now Bernard must be frantic," Janee murmured.

The barrage continued at regular intervals through the afternoon. By nightfall, heavy artillery added to the mortar rounds. The continued pounding of Khe Sanh had the team's nerves on edge. Janee thought she was going mad! They hadn't seen anyone, and they knew nothing!

Chapter 27

Fear

The attack on the base of Khe Sanh was relentless through the night. The continued pounding of mortar and artillery shells numbed the USO team's senses. Dawn found them weak and exhausted. They were nearly twenty-four hours without food and sleep. What little water they had ran out in the night.

Doc attempted to go outside the bunker to find more water - maybe some food. He was soon driven back inside by the ferocity of the enemy blasts.

"Don't see how anyone out there could survive!" he stammered.

They knew from a thin thread of light outlining the door that the sun was up. As quickly as the shell explosions had begun, they stopped. The team sat motionless, afraid to breathe that the attack might start again. They sat silent in the darkened room, staring. Janee could barely make out the men's faces. She knew by Phil's shaking he was on the verge of a breakdown - maybe he had already had one. Juju never blinked. He seemed frozen like a rock. Buster was pale; Doc had his face buried in his arms. Compton seemed to carry the weight of responsibility for their safety on his shoulders. Weariness showed on his face!

Huggie's eyes were wide and darting everywhere, like he was searching for a joke to ease the tension, but for the first time in his life coming up empty.

Jason was drawn and tired, but when Janee's eyes met his, he attempted a weak smile that appeared to say, "We'll be alright. I'll take care of you. I'll protect you from harm!"

Janee was amused and smiled herself. Jason Finn couldn't fight his way out of a string of cobwebs. This was he-man stuff and way out of Jason's league.

The team remained in the bunker for the longest time. The silence that had fallen on Khe Sanh was eerie. They were jolted, then relieved when Gunney burst through the door.

"I gathered some C rations and water from the mess hall for you."

The team ripped into the rations and ate like animals; Janee was so hungry she didn't care. The thought of table manners seemed an intrusion and would not be entertained at this moment.

"What have you done for a latrine seeing as the nearest one got blown up during the night?" Gunney queried after the eating slowed down.

"We used - Janee's - room - I mean since - she stayed - out here," Compton appeared ashamed to admit.

Gunney studied the group hard. "Good! That's good!" he finally replied.

"Please tell me it's over, and I can go home!" Phil burst out.

Gunney's eyes dropped, and he struggled to speak. "Wish I could - tell you that," his cheerfulness faded to a somber tone. "The enemy pounded the hell outa us last night. We took casualties, but we made Charlie pay. Just isn't V.C. out there, but North Viet Namese regulars with heavy stuff. Recon tells us there is a large build-up - one we never suspected - all around our base."

"Maybe I can go laugh them to death," Huggie offered, but garnered only a few smiles.

"How - large - a build-up?" Jason asked.

"Three to five times our number, maybe more."

Janee felt the sense of despair that hit the team.

"What will you do?" Juju asked with quivering voice.

"Soon as they show themselves, we'll call in air strikes - and fight for our lives!"

"Can't they just give up and go away?" Buster was trying to overcome his own fear.

"I wish to God they would, for all our sakes, but this has been the plan all along - to lure them out. We are the prizes!"

Janee felt her throat tighten, "You - you mean?" she felt sick.

"Yes, Ms. Stemper, they intend to overrun us!"

"We'll be taken prisoners - won't we?" Phil choked on his own words.

Gunney's face turned ashen. "Sure, they'll take some prisoners. Two or three will be kept alive after torture to air their propaganda on TV. Those will live the longest. Most others will be executed; some will be tortured for information and amusement."

All eyes turned toward Janee as if to say, "What about her?"

Gunney shook his head.

"What will - they do to Janee?" Compton insisted.

Gunney evaded the question.

"Tell us, Gunney!" Jason shouted. "What are we up against?"

Again, Gunney shook his head and turned his face aside.

"Please tell me, Gunney, I have a right to know what will happen to me," Janee implored.

Gunney's look was hard and steady as his gaze turned to Janee. Her hands were trembling.

"The soldiers will rape and mutilate you until you go mad - or bleed to death," Gunney spoke gravely.

"God, help us!" Jason gasped.

Janee felt something cold and black crawl inside her nerves. It clutched her heart - her lungs - it fought to envelope her mind. Her knees wobbled, and she reached out. Huggie was closest and caught her! She struggled not to pass out, her hands grabbed at the circle of men surrounding her as she used them to regain her footing. The next thing she remembered was sitting on one of the chairs. She studied the worried faces of the men. Their contorted expressions looked so foolish she had to laugh.

"Darn, woman, what's so funny?" Compton threw up his hands in exasperation.

"You all are! You should see your faces!"

"Well, yours doesn't look so grand either!" Phil snarled. The men turned away from Janee and addressed Gunney. Janee sensed she hurt them all by belittling their concern over her.

"When will - they attack?" Compton asked.

"Probably after dark," Gunney answered as he left out the door.

The team stayed inside the bunker. Conversation felt empty, and minds refused to concentrate on attempted games of cards. Everyone dreaded what no one spoke of - the setting of the sun!

Gunney's predictions were correct. With the darkness came the renewed barrage of mortar, machine gun and heavy artillery bombardment. Janee could make out the screams of men that grew from a low roar to a high-pitched rumble. The velocity of cries of pain and death was so close and so clear; Janee could swear the fighting was taking place right outside their bunker. She totally expected the enemy to come busting through the door any second. They all cried out in unison when Gunney threw open the door. His face carried a look she had never seen in any human before. All eyes were intent on him!

"It's a fierce fight!" he exclaimed. "Got helicopter, gun ships, Puff and air strikes - but there are so many of them - I don't know if we can hold 'em back. They are breaching the east side, and close to overpowering us on the north."

Gunney took a pistol out of his belt and laid it on the table.

"There are eight rounds in the clip. In the - event ..." Gunney's voice trailed off. Unspoken words and feelings were relayed in the glance he gave everyone.

"Oh, no!" Phil groaned. He crawled under his cot, curled up in a fetal position and began to sob like a child.

Buster vomited where he stood. Huggie grabbed his chest and sank heavy into a chair. Juju stood with hollow stare, while Jason dropped to his knees to plead with God. Compton stared in wild disbelief. Doc covered his head with his hands.

Janee felt fear, as she had never known it! She studied the men's reactions around her, and she felt alone. There was no one to help her! Then the image of vile, dirty, ugly little men bursting into the bunker, ripping off her clothes, forcing her to the floor, having their way with her until she passed out - only to awaken to more of the same - that horrible image overwhelmed her ability to even imagine. Fear gripped her with its paralyzing effects! She could taste it! Her blood ran cold - her mind went numb and refused to think! All she knew was somehow she must survive!

Chapter 28

Of Courage and Cowardice

Every eye stared at the loaded pistol placed on the table. They knew without being told its purpose.

"In case," Gunney gave one last look around then headed toward the door.

"Wait!" Jason spoke up. Gunney turned around.

"Put a rifle in my hands!" he spoke with resolve.

"Can you use one?"

"I'll take the crash course!" Jason seemed to gain a strength and determination from some unseen force. "If I'm going to die let it be by the hand of the enemy - not by my own - or by - my friends!"

"I've done my share of hunting," Compton joined in. "I have family to fight for!"

"Round me up one of those rifles too," Doc held up his hand. "I'll fight!"

Gunney smiled and nodded. "What about you, Huggie?"

Huggie dropped his eyes. He could barely be heard above the explosions and shouts and cries of battle outside.

"I've been good at slaying people with my jokes, but nix the guns."

"Buster?" Gunney questioned the man cowered in the shadow of the flashlights. With quivering lip Buster shook his head.

Gunney shined his light on Phil who was shaking, lying under his cot. Juju slipped into the little side room now used as their bathroom. "Follow me," Gunney motioned to Jason, Compton and Doc. They disappeared out the door into the war!

The bunker shook with each explosion from mortar or artillery shells. Particles of dirt fell from cracks in the ceiling and walls. Janee watched her four companions - their outlines silhouetted by the flashlights. Her gaze rested on Huggie. She felt something stirring within her - rising to overcome the fear and beat it into submission. She realized that out of her fear and tiredness two desires rose - a sudden, strong desire not to let her friends down, and an overpowering desire to defeat the enemy. She waxed hot with anger!

"Shame on you - all of you - cowards! Hiding while Jason, Compton and Doc are out there - fighting - for us - for their lives! How can you just - sit here?"

Huggie looked up at Janee without his trademark smile. His eyes glared!

"Don't be a hypocrite, Janee! I don't see you doing anything!"

"Just watch me!" Janee yelled over her shoulder as she bolted to the door.

The noise outside was much louder than what could be heard in the bunker. An explosion nearby threw her on her face. When she cautiously lifted her head, for the first time she became conscious of the scene around her.

Flares lit up the sky in all directions. Helicopters were buzzing in and out, spitting fire like a nest of hissing hornets. Jets roared across treetops to leave long columns of flame and destruction. She saw white streaks flashing back and forth caused by tracer shells. Cries of rage, pain, confusion, and yes, death became more distinct. Janee shuddered as she crawled on her hands and knees. She made her way along bunker embankments and piles of sandbags toward where she remembered the hospital to be. The concussion from a mortar round threw her into a row of sandbags and covered her in dirt. She sat up, spitting and coughing, attempting to brush herself off! She looked up into the face of a medic.

"You okay, Ma'am?"

"Yes."

"Can you help me?"

"Yes."

Janee ran behind the medic in a crouched position for a few feet and dropped beside two wounded soldiers.

"Stay with these men until I can get them to the post hospital."

Janee turned her attention to her part in this dirty war. Keeping two shot-up GI's company for the moment didn't seem like much, but that was her assignment for now. One of the men screamed out in harsh pain. Janee held his hand and tried to comfort him. He clutched her arm.

"I don't - want to - die - yet!" the Soldier's words came in gasps.

"Don't you worry none, Preacher. When your time's up, your time's up," the other Soldier spoke in a low voice.

"Let's have no talk of dying tonight," Janee wiped sweat from the forehead of the one called Preacher and smoothed his dirt-matted hair. The man covered his mouth to keep from crying as pain racked his body again. It left him gulping air! He spoke with labored words.

"I'm not afraid - to die - jus' - life seems too short. Good Book says - we have - an - an - appointed time."

"She - shhh. Be still, Soldier. You'll be just fine. Soon we'll get you to the hospital."

"I don't... I jus' - don't know - if - this is - my - appointed time. Seems too soon!"

Visions of Janee's Grandpa Farmer and his untimely death resurrected from somewhere in Janee's memory where she had laid them to rest. She didn't like the feelings it brought!

"Why would the Almighty give - me - dreams - of - a - wife - and children - an' - an' let me die - here? Tonight?"

"Hush this talk!" Janee instinctively scooted around and propped his head in her lap. He looked up at her, yet didn't seem to see her.

"I - I - see - an angel."

"You are dreamin' sure nuff, Preacher. This is a movie star, Janee Stemper. Remember, she acted and sang for us."

"I - see - an angel..." his voice faded.

Janee felt the Soldier breathe out and become very still. She called to him, she patted his face, and she tried to feel a pulse from a heart that no longer beat.

"Hey, Preacher, you hang in there," his comrade encouraged.

"He's gone!" Janee snapped. Old feelings and anger ripped open buried wounds.

"Preacher's dead!" she yelled. She wanted to beat God in the face with her fist for this inexcusable injustice!

"I hate you, God!" Janee screamed into the flare-lit night. "You hear me?"

"God didn't kill Preacher, Miss, the Viet Cong did," the Soldier tried to calm the distraught woman.

"Oh, shut up! What did God ever do for you?"

Anger burned red hot, streaming into Janee like molten lava. A flare burst above, making the night as bright as noonday. Janee spied Preacher's rifle. She crawled over and took hold of it. One memory she recalled was of her grandpa teaching her to shoot a gun when she stayed the summers in Oregon.

"Show me how to use this," she demanded, dropping the butt with a thud on the ground near the Soldier's head.

With great effort he pointed to a small handle on the rifle.

"Pull that all the way back until it clicks - then it's ready to fire."

Janee crawled toward the sandbag trench nearest her. The noise, which had never let up for an instant was deafening now. Bullets whizzed above her head striking sandbags and bunkers. She peeked over the trench mound and saw a sight that caught her breath! Armed men by the hundreds - thousands were appearing in the light, advancing at a charge pace. Fire from the Americans was rapid and constant. Some of the enemy reached the perimeters of the base, throwing their bodies across the barbed wire so as to create a bridge for the others who followed. They came faster than the G.I.'s could shoot them! Janee cocked the rifle. Some of the enemy was so close she could see their eyes flash in the bright flares. She picked a North Viet Namese soldier who was running toward the trench. She tried to remember what grandpa taught her. She aimed - then hesitated - then squeezed off a round. The soldier kept coming. She fired again; the soldier went down.

Janee fought bravely, not realizing her position above the Marines and Soldiers in the trench left her exposed.

"This one's for grandpa!" she yelled as her bullet hit its mark. "And this - for Preacher!" She fired again and again!

Janee was so intent on killing the enemy; she had abandoned her own safety! Her ammunition spent, she crawled back to see to the wounded Soldier who still lived. She took his rifle and extra clips. The Soldier who identified himself only as "Shotgun," showed Janee how to change clips. She crawled back to her position on the mound.

How long she fought into the night was hard to figure out. How many of the enemy did she kill? She lost count.

Close air strikes followed one after another, dropping bombs and Napalm across the clearing and into the trees. The roar of war drifted into a dull noise, and everything went into slow motion for Janee. She saw pain and fear cross the faces of the soldiers she shot. It didn't matter she was taking lives. She even pictured she was doing God a favor - if there was a God! How could there be one to allow such chaos, death and misery?

A mortar blast lifted her off the ground and sent her rolling down the side of the mound. She collected her senses and crawled back up to the top. When she peeked over she was face to face with a North Viet Namese Regular coming straight toward her. His eyes met hers, and he threw his rifle up to his shoulder. She pulled her rifle up quickly and squeezed the trigger.

"Click."

Her rifle was out of shells! She stared down the barrel of the enemy's gun, and froze! Instantly, the distinct crack from a GI's rifle sent the enemy soldier flying backward. Janee looked over into the trench below her to see the Marine who shot her assailant. Her heart was beating so fast she feared it too would explode!

The assault that lasted for hours had been beaten back. Janee drug her rifle in the dirt by the shoulder strap. She collapsed beside the wounded Shotgun and the dead Preacher. Tears washed tracks on her dirt-stained face as her emotions collapsed. She just wanted to go home.

A different medic happened on them. Huggie followed him. Huggie flashed that old familiar grin which seemed to say, "You were right, Janee, freedom can only be bought by courage - not cowardice!"

Chapter 29

A Time of Shame

Janee trudged slowly back toward the team's bunker. The events of the nightmarish night replayed in her head. The reality that they all might die gave her a fear so heavy it had a taste! The suicide pistol so starkly outlined in her mind as it rested on the table. The reaction of the men... Her reaction! She could hear Preacher's last words - "I - see - an angel!" and feel life slip out of him. What had he seen in those last seconds? She must think of something else, something beautiful and pleasant.

She tried to remember the faces of her parents, Grandmother Emile, Bernard, but the faces of the men she had just killed charged their way to the front of her mind's eye. She shook them off!

She asked the medic who Huggie came with about the first medic and was told he never made it back to the hospital. Poor, brave Preacher. She waited and stroked the lines in his face until some Soldiers came to carry him away. She didn't want him to be alone!

And Huggie! He most likely shamed himself into action - or was it Janee's cutting, angry accusations? Whatever it was, Huggie was helping the medics carry the wounded on stretchers to the hospital. Once inside, Janee knew he would lighten suffering with laughter.

Jason came to mind! 'What had become of him, Compton and Doc? Did they survive the attack? Were they wounded - maybe dead?' Janee's heart sank with the dread of their welfare. The last she saw of them was when they exited the bunker with Gunney. 'Dear God, what about Gunney?'

Janee stopped to look around and get her bearings. Lost in thought and in the early morning darkness she had wandered carelessly into an unfamiliar part of the base. She was uncertain as to where she was or how to get to her bunker. It was then she saw the red glow of a cigarette in the dark shadows. A man spoke slowly.

"Tired of this worthless war and the hell it brings? Had your fill of blood, guts and death?"

"What do you know about it?" Janee was curious about this soft-spoken lad.

"I know plenty, and I've seen my fill. Enough to last my life..." The man's voice was deep and slow.

Janee stepped closer but couldn't see his face.

"I'm with the -."

"I know who you are, Miss Stemper, but I wouldn't give a damn if you were Mother Goose."

"Who are you?" Janee asked.

"We're the dopers. The gooks will be back again – soon. You can bet a paycheck on it, but we live to escape – to fight another day."

"You mean you are a coward and you hide?"

"Aw, see the problem you have Miss Dumb and Fancy is, you've been listening only to the straight folk."

"Who are you?" Janee was more pointed.

"I'm known as Broken Cross. Won't you join us in our sanctuary?"

Broken Cross opened a door near him to disclose a candle lit room in a barrack's bunker. The light revealed the bearded face of a lean, good looking young man. His hair was shaggy and longer than regulation. From what Janee could make out, his uniform was worn and sweaty, with missing sleeves.

"You expect me to just walk into that barracks with you Soldier? I'm not as dumb as you think. The last thing I need right now is to spend time with a bunch of dope heads. I just need to get back to where I belong."

Without warning she was grabbed from behind.

"You – belong – with us!" came a voice next to her ear – gasping out words. Next they were mixed with low guttural sneering laughs. Whoever gripped her put his hand over her mouth so she couldn't scream.

"Don't you know to insult our hospitality ain't neighborly?"

Janee struggled as the man forced her into the bunker! He was too strong for her. A small group of men stood to their feet as she was roughly shoved into the barracks. Janee spun around to face a man who displayed the look of insanity. She swung her fist towards his face but he grabbed her arm. She kicked his legs hard and furious. He went down to the hilarious delight of the other men. Instantly the marine was back in her face poised to strike. Broken Cross threw him down.

"Now Powder Keg, is that any way to treat our guest? Save that hate for the war mongers."

Broken Cross helped him to his feet, then turned to Janee, "Men we have the honor of having Miss Stemper. You remember her from the USO Show."

"We had a USO Show?" one laughed.

"You were too stoned Fried Egg, to remember," another man replied.

"Miss Janee Stemper," Broken Cross went on, "has been outside fighting the war for us, and we need to show our appreciation."

The men circled her and suddenly Janee felt like a doe, surrounded by a pack of wolves.

"Forgive me for forgetting our manners." Broken Cross continued. "You already met Powder Keg. He's just a little crazy, and Fried Egg, Yankee Dog and Gater – hey where's Gater?"

Everyone turned to look for Gater.

"There he is," Fried Egg laughed, pointing to a Marine sprawled out on the floor. "He done passed out!"

"Ok, Gater's over there. Behind you is Alabama and Bally Hu."

"Don't any of you have normal names?" Janee coughed nervously.

"Don't you know? Every marine at one point in his duty tour gets a nickname that sticks for life. Alabama got his in boot camp because, well, he's from Alabama. Fried Egg and Powder Keg got theirs changed after they got to Nam. Ones mind is fried – the other, he explodes all the time."

"I got mine from the southerners," Yankee Dog grinned. "Gater came from the swamps of Louisiana."

"I stand for peace," Broken Cross added, "and we can't figure out what the hell Bally Hu means. He transferred from another unit, and he won't tell us. So he's just plain ole Bally Hu."

Janee took in the faces of each of the men. They were like little boys in a candy shop, but much more volatile. When her eyes met Bally Hu's, she saw something there that made her feel very uncomfortable

"May we offer you a drink, Miss Janee," Alabama suggested.

"I am thirsty, for some water."

"Try this!" Fried Egg produced a cup.

Janee took a long swallow and came up gagging and spitting.

"I asked for water!" Janee stormed.

"Waters kinda hard to come by. That's a Hoochie blend," Yankee Dog commented dryly as he lit up a marijuana smoke.

"Well thanks for nothing, but I really don't enjoy spending time with a bunch of spineless cowards while the real men are out fighting for their lives."

"You don't think we are real men?" Bally Hu bellowed. He grabbed her arm and twisted, making Janee cry-out.

"Let me go!" she struggled, "or I'll report – umph –you – umph – to your commander!"

The lot of them howled in laughter.

"Do you think anyone here has time for anything like that, damn, or even cares?" Alabama snarled. "We'll just all testify seven against one, you broke in on us crazy with rage and such, and attacked us. It'll go under the mat and you will go home – alive or in a body bag!"

"You dirty . . ." Janee screamed pounding at Bully Hu's face with her free fist. She fought, kicked, bit with all her strength. She felt rough hands on her and heard their coarse voices. She managed to break free from Bally Hu, her arms flaying wildly in all directions. A sharp blow to the side of her head knocked her to the floor. She pulled her knees tight against her chest holding them with her arms. She cried for help until another blow hit her face, rolling her to the other side. She groaned and wept – mostly because this extreme cruelty that she had feared most was being inflicted on her not by the enemy, but by those she had trusted to protect her.

Strong, eager hands manhandled her body and tore at her clothes. She lost count of how many times or who was doing what until the shame and pain became more than her body or mind could handle. She passed out.

Chapter 30

Escape

It was deathly silent when Janee was jolted awake. She found herself tangled in a mass of human flesh. The men were asleep - no - they were stoned. When she raised up on one elbow and looked around, the single candle which had survived the night, revealed that all of her clothing was gone.

"Oh no," she moaned. She detected splotches of blood on her legs and her attempts to move sent jabbing pain into the lower part of her stomach. She felt sick and disgusted! She had the strong urge to clean herself, to stand for a long time in a soothing shower seemed of utmost urgency – but it was only wishful thinking. How much soap and water would it take to wash away this filth? She wanted to throw up.

She sat up, fumbling with her blouse and began searching for her clothes. Fried Egg had her bra on his head; Bally Hu clutched her panties in his hand. The rest of her clothes were thrown carelessly about and her shirt was torn in several places. Hate raged through her as she remembered the insults and abuse inflicted on her by these men. She wanted to brutally kill them! Without hesitation, she grasped the handle of Bally Hu's sidearm and slipped it from its holster. She pressed it against the Marine's temple as she pried his fingers from her underwear.

Janee Stemper had come to a war zone to lighten spirits and encourage a group of GI's, but these men had brutalized her. Their despicable acts were inexcusable, unforgivable. Hate of intensity Janee had never felt before now demanded revenge. She felt her finger tighten on the trigger of the weapon still pressed against Bally Hu's head. Was it she or someone else controlling her? She couldn't stop and knew her squeeze on the trigger was slowly raising the hammer. In an instant it would be over and the bastard dead!

"Please don't Miss," a pleading voice interrupted her outraged rush to take a life. Janee slowly turned towards the direction of the voice. It was the one named Gater.

"I know we deserve ever bit of what you are intending to do, but we are a sorry lot who have lost all sense of decency, we've lost our way. Not a one of us is worth you going to prison fer."

Fires of indignation still burned hot in Janee. She slowly raised the gun and leveled it at Gater. For an instant their eyes locked and his seemed to beg her, 'go ahead, please do it, I don't want to live like this anymore.'

She threw the weapon down and hurried to dress. She glanced several times at Gater to see if he was watching; one last thrill. His head was buried in his hands. She had to get out – she was suffocating in the filthy stench. It threatened to close in on her. She held her breath to keep from vomiting! Alabama and Broken Cross began to stir as she zipped her pants. Grabbing one of the marine's jackets, she bolted through the door!

It looked to be late morning. The sun was bright, and for the moment the fighting had subsided. She saw Marines moving ammunition, probably to re-supply the troops in the perimeter trenches. There was a rush of activity, and the Soldiers were so intent they failed to give any recognition to her.

For the first time she realized she could barely walk. Pain made each step labored.

She called out to two medics carrying a wounded Soldier, but they failed to hear her. She hobbled after them to the hospital bunker.

"Are you okay, Miss Stemper?" a corpsman had watched her intently from the time she entered the hospital. She felt like she was wandering in a daze.

"Do I look well? I could - would - appreciate some - strong coffee and water." Her tongue felt thick and dry; her speech was slow. Her mind seemed mired down in a dismal bog! She could feel their scent on her, in her hair, everywhere. It was foul.

"Coffee's down the end," a doctor pointed with his nose, reluctant to release the corpsman for even a moment from the pressing tasks at hand.

Janee made her way past beds looking almost absentmindedly at faces of the hurting. Suddenly, she gasped and held her mouth.

"Compton," she whispered. A hand came out from under the sheet and held out to her. She reached to take it.

"Oh, no, Compton, not you," she stifled a cry and fought back tears.

"Janee," Compton could hardly talk. She drew closer to hear him. "I'm so glad you are safe. We have been worried sick over you."

"What happened, Compton?"

"Took a mortar round. Fell right in the dang trench. Killed the ones close to me!"

"Oh, dear God!" Janee cried out. "Please don't - let it - be!"

Compton read her thoughts.

"Jason and Doc are fine - so far. But I'm afraid Phil isn't doing so well. He lost it, and we had to get him in here. He's across the - way, a few beds down. Got him so - doped up. He won't even know you - or remember - …"

Compton held tight to Janee's hand. His expression changed, his smile faded and his keen eyes searched hers.

"I got blowed full of metal pieces. The doctor told me I needed to be back in the states to a good hospital. I told him we were trying, but this darn war... Anyway, he's having some trouble stopping the bleeding - already had one transfusion. Pray for me, Janee, and promise you'll tell my family - I fought for - them -."

"Oh, stop it, Compton! I don't pray; besides, you're not going to die. Don't expect me to go back to your family - and explain - " Janee motioned around - "all this hellish nightmare. So stop this talk, and stop bleeding!"

Compton smiled and drifted off in sleep.

By sundown another wave of North Viet Namese heavy artillery pounded the base of Khe Sanh. In the dark, the crazed screams of charging soldiers increased until it threatened to drown out the explosions of the cannon rounds. Janee couldn't bring herself to take up a rifle. She retreated to a corner and curled up in a fetal position. If the gooks were going to overrun the base and rape her until she was dead, she wished they would get it over with – or leave! The hours dragged on, especially in the dead of night. It was evident yet unspoken that everyone longed for the dawn to arrive. Perhaps with the light would come a withdrawal of the North Viet Namese.

The hospital was chaos! The wounded were carried in faster than they could be looked after.

"Leave the dead where they fall!" Janee heard a doctor shout angrily at a private who carried in a fallen comrade.

"Can't help the dead, Soldier!" the doctor tried to deal with his own frustration.

"Don't let my buddy die!" the private pleaded.

"Get him out of here!" the doctor yelled.

"Marine, get back on the line and hold it!" a corpsman ordered.

The battle went on into the next day. The American casualties were high, but Janee figured the body count of the Viet Cong and North Viet Namese to be enormous. The plan all along was to lure them out of the jungle so they could be massacred by machine gun fire and air strikes. Some of the Napalm drops were so close the heat was felt on her face! Janee attempted to help and was exhausted by late afternoon. Dealing with their wounds was difficult enough, but to watch some die pushed her emotions to the edge of collapse. The constant noise of the battle ground her nerves, adding to the long hours. She drove herself to keep going. When she couldn't lift a hand or take another step, she retreated to the side of Compton's bed to check on him. She held his hand and fell into a fitful sleep, semi-conscious of the ferocity of the battle outside. Only a short distance separated her from death, with a thin line of Soldiers and Marines between.

It was lying on a Viet Namese mat near Compton's bed that Gunney found her the next morning. He had come for Phil and Compton. He shook the young movie star from a heavy sleep. Startled, she sat up!

"Miss Janee, are you a sight for my sore eyes. Been looking everywhere for you! I am sure relieved you ain't hurt - or dead - which I was afraid you were. Got word you was shootin' Charlie! My God, you look a mess. I see you got yourself a bruised face. Some Marine will be proud you're wearing his – er uniform jacket."

Janee blinked her eyes, and looked around to get her bearings. She pulled the jacket tight around her to cover the ripped blouse.

"Come on, the rest of your team is outside. Some choppers are inbound for bodies and wounded. We are hoping to get you into one and outa here!"

"But my things!" Janee struggled to get up. Her body was badly bruised and the flesh swollen. Every movement was painful.

175

"No time! Let's go. Medics, we have USO team members to get loaded. Two of them fought alongside us, so you give special care."

Janee limped outside. There was Doc Martin, Buster, Juju, oh - Huggie, who waved a happy greeting to her, and then she spotted Jason.

"Jason!" she screamed as she fell into his open arms.

Within moments a helicopter set down in the clearing near the hospital. With the engine still running, Compton and Phil were slid inside and their stretchers secured. The rest of the USO team scrambled to get aboard as the chopper immediately lifted off the ground. Janee blew a sad Gunney a goodbye kiss.

"I feel like we are in a movie and making our escape," Jason laughed.

"Except these are real bullets they're shootin' at us, Mr. Finn," Janee replied as she poked her finger into a small round hole in the fuselage. She sat in sullen silence. She believed in her heart that there would never be an escape from what happened to her.

Chapter 31

Freedom Bird

The siege on Khe Sanh would go on until April of 1968. What would be found out later was that during those three long days the USO team was in the thick of battle, the Americans broke the back of the enemy in that region.

The team was checked over in the military hospital at Saigon. Since Janee, Jason and Huggie were celebrities; there was immense pressure to get them back to the states. It also was imperative that Compton receives civilian medical attention. Thus the team was hurried onto what the GI's affectionately termed as a Freedom Bird.

Janee looked with sadness out the plane's window as it lifted into the air with its human cargo. Servicemen and women in coach chattered animatedly, happy to be alive and excited to be heading home.

The USO Tour group was silent and reflective in their first class seats. No longer the jovial bunch on a worthwhile mission to cheer up the military, they were drawn and tired. They had neither the inclination nor the energy to have any further contacts. They too, just wanted to go home.

"You okay?" Jason slipped into the seat beside Janee. He studied her face with gentle steady eyes. "You're all banged up."

She could hardly hold eye contact. Jason had changed. Something had happened to him at Khe Sanh. He was stronger, more confident, sure of himself. She saw the change, sensed it the instant she was in his arms outside the base hospital. She felt it in his embrace, heard it in his soft, low whispers of concern and relief that she was safe. Deep in her heart she knew he cared for her - more than just a friend. She had come to admit to herself those feelings were mutual. She was falling in love again.

"Janee?" Jason was waiting for her answer.

"Wha - oh, Jason, I was lost in thought."

"Word spread around the base how you grabbed a rifle and was on the top of a sandbag wall fighting. They said you were a tiger, and thought you killed your share…"

"Jason, it seems, so, so long ago. I killed them, and didn't even care!"

"I know how you felt. At first I was just scared of dying. I wanted to run and hide, and then I got angry - so angry I turned into a vicious animal. We were fighting for our lives, but we aren't monsters - we do care!"

Janee looked up into Jason's face. He put his arm around her and held her. She felt secure and warm there and wished to stay forever. She whimpered as she laid her head on his shoulder.

"When I heard about you - fighting like that, I was so proud of you, Janee. There was a journalist on base, and he saw you and took some pictures."

"You've got to be kidding, Jason!"

"I swear. I saw the one that the papers in the states are printing. Your face and hair covered in dirt; there is a distinct tear line on one cheek highlighted by the light from a shell burst. You are dragging your rifle by the shoulder strap. Your clothes torn, Janee; you are a hero!"

"No more than you, or Doc, or thousands of Soldiers and Marines, or… Preacher."

"Who?"

"He died in my lap. Said he saw an angel."

"He saw one no doubt, Miss Stemper."

"It wasn't me. There was something - someone - they were all so young," Janee began to sob. The tears flowed until she fought them back.

"I know, Janee, but you did a brave thing."

She moved from his arm to look him in the face. He was puzzled.

"When they came to carry Preacher away, I was so tired from it all - my emotions numb - raw. I worried over you, and Compton, Doc, I wandered trying to make my way back to our - bunker, and got so turned around I didn't know where I was.

"I ran into a marine outside a barracks who said his name was Broken Cross. I meant to ask directions, then another GI grabbed me and took me inside the barracks where a bunch of dopers were hiding . . ."

"Janee, you don't have to explain. You finally found a group of guys to do what you wanted." Jason shrugged his shoulders, "I understand."

"What?" No one had ever said anything to cut her so deeply. "Jason, it wasn't like that!"

"You said!" Jason realized he was raising his voice. He looked around and spoke low, "you said you were looking for men to love. So you slept with this Cross man!"

Janee was in-sensed that Jason would jump to such a conclusion!

"No, Jason, I slept with them all!" she snapped. "I was naked when I woke up; we had a stupid party – that's how my face got busted!"

She immediately saw the hurt in Jason's face. Her revelation had cut him to the quick. She wished she could retract those hot words; she wanted to undo the damage, just to share with him the truth – her pain.

179

What Jason was experiencing was evident. His eyes watered up. He had difficulty finding words to respond to what was an outrageous and unforgivable act.

"Janee, I'm shocked!"

"Well, you shouldn't be. Haven't you ever - known a woman?"

"I've been waiting - for that - special one." The words seemed those of a man whose dreams had just been shattered. Now Jason was whispering, "The litmus test of my feelings is this – tell me you are a virgin."

Janee wanted more than anything to lie, but knew in her heart she and Jason could never build a relationship on a lie. She sat silent.

Jason got up to return to his own seat. Janee reached out to touch him.

"I'm so sorry, Jason," she whispered. "Please let me explain."

"No, I'm the one who is sorry," he replied. His eyes locked with hers for a brief moment. Something that had been there before was gone; she had killed it. She turned her face to stare out the window.

She was furious with Jason and with herself. Why couldn't she have just told him the truth? Why did she have to be so proud and heartless? She was filled with shame, anger, guilt and sadness. She wanted nothing more than to tell him what had really happened. 'No, forget it, if that's what he wants to think, then let him. It doesn't matter.' Her heart was reaching out for him but her pride was holding her back.

Hours later as the Freedom Bird neared the California coast, one of the pilots made the announcement over the plane's speakers that Miss Janee Stemper and Mr. Jason Finn had been nominated for Oscars. Cheers and whistles and wild clapping came from the passengers behind. Amid the laughing and congratulations, Janee put on a happy face, but her heart was breaking.

When the commotion quieted down, suddenly Phil stood up facing the team. His voice was emotion-packed as he spoke.

"I owe all of you an apology for the way I acted at Khe Sanh. I've never been that scared. I hid like a coward!"

"I saw some men who ran and hid and were cowards. You weren't one of them, Phil," Janee shot back.

"I think I know now why they call this a Freedom Bird," Phil concluded.

"Here, here!" Huggie agreed and began his slow clap. The others joined in and reaffirmed their love and acceptance for a broken comrade. Janee only wished Jason would do the same for her.

Coming off the plane was a blur. She searched through the myriad of faces of the news media making absent-minded comments to their barrage of questions until she saw - her mom and dad, and faithful Bernard. Tears were flowing freely at sight of her. She pushed her way through the crowd into their arms. She felt like a little girl - safe at last. A Freedom Bird had brought her home!

Chapter 32

Wake Up, Janee!

The upcoming Academy Awards opened phenomenal doors of exposure for Janee. Not only was she up for an Oscar, but she had also emerged as a Viet Nam War hero. The Front Page image of a tired, embattled movie star dragging a for-real rifle made her a household name all over the world. Unfortunately, the same coverage was completely lacking for Jason, Compton and Doc who had fought even harder and longer. Janee felt embarrassment concerning the men's lack of recognition, and badly for her friends. She tried to redirect some of the attention toward the men when she did interviews, but the media couldn't care less.

Jason was cool toward Janee. It was obvious to her and to those who knew them both.

"Go talk to him, for goodness sake; swallow your pride," her mother advised the morning Janee had stopped by to "cry on mom's shoulder."

"It's not pride, Mother. I hurt him deeply and can't fix it!"

"Nonsense, nothings too deep that can't be worked out by two people in love."

"I killed that love, Mother, I know it!"

"Then it wasn't love Jason felt."

"You don't understand, but I can't discuss it with you right now."

"Janee, what have you done?"

"Nothing! Nothing!" Janee cut off any further questions.

Janee did several pre-Oscar interviews together with Jason. After the taping, Jason avoided her and hurried off. When their picture was taken together both smiles were plastic and Janee knew that Jason only accommodated because it was expected.

She did manage to wish him luck as sincerely and lovingly as she knew how the night of the Academy Awards, when she took her seat near the actor.

"Thank you," was his simple and disappointing response.

Janee was on the edge of her seat. She couldn't wait for the "Best Actress" category to come up. A thrill jolted over her body as they announced the nominees and showed short film clips of each actress in her role. Her dad, Harold, sitting next to her squeezed her hand and winked when they came to her.

"Janee Stemper for 'Maggie' in, 'A Bowl of Dust'."

Janee's heart was racing when they called for the envelope. Bernard reached across her mom to touch her arm in excited support.

"And the winner is - Molly Dugan for 'Heidi' in 'Swiss Miss'!"

Janee's world collapsed. The letdown was brutal. She wanted to die!

Moments later were the, "Best Actor Award." In a daze, Janee heard the announcement.

"And the winner for Best Actor - is - Jason Finn as 'Rupert' in, 'A Bowl of Dust'." The cast of the movie went wild; especially when it went on to receive an Oscar for "Best Picture."

Janee was thrilled for Jason, but crushed they would not be able to share the excitement together. She carried a smile, but her heart was black. When everyone stood to leave, Jason was surrounded by well-wishers. Bernard helped her with her coat.

"If it helps, I would like to point out that our director didn't win either," Bernard spoke hoping to bolster her trampled ego.

"You are so stupid! How is that supposed to help me? I don't care he didn't win - I didn't win!" She pushed her agent aside and stormed up the aisle.

Post Oscar celebrity interviews featured Jason and Molly - Molly and Jason. Their picture together was in the papers and would soon grace magazine covers and articles. A few weeks passed and rumors circulated that the two were dating. Janee grew desperate! If she was ever to win him back it must be now before he became too involved with Miss Dugan.

There were nights full of fits of jealousy. She wished Molly Dugan would grow old and wrinkled - or succumb to some disease - no, that was not swift enough. A car accident - no, a bullet to the head – 'Oh, why do I feel this way - think such dreadful thoughts?' She called Jason and asked him to meet her for a quiet dinner. She nearly fainted when he accepted.

They met at the LeFount, the same restaurant they went to the night before the tour left for Viet Nam. She arrived early to secure the same table they sat at that night. It was quiet and romantic. She had a small gift for Jason.

He smiled and waved when he saw her as he entered the room.

"Hello, Janee," he took her hand. She reached up and kissed his lips softly.

"This is a surprise," he said with a smile.

"I want - to give - you this," she produced her gift.

"What's the occasion, Janee?"

"Nothing, except I just wanted you to have this - little memento."

Curiously, Jason unwrapped the small box. Inside, he discovered the battered ring he had worn as the character, Rupert, in "A Bowl of Dust."

Jason was surprised and pleased.

"How did you get this - ring?"

"It wasn't easy - I paid them off."

Jason drew a strange face.

"Not that way, silly. I just wanted to - convey how - happy - and proud - I am of you for winning the Oscar." Janee realized as she spoke, she was sounding exactly like her Grandma Emile.

Jason studied her for a moment before he replied.

"I'm sorry you didn't, Janee. You did an Oscar performance."

Janee waited until after they ate to make her move.

"Jason, I hurt you very deeply by the things I told you on the plane."

"You only acted upon what you had bragged about when the team went on tour."

"But how do you know I did - those things?"

"You said so."

"Oh, Jason - just words - words - empty words! I would take them back - erase them!" she wailed.

"Why would you be so careless with empty words about something so - special?"

Janee reached out with a trembling hand. She was pleading with her eyes. Jason gave no indication he understood - or cared, as he continued.

"I've dreamed of keeping myself pure for my wedding night and want my bride the same. Sounds out of step with today's demands of free sex, but still it's - important - to me."

Jealousy took control. "Do you think Molly Dugan is lily white? That she's never been -"

"I don't think that's any of your business!" Jason cut her off. He looked like he had been blindsided by her question!

"Jason, I'm sorry, that was so cruel and judgmental. I just want us to go back to the way we were."

"If I can afford to buy a new car, why would I want a used one? I would never be sure I could trust you. Your past would haunt me. I would always be afraid I was not the one and only, but just another in your long list of - encounters. I really wonder, Janee, if you will ever be worth anything."

"Worth anything?" Janee exploded. His words had dug deep like a red-hot poker!

"Worth anything?" she continued, " I've played roles equal to yours. I performed on stage with you. I fought for our very lives beside you. I was - nominated for an Oscar; I'm a successful movie star. Just let me explain!"

"Fame and wealth don't compensate for character and integrity, Janee," Jason concluded with a note of sadness. "You don't need to explain. Good evening. Thank you for dinner and the gift."

It was one of the few times in Janee's life she was left speechless. Her heart and hopes sank. She had lost - lost the love of her life - and a good friend.

Again, the one she loved was taken away. She buried her love deeper that ever. It wasn't fair – Jason wouldn't listen to the truth. He only accused. She vowed to never love again. If Jason thought she was a slut – she would be a slut!

She needed something to remove the pain that constantly racked her brain. She began to party late and come home high. She became a chain-smoker, drunkard and pothead all mixed up into one big, ugly excuse for a movie star. She lost count of the men she slept with, for she no longer cared!

Bernard was the first to confront her about her behavior.

"Janee, I'm concerned! Your acting is slipping, along with your career."

"What do you mean? My last part was my best - acting ever," she bellowed.

"No, Janee," Bernard shook his head. "Your worst movie was better than this last part. No one wants to touch you!"

"You mean you've lost your touch! You just can't do your job anymore, wise guy."

Bernard's face darkened. He was determined not to cow to his boss. Too much was at stake!

"Look at these articles, Janee! 'Actress Janee Stemper passes out at drug party.' Another- 'Cited for D.W.I.;' the reviews on your last movie were damaging. And what's this? 'Janee Stemper speaks at anti-war rally. Concludes by throwing her bra into a frenzied crowd.' Have you lost all reason?"

"The war is all a horrible mistake. I'm ashamed to call myself an American!"

"But you - fought in it! You are a war hero."

"I was a fool! That was when I lost all reason - now I've found it!"

"You're drowning yourself in liquor, marijuana and..." Bernard checked himself.

"Go on - say it, Bernard! Sex! Men! Yes! I'm a slut and proud of it. I can't tell you how many men I've - but I see their faces - their bodies, and it's a lot of them! I'm the happiest I've ever been. I'm a free spirit, and I don't answer to anyone. Not you! Not anyone! You're outa step, so if you can't hack it and don't like what I do - go packing, and don't let the door slap your butt on the way out!"

Bernard had that crushed look he always did when Janee verbally flogged him, but this time it had taken its toll - it took a different turn that Janee had not seen before. She glared angrily at her agent as he turned and walked toward the door.

"And don't come back," she yelled at him.

He turned his head and said in a low coarse voice, charged with emotion, "Goodbye, Janee."

Many things divide people. Viet Nam was the war that divided a nation. Janee became a flower child and advocate for free speech, drugs and love. She decided to take part in a huge anti-war demonstration at Berkley, as she felt sure all three of those precious components would be present for her to indulge in.

The event at Berkley was not one of the more prominent demonstrations, but it did draw a lot of media attention. Viet Nam Vets against the War were present, along with many other notables. Draft cards were burned, and a North Viet Namese flag was flown, which started a riot. It was an exciting rush to run from riot police and dodge bursts of tear gas.

That afternoon she was scheduled a few minutes on the podium. She faced thousands of chanting, screaming anti-war activists. She denounced the war and her brief part in it. She even apologized for cheering on the war effort, and her statement, "I'm ashamed to call myself an American," is what hit the morning papers.

Her reputation was ruined. Her career was a collapsed house. Her life a shambles, focused on empty things, yet Janee said she was a free soaring spirit. She was crusading for a cause she truly believed to be right. For once in her life by bucking the system, she was doing good and her part to change the world. She slapped a reporter when she came off the stage, who implied her main interest in being at the demonstration was the free access to drugs. She spent two hours in jail until the television network dropped its charges. She agreed to pay for the camera she damaged. This made her a hero of the movement.

That night she attended a small elite party of carefully selected members of the anti-war movement. A friendly stranger slipped LSD to the film star, which sent her on a wild trip.

Janee began to see strange sights and hear warped sounds, enhanced by the beating music and flashing colored lights. She was walking through fields of beautiful blowing flowers of brilliant colors. Peace signs were everywhere - even in the sky, which also was constantly changing colors. All the people around her were holding up two fingers saying, "Peace, be still," in a melodious harmony that struck Janee as most profound.

Suddenly, the trip turned into what seemed to Janee some sort of deep spiritual journey. She found herself walking hand-in-hand with Jesus across the flower field. He smiled at her and winked. He wore his long hair tied back with a string of beads on his head for a crown. His shirt was open, revealing a peace symbol strung on a piece of leather lying against a hairy chest. She laughed and laughed 'til tears wet her face to see Jesus in flip-flops and shorts.

Next he stood on the other side of a large room filled with people. He beckoned to Janee with gentle words, "Come to me, Janee. Give yourself to me - come to me..."

She had the sensation of sweet surrender as she made her way to him. The scene changed to a wedding. She was the bride walking the aisle; Jesus had become Jason. The instant she put her hand in his, her trip became a road race to hell! Jason's face turned into that of a hideous demon. She tried to pull away, but he clutched her tightly in a hammerlock. She cried out for help, but no one paid her any attention.

To her horror, the floor beneath her feet opened to reveal hot, leaping flames. "You're mine, whore, now burn!" the demon declared with a wicked laugh.

Janee screamed and screamed. She fought, but couldn't break the hold. She knew she was in a nightmarish trance and desperately needed to wake up!

"Wake up, Janee," she screamed.

"Wake up, Janee!"

"Wake up, Janee!" The flames were burning the soles of her feet. She kicked violently!

"Wake up, Janee!"

"Wake up, Janee!"

Chapter 33

Secret Arrival

It was after dark in September 1983 when Janee slipped into the small lumber community of Douglas Landing. She had wanted to arrive unnoticed before the rest of the family. In fact, she didn't want anyone on the planet to have an inkling of where she had gone, not even Bernard. She borrowed his flashy convertible so that her own car appeared in her Beverly Hills driveway, and swore Bernard to total silence as to her whereabouts.

Janee grew serious as she recalled the look of panic on Bernard's face.

"Janee, you aren't going to do something foolish – er like you've done before?" Bernard's face clouded in concern.

"No Bernard!" Janee's reply carried that biting edge she had become noted for. "Do you think I'm stupid enough to return to those years of jabbing needles in my arms or drinking myself into a mindless stupor? I assure you My Dear; I carry no homesickness for any of those re-habs I spent so much of my life in. Don't think it was the time of my life there because it wasn't. Bernard, your question was ill thought out – in other words, it was dumb. I'm making a strong comeback in my career. It has taken years to get back to this point. I wouldn't throw it all away again for a fix.

Don't ever consider it or question it Bernard, or I'll – I'll fire you so –"

"Like you've done forty seven times?" He interrupted her. "Yes, I've been counting." He gave her a befuddled glance as he handed her his car keys.

"I just would like to know where you are going!"

"I'll call and explain," she returned a half-hearted smile and waved his keys to him as she disappeared out the door.

'He couldn't tell anyone where I am, even if he wanted to,' she thought. 'However, he could figure it out, and he better not report his car missing or stolen.'

"I'll fire him!" she spoke part in jest, but also realizing Bernard was known to make some stupid moves.

"That's after I kill him," she laughed.

As Janee drove into town she could barely make out the outline of the old Cascade Mountain Lumber Mill. Scattered lights lit up the yards of lumber, but the mill was quiet and dark, an operation no longer able to sustain a night shift.

She slowed down, passing the station and café - both closed for the night. In the darkness, she missed the first street, Myrtlewood, but she remembered that Aspen was between the post office and the bank.

The town had grown slightly since Janee's last visit. She caught a glimpse in her headlights of a few buildings she couldn't identify. One thing hadn't changed; everybody closed shop at sundown, and what sidewalks the town boasted were pulled in and locked up as well. Of course, Janee had counted on that.

'Fewer people to see me arrive,' she thought.

Her headlights picked up a faded street sign that read Aspen. She turned left onto the street and drove to the end - stopping briefly. She looked to the right down Breach Road to the house on the corner of Peppertree.

The night air was still warm from a hot fall day, but the house on Peppertree looked dark and cold.

Janee shivered, then slowly inched onto Breach and drove toward a place that called to her fondly from child-hood memories.

She stopped the car in a place made for cars to park, now grown up in grass and weeds. She shut the engine off and sat thinking.

What had she expected? The house warmly lit up? Did she think Grandma would be running out the front door, onto the porch, and down the steps to sweep Janee into her arms?

For an instant it seemed real! Janee shook those thoughts off, and for the first time she became aware that her long blonde hair was tangled and wrapped around her head and neck. She had driven nearly the length of the State of California with the top down, wind in her face, blowing her hair. What a relief and freedom she felt leaving Los Angeles. For many of the miles she seemed to recapture feelings she had known in her twenties - wild and loose!

Janee sighed. She started to put the top up, then thought, 'What the heck,' and left it down. She fumbled in the glove box hoping to find a flashlight, coming across a pack of ciga-rettes and a lighter instead. She scooped up both and made her way carefully around the side of the house, feeling along the wall until she touched the gate that led to the back. The latch was stubborn and held fast. Janee finally flicked the lighter to see what she was doing.

"Grandma, I hope you left the back door key in our secret place," Janee whispered as though her grandma was quietly listening, "Otherwise I'm going to break out a window."

Janee walked along the side of the porch to where it came against the wall. She could hear her Grandma Emile telling her as if it were only yesterday.

"Janee, when folks hide a key they put it in a would-be place. Why even the worst of crooks can look under a flow-erpot or over the doorframe. So I got your grandpa to fix this last board on the porch where you can raise it, and underneath on that beam is the key."

Janee lifted the board and held the lighter close. She couldn't see for the spider webs. Locating a stick, she cleared the matted webs and held the light - searching - yes! There in the dim light of the flame was the key - rusty with age but still in its place.

Janee grabbed it up and dropped the board. She hesitated, and for a moment her eyes grew misty. She recalled the last conversation she had with her grandma.

"Janee, it has been so long since I have seen you, and I miss you terribly."

"You can't imagine how busy I am. We are shooting again - in fact I have a five a.m. call on the set tomorrow."

"Janee, I'm not sure how much longer I have, and I so want to see you - hold you. I love you"

"Grandma, don't try to run me on a guilt trip. Besides, whenever we're together we just argue! I'm tired of it!"

"I've never stopped praying for you, Janee. One of the last prayers I remember hearing your Grandpa Farmer offer up to the Lord was that you would find Jesus as your Savior."

"Don't bring grandpa into this. I respect your faith, but it's not for me. I have my own beliefs. I have to go, grandma!"

"Janee, I want you to know you are always welcome here - to come anytime - you know where the key is."

"Yeah, sure, grandma. Goodbye!"

"Goodbye. I love you, Janee."

A wave of guilt and regret penetrated Janee's thoughts as it hit her how long it had been since she had told her Grandma Emile she loved her too, all because of a difference in religious beliefs.

"Damn!" Janee muttered and shook those feelings off. She unlocked the back door and turned on the kitchen light.

Chapter 34

A Knock in the Dark

Nothing had been touched in the house. The utilities were still on. Janee tried the water and then lifted the kitchen phone receiver off the hook. She listened to that familiar buzz that indicated the phone was still connected. Janee followed the line and disconnected it at a wall jack.

She next flipped on the lights in the living room. Grandmother had a new sofa and easy chair. She had rearranged the furniture, but Janee recognized most of what she saw.

She spied another telephone on a small table by the easy chair. What an antique it was.

"I think they kept everything they ever owned," Janee muttered, and she disconnected that phone also.

She next turned on the light to the room where her mother grew up, and Janee stayed when she came to visit. Nothing had been moved - nothing had changed from the last time she saw it. She lingered here for a while before walking to the next door. It opened to Walter and Clifton's room, used no doubt for guests, and it would again be occupied tomorrow. Janee finally brought herself to switch on the light in her grandmother's bedroom. This is where they discovered her grandmother's body.

'She died all alone!' Janee thought. 'How sad for her!'

The mattress, sheets and blanket looked like they still held the faint outline of the person who had lain down there to rest and sleep - until one night, she never woke up - or woke up somewhere else, perhaps in a beautiful woods.

Janee ran her hand along the bed. The light cast an eerie glow into the room, almost as if there was a presence there.

At one angle looking at the bed it struck Janee that it appeared her grandmother's body was positioned at the foot of the bed.

"How odd!" Janee thought out loud, and the sound of her voice broke a heavy silence. A cold icy shiver rose up her back to her neck. She wasn't certain she could spend the night, and if she did, it would be a sleepless one. She retreated to the kitchen, turning out lights as she went.

Janee opened the refrigerator hoping she might find something to drink. She surveyed the meager occupants and settled for a cola.

"Hell, should of known! Grandmother never tasted anything stronger than tea her whole life," Janee grumbled.

She took her soda into the living room and set it on the table by the phone and collapsing into the easy chair she lit up a cigarette. She became lost in thought.

"Bam - bam - bam!" came a loud knocking on the front door. Janee was so startled she screamed!

Chapter 35

A Message

Janee sat frozen in the easy chair, her heart pounding so loudly she was sure that whoever stood on the front porch could hear it!

"Bam - bam!"

Janee's mind raced - what to do? If she refused to answer the door, would they go away?

"Bam - bam - bam!" Only this time: louder and more persistent.

Janee tried to think. Wait! She was the counter intelligence heroine in the movie, "Aegean Agent." She had fought off a multitude of spies then, so why was she afraid?

"Bam - bam - bam!"

She heard a muffled voice; however what was spoken was inaudible. She went to the front door.

"Who is it?" she asked.

"I have a message for Miss Stemper."

"Oh, good Lord, what is it now?" Janee was annoyed. She threw open the door to see an aged white-haired man holding up the cane he had been knocking with.

"Oh! It is you, Miss Janee. I'm sorry to bother you, but I saw lights on in the Trevor house."

"How do you know who I am?" Janee snapped.

The old man laughed.

"Well, I saw you - lots - when you would come up to visit your grandma - an' grandpa while he was still - well, anyway saw you 'til you stopped coming. Then we saw you - mostly in your movies 'til -"

"I don't believe I know who you are," Janee interrupted.

"I'm Gordon. Gordon Brooks. My wife, Ella May, an' I live down at the end of the street."

Janee stood staring. She looked him up and down. It appeared he had yanked his overalls up over a red flannel undershirt then pulled on a pair of logger boots. The smile he held when the conversation began was gone. He peered at her through old-fashioned glasses, but his eyes were clear as he studied her face. He steadied himself, applying weight on his cane. He waited.

"Oh!" Janee spoke after an extended silence. "Yes - of course. Won't you come in?"

She went to turn on the living room light as the old man hobbled toward the sofa.

She spun around and returned to face Mr. Brooks. If he ever got seated on the couch, he would probably be there for hours.

"You said you had a message?"

"Yes, yes I do. The sheriff came by my place earlier this evening. He had been down here."

"The sheriff!" Janee gasped. "Whatever for?"

"Well, seems like - your manager -"

"Bernard Swift?"

"Yes! That's the fella. He seems desperate to find you. Afraid you ran away or…"

Janee threw up her hands in amazement.

"That bast… I'm sorry. Bernard is such an idiot!" She was raging inside. She started pacing the floor resisting a strong urge to throw things.

"Your grandpa used to walk the floor like that when he was upset or thinking hard."

"What?" Janee stopped and glared at the old man.

"Pacing the floor like that."

"What?"

"Your grandpa used to do that way."

"Mr. Gordon, thank you for delivering that message, now if you don't mind -."

"That was just the first message. I got another one," Mr. Brooks hobbled to the sofa and sat with a thud.

Janee was angry and irritated. She began to pace again.

"I mean to deliver the second message now 'cause I may not have a chance later," Gordon continued.

"We all - everyone was shocked and hurt when your Grandpa was - shot."

Janee stopped and looked squarely at Mr. Brooks. "Is that your message?" she snapped.

The old man set his cane and struggled to his feet. He walked slowly to Janee until their noses were almost touching. He straightened up and spoke.

"Listen here, young lady, you get down off your high horse! Hear me out! I'm trying to tell you something about your family."

The old man's voice that had been gentle and sort of shaky now thundered. Janee suddenly wanted to break down and cry. She felt tears coming to her eyes, but she turned her back on Mr. Brooks and fought off the tears.

"Then get on with it!" she growled, keeping her back to the old man. She walked to the wall and occupied herself picking up some knick-knacks from a shelf.

"Your grandma especially, took your grandpa's death hard," Gordon went on.

'So did I!' Janee thought as some old feelings attempted to surface. She pushed them back. She wanted them so buried; she would never feel them again.

"It was like my misses, Ella May. When our Gordie was killed in the war - we never knew we could hurt so bad. Ella just has never seemed to get over it. She still grieves!"

"What's this have to do with my family?" Janee spoke harshly giving him a brief glance that was certain to display her displeasure with the topic of conversation.

"That's my point. Emile never got over your grandpa's death. She missed him terribly! Oh, she lived a long and full life, but most of us around here who knew her think she just got to the point she would rather go be with her Lord and Farmer. She just longed to be - somewhere else - to see..."

Gordon's mind seemed to drift off in thought for a moment.

"We felt bad when we found her. We think she passed peaceful in her sleep - we think, but she was all alone. That was the bad part, and it was two days before... Well, we was puzzled. She was lying at the foot end of the bed - reaching out - like toward the door. Maybe she was trying to get help... We all are sorry about her passing and sure will miss her."

"Mr. Brooks, I think it best you leave!" Janee spoke angrily. She moved toward the front door.

"I ain't given you the message yet."

"For heaven's sake, get it out!"

"Well, that's it. It's from your grandma. She wanted to be sure she would see you in Heaven someday."

"There is no Heaven, you foolish man. Is that what she told you to tell me?" Janee yelled in a loud voice.

Gordon Brooks remained calm.

"She seemed to sense her time was near, and she wouldn't see you again in this life. She gave lots of folks here in Douglas Landing a message for you. Mine was this:

'Janee,' she said, 'God has given you a beautiful talent and has blessed you. He wants you for His own. Like when He walked in the garden calling His children, He calls you now. Please let Him find you.'"

Tears rolled down Gordon's cheeks from under his glasses. He stood quietly now.

Janee fell into the easy chair, laughing hysterically. She laughed until her face was wet.

Gordon Brooks watched her. He was bewildered at this weird behavior.

"Oh, Gawd!" Janee coughed through her laughter. "My grandmother never gives up. She preaches to me still from beyond the - grave."

Her mood turned sullen as sudden as the laughter and tears had come.

"Anything we can do to help, Miss Janee?" Gordon showed concern.

Janee covered her face in her right hand and pointed toward the door with her left.

"Get out!" she ordered. "Get out! Leave me alone!"

The thump - thump - thumps - thump of Gordon Brooks' cane could be heard - then the gentle closing of the door. Janee had the urge to break down and cry, but she fought it off. She sat fuming for a long time.

Finally, she got out of the chair and reconnected the ancient phone, which was near the easy chair. She stood as she dialed. The connection was made, and it rang several times before she heard a sleepy, "Hello."

"Bernard, you moron, I have a message for you! You still don't know where I am or why, but get this into that thick head of yours! If you ever call the authorities on me again like you did today - if ever - I'll fire your butt so fast smoke will come out! And to finish you off, I'll fix it so the only one you can find to represent is some old slop jockey from the mid-west!"

Chapter 36

A Discovery

It took some time for Janee to settle down! She paced the floor in her Grandma Emile's house. She smoked several cigarettes before she realized she'd better save some for the rest of a long night. The thought of going out to buy a pack next morning repulsed her. She felt exhausted, but sleep was nowhere near.

'What the heck,' she thought. 'I'm used to long hours on a shoot. This is just the first take - no rehearsal. Lights - camera - action - hell!'

She flopped down on the sofa and closed her eyes. That lasted about two minutes and her eyes were wide open looking up at the ceiling. She sat back up.

Her eyes scanned the room, which by now was well embedded in her mind. Her attention slowly focused on the hallway and the dark room that had been her grandmother's bedroom. The thought of Grandmother Emile lying dead on that bed sent a chill up Janee's back. For an instant she wished for daybreak and the family to arrive.

Janee didn't want to go back into that room. It felt strange - disrespectful, yet a strong force seemed to draw her. A twinge of fear gripped her heart. She shook that off.

"All that Janee Stemper has been through, why should I be afraid of an empty room?" she spoke loudly as she marched down the hall. She reached into the dark room, felt on the wall for the switch, and flipped on the light.

"If your spirit is in here, grandmother, speak to me! It's me! Janee! Your rebellious granddaughter. See! I was right! There is no Heaven or hell! You're just in a beautiful, peaceful place - or just - here - in this room."

Janee examined the bed more closely.

'What was she doing down here?' Janee wondered. 'Was she trying to get help?'

It appeared as if Emile was trying to crawl right off the end of the bed, but to where? The door? No, the angle of her body was not pointing in the direction of the door - it was toward - the dresser. Did she want to reach for some of her clothes - or something else?

Janee hesitated. Her grandma's drawers seemed like sacred ground.

"What's the difference, for cripes sake!" she muttered walking to the dresser. "Family will rummage through everything anyway when they arrive."

Janee started with the top drawer feeling amongst bras and underpants. She pulled a girdle from the next drawer.

"Never knew grandma wore one of these!" she laughed.

Janee found nothing of importance in the top two drawers. She opened the bottom drawer. It displayed some sweaters, an array of scarves and a wad of nylons. She felt around, and in one corner her hand came upon a book.

"Oh, ho! What's this, grandma?"

The book was very old and worn. The cover was almost completely detached from the binding. Janee opened it up and instantly treated it with great reverence when she realized it was Emile's personal journal.

She walked slowly away from the dresser, eyes glued to what she was reading. She sat cross-legged on the small area rug, leaning up against the side of the bed. It felt like a sacred moment. She was reading about thoughts, feelings, and events of her Grandma Emile's life. She was reading something that perhaps no other person, maybe even grandpa, had ever seen. What a discovery!

Chapter 37

Entries

First entry: **March 30, 1925**

'Tomorrow morning we depart on a long journey to a strange land and different life. Tonight Walter and Clifton were so anxious to leave they had difficulty falling asleep. If only they knew what lay ahead and the hardships. Clifton thinks we will be in Oregon by supper. Oh, God, I am so frightened for them - and what if I am with child! But Farmer is so eager and excited to be off - I dare not let him see. Help me to be brave!'

March 31, 1925

'It was sad for Farmer and I to say "goodbye" to our farm in Texas which afforded us so many wonderful memories. Farmer felt it too - I could tell - but it is good to be on the way. I think I am absorbing my husband's enthusiasm!'

April 1, 1925

'We arrived at Mr. Redkin's Ranch. Farmer played a joke on me, and I believed him. He said we were really going to live here and work for Mr. Redkin. It is so nice here, and everyone has been so kind. I almost wish the joke were true - God forgive me!'

Janee's eyes fell on a note Emile had penned a few days later making her laugh out loud!

'We have seen automobiles in abundance and even an airplane. What amazing sights! In Amarillo many of the women have their faces painted and wear dresses up to their knees. I was shocked!'

Janee skimmed over the next few entries as the pioneers passed through west Texas cattle towns, but two sentences stood out.

'I am positive I am pregnant. I could tell today.'

Further journal entries referenced travel accounts through Glen Rio, Tucumcari and on across New Mexico. Suddenly, the words caught Janee's attention.

'The good Lord spared us from death last night. Farmer felt warned and moved us to high ground just minutes before a wall of water came rushing unannounced down what had been an almost dry creek bed. So powerful was the force it tore out the bridge. Poor Farmer, he stood out in the downpour with a lantern to ward off other travelers in the night that they might not perish in this dreadful storm. God save us all! My heart stopped when I saw headlights approaching from the other side of the swollen creek. I cried out to them and You when it seemed they would disappear into the black rushing water, but at the last instant they saw Farmer's lantern. Thank you, Father, for your mercy in sparing the Buchwalds and their precious children - and us!'

The next few pages had water stains, and Janee just assumed they were from the rain. However, as she read on she began to realize they were not from the rainstorm but were her grandma's teardrops.

'Farmer is getting something. A fever? Maybe something from the cold and soaking of the thunderstorm.'

'Farmer was too sick to travel this morning. Dear God, please help!'

'For two days and nights, Farmer has been delirious. He is burning with fever. He kicks and beats the air. Now he has grown so weak he barely moves or breathes. Farmer, you've got to fight! For me! For the boys! For our unborn baby! We need you! Don't leave us alone out here! Farmer, get well!'

'Dear God, I am lost! I don't know what day it is, I don't know where we are, what I am to do! There is no one here to help us but you. Unless you heal Farmer, I fear we are all doomed in this wild place!'

'Oh, joy of Heaven! In the dark of night Farmer called out my name. That was the most wonderful sound I have ever heard. He said he was so hungry he could eat one of the horses! Praise be to God, He has spared us all!'

Janee's face was wet from her own tears. She swore in anger and hastily wiped her eyes. She continued on - captured by the journal's contents. She turned each page carefully as the paper had become brittle with age.

The entries chronicled the Trevors' trip on through New Mexico and Arizona. Janee read with interest about Flint Parker and his Model T Pickup, the camp on the Rio Grande, the theft in Gallop, Two Guns and the mountain lion in timber country around Flagstaff.

"Make a great movie script!" declared Janee.

She read where Emile wasn't feeling well. The bouncing of the wagon and the desert heat was getting her down. Then there was a blank page before the next entry. Janee wondered why that was until she read on.

'My recollection of several days into Utah are as blank as the prior page. As I grew weaker I fell in and out of consciousness. I became aware of Farmer's grave concern and the motions of the wagon told me he was pushing the team to move faster.'

'The next thing I remember was a strange woman standing over me, and I was in someone's house. She told me to hang on. That I and the baby would be fine.'

Janee turned the page.

'I feel much better and am regaining my strength. The rest has been good for me.

The most wonderful and exciting news. Farmer led Ruth Riggs to trust in the Lord today! I can see such a change in her - she is truly happy and at peace!'

"This is ridiculous!" Janee slammed the book down dislodging some of the pages. "People determine their own fate. What's left is written in the stars! I'm sick of all this God and saving junk!"

Janee walked into the kitchen. She opened cabinets until she found a jar of instant coffee.

"This will taste like crap, but will have to do," she complained as she filled the kettle with water and set it on the stove to boil. She was still fuming as she sat at the table later sipping her coffee.

Janee remembered one such conversation, 'grandma, why must you insist everyone believe as you?'

'Janee, you know that I don't expect that. I just want to share my faith with you.'

'Then I would appreciate it if you shared with someone else. There are millions of gullible idiots in the world to pick from.'

No more was spoken of it, but Janee could see the hurt in her grandma's face.

Janee sat with both elbows on the table clutching her cup. She couldn't get her mind away from the last entries she had read in Emile's journal. After a period of some honest soul searching she had to admit that it wasn't her grandma's joy over the midwife becoming a Christian that upset her so - it was something before that!

The baby who was almost lost out there in Utah was her mother, Leah.

She took another swallow of coffee. She stared straight ahead, but saw only something from her past. She shook her head at the paradox. Her grandparents fought to save a baby; she had fought to get rid of hers. No one had any knowledge of her abortion, except the doctor.

It's legal. Women have the right to choose - Janee rationalized what she had done. It wasn't even a life yet - just a growth in her body.

For an instant she felt the sharp sting of guilt, but just as quickly dismissed it refusing further thought in that arena.

Curiosity finally demanded more dwelling into the journal. Janee rose from the table, returning to her grandmother's bedroom. She plopped down on the rug and reached for the journal that lay on the floor. She found where she had left off.

The journal followed the Trevors' trek west until they reached their promised land in Oregon. Emile's words described their homestead in beautiful - flowing words.

Janee paused on one entry.

November 4, 1925

'Last night a little after midnight God gave us a beautiful daughter, Leah. The birth was not without great stress and event. Beth walked to our house to stay on November 3rd. That day seems hazy to my recollection. It snowed heavily then froze. I went into labor, and my water broke soon after. Farmer rushed out for Doctor Put, and I was relieved he soon returned until he informed me that the truck was stuck, and he came for the horses. I tried to hold back labor. Beth was taking this delivery harder than I for she was as white as my bed shirt.

It seemed Farmer took hours to retrieve the Doctor. Just when I felt the baby would wait no longer, Farmer arrived with Doctor Put. I heard Leah's first cries of life a few minutes later. She was so noisy and restless for a long time. I fear this girl will be a wild one. Farmer held her and was so proud. I pray she doesn't have his restless spirit.'

"Don't know if mom did, but I sure have it!" Janee mused.

The journal told of glad times, described the horrible Depression years and the loss of the ranch. Janee read how banker Rollin Graves deeded them the small house on Peppertree and Breach Street. Her grandpa was fortunate enough to get a job at the mill.

She was shocked at the entry about her mother and father. Not that her mother was pregnant out of wedlock, she knew that, but her father ran away and disappeared?

'Walter and Clifton displayed a hate toward Harold that frightens me,' Emile had written. 'I fear they will kill him if they find him.'

"I can understand Uncle Walter and Clifton feeling like that," Janee perceived. This was part of the past the family never spoke of to her, nor would she have ever suspected it had happened.

The journal shared Emile's perspective on the atrocities of a World War, from news of Europe's eruptions to the surprise attack on Pearl Harbor and more tearful entries.

December 1941:

'Dear God, my whole world is crashing down around me. I don't know what day it is, who I am, what is happening. Farmer returned with the boys and announced they had all tried to enlist in the service. I was so mad at Farmer I wanted to beat him. He would leave me alone to go off to war. My mind cannot think like a man. Why are they so in a hurry to run off to fight - and for what? To prove how quickly they can be shot and die. Walter was not accepted. I was relieved and happy while dear Walter was devastated. My poor dear Clifton joined the Army Air Corps. Words fail!

It's a black Tuesday, December 1941. I am writing this journal early because I know I won't have the will or the heart to do so later. All of my children leave today. Walter will take Leah in his car to join Harold in Southern California. They will get married, and I can't even be there to love them and cry. Farmer has been cheated of the special experience of giving his daughter away. Walter will get a job there, but at least he is safe. But Clifton is going off to a strange land to fight a war. I watched him at breakfast - he seems still a little boy joking and laughing as he eats. My hurting heart has made me numb.'

Janee came across the entry, which announced her birth. She reflected with a smoldering anger how most folks soon figured out she was in the oven before the wedding of Harold and Leah Stemper occurred.

"Do the math," Janee frowned in disgust. "Married in January; baby in March! That's a damn short nine months."

She remembered how the tabloids crucified her and her parents when she got older, one even suggesting that Harold was not actually the father for he was a half-breed Indian of dark skin and black hair, while Janee was of fair complexion and ash blonde. She dismissed those thoughts and turned her attention again to the journal. Janee thumbed through more pages, glancing over the entries. She could not bear to read of the worry and fears of the war years. She stopped at the ones which told about the trip Farmer and Emile made in 1945 to California and Texas. Janee closed the journal for she had a memory of her own in mind.

She pictured the first time she saw them. She had talked to them on the phone, but here they were - face to face. She instantly loved her Grandma Emile. Grandpa Farmer was different. He appeared a western man - strong and somewhat gruff and reminded her of the pioneers in the movie of which she played a part. She thought it best in her little mind to approach him in like manner - big and tough.

By the time their visit was ended, she had come to love her grandma deeply, but grandpa she adored! She had won his heart as well.

Janee passed over many happy entries in Emile's journal of family visits with her Uncle Walter and Uncle Clifton, Aunt Rachel and baby cousin David Lee. There were relatives in Texas, and those years following the war, all were entries of growth, prosperity, wonder and loads of laughter. Janee's family was fast becoming wealthy, and she was emerging as a movie star.

Then her eye fell on an October 1951, entry. Janee knew instinctively what it was. Did she dare read it? She wanted desperately to close the book, but her fingers would not move. With trembling hands and racing heart her eyes followed Emile's handwriting.

'They told me this evening they found Farmer's body on our ranch - our ranch? Dear God, what was he doing out there? He vowed never to return until we could once again own our old place. Was he working on a surprise? Or did old memories compel him? He did appear troubled last night - and I recall his words that seemed born of some kind of confusion and doubt. A young hunter who mistakenly took my sweet Farmer for a deer shot and killed him. I should hate this hunter as I do all hunters and their guns right now, but I - only feel pity for him. I am suddenly alone! Dear God, what am I to do? I feel a part of me, the man I have loved all of my life, my husband, the father of our children, has been ripped away from me! In my whole life I have never hurt like this! It's as though I too was shot. I am dying inside.'

Janee silently closed the journal and placed it back in her grandma's drawer. She cared not to read further – maybe at another time.

She got up, turned out the light and returned to the living room. She plugged the phone back in and dialed Bernard's number. It rang and rang. Janee thought to hang up when the receiver at the other end clicked, and she heard a sound resembling a groan.

"Bernard?"

"Janee . . .?"

"I called to tell you I was sorry for the way I spoke to you earlier."

"Janee, what time is it?"

"Nearly 4:30."

"Are you – alright? I mean ..."

"I'm fine. I'm at my grandma's house in Oregon."

"Why didn't you tell me? I've been sick with worry!"

"I didn't wreck your car."

"Damn it, Janee, you know I don't care about my car! You know it's yours to use. I just don't understand why you didn't let me know what you were doing."

"My Grandma Emile passed away."

There was a silence.

"Janee, I am sorry to hear that."

"I was afraid word would leak out. I would die if the media showed up here!"

After another long silence, "Janee, we've known each other for twenty-one years, and you can't trust me?"

"A sheriff or somebody like that came into town looking for me."

"I know," Bernard coughed. "I called every place I could think of – now don't get mad again. I was just trying to locate you. I never implied you were missing. I panicked and was desperate. I asked the local law enforcement to check to see if you had arrived there. I had no idea Janee . . . I was just worried about you. If you would have asked, I'd have gone with you."

"I know you would have. Just understand how furious I was to learn a sheriff was here looking for me."

"I'm sorry. Is there anything I can do?"

"Actually, Bernard, right now I wish you were here..."

"I'm on my way! I'll be there as soon as I can."

Chapter 38

What Upset Her?

Janee sat up with a startled, wild look. It took a moment for her mind to focus. Loud noises and voices jerked her out of a dead sleep. Her head ached!

"Janee, you look like you have encountered a ghost! Were you having a nightmare?" her mother spoke as she marched into the house. "Oh my goodness, it smells awful in here! What were you thinking smoking inside your grandma and grandpa's house?" Leah set about opening windows to air the place out.

"Yes," Janee mumbled. "I dreamt my mother was here waking me out of a sound sleep."

"I'm sorry, honey -."

Janee waved her off. "What time is it?"

"Five minutes to twelve," her dad answered. Janee squinted at him in disbelief.

"Gaaa, I must have been up all night." She stumbled to the bathroom to wash her face and brush her teeth. She could make out the noise of a commotion outside.

"What's that noise?" she yelled to her mom and dad through the bathroom door.

"A news crew is setting up," came a reply after a brief interlude.

"Damn!" Janee exclaimed. "I swear I'll kill the lot - and Bernard along with them!" She stood with her head down, holding the sides of the sink for a long time. How she wished the gathering outside would just go away!

"Damn it to hell!" she exclaimed again. No back door or alley to duck through here. For an instant she wished herself astride Dusty riding like the wind for the trees.

She emerged from the bathroom slamming the door behind her. She sat down on the sofa and stared blankly at her parents.

"I tried to keep my whereabouts secret. I even drove Bernard's car, but he went into a dither and called the Sheriff. That alerted the whole world," Janee threw her hands into the air, as if to give up.

"You'll just have to be brave," her dad, offered.

Janee felt her temper boil, and hot words came to mind. Better judgment would halt those words, but anger propelled them out anyway. Janee was never one to hold her tongue.

"Be brave? Be brave? How can you give me advice like that when you abandoned mother at a time she needed you most. Is my shame not enough that I am a bastard child - now to have a coward father?"

Harold and Leah were shocked! With her accusation, Janee brought out into the open things never spoken of by the family. Harold was devastated, and Leah stood up defensively.

"Who told you this?" she demanded.

"Every family has its skeletons! Believe me, I spent the night in the closet. Grandma told me!"

Leah sank under the blow! She shook her head in protest.

"I found her diary last night. I read every page. Daddy, how could you? You ran away - like a coward!"

Leah rushed forward as if to slap Janee's mouth. Harold stopped her with a firm hand.

"No, Leah, don't. What she says is true. I did run away. I was afraid. I abandoned you - and our baby. Oh, God, how I asked His forgiveness. My guilt drove me to Him!"

"Oh, great! Dad felt guilty and got religion. Now that makes everything just peachy sweet."

"And my love for Jesus Christ, and you both, drove me back to Douglas Landing - to make - things right…"

"Ha! What a joke! My mother slept with my coward father before they considered marriage. Why bother? Just a scrap of paper with no meaning, and I'm still the illegitimate child from your unholy union. How do you make - that right?"

"Oh, Janee, your words - so cruel - and - heartless!" Leah cried. Harold held his wife. Janee felt she had pushed her parents to the limit, but didn't regret her words. Leah made haste to hide her tears as she saw Clifton and his family coming to the front door.

"Hello, everybody. We're here!" Clifton shouted as he threw open the door. Rachel followed with their son, David, his wife, Cynthia, and their daughter, Mary, close on their heels.

Greetings, embellished with hugs and kisses, were passed around. Rachel eyed Leah, then Janee with a questioning look. Janee rolled her eyes and turned away. Mary took hold of Janee's hand and held tight. Janee looked down into dark brown eyes filled with the wonder of seeing a movie star. She hugged her cousin's daughter and kissed her cheek. Mary giggled but held tightly to her hand.

"Where's Morgan?" Harold asked Rachel, looking outside.

"She's with the news people," Cynthia answered.

"She's talking to the media?" Janee was aghast.

"No, not Morgan," Clifton laughed.

"Joseph's talking to them?" Leah gasped.

"No, Joseph had an emergency at work at the last minute and couldn't come," Rachel continued. "It's little Caleb."

"Caleb?" everyone said in unison.

"Yes, he's telling the news crew how he trusted Jesus as his Savior a few months ago in church," Cynthia smiled.

Everyone laughed except Janee.

"Now the whole world will know my family is a bunch of Jesus Freaks," she groaned.

Chapter 39

Family

Walter flew into Douglas Landing that afternoon in his own small plane, and Bernard drove up in front of the house as the sun was dipping out of sight. He engaged in conversation with news crews who had waited patiently for a glimpse of the film star, Janee Stemper. When he came into the house he held up both hands to Janee.

"I swear, I didn't tell anyone!" He begged forgiveness with his expression.

Walter was Janee's favorite. She loved talking to him and enjoyed his dry, casual humor. He reminded her of Grandpa Farmer. She ignored Bernard for the most part; however, he busied himself visiting with family members. Janee tried to spend time with everybody, even the children.

Walter was an airline pilot. For some unknown reason that only Janee could understand, he had remained a bachelor all these years. He was considered a prime catch, but never got hooked.

David was an airplane mechanic along with his father, Clifton, with the same airline as Walter flew for. They all lived in Alaska. David married Cynthia sometime in 1972, but Janee forgot the day and month. Two years later they had

Mary. Mary, from the few meetings she had with Janee, idolized her celebrity relative.

Morgan, on the other hand, was another story. Clifton and Rachel's second child was a mere ten years younger than her cousin Janee. When she graduated high school she left Alaska to study in the east. She met and fell in love with a Jewish boy named Joseph Hillag. Before the birth of their first child, the marriage seemed doomed. Joseph and Morgan argued violently over their differing beliefs. Both were stubborn in their faiths, but when little Caleb was born, something happened to Joseph to turn him to embrace the Messiah of his wife. Morgan's people were saddened to see Joseph made an outcast from his own family, but lovingly took him in. The Hillags settled in Seattle, so Morgan could be closer to her family.

Where Mary was quiet and gentle, Caleb was a handful. He had given the media a six-year-old's version of the condition of the world. As Janee pondered over what the lad might have said, she felt a healthy tug on her sleeve. She looked into the face of a boy who seemed to view everything around him as wonder and magic.

"Hello Caleb," Janee acknowledged him.

"Mema Emile had her a question for you that I don't spec she ever got answered."

"And what question was that?" Janee was curious.

"How long you gonna stay mad at God for taking your grandpa away? She hoped it wouldn't be for your whole life. That's what she told me. Are you mad at God?"

"What makes you think I'm mad at God?" Janee glanced up nervously to see Bernard carefully listening to the conversation.

"You don't seem very happy, and when you smile, I don't believe you."

"Well, Caleb, how can I be mad at someone who isn't there?"

"Oh, Jesus is there, I know! I talk with Him all the time, and He lives in my heart. I'm in God's Family now!"

Janee wanted to retaliate, but held her tongue. Caleb's childish words and simple faith had stirred something inside her soul. There was no rebuttal for it.

Chapter 40

A Long Evening

T he evening hours wore on, but there was a reluctance to
leave. Emile's room had remained hallowed ground, and
no one approached her door. It was as if, though unspoken,
the family didn't want to let her go.

"I keep expecting her to walk briskly out of her bedroom,"
Rachel murmured, "like she always did."

"She lived a long time after Pa…" Clifton reflected.

"Remember that fella which hung around from Applegate
and tried to court Ma. She finally ran him off!" Walter
laughed.

"Grandma was tough as nails," Morgan added.

"I met her several times - when she came to Los
Angeles," Bernard spoke up. "She was an intelligent and
elegant lady."

"She was old-fashioned and out of her place in high
society. People thought of her as comic and only put up with
her to be polite," Janee snapped. "Bernard, you amaze me
with your senseless insights!"

She saw the family stare at her, then Bernard. They turned
their heads to private conversations. That had always been
their way of shutting her out when they were annoyed. Janee
grew sullen and finally walked out on the back porch. She

was shocked to see a stranger sitting on the edge, leaning against the wall.

"Who?" Janee started to speak but stopped when the man put a finger to his mouth for her to be quiet.

"I'm from 'Star Expose'. I was hoping you would come out the back; that's why I sneaked around here."

"Are you here to rape me or interview me?" Janee spoke sarcastically.

The man coughed.

"I had hoped - for an interview."

"You people are unbelievable. For years I've been old news; now on the eve of putting my grandmother to rest, you want an interview?"

"Miss Stemper, you are an incredible woman. You are one of the few who licked a hardened alcohol and drug addiction. You have made a powerful comeback in your last film. I just saw some clips. You'll get an Oscar for your performance - you can bank on it! I just want your story."

"You have just told it, sonny. I got messed up, tore up relationships, smashed my career, went to hell and back in rehab, played a strong role in a great movie. Was I close to my grandma? Not really. I – I – loved her but we had–sharp differences. Now please leave us alone!"

Janee walked back into the house. Mary and Caleb were playing in the kitchen; the men were visiting in the living room. The women had finally ventured into Emile's bedroom. Janee joined them.

Rachel and Morgan sat on the bed's edge. Leah was looking through an old photo album as Cynthia looked on.

"I could still see the imprint of where grandma was lying," Janee said slowly.

"I know! I see it too. I wonder what she was doing at the foot of the bed?" Rachel eyed the mystery indentation.

"Like she was trying to - go - somewhere," Morgan rubbed her hand on the quilt.

"I'll ask her when I see her," Leah replied matter-of-factly.

"I doubt that," Janee answered with her familiar cynical tone.

"You don't believe we'll see grandma again?" Morgan sounded hurt.

"Not like that!" Janee was ready to assert her beliefs.

"Of course, we'll all see her again. She's in a most beautiful place, and she's finally with grandpa!" Leah tried to be cheerful. "Now, Janee, you said you found grandma's diary. Where did you put it?"

Janee pulled the worn ledger from the drawer and handed it to her mother. The other women gathered around, intensely curious as to its contents.

It would be a long evening. They took turns reading, as they wanted to savor every word. It became so real, Emile herself could have been there reading to them. They could imagine her laughter over funny little things. The women cried over her pain and sorrows. Leah bravely read the entries of her own unexpected pregnancy, having to stop often to wipe her eyes. She left her own teardrops mingled with her mother's on the pages, which told of Harold's disappearance and his return. They laughed and joked over happy entries of the arrival of each grandchild. The women became very quiet when they came to the news of Farmer's death. Rachel was reading.

"I don't think I can do this!" she cried.

"You are all nothing but a bunch of sentimental mush heads!" Janee snatched the journal from Rachel.

Janee read quickly and dry-eyed, but all the while her heart was aching.

Looking at the entry date, it was almost two years before she wrote in the journal again, and then it was mostly joy over her family, displeasure with men who wanted to date her. There were many entries concerning the empty pillow next to hers.

"She was tired and just wanted to be with daddy," Leah spoke softly as she concluded the last entry and closed the journal.

"That entry was written the day before she passed away," Morgan commented. "Do you think she knew it was her time?"

"I think Jesus told her," Rachel murmured.

Janee just shook her head.

The evening was spent, and weariness overtook them and the funeral was to begin at 11 a.m. next morning.

Clifton and Rachel piled Morgan and Caleb into their rental car to spend the night with Rachel's mom.

David, Cynthia and Mary had a room in Applegate, so they took off for the motel. Harold and Leah was guest of Donald and Beth Parrigan at their ranch. Walter gave Bernard his old bed and found a couch for himself. Janee retired to the spare bedroom. She would find no peace in the dark and dreaded facing tomorrow.

Chapter 41

Putting Emile to Rest

D avid and his family were late coming from Applegate. Leah was fretful!

"Oh, where are those children?" she kept looking out the living room window. "Everyone will be waiting in the church!"

"Well, one thing, they can't start without us," Walter responded in his slow drawl.

Leah paced back and forth between the kitchen and the front window.

"This is dreadful!" she fumed.

"You're dreadful, Mother, and you are being a bore!" Janee snapped.

Caleb came bursting into the house from his vantage point in the front yard.

"I seen them turn the corner!" he announced.

The funeral home had provided cars for the family. The processional made its way slowly out to the Church in the Woods. Janee was relieved that most of the media had left their posts outside Grandma Emile's house, but became agitated when she discovered them camped near the church.

Janee ducked her head and turned quickly toward the church. They took pictures and rolled footage; however displayed courtesy toward the family. She knew that would end after the graveside service, crawling all over her like ants on a piece of sugar!

The church was overflowing. The others that couldn't get inside crowded the doors and windows. Janee wondered if they were really there to see the remains of Emile Trevor or to see a movie star. She mused over that.

The family was ushered to the seats in the front. Leah and Rachel immediately burst into tears. They had held up well until they saw Emile lying peacefully in the casket. Morgan and Cynthia also began to cry, and Janee saw Walter and Clifton out of the corner of her eyes draw handkerchiefs. Only she and her dad remained dry-eyed. She fought back emotions with all her might and will. She had not been inside this church since her grandpa's funeral, and she did not like the way it was making her feel now.

Some of Emile's favorite hymns were being played until the family was seated. The service opened with a scripture and a prayer. The small choir of the church sang, "Jesus, Lover Of My Soul," followed by the Pastor's short message. Janee tuned it out and thought of other things - pleasant things.

"We are here today to celebrate a life well lived. Perhaps there might be some who would like to stand and say something about Emile," the Pastor invited at the end of his message. There was a moment of silence, and the Pastor again opened the way for any who wished to speak.

"Anyone," his eyes swept the whole room.

"Well, I never been one to keep my mouth shut," an aging old man stood. "She be still as pretty a flower as there could be. She lived fer others and longed to be with Farmer. They be hand in hand walkin' them golden streets, glad to be together - forever."

Janee shook her head. She could hear many behind her sniff and weep. Some were blowing their noses.

'Such sentimental trite!' she thought angrily.

The old man's wife stood next. "I'm Beth Parrigan, Donald's wife," she said with a shaky voice. "Farmer and Emile took me in, a widow all alone in a strange place. They made sure I had a home - here - and one for my mister and me in Heaven. They helped us find Jesus." She paused as if to gain strength to go on. She looked at Leah. "I was with her when Leah was borned, and she with me when I delivered Beverly Ann. I sure miss my friend -."

Another elderly woman stood to speak. "I'm Ella May Brooks. Our children played and grew up together; we lost our ranches at the same time. Farmer and Emile always seemed more concerned about us than themselves." She began to shake and had to stop. Janee could see tears flowing freely down her cheek. She fought back tears of her own.

"They were first to - our house - when - when..." she stopped again. Her husband, Gordon, had to stand up to help steady her. "When we lost our son, Gordie, in the war," Gordon finished her sentence. "Emile spent many a day and night with Ella May during those dark days."

Janee had crying and grief up to her ears. She quickly stood as soon as Mr. and Mrs. Brooks sat down. She commenced to put on her made-for-the-fans smile. She began in a sweet but mature voice.

"While driving to Douglas Landing - in my agent's car -" she gave a little laugh. "I came upon a beautiful meadow, shining in the sunset. Out in the grass I saw two deer, peacefully feeding. One was a buck, I could tell by its antlers; the other a doe. 'It's a sign,' I thought at that moment. There are my grandparents - together - at peace - in a beautiful place."

She turned around to be confronted by a multitude of blank stares. She was amazed nobody got it!

"Anyway, that's how I see them," she concluded.

As she sat down, she had the sensation of being in a theatre of blind fools. She just wanted this funeral to be over, and it appeared her words had killed the momentum that had built in the testimonies. The Pastor started to close the service when a stirring could be heard in the rear of the church. Everyone turned to see an Indian woman make her way through the door.

"Please let me say something," she pleaded. "I have come a long way. I saw a newscast about Ms. Stemper's grandmother's passing. I remembered the name."

The Pastor glanced at the family. They were puzzled by this person and didn't recognize her. He nodded to the woman who had come down the aisle to stand by the family. She addressed them tenderly.

"Many years ago, my mother and father took me and my brother and escaped from the reservation in Montana. We walked for many days in the heat of day, and the night air was cold. We grew tired and were very hungry and thirsty. We saw a fire in the desert darkness and walked towards it."

Janee heard Walter gasp, and he turned to whisper something to Clifton.

"My father and mother were Henry and Hettie Wild Eagle, and I am their daughter, Omney. We walked in on a family - your family - traveling in a Chuck Wagon, camped in the Arizona desert. You shared your fire and gave us food to eat and water to drink. I have never forgotten you, Walter and Clifton. You gave my brother Curtis and me your airplane. But I want to say this; the greatest gift was your father's Bible. Written inside were your names, but best of all it revealed your father and mother's Savior, Jesus, so we all believed, and because of our faith, I know they are all together again - in Heaven..."

A collective cry of emotion and praise to God rose in the church.

After the service, family and friends filed slowly into town to the small cemetery. Emile's final resting place would be next to her husband, Farmer.

Chapter 42

After It's Over

❧

Donald Parrigan approached Janee near the cars. "Ms. Janee," he removed his cap. "I'm as curious as a beaver in a new stream. Do you really believe what you said - you know, about the deer?"

"I sure do, Mr. Parrigan. Someday you'll see the truth and believe as I."

"I'm a wondering what gave you that idea? Was it something one of your movie friends dreamed about?"

"It isn't a dream. It came from the writings of a brilliant man, ' course, I doubt you ever read anything that deep."

"The Bible is 'bout as deep as I get, Ms. Janee."

"That's just an ancient book, written by uneducated men." Janee was defensive, and that made her uncomfortable. She always wanted to be the aggressor, but before she could begin her barrage, the old man disarmed her with a broad grin.

"I was watchin' a flock o' geese one spring flying back to where they hatched out. 'Who taught them how to do that I wondered?' I answered in my thinking, 'Musta been the good Lord, 'cause they sure didn't study no books to learn how to go home.' That reminds me of a question yer grandmother told me to ask you."

Janee let out a sigh, "What- is- it?"

"She wanted to know when was you coming back to what once was precious in yer life?"

"Never!" Janee retorted as she spun around and climbed in one of the cars.

Exasperation dumped on Janee as she saw the media news already gathered around her grandma's house.

"Don't they ever give up? Won't I ever have a rest - from them!" she muttered to Bernard who took her hand.

She looked through the tinted window at a group of vultures, ready to descend on their prey and tear its flesh from the bone. She braced herself, put on her media news face, and stepped gracefully from the car.

Instantly mics were shoved toward her, and cameras were rolling.

"There's rumor you're getting an Oscar nod, Miss Stemper. How do you feel about that?"

"I would feel very happy and pleased, however, the outcome is yet to be revealed," Janee smiled.

"Have you got the monkey off your back?"

"Absolutely," Janee resented the question directed at her past drug abuse.

"Some say you differed with your grandmother. Can you elaborate on that?"

"No! I loved my Grandma Emile, and she is at rest."

"That's all, people," Bernard stepped in to rescue her. "Please respect the family's privacy at this time of grief!"

He hurried Janee into the house.

"I'm not grieving," Janee made it clear.

"Sorry - sorry!" Bernard held up his hands. "I was refer-ring to the rest of us."

"Cry your damn eyes out!" her words carried the deadly sting of an adder. She disappeared into the bathroom.

All afternoon friends dropped by bringing food and condolences. They wanted to share their love - some lingered to pray with family members. More than just a few sought out Janee to give messages from Emile that she had made them promise to deliver. One after another they came - some getting right to the point - others more timid. One could almost have viewed it as comic, but it certainly was not for Janee. She exploded in fury!

"I've heard all of this for so long it's rotted in my gut and comes up as foul garbage! My Gawd, even after it's over my grandma is still trying to preach to me!"

Janee headed toward the spare bedroom.

"Bernard," she yelled over her shoulder, "if there are any more visitors - I'm unavailable!"

She slammed the door shut!

Chapter 43

A Most Exciting Time

J anee, indeed, received an Oscar nomination early the next year; however, a nagging cough, she simply attributed to her chain smoking, became so serious two days before the Academy Awards, she had to be hospitalized.

Janee's disappointment was intense, but she had a growing fear that something was going on in her body. Something had changed, and she could feel it. She grew weaker, and her doctor ordered tests. She tried to focus on the Academy Awards.

"Tell me I'll be up for the Awards tomorrow," Janee studied Doctor Davis' expressions as he examined her, and tried to analyze them for some sign of positive news.

Her doctor of many years shook his head.

"I don't think so, Janee," her old doctor spoke kindly, but displayed a firmness that would not allow his patient to do any stunt that would jeopardize her health.

Janee threw her head back into the pillow in despair. She crossed her arms like a pouting child.

"This is terrible! It's a bunch of crap," she spoke angrily before her voice degenerated into sporadic hacking, leaving her gasping for air.

Dark gloom filled Janee's room the night before the Academy Awards. She had convinced her parents to attend the ceremony and that she would be fine, but Bernard refused to leave her alone to watch the results on television. She threatened to fire him, but his mind was set - he would be there with her in the hospital.

The doctor had not disclosed anything, only that he was waiting on test results. Janee had the unsettling, sinking sense that Doctor Davis was holding off giving his diagnosis until after the Awards, and what he had to say would not be good.

That night after everyone left, Janee knew she had to make two phone calls. She nervously dialed the first, and after a few rings heard a familiar voice.

"Paige…"

"Yes - oh my gosh! Janee?"

"Yes, it's me. It's so good to hear your - voice - after - so long."

"Janee, are you - okay?"

"I'm sick, Paige; I'm in the hospital."

"Oh, no! What's wrong?"

"I don't know for sure - yet. I have this aggravating cough, and I - I feel very weak and tired."

"I must come see you, Janee!"

"No! No, not yet; I have a favor to ask."

"Of course."

"But first I -," Janee fought back tears, rubbing her eyes.

"I must apologize to you for all the awful things I said, and the horrible way I treated you when I - was - so messed up and stupid."

"Janee, you know I have never ceased to be your friend. What is the favor you need?"

"I'm too ill to attend the Academy Awards tomorrow night. I know this is short notice, but - will you go in my place - no - I mean in my agent's place. He won't be attending - my seat will remain empty, but he was to sit next to me."

Paige didn't answer.

"Please, Paige, for me!"

"Yes, I will be honored," came a soft reply.

It took a long time for Janee to get up the courage to make the second call. The hour grew late. She finally grabbed up the phone and dialed quickly before she lost her nerve. She heard a female voice.

"Molly?"

"Yes."

"It's Janee Stemper. I'm sorry to call so late, but I need to speak to Jason a moment."

"Sure, Janee, I'll get him."

It was several minutes that seemed hours before Jason answered.

"Jason, it's Janee," she hoped for kindness in his voice.

"What is it, Janee?" he was abrupt, but her heart warmed just hearing him.

"I'm sorry to call you so late, but I have a favor to ask of you."

"If I can," he was short.

"I'm in the hospital and too ill to attend the Oscar Awards tomorrow night. I don't know if the evening will be a great disappointment to me, and I'll get beat out as I did - when you won your Oscar, or if I even have a chance. Oh, Jason, at times I've felt good about my performance, and - other times - like a - girl in a high school play - and no one would like it."

"Your role was magnificent, Janee, but how can I help?"

"Jason, if I win - would you - accept - for me?"

Janee could hear Jason draw a breath, but he gave no reply. Janee waited until the silence crumbled her confidence. She went on.

"Jason, we were once good friends - close friends. I ruined that! I was such a fool! Someone else stole your love that could have been mine. I still love you! If you have any feeling left at all - any compassion - please do this for me. Please don't hate me!"

Jason did not reply for some time. Janee feared he would slam the receiver down. Finally he spoke. His voice was low and the harsh edge gone.

"Yes, Janee, I will accept for you if you win. What would you like me to say?"

"Whatever comes to mind. Thank you, dear!"

Janee was saddened as she watched the Academy Award arrivals walk the red carpet. She should have been among them instead of in a hospital room. She fought off tears and tore away from self-pity. She struggled when inside shots panned her row, and she saw the producers, director and cast of the film that had earned her this nomination. Then the camera passed her mother and father. Mom gave a quick little wave, and Janee thought she caught her dad's wink. Then on to Paige who looked stunning, stopping at Janee's empty seat. The narrator made a comment of Janee's absence before cutting away to a commercial break.

Bernard came through the door laughing and making comments that annoyed Janee more than amused her. His arms were loaded with junk food and some flowers for her. He talked nervously and often made little sense to her. Finally, she blurted out, "Shut up, Bernard, so I can hear this!" pointing to the television.

Janee's heart was racing when the Award for Best Actress came up. She held her breath!

"And the winner is —." Janee thought she was about to die. Bernard held her hand. The envelope was opened.

"Janee Stemper, for her role of "Crystal" in "Street Smart!"

Janee screamed and then went into a coughing fit. Bernard shouted, jumping up and down, laughing and trying to pat Janee's back to help her get her breath. Janee held her mouth so she could hear. She shook her head to fight off the cough and tears that so wanted to flow.

"We understand that Ms. Stemper is in a hospital and not here tonight. We give our congratulations - wait - someone is coming to accept for her!"

The camera turned to catch Jason walking down the aisle.

"It's Jason Finn to accept for Janee Stemper!" the presenter announced. The whole Academy rose to their feet. Jason took the Oscar and held it up for all to see.

"Last night I had a late night call - from an old friend. She asked that if she won, would I accept for her. She told me to say what came to mind, so here goes! I'm positive there are many persons Janee would like to thank; starting with her mom and dad I see sitting down there - to countless others, however, I'd like to say a few words about Janee.

We went on a USO Tour together years ago. She not only lifted the spirits of the troops, she took a rifle and fought alongside of the men. Who in the world hasn't seen that famous picture of Janee in Viet Nam? We starred together, and we fought in the film, "A Bowl Of Dust." But Janee's biggest battle in life was with herself - she fought it and won - making an incredible comeback. If ever anyone deserved this Oscar tonight!...

The Academy began to clap and cheer, coming to their feet again! Jason held high the Oscar.

"Janee, this is for you!" he declared proudly.

"Would you listen to that?" Bernard pointed. Laughing and crying, he hugged and kissed the actress, who was trying to see the television screen. Janee was thrilled! She laughed and coughed until she gasped for breath.

The rest of the evening family, friends, hospital personnel, and total strangers filed in and out of her room. It was an Academy Award Party that lasted until Janee was exhausted. Jason and his wife, Molly, even stopped by to give Janee her Oscar. The last to leave were the proud parents: Harold and Leah Stemper, and the faithful Agent Bernard. It was the most exciting time in Janee's life - even if it were in a hospital room!

Chapter 44

Shocking Truth

It was right after breakfast that Doctor Davis made his rounds. He offered his congratulations.

"My wife and I watched the whole show. What a night for you, Janee, and a long time coming. We couldn't be happier for you - "then he saw the Oscar standing on the window ledge. He had to walk over and touch it. When he turned back around, he was serious.

"Let's get to business at hand, Janee. You didn't eat much breakfast," he eyed her untouched food, but avoided eye contact with her.

"I had no appetite," Janee spoke quietly, trying to suppress a cough. "It isn't good, is it?"

The doctor sat on the edge of Janee's bed. He assumed more the appearance and manner of a dad rather than a doctor. His facial expression softened, and sadness filled his eyes.

"I'm a grown girl, Doctor. Lay it out!" Janee braced herself.

"Janee, you have tuberculosis," Doctor Davis said bluntly?

Janee was stunned! She stared at Doctor Davis, 'how could this be?'

"You mean it's not from my smoking?"

243

"That certainly aggravates your condition, and you must quit, but you do have TB."

"I thought tuberculosis was eradicated years ago!"

"It was. It is still around, and there is exposure, but most healthy individuals throw it off."

"Are you implying I'm not healthy? I've felt fine until a few days ago. Can this be treated?"

"The tuberculosis we can treat, and successfully, I believe, however, it is an opportunistic infection..."

Doctor Davis' explanation trailed off, and his expression turned grave.

"Janee, tests are conclusive that you have Acquired Immune Deficiency Syndrome, known as 'AIDS'."

"AIDS?" Janee choked on her own words. A sick, sinking feeling began forming in the pit of her stomach.

"I thought that was in people in - in Africa," Janee was reaching for some kind of hope. This was far removed from her - a huge mistake - a gross error.

"It seemed to have its roots there, but reports of cases here in America started in '81."

"I don't understand! How could I have been - caught it?"

"It generally is transmitted through sexual activity, or a blood transfusion."

Janee threw her hair back with a laugh.

"Well, I haven't slept with anyone for two years, and I've never had a blood transfusion, so there, my fine doctor. Besides, I've heard it's transmitted by homosexual men, and I ain't been in bed with any of those, as if they would be interested in me! Ha!"

Doctor Davis never cracked a smile but looked on Janee with pity.

"Janee, symptoms may not appear for 10 years or more. If you had sexual intercourse with someone infected with the virus, it may have entered your body through the walls of your vagina."

Janee clenched her fist and closed her eyes. She calculated 10 years back, 1974. She was at the zenith of her promiscuity. Who could it have been? She tried to review faces and names; she couldn't remember many others who were mere bodies for an evening of pleasure. She wanted to undo her deeds; she wanted them all to never have existed. She wanted to kill whoever did this to her. She covered her face with her arm and groaned!

"The disease can also be transmitted by a dirty needle," Doctor Davis continued. "I see some scar remains of needle marks on your arm, Janee; I know your history."

"Oh, no," Janee moaned. There were times that she used a needle - many times, and often when she shot up, she was so high and out of it, she just used any handy needle.

She struggled to sit up. She threw off the urge to throw up and shook off tears! Was this the end, or was there hope? She tried to prepare herself for her doctor's answer.

"Can I beat this?" she asked.

Again, Doctor Davis dropped his eyes.

"The HIV has been destroying your body's ability to fight off infections and has a head start on us. That is why you have TB now. Before you got AIDS, you had a healthy blood count of over 1000 CD4 positive T-cells. Tests yesterday came back 197 T-cells and dropping I'm sure. We can try to keep you clear of the opportunistic infections, such as other viruses, bacteria, fungus or even some parasites, but, Janee, your immune system is so devastated by the HIV, even a cold or flu can be fatal."

Janee hesitated, swallowing hard. She asked her question again.

"Can I beat this - AIDS?"

Doctor Davis looked up at her with tear-filled eyes.

"I'm afraid - there's - no cure . . . Janee," Davis dropped his head again as a man defeated.

A shock jolted through Janee driving itself to the very core of her soul. She had survived Viet Nam; she had abandoned a stupid and destructive lifestyle; she had beaten drug and alcohol addiction, and even though she was dying for a cigarette, she would beat that too - but AIDS! She was at the height of her career! She won an Oscar last night! How could life be so cruel - how could - God?

Janee took a deep breath. A nurse came in, but Doctor Davis waved her off. Janee and her doctor's eyes met.

"How long?" she asked nervously.

"If we can get the tuberculosis under control and keep you from other sicknesses - maybe with luck -."

"Luck ain't got nothin' to do with it!" Janee was surprised to hear her self speak.

"What?" Doctor Davis questioned.

"I heard my grandparents say that once," Janee murmured - in a daze.

"As I was telling you, Janee, based on what is happening to other patients with AIDS, you may have three or four years left, but let me prepare you for what's to come. As HIV continues to ravage your immune system, and understand, that's the part we have no treatment to stop. As your system worsens, other symptoms may appear, growing in severity. You could even develop cancer. Janee, you may be so debilitated you can no longer work or even do household chores. There will also be many, including friends or loved ones, who will no longer be around you for fear they will catch your - illness."

"Three or four years?" Janee had retained little else of what her doctor was detailing.

"I'm afraid so - I'm sorry, Janee..."

Chapter 45

An Unexpected Invitation

‽

Medication and rest did wonders for Janee. By the summer of 1984, she felt strong enough to ask Bernard to get her some parts. She accepted two smaller projects that extended into 1985; however, to her frustration her energy level was far below what she was accustomed to. She was forced to admit her inability to do a major role, and that compounded her anger.

It also hurt her to discover there were people afraid to work alongside the Oscar winner. Even though Janee explained HIV is spread only through blood contact, fear of infection was not alleviated. She finally succumbed to keeping her illness secret. That was nearly impossible for a person of her notoriety.

Work was cut short in February of 1985 by sickness. A twenty-four-hour flu hit Janee so hard she had to be hospitalized again. She had bouts of coughing and sneezing, intensified by high fever. All of this aggravated the tuberculosis, which was still present. She dropped several pounds, which she really could not afford to lose. She had days of extreme fatigue, making any mobility out of the question.

Visitors flowed in and out of her room. She was thankful for most, even though the constant speaking left her exhausted by day's end. There were two visitors however, that she did not appreciate.

The first was a hospital Chaplain, who stopped by to comfort and pray with her. It mattered little that he was gracious and had asked permission to pray for her. Janee was incensed he was even in her presence. She argued with him over beliefs, refused his prayers and insisted he leave.

Her parents' Pastor's arrival was the final straw!

"Get out! I don't need your dumb religion, and I resent you invading my privacy! Leave me alone! Nurse! Nurse!"

The Pastor made a hasty retreat. Janee smiled after her coughing ceased.

AIDS was a sickness shrouded by mystery, and one most greatly feared. Stories had circulated the virus could be spread by kissing, sweat from the palm of your hand, using the same towel, even sitting on the same toilet seat as the infected person. Armed with those kinds of rumors and the media coverage of her HIV infection, it was no wonder that Janee's visitors dwindled to only close friends and family. She didn't think the absence of so many would bother her as much as it did. It tormented her in the night that friendships she took for granted as strong and loyal ones were so shallow and easily frightened away.

Spring had begun in all its splendor the day Janee was released from the hospital. Her mother arrived early to drive her home.

"You look good and healthy today," Leah greeted her daughter cheerfully.

"Thank you, Mother. I can't wait to be home! The hospital stay has drug on such a dreadfully long time. Some days I swore the clock stopped! Where's Bernard?"

"I don't know, Janee. I haven't seen or spoken to him for several weeks."

"Hum, come to think of it, nor have I. Only spoken to him on the phone - the last few days he hasn't returned my calls."

"This is so unlike him, Janee. Perhaps he is seeing someone."

"Bernard? Ha! Mother, he is so dense, no woman would last a day!"

Both women laughed, but a sickening dread found a cracked door in Janee's thoughts and now threatened to barge in and fill her mind. Janee was not as concerned over Bernard having a girlfriend as she was over the possibility her agent was backing away from her like all the rest of her so-called friends. Why should that upset her? How many times had she threatened to fire him - actually fired him - driven him out - still he always came back - like a little puppy. Yet, the thought of losing him left her unsettled, and if she imagined him walking into a familiar dining establishment they had frequented with some strange woman - oh! This is ridiculous! Bernard is just my agent; nothing more. What's to lose? Let him represent someone else! He's not getting me any work now, so what do I care, and if he finds some bimbo - she can have him. It won't take her long to see what an idiot she has found.

"Janee, here's your house. You have been very quiet. What were you thinking?"

"Nothing, Mother, just how beautiful it is today and how good it is to be home."

Janee tried to stay busy. She stayed on the phone trying to set up meetings and appointments. All who spoke to her were concerned of her health and were sympathetic. She didn't want sympathy; she wanted them to meet her for lunch or dinner. She knew that their, "We'll have to get together someday soon," really meant - never!

Producers and directors who would have wined and dined her months ago now made excuses and put her off.

None would commit to even meet with her. Those who once approached her with contract and pen were now never in their office or at their homes, so the ones who answered their phones said.

And where was Bernard? Why wasn't he getting her any work?

"Bernard, if you don't answer my calls and get me some work, you're fired for good!" Janee yelled into the receiver before hanging up.

What does one do, what does one think about when they realize their life is coming to an end? Janee tried to push it into oblivion – hoping it would stay there.

At first she raged at how unfair and dirty life was. She hurled taunts and accusations at a God she didn't even believe in. She spent hours in the library pouring over any information about the deadly disease she had contracted. She searched endless days for any hope of a cure, but it proved futile. Friends continued to send her articles and advice, hoping to help.

"Janee, I heard of this treatment in Mexico that they claim has done wonders," her mother told her one evening while they were in the kitchen.

"That's right, Janee," her father agreed from the living room.

"Stop it, Mother! I'm dying, and that's that!" Janee could tell her mother was heartbroken, and said no more.

Janee retreated into her past. Sometimes she studied awards displayed in cases and framed on her walls. She went over pictures in her albums and remembered. One night she caught herself carrying her Oscar around in her arms. She purchased videos of her movies and watched them over and over, reliving every moment of their making.

Phone calls became fewer and farther apart. Now she lunged when it rang and grabbed it up like a morsel to devour! She drove by Bernard's house many times but never found him home.

One morning in late April 1985, the doorbell awakened Janee. She rose up on one elbow to eye her bedside clock. Ten in the morning!

"Gaa," she fell back on the pillow, hoping the person would go away. She figured it to be someone selling or soliciting something.

The doorbell rang again.

"Go away - don't want none!" Janee groaned.

Her bell kept ringing. By now, Janee was mad!

"Alright - alright. Quit your damn twitch on my buzzer already!"

She stumbled to the door - throwing it open. There stood her agent, Bernard Swift. She stood dumbfounded for a minute. He smiled.

"Good morning, Janee," he spoke cheerfully.

"Nothing good I see," she answered. "Where the hell have you been?"

"May I come in, or am I fired?"

"Yes, you can come in, and yes, you are fired! Make me some coffee."

"I didn't come here to make your coffee; I came to talk to you," Bernard spoke nervously.

Janee glared at him for a moment. Bernard could be so irritating.

"You are so stupid! I don't see you or hear from you for weeks, and you show up when I look a fright, I'm half awake, and in a crappy mood, so - mister, if you expect me to talk and be civil, you better get going on that coffee - and make it black - strong black!"

"Fine! I'll be glad to, but you don't have to prove your beauty by fixing yourself up," Bernard commented as he headed for the kitchen. Janee went back into her bedroom.

'Leave it to Bernard to assassinate a compliment,' she thought.

She took her sweet time getting dressed. She fixed her hair and put on some makeup. Bernard was asleep on the couch when she finally came out. He jumped up when he heard her and preceded her into the kitchen where he poured her a cup of coffee, then one for himself. They sat facing each other on two bar stools.

"Why didn't you answer my phone calls, Bernard? Where have you been? Not home! I checked!"

Bernard didn't answer immediately. He sipped his coffee, perhaps searching his mind for the right words. Janee studied his face. He seemed - somehow - different? Something new - almost fresh - was there.

"Janee," he started, choosing his words carefully, "so much has happened; I had to get away, and, I guess, find myself. You getting sick - that was a low blow - to both of us. I felt so, well, helpless."

"That you are, Bernard, but I can assure you I can take care of myself. Is that what you came to tell me?"

"No. Something wonderful has happened to me! I'm not the same Bernard Swift you've known for so long, but it has taken me this long to get up the courage to tell you, because I knew you would be upset and not understand."

"I'll be darned if you haven't fallen in love, Bernard!"

"Yes! I have, but not with a woman - I mean -."

"What?!" Janee was shocked and wanted to get sick and slap him at the same time.

"No! No, not what you think. I get so tongue-tied around you."

"Then what, Bernard?"

"It was a cold, windy day in March on a Sunday. I was depressed and - and lonely, so I was walking the beach - watching the waves come in. I happened into this little inlet surrounded by high cliff walls. I walked up on a group of people. There were guitar players and everyone was singing and clapping. It made me think of Sunday school and church when I was a little boy. I started to leave, but several people motioned for me to come join them. I was curious and found they *were* having church - on the beach. A young minister spoke, and Janee, it was like he was feeding my soul. I've been going back every Sunday, and last week - something happened to me I can't explain. Please don't be mad at me, but I couldn't wait to tell you. I accepted Jesus Christ as my Savior. He came into my life and filled the emptiness. I have never been so happy!"

Janee was aghast! She felt betrayed, but there was no denying the change she saw and heard in Bernard. His face seemed to glow.

"Janee, I invite you to go with me - I so want to share this with you. Say you will! I've never asked much of you, but I'm asking you now - please come with me to this church!"

"I can always count on you to do something dimwitted. And to think I gave you more credit for brains. I have never seen such gross weakness in a man. Not only are you fired, you are never to see me again, and you can put your invitation where the sun doesn't shine, along with your asinine happy heart change!"

Chapter 46

A Great Wrestling Match

ॐ

Janee was so infuriated by what Bernard had done she couldn't sleep for nights. How could he be so disloyal? He knew her strong feelings about any kind of organized religion - even talk of God Himself. She felt that her trusted and faithful servant had become a traitor and defected to the enemy.

A church meeting on the beach undoubtedly had no resources for property and a proper building. They were probably some kind of cult, brainwashing Bernard to get his money, and he proved such an easy target for them. Bernard had always been a weak-willed man who would flee like a coward or just follow a crowd.

Now, Bernard's silence provoked her the more! He did not call, nor had he stopped by her home. In times past, he would have crawled back to her feet begging to be forgiven and restored into her graces.

"Well! Two can play this game," she declared late one Saturday night. "I'll show him to ignore me!"

The next morning she attended a service that she heard enlightened members in many of the same ideas she embraced.

She felt inspired and secure to hear a teacher articulate so intelligently beliefs that matched many of her own. He made so much sense, and she was encouraged to learn she surely must have been correct all these years. Still a nagging doubt pervaded her heart, clouding the church service, leaving her feeling cold and empty. Bernard's words kept coming back to her, "I accepted Jesus Christ as my Savior. He came into my life and filled the emptiness."

A week passed and no contact with her agent, but Janee was too stubborn and proud to call him. One night she got in her car to go to his house. As she started to back up, her parents pulled into her driveway behind her. She was glad to visit with her mother and father; however, there was no comment about what Bernard had done, nor was religion discussed. Her parents had learned to leave that topic alone - maybe they just took it for granted her early conversion was real.

The next Sunday, Janee sought out a church she thought to be similar to the Church in the Woods where grandma and grandpa used to attend.

The people were friendly and well dressed. Janee enjoyed singing some of the old hymns - two she remembered from when she was little and went to Douglas Landing for summer visits.

The minister moved into his sermon, getting louder as he went. He threw his arms up and down, pacing back and forth in a frenzy. His eyes blazed with passion for his message, and beads of perspiration dotted his face. Janee was little moved, mostly startled. When an altar call was given at the end, the preacher gave an appeal to come as the music played and the congregation sang. When he called for those who were ill to come for prayer, Janee thought, 'What the heck,' and walked forward with others. Soon an older woman with her hair up tightly on her head and little makeup took her hand. She looked intently in Janee's face. "How can I pray for you?" she spoke abruptly.

"I - have - I'm sick," Janee dropped her eyes. Nothing was said. Janee looked up to see the woman staring at her.

"Aren't you that movie queen?" she asked.

"Yes."

They both bowed their heads, the woman holding Janee's hands. She seemed gentle and kind enough, until she began to pray.

"Oh, Lord," she hesitated. "I perceive this poor woman is sick because of the evil work she does. Lord, give her strength to confess the ways she has offended You and to forsake the movie business. Then and only then can You heal her sickness."

Suddenly, Janee wondered what she was doing there. If it meant leaving the film industry to know God, she guessed she would never know Him. She pulled her hands away from the woman and crossed her arms. She wanted out of that place. The woman placed her hand on Janee's shoulder. Janee yanked away.

"Just let it go," the woman pleaded. "Ask His forgiveness, and He -."

"For what? I came for prayer to get well, not to be told what a sinner I am!"

"But both are inter-related. Jesus wants to forgive your sin and heal your heart."

"My heart's fine," Janee snapped, "you holier-than-thou freak!" Janee stormed out of the building, convinced she made a grave mistake seeking anything from God or His so-called church.

By the end of the next week, she could take Bernard's absence and silence no longer. She called him and was relieved to hear him pick up.

"Hello."

"Why haven't you called me, Bernard?" she demanded.

She could hear him sigh before he answered.

"You fired me," was his calm reply.

"That never stopped you before!" She was angered and confused by this change in him.

"You ordered me never to see you again."

"I've told you the same thing at least a hundred times over the years. You never paid any attention to me!"

"I'm not the same man I was then."

"Don't be stupid and ridiculous, Bernard. I want to see my agent - tonight!"

"I'm not your agent - anymore."

"What?"

"I never will be - again. If you want to see me you can come with me - to church - next Sunday."

"Then I guess we'll never see each other again!" Janee slammed the receiver down so hard the phone flew off onto the floor. Janee went into a fit of rage. She started throwing things! She rampaged through her house sweeping vases, pictures and collectibles off of tables and shelves with a swoop of her hand. She went into the kitchen smashing cups and plates onto her tile floor. She yelled and cursed until finally she plopped, exhausted, into the midst of the rubble. She sat in silence for a while, and then screamed, throwing pieces of plates against the wall. This ritual continued into the early hours of the morning and her strength was completely spent. She slowly and carefully made her way to a phone. Her trembling, blood-smeared hand dialed Bernard's number. She woke him.

"I'm not your agent anymore," he mumbled.

"You win, Bernard! I'll go to your damn church with you! Pick me up Sunday."

Chapter 47

Church on the Beach

J anee phoned Bernard early Sunday morning.

"I'm a mess!" She was exasperated. "I don't have a thing to wear! What do they wear? To the beach church?"

Bernard laughed.

"What's so funny? This isn't a joke! I need a new outfit!"

"I'm sorry, Janee, I thought you were calling to bail out on me."

Janee stood waiting for an answer, tapping her foot nervously.

"You have a bathing suit?"

"Yes."

"And a beach wrap?"

"Yes, of course, dummy."

"Wear that."

"To church?"

"It is on the beach, Janee!"

"What are you wearing?"

"Shorts and a t-shirt. I've got a pair of deck shoes, but flip-flops are fine."

"Okay, if you say so."

It wasn't long before Bernard arrived. He had breakfast and two styrofoam cups filled with hot coffee. He gave Janee an admiring glance when she opened the door.

"I feel totally - undressed!" Janee exclaimed as Bernard parked his car near the sand's edge. They walked toward an outcropping of cliff. They followed several people walking in the same direction, and throwing a look over her shoulder with a toss of her hair, she saw more following behind.

The other side of the cliff opened into a small sandy inlet. The water came in rhythmic waves onto the shore. It seemed so peaceful to Janee; a gentle breeze blew across her face. A group of people had already gathered, who greeted the couple warmly. Several gave Bernard a warm hug, and turned to Janee to do the same. She waited for someone to go on about a celebrity in their midst or say something about what she was wearing, but either they didn't notice or didn't care. Everyone seemed intent on something more important, just loving each other!

One young woman stood up as Janee drew near and threw her arms open as wide as her smile. Her husband or boyfriend also gave her a hug - strong and meaningful like she remembered her grandpa giving.

The musicians assembled to begin the singing, while everyone else either sat or stood in the sand. The music began with some men and women leading, accompanied by two guitar players and a fellow on what Janee knew as bongos.

The words to the songs were easy to pick up. It wasn't long before the group was singing from their hearts in beautiful harmony. The melody lifted up to the sky, and Janee found herself singing, not about Him, but to Him. She shook that off and instantly became sullen, yet something was astir deep within her own heart.

The minister was young with a slight beard. Janee thought it curious to see a preacher in shorts and a colorful Hawaiian shirt. She expected him to quote out of some weird book, but instead he opened a Bible.

"He just started a study from the book of John," Bernard explained as he opened his own Bible. It was odd; Janee had never seen him with one before this day.

"He finished chapter three last week."

Everyone was quiet. Only the low roar of the waves and the intermittent shrill cries of gulls mingled with shouts and laughs of beachgoers beyond the rocky cliff could be heard. The minister smiled, and then took a deep breath to begin his message.

"Two weeks ago we learned in John 3 that Jesus told a ruler of the Jews, Nicodemus, that we must be born again. Nicodemus thought that to be impossible. Jesus explained that just as each of us is born physically, we must also be born spiritually. He went on to say in verses 15 through 17, 'that whosoever believeth in Him should not perish, but have eternal life. For God so loved the world, that He gave His only begotten Son, that whosoever believeth in Him should not perish, but have everlasting life. For God sent not His Son into the world to condemn the world; but that the world through Him might be saved!'"

"I've thought a lot about these three verses the last two weeks, and have come to this conclusion which leads into chapter four."

Janee had attempted to tune this young speaker out, but was having difficulty. He didn't shout or beat the air with his arms; he simply taught in a mild-mannered voice that carried an appealing charm. He displayed a commanding confidence in his Lord and the message that invoked her attention. His next statement struck a chord with her.

"It seems that everyone ever born since the fall of man, except for Jesus Christ, has been born with a gaping hole inside of them - empty - and wanting to be satisfied. Take a newborn baby, so innocent and helpless, it starts with that hole; it just isn't evident. Our children are so cute and sweet when we watch them. In our own eyes, they can do no wrong, 'til they grow. Something happens when they get older! An ugly nature begins to reveal itself, and that hole gets bigger - and bigger - and darker - and bigger - making people change. That's when they try to fill the emptiness in their lives. That emptiness is in us all, man, woman, rich, poor, all races, and smart, not so smart, no one excluded. The woman in our story today discovered she was empty."

Janee became lost in her own thoughts. Something was tugging at her heart - she felt like she was suffocating - being buried under a mountain of weight on her back! She heard the preacher explain how the Jews hated the people of Samaria, looking on them as half-breeds. Most Jews went around the country of Samaria, but not Jesus; He led his band right through the country stopping at Jacob's well to rest. While His disciples went into the city, Jesus waited.

"Soon a woman of Samaria came for water. Jesus asked for a drink."

'I remember this story,' Janee thought. She glanced at Bernard who was intent on the message. She watched the people congregated around her until the Pastor read a verse that snapped her back into the story. Only the last part caught her attention.

"He would have given you living water."

Suddenly in Janee's mind's eye she could see a figure offering her water. She heard herself as the woman in the scripture asking, 'Where is this living water?'

The preacher read the answer. "Jesus answered and said to her, 'whosoever drinks of this water shall thirst again: But whosoever drinks of the water that I shall give shall never thirst; but the water that I shall give him shall be in him a well of water springing up into everlasting life.'"

Janee did not like the un-comfortableness she was beginning to feel. She wanted to jump up and run to Bernard's car, but she seemed planted in the sand.

"This woman was empty and was trying to fill the vacuum in her life with something that would not satisfy. She asked for some of this living water, but Jesus knew her problem. He told her to go get her husband. She answered, 'I have no husband!' Jesus said to her, 'You have well said, I have no husband; for you have had five husbands; and the one you have now is not your husband!' You see, brothers and sisters, this woman wanted to be loved. She thought these men would fulfill her needs, yet she still was thirsty!"

God's Word cut like a searing bolt of lightning. Her life took on a blackness that seemed impenetrable as she identified with the Samaritan woman. Situations and men began to fill her consciousness; beginning with Aaron Mocknour, to the potheads in Viet Nam, to every man she had ever slept with. Then the guilt of her abortion drowned her, she was doomed! Drug abuse and drinking memories hammered at her with a vengeance. She heard no more of the message as she struggled with her life of sin, which appeared immensely ugly beyond belief. She was condemned! The contortion of her face prompted a query from Bernard.

"Janee, are you alright?"

She refused to even look at him, but stared straight ahead. She wanted to die!

"Jesus offers us His living water today. If you have a big empty hole you have been trying to fill with - things - whether it is money, fame, sex, drugs - nothing will fill it except Jesus Christ, because the emptiness is a spiritual one. He says, 'Come and I will wash you clean on the inside. Invite me into your heart - here - right now!'"

The singers began to sing softly. Janee listened to the words. It was an old hymn set to a more contemporary sound. As they sang, she felt her heart respond.

"Come Thou Fount of every blessing; tune my heart to sing Thy grace."

Janee's sin was so monstrous and enormous it was not only crushing her, it was wounding her heart. She was feeling something down deep, too long suppressed, from long, long ago. She was dying inside from shame! Now came the third stanza of the song:

"O to grace how great a debtor-daily I'm constrained to be! Let Thy goodness-like a fetter, bind my wandering heart to Thee."

Janee felt herself crumbling.

"Prone to wander, Lord, I feel it, prone to leave the God I love..."

"Oh, dear God!" Janee cried out in a whisper as the tears began to flow.

"Here's my heart, O take and seal it, seal it for the Thy courts above."

Janee buried her face in her hands. With all of the understanding and faith she could gather, she believed on the One she had loved as a little girl. She had lost something precious then, and she desperately wanted it back. She surrendered to the Savior she had tried for so long to hate and abolish. Wave after wave flooded her whole being as the blood of the Lamb washed every sin away into the deepest part of the ocean to be remembered no more. Jesus filled her emptiness with an incredible peace and joy! The weight of sin dropped from her back! Janee was born again! She sobbed uncontrollably as years of anger dissolved into love.

Through blurred vision she saw Bernard's knees in front of her. He had her in his arms. She could feel other hands on her and sensed they were praying for her. She cried so hard her body shook in convulsions. She still didn't understand why God took her Grandpa Farmer, but it was okay! The rejection of Mocknour and the abortion – forgiven! The guilt and shame of the dopers' cruelty – cleansed! The emptiness of Jason's lost love – filled! Sins of drug addiction, drinking, sex – all washed whiter than snow! She cried over how she had treated people, especially the ones closest to her. How thankful she was that Grandma Emile had never given up on her - that God hadn't given up on her. And dear Bernard - he brought her - to hear - to receive! She wanted her momma and daddy - she wanted to tell them how much she loved them and how sorry she was for the terrible ways she must have hurt them.

She looked up at Bernard and the others gathered around her. Her hands and face were soaked with tears and speckled with sand. Snot streamed from her nose. She was a sight, but didn't care. She placed a wet hand against Bernard's face.

"I'm so sorry, Bernard," she whimpered.

"Why?" Bernard was laughing, "This is one of the happiest days of my life!"

A young woman next to Janee offered a tissue for the actress to wipe her face and blow her nose.

"Did you?" Bernard asked.

"Yes! Yes! Bernard. I threw open my heart to Jesus! I found Him again!" Janee shouted.

Sounds of rejoicing were heard that day all the way into the courts of Heaven! A woman named Janee Stemper was saved at a Church on the Beach. Her fame didn't merit it; her fortune couldn't buy it. It was a free gift, purchased on a cruel cross 2,000 years ago.

Chapter 48

Through the Eyes of the Heart

🤖

J anee could not wait to tell her parents what had happened to her that morning in church. Bernard drove her to the Stemper home, but no one was home.

"Shall we have lunch and return?" Bernard suggested.

"We must wait, Bernard, there can be no delay in telling them what has happened. Oh, dear, my heart is racing with excitement - like it's about to soar into the sky. I'm sure my parents will arrive soon!"

Bernard sat on the front steps while Janee paced back and forth on the lawn.

"You are a curious one, Janee," Bernard remarked casually. "I've often wondered why you pace like that - what causes it?"

Janee stopped and stared at him - thinking - now conscious of what she was doing. She laughed - not a cynical laugh, but one born out of a newfound freedom.

"My grandpa did that. I used to watch him - pace back and forth - when he grew impatient or troubled. One of my grandpa's friends pointed it out to me at grandma's funeral. I didn't really pay attention to what he was talking about at the time; but I guess I do it too!"

Time drug on, and Janee ignored sounds of hunger from her stomach. She would not be driven away from what she was determined to do. She prayed her parents would hurry home.

Finally, she caught sight of them turning the corner onto the street where they lived. She could tell they were surprised when they pulled into the drive to see her and Bernard waiting for them. Janee ran to them throwing her arms around her mother almost before she could get out of the car.

"Oh, Mother! The most wonderful thing happened to me this morning!" Janee bubbled over. "I went to church with Bernard, and I accepted Jesus into my heart!"

Leah held onto the car to brace herself. She had a bewildered look on her face, not quite knowing if she should smile or frown.

"But, Janee, I thought you did that when you were young. Remember, you went forward in an altar call. You were even baptized."

"I just went 'cause other kids were going. I loved God then, but hated Him later for taking grandpa. I was mean and horrid, to Him, to you, to everyone. Please forgive me Momma, for hurting you."

Janee saw a tender love in her mother's face she hadn't noticed in many years. Leah took Janee into her arms and held her like she used to when Janee was a child.

"You haven't called me - momma - since..." Leah's voice trailed off as she wept with her daughter.

"I am overwhelmed by all this that I don't fully understand. All I know is that my heart is singing! I only wish your grandma were alive to share this moment."

"So do I," wailed Janee, "but I shall tell her - someday - soon!"

The crying of the women turned into laughing as they rejoiced together over Janee's newborn faith in Jesus Christ. In the midst of the excited talking, Janee caught sight of her father standing nearby. She abruptly ended what she was saying and turned to him. He was overwrought with emotion, but managed a smile.

"Oh, Daddy, I am so sorry for the awful things I've said to you - accused you of - done to you. I hurt you - deeply - I have been a horrid daughter!"

Nothing was said. Harold Stemper silently held his daughter close for the first time in many, many years. He felt a peace in his heart that his daughter truly knew the Lord.

Janee had no doubt she was forgiven. Her life was totally turned upside down; she was a new creature in Christ, and couldn't wait to share her good news with Jason Finn. She forced herself to hold off until late, making sure to catch him at home. She was disappointed to get their answering service.

"The Finns are in New York; may I take a message?"

"This is Janee Stemper. I must speak to Jason tonight. It's an emergency!"

In ten minutes Janee's phone rang. It was an annoyed Jason Finn.

"You better be dying!" Then he hesitated, realizing what he had just said.

"I am," Janee laughed and went right on talking, taking no offense. "This couldn't wait, Jason. This morning I went to church. Janee Stemper went to church and got saved. I'm so excited! I had to tell you first!"

After a long pause, Jason responded. "Janee, have you been drinking - or…?"

"No, you funny man! I'm just happy! I'm high on Jesus! You were right, Jason, I was wrong - so misguided. For all the hurt I caused you - I'm sorry. I beg your forgiveness!"

"I hold no ill, Janee. I'm glad for you. I hope you've made peace - with yourself." With that he hung up.

Later that week she went to Paige's home. Paige was married to a man named Billy Hughes. After the marriage,

Janee and Paige had drifted even farther apart. Janee rang the doorbell not even sure if Paige would be home. After several persistent attempts at the doorbell, Janee knocked loudly. Slowly, the door opened to reveal a thin and weary-looking woman whom Janee almost didn't recognize.

There was only a half-hearted greeting from her old friend as Paige ushered Janee into a dirty, untidy house. Paige cleared a place for Janee to sit.

"Please excuse the mess, didn't know you were coming," Paige mumbled.

"I should have called, but I was so anxious to see you."

Janee began to cough uncontrollably!

"Can I get you something?" Paige asked, concerned.

Janee shook her head, trying to stifle the nagging coughing. She held up her hand to indicate she was all right.

"I'm a mess," Janee tried to catch her breath, laughing and choking between words.

"It's so good - to - see you," Janee managed to say.

"Good to see you - too," Paige replied, straight-faced.

"I wanted to tell you that something wonderful happened to me last Sunday. I'm not the same person you knew, Paige."

"Oh?" Paige eyed her keenly.

"I went to church, would you believe? This church meets, of all places, on a beach. Anyway, I felt something that had been lost since I was a little girl. What that was, I discovered, was a love for Jesus Christ, and I was empty without Him. Paige, I believed on Him and what He did on the cross. I opened my heart to Him, and He came in. I have never been so happy. I couldn't wait to tell you!"

Paige sat for some time with downcast eyes.

Instead of the expected gladness that Janee expected to see, Paige burst into tears. She began to pour out pent up feelings and hurts.

"Janee, I too am empty - and unhappy. You - look - beautiful! Look at me! My life is reflected in my home - look at it! I'm the mess!"

"Paige, what is it?" Janee went to her friend.

"My marriage is in shambles!" Paige sobbed. "Billy doesn't want children - I do! He bounces from job to job - he's never home - we argue all the time - over that - money - I think - he's seeing - someone - else!"

Janee held Paige and tried to console her. Janee had no idea that Paige and Billy were having marriage problems. She tried to collect her thoughts and searched for words that would offer some advice and comfort. They just wouldn't form in her mind, so she simply let Paige talk and cry herself into a subdued quiet.

"Paige, please come to church with me, Sunday." The invitation seemed to pop out of her mouth, but both women sensed that answers would be found there.

Without looking up, Paige nodded an acceptance.

The next person Janee felt compelled to see took some time and much prayer before she mustered the courage to pick up the phone and make the call.

"Aaron Mocknour's Productions."

"Hello. This is Janee Stemper. May I speak with Mr. Mocknour, please?"

"Mr. Mocknour is in a meeting. May I take a message?"

"It is urgent I speak with him. When can I call back?"

It took over a week of hounding calls before Janee finally got Aaron on the phone. It was only after her threats of coming and parking herself in his office did he acknowledge the actress. She grew faint when she heard his deep, manly voice that had not diminished with age.

"Well, well, Janee Stemper, it has been a long time," he tried to be nonchalant and cheerful. "Congratulations on your Academy Award. Your performance was outstanding, but I have been concerned about your health. Tell me how you are?"

Janee looked at the receiver and scowled.

"I'm dying, Aaron, but I'm okay right now."

"I heard that; I'm so sorry, Janee."

"No, no, it is okay, Aaron. I settled things with God, and I know where I'm going."

Janee drew a deep breath and gathered her courage.

"What I called about is to tell you I have been going to church that meets on a beach - oh, well, where they meet isn't important, but what is - important - I found Jesus Christ and trusted Him as my Savior. He changed my whole life. He forgave me, and I wanted to tell you that I forgive you - for everything."

Aaron Mocknour said nothing for a long time, and then she heard that familiar grunt she had learned to recognize as a sign of disgust.

"You forgive me? You forgive me?" Aaron shouted into the phone. "Do you realize how much embarrassment and humiliation you have caused me? You have been nothing but a pain in the rear since I first met you, and your acting was a performance only to be tolerated at best. I was dismayed that the Academy awarded you an Oscar this time. I think it was because they felt sorry for you!"

Janee felt her face flush and her blood run hot. She prayed for words and control, and as she did she felt love fill her heart and dispel the rage that wanted to erupt!

"So you found religion after you discovered you are sick and dying," Mocknour raged on. "How nice - how convenient. That solves all your problems, does it? How dare you forgive me! You should be asking, no begging, me to forgive you!"

"You are right, Aaron, will you?"

"Will I what?"

"Forgive me?"

"Ms. Stemper, I regret the day we ever met. I loathe the sight of you - even hearing your name. I'm ashamed of the work you did for me – ashamed your name was connected to it. Nothing good ever came of our relationship, stop clinging to me, and don't ever - call me - again! Never mention my name to anyone - don't come near my office, my house or me. If you attempt that, I'll have you committed for the psycho broad you are. Hollywood will be a better place when you are dead and gone, so have a happy hereafter!"

With that verbal barrage, Aaron hung up.

Janee grieved for weeks over her misfired attempt to reach Aaron Mocknour. She knew in her heart she had been sincere, and made the effort toward some sort of reconciliation. She could do no more; the ball was in Aaron's court. She was amazed one day to realize that the feelings she carried for him had transformed. She loved him as a person Jesus loved, not romantically as she once did. She wondered how this could have happened; then concluded it had to be a transformation God was accomplishing in her.

That summer of 1985, Janee cut her finger while fixing dinner for Bernard. Even though she dressed it, infection set in and soon rampaged through her body. Back into the hospital she went, filling her full of antibiotics. She slept most of the time the first few days, not being aware of much that occurred around her. It was in the heavy hours of the early morning that something strange, wonderful, and magical happened to Janee.

She opened her eyes. She was in her hospital bed, the room dimly lit. She was not groggy but alert. She felt stronger. She rolled over to retrieve her watch from the bedside stand. She squinted and held it to the light to see the time - 3:37 a.m. Then she saw Bernard asleep in the chair beside her bed. Faithful Bernard!

She studied his sleeping face, almost comic in his expressions. Her eyes went over his rumpled hair, his twisted shirt covering the gentle rise and fall of his chest. Her gaze stopped at his hands. One held the open Bible he had been reading - probably to her. The other held a flower that was droopy - no doubt to give to her when she woke up.

That's when it happened. She no longer viewed him as her agent - an associate in business - no, not weak-willed or as a gawky annoyance - certainly not stupid - not even just as a friend.

For the first time, she saw him as a man - a man who loved her, and could be loved, by her. Something wonderful and beautiful came alive that moment in the early hours of the morning as Janee saw Bernard through the eyes of the heart.

Chapter 49

Fallen

It happened late one night in the summer's close of 1985. Janee had tried to sleep, but her mind was far too active to shut down. She walked in the cool of her garden; she prayed quietly there, only to return to fitful tossing, wide-eyed in her bed.

She drank some milk; she even tried a sleeping pill, which only heightened her alertness. She got back up after a futile attempt to fall asleep. The actress wandered from her bedroom and plopped down on the sofa in her game room and grabbed up the TV remote. A dull, unimaginative movie would surely do the trick and have her out in no time.

She was surprised to see herself so vivid on the small screen. There she was - "Maggie" in "A Bowl Of Dust." It was near that famous love scene between her and Jason Finn, the one that had convinced the whole world there was a love affair between them. Yes, there came Jason as "Rupert" into frame - "Rupert," the part that landed Jason an Oscar. She watched as love unfolded on the screen, then Rupert gave a timid and shy kiss to Maggie. Janee could still feel that kiss that had held more meaning than just play-acting.

But as Janee watched the movie, a slow dawning emerged in her thoughts. Instead of thinking of Jason and old feelings being dredged up from the past - she was remembering someone else - it was Bernard!

The television screen had blurred. The movie played on, but Janee wasn't seeing it. Jason Finn, old feelings, making the movie and its memories drifted into a thick cloud until they were obscure.

Instead, what Janee remembered was the day Bernard came spilling out the news he had got her an audition for the part of "Maggie." She could picture his excitement when she landed the role - and his look of hurt and disappointment when she didn't win the Oscar that year. As she watched the movie coming to a close, it felt like a new story demanding to be told. Suddenly, she wanted to be in Bernard's arms - not Jason's! She hungered for a kiss - Bernard's!

"What am I thinking?" she blurted out loud. "He's just my agent - no, I fired him – no. He's just a friend!"

Then a revelation hit her as powerfully as a thunderbolt sending a shower of sparks through her body, igniting an eternal flame in her heart. She had somehow fallen in love with Bernard Swift. Her feelings were so strong she cried out. She wanted to laugh and cry all at the same time. She was so happy she wanted to dance. Her heart and spirit soared with the eagles amongst the mountaintops. Her love overflowed so strongly with the admission, Janee thought she would be swept into the sea of passion. She had an overwhelming desire to confess her love - to Bernard. She must tell him - right now! She ran for a phone and jerked the receiver off the hook. She punched in part of Bernard's number - then hesitated - she hung up.

'For years, I've called Bernard for one thing or another,' she thought. 'I can't do this over the phone. I must go to him!'

She walked back to her bedroom and sat down at her makeup dresser. She eyed herself in the mirror. The ravaging AIDS was taking its toll. Dark circles ringed her eyes.

Her once glamorous face now revealed wrinkles and red splotches. Her beautiful blond hair now exhibited a dullness that no longer responded well to tints or perms; however, Janee wanted to look her best for Bernard. She would fix her face and dress up for him.

Then, she could see Bernard opening the door, half asleep, in his PJ's or robe, hair in his face - and her all dressed up? What an unfair position to place the man she loved. She did not wish to be above him - only his equal.

She hurriedly powdered her face and applied some lipstick. She threw on her jogging outfit and raced to her car. She glanced at her watch as she started the engine. Nearly 2:00 a.m.! Bernard would want to strangle her - until he learned what she had come for. Janee smiled, as she flew backwards out her drive and then peeled off down the street! She drove hard the short distance to Bernard's place, her car bouncing when she hit the street dips. It couldn't have been soon enough when her headlights flashed upon Bernard's home. She jumped out of her car. She forgot to turn out her lights - she didn't care - she was in love. She was alive and crazy; all jumbled up! She rang the doorbell so fast and furious surely it would knock Bernard out of bed onto the floor. When she saw no lights come on she banged on the door, calling out to him. The neighbors' lights flashed on, so Janee went back to the doorbell.

Suddenly a dim light over her head came on, and the door cracked open.

"Who's there?" she recognized Bernard's voice; the sound sent a thrill through her!

"It's me! Janee!"

"Janee." Bernard sounded exasperated. He opened the door and motioned her in. His hair was all over his head, and he was in his robe. He looked more handsome in that instance than Janee could ever remember. He gave a sleepy yawn.

"Janee, don't you ever do things during the day like normal people?" he grumbled.

"Not this time - this is far too important!"

Janee could not hold back. She threw her arms around Bernard's neck and kissed him with a love and passion erupting from the depths of her heart. She felt Bernard stagger under the weight of her body. He was shocked and at first unresponsive - then he enfolded her in his arms and no longer was being kissed but returned her kiss. Soon they had to get their breath. Janee was laughing and crying. Bernard looked bewildered, yet somehow pleased.

"What are you doing?" he stammered as he released her from his embrace.

Janee put his arms back around her as she stood against him. Her heart was pounding! She looked into his questioning eyes.

"Bernard, I'm in love with you. I realized it tonight - maybe admitted it - I don't understand it all - I just know I love you - very much!"

Janee spoke words of a gentle, quiet, spirit she had never heard come from her lips. It was like hearing her grandma - or her mother.

Bernard looked like a man shot in the stomach. He braced his weight against the wall where they stood, slowly turning to make his way down the entrance hall.

"Bernard, what's wrong?"

He only waved her back. She followed him. What had she done? He held on to the wall, then furniture as a man about to collapse. He turned on a table lamp in the living room. He fumbled for the couch and fell into it. Janee sat beside him. Tears fell from his eyes, wetting a ghostly pale face.

"Are you - alright?" she asked again.

He broke down and wept, pulling her into his arms. She held his shaking body. She was frightened and confused. She had not intended to hurt or upset him so. She had never seen him react with such emotion. Her next words were her heart speaking and not her head.

"Bernard, I had hoped you loved me too, but if you don't, I understand. Maybe one day…" she said softly as her voice trailed off in thought.

She came back to the moment when she felt Bernard shake again and knew from his sounds he was crying. She held on tight and buried her face against his neck. When he finally spoke, his voice was packed with feelings.

"Janee, love you? You don't know how I've longed - dreamed of you saying those words! You have no idea how much I wanted to be the first person you looked for when we went to parties, how I hurt when I was - ignored. I thought I'd lose my mind when you went to Viet Nam. Hoping against hope that you - Jason - other men - I died when I found out the things that you did. I grieved, watching you destroy yourself; I applauded and cheered when you beat off the demons and came back! I was so excited when you won your Academy Award, and so proud!"

Bernard pulled back so he could look her in the face.

"I fell in love with you the first time I met you. Remember the night - you hired me as your agent. I felt I acted like a love-struck teenager."

"I remember," Janee smiled, "and yes, you did - act like that, but you were cute!"

Bernard grew solemn.

"You don't know how I longed to be - more than an agent or even your friend. I wished and hoped, but my hopes were dashed, and over the years my chances were constantly scattered, especially when you were running loose and wild. The possibility of you loving me the way I loved you seemed slim to none. When you were diagnosed with AIDS I saw the door close, and we would never be - together. Janee, I have died a thousand deaths."

Janee's heart welled up overflowing with love for this man. She so wanted to undo all the pain she had inflicted on him, but knew that could never be. She had so little left to give him. She cupped his face in her hands, looking deep into his eyes.

"I am sorry beyond words and feelings, Bernard. I have little left to give - of me - of time - perhaps it's not too late. I have fallen madly in love with you. I want to spend every moment I have left with you - if you will have me. I give you - my heart and soul - to love," Janee murmured.

Bernard took her hands from his face and held them in his. He slipped off the sofa onto his knees before her. Sadness clouded his face, and then he seemed to brighten.

"I have a confession to make, Janee," he began. "There were other women in my life."

Janee dropped her eyes. She couldn't recall Bernard with any other women. Somehow, it seemed out of place or character for him.

"Some I went with because I was jealous and wanted to hurt you - others were stupid one-night stands. This may not make any sense and sound strange to you, but I must say it in light of what I'm going to say next."

"Because of what Christ did for us and His forgiveness - His blood washed away all our sins - yours and mine. I feel He has purified our love - for each other. It's as though we have never - sinned or known anyone else. It's like two teenagers falling in love - innocent and pure - it's -"

Janee freed her hand and stopped Bernard by placing her fingertips gently upon his lips. She was silently saying, 'Yes, I understand. I agree. I love you no matter what!'

Bernard took on the look of a man whose every wish was coming true - a man who dreamed that one day would come and he'd awakened to find that day was here - a man who had prayed in childlike faith now to realize his prayer answered.

There he was in his robe, his hair mussed up, unshaven, on his knees. He was her Prince - her man!

Bernard swallowed hard and smiled. He took the next step which seemed only natural and at the center of both their hearts.

"Janee, will you marry me?" he asked in a husky voice.

Chapter 50

The Wedding

The tabloids and news media never seemed to lack some tasty morsel to feed the public concerning Janee Stemper; she was such a bag of tricks. First to hit the headlines was Janee's rejection of her parents' church following the accidental killing of her grandfather. Media hounds nipped her heels all through her growing up years. They had a heyday when she did the film for Aaron Mocknour, trying to prove there was something going on between the actress and the famous director. Later, the media went crazy with the whole Viet Nam tour and Jason, then the sinking of a beautiful, bright movie star into the morass of drugs and drinking. There was news some years after that of Janee's conquest over her addictions; although for most, news of her upward journey to recovery was far less interesting than her slide down had been.

Her comeback Oscar Award and subsequent announcement of AIDS was headline news, but over the summer had pretty much run its course. Now when the engagement of Janee Stemper to her agent, Bernard Swift, leaked out, the media went into another news casting frenzy!

The wedding was set for October, and Janee and her mother had one month to get the many arrangements and details taken care of. They acted like two women who had recently discovered each other and set about their busy schedule, determined not to let themselves get stressed out, but to make it a happy time.

"I had so hoped you would marry in a church," Leah expressed one day, "but your church meets on the beach, and the days are cooler."

"What could be more lovely and meaningful than to marry at the spot where I found my Lord, Mother? It will be alright - it will be beautiful, trust me."

As the time of the wedding grew closer, Bernard was concerned about the pesky media.

"Shall I make arrangements with the police to keep them away?" he asked her one afternoon.

Janee thought a moment.

"No, Bernard, let them come. All I ask is that they respect our day, and our guests. If they stay back and quiet during the ceremony, I'll be okay. Do you remember that nice man on the Christian station we listen to - the one who interviewed me in July?"

"Yes," Bernard answered.

"Would you see that he gets a personal invitation to our wedding?"

Bernard smiled and kissed her as he left out.

The weeks flew like paper sheets in a windstorm. The much-anticipated day arrived, and people gathered at the beach site for the Swift-Stemper wedding. Three hundred and seventy folding chairs had been set up early that morning, along with a white gazebo that was now adorned with pastel-colored flowers. Janee peeked from inside the pavilion, which had been erected for her and the bridesmaids. The crowds were swelling, and Janee giggled to see men in suits and women in dresses struggle to walk in the sand. She was thankful the ocean air was cool and the sun beginning to break through the overcast.

Paige was beside her when she turned back inside.

"You are so beautiful today, Janee."

"You're a looker yourself!" Janee gave her a hug. "I love your jade dress."

Leah, who had been flitting from one person to the next like a hummingbird, shouted.

"It's Walter - Clifton - oh! Oh! Rachel! In here!"

Leah was already there greeting her brothers and sister-in-law. When Walter saw Janee, he held out his arms. Resting in his embrace, she couldn't find words to say, so she spoke what first came to mind, and then felt dumb.

"I trust you had a good flight here, Uncle Walter."

"Naw, twas miserable. 'Bout drives me loco to let someone else do the flyin', but aren't you a sight! Janee getting' married! I hed 'bout given you up."

"Least you won't have ta change yer initials," Clifton laughed as he hugged her.

Janee got hold of her emotions and spoke from her heart.

"I am incredibly thrilled you are here. This wedding is very special to me, and I needed your loving support- all of you here with me."

"We are so sorry that David, Cynthia and Mary couldn't make it. They were very upset and desperately wanted to be here," Aunt Rachel spoke softly as she took Janee in her arms. "You are such a beautiful bride. We are so happy for you!"

Morgan and her husband Joseph burst through the pavilion flap. She spied Janee and hurried to her. She was a bridesmaid and carried her shoes in her hand. She reached out to Janee. "Hi, cousin, sorry we are late - traffic here from the hotel was - unreal! I love your gown Janee. I'm so excited for you! Have you seen Bernard this morning?"

"No, nor has he seen me," Janee and the women laughed and carried on while the men watched. Janee felt a tug on her hand and looked down to see Caleb. His eyes were wide and his face shone!

"You sure are pretty, Ms. Janee," he spoke in boyish exuberance. "I have a question?"

Janee squatted down to get eye level with the boy. She took his hands.

"You always question, my handsome little eight-year-old, and don't you ever stop!"

"Mom and dad said you believed in Jesus?"

"Yes, I did, and He lives in my heart. I will never forget what you asked me at Grandma Emile's, Caleb. I was angered, but you helped me find Jesus. Thank you...."

Janee held Caleb and squeezed him.

"I reckon Emile is dancing in Heaven right now," Rachel reflected, and the group gathered around Janee acknowledged agreement.

As Janee stood up, she saw her father standing in the light. He was dashing in his tuxedo, and Janee could see why her mother had fallen head over heels in love with him.

"It's time," he announced. Everyone made a hasty exit through the pavilion flaps, leaving only Harold and the bridesmaids with Janee. Morgan stood proud at the opening, waiting for the signal to start walking. Janee had befriended some of the women in the church. She asked the one who offered her the tissue the Sunday she got saved, along with the woman who taught her Bible study group, to be bridesmaids. The two had bubbled and gushed the whole morning.

Then there was her Maid of Honor, Paige. Paige looked at her as they waited and gave that familiar, 'go get 'em, girl' smile. She had responded to Janee's invitation to accompany her to the Church on the Beach, and on the fourth Sunday also responded to the Savior's call, 'whosoever will, may come.'

Morgan motioned it was time, and the other two bridesmaids went first, followed by Morgan.

"Pray I don't fall down!" Paige snickered.

"Let's go barefoot," Janee giggled. They looked at each other an instant, laughed, and kicked off their shoes.

Janee took her father's arm, and the two emerged from the pavilion. Everyone stood, nearby media had cameras rolling. Janee searched for Bernard, and their eyes and hearts locked.

"Janee, this is the happiest, saddest day of my life," her father's voice broke. She looked into his eyes and saw tears. She had never seen him cry.

"Daddy, don't cry. Be happy."

"I am; it's just hard letting you go."

"I'll still be here."

Harold was silent. They were coming closer to the assembled crowd.

"I must tell you something, Janee. I want you to know that even though you were unexpected, you were never unwanted."

Janee fought back tears, but could not.

"I ran from a painful situation I didn't know how to handle, but I never stopped loving you or your Mother. In fleeing, I ended up running to God - just like you did, Janee. I have loved you, my daughter, and it's a special privilege to give you away today."

Janee and her father stepped onto a white sheet that had been spread down the aisle leading to the gazebo altar. The bridesmaids had reached Bernard, who was standing by the minister. He was the most handsome man in the world to her. She was eager to stand by his side – to be his wife.

There were countless faces of people she didn't know. Many had gathered from the beach and were standing in groups behind the rows of chairs. Hands reached out to her, and she heard voices saying, "We love you, Janee." Rows of people became a blur except for some near the aisle who she recognized.

Jason and Molly were clapping as she passed them. Others she had worked with gave little waves as she went by. Uncle Walter tipped his hat with the look of Grandpa Farmer. It suddenly seemed her grandparents were there in the spirit of their family.

Uncle Clifton winked, and Aunt Rachel blew a kiss. Her mother, standing in the front row, was weeping.

'Oh, Mother,' Janee thought, but smiled, 'I'm fine. Be happy for me,' when her mother's eyes met hers.

"Momma," she whispered.

Janee acknowledged Bernard's family just before she took her place beside their son.

It felt like hours before the minister made the pronouncement. He had Bernard and Janee turn around to face their overjoyed guests.

"Family and friends, let me be the first to introduce, Mr. and Mrs. Bernard Swift!" he announced loudly over the roar of the waves. A thunderous response came from the crowd!

Chapter 51

Happy and Active

T he newlyweds had the time of their lives during a two-week honeymoon in Hawaii. When the couple returned, Bernard moved into Janee's house, and they rented out his place to a family from Boston. Janee took some time to rest and build up her strength.

The first item on Janee's "to do" list was to aid the church in finding a building. With the impending winter weather around the corner, the congregation was in need of a sheltered place to worship. An empty storefront building in a strip mall was discovered and soon secured. It was perfect, located in a small community near the beach where the church had been meeting, and a mere block away from the ocean.

A contract was signed and permits obtained, thus Church on the Beach became Oceanfront Christian Fellowship. The congregation raised monies to renovate the building into a beautiful church, while Janee and Bernard paid in full five years of the lease.

Their first Christmas together as husband and wife was a joyful one. Janee opened their home to feed families who were hungry and struggling. She and Bernard prepared meals and gave out countless Christmas gifts - targeting children who would otherwise have had no Christmas.

Bernard became concerned and voiced his objection.

"Surely, you aren't worried we are spending too much!" she shot back at him.

"Of course not! That has nothing to do with it. We are constantly around the poor and sickly, and I'm afraid you'll catch something -," Bernard turned his head. "That could be - fatal."

"Do you expect me to stay in my - our home and never entertain - never go outdoors?"

Bernard looked up at her wistfully.

"Yes, Janee, if it will keep you here with me longer. You know you drive Doctor Davis nuts with your running around and all your exposure…I'm afraid for you!"

Janee didn't answer because she recognized Bernard's sincere love and concern. She knew he was right. Yet it didn't seem fair that she isolate herself. In fact, something inside her revolted against the very thought. She had never been so happy and felt so alive. Maybe God had healed her! How could she feel so good and be so sick?

She wrestled with Bernard's words for several nights. It weighed on her mind, making her unusually quiet. She evaded Bernard's questions by, "I'm fine - doing good!"

She prayed, seeking God's wisdom and leading for her life, but it was no longer just about her. She had to consider her husband, her love. It came to her one morning while she was praying in the shower. The still, strong voice of the Holy Spirit was clear, leaving no doubt in Janee's mind what her Lord wanted of her. She would share it with Bernard when she joined him at the table for some juice and breakfast.

"Bernard, will you be my manager?" she asked sweetly. Bernard looked up, surprised.

"No!" he answered abruptly. "Nor am I your agent."

"I need two things done."

"We can hire somebody."

"No, I need you. Will you do this as my husband?"

She could see Bernard's resistance melt. His face softened.

"Of course, dear, I will do it as your husband."

"First, I want to travel everywhere - with you. There are so many countries I long to see - so much to do. Second, as we travel, I need you to get me on as many interviews as possible."

Bernard groaned and buried his face in his hands.

"Bernard! Look at me! Bernard!"

He looked up with pained worry.

"Look at me. I know the truth of what you said the other day; believe me I don't want to die. I don't want to leave you, but I know what God wants me to do. I have wasted my life! I have nothing to offer Him now, and I may not have much time, so we've got to make every minute count. Please, Bernard, He spoke so clearly to me about it this morning. I must share the happiness He has given and tell as many people about Jesus as we can. Please help me, Bernard. We can share this together."

"I know, Janee, I know. The Lord has been talking to me about it for some time, and I've been fighting Him. I'm so afraid - for us! I can't stand the thought of losing -."

"Shhh, we'll just have to trust Jesus to keep me well. Okay?" She reached her hand across the table toward Bernard. He quickly enveloped her hand in his and held it tight. Their eyes locked, followed by their hearts in firm agreement and resolve.

The next twenty months were times of happy memory making and much activity. Everywhere the couple went there were sights to see, people to meet, a witness to give. They visited hospitals and orphanages in far away places, praying with the sick and loving the children. These brought wishes she and Bernard could have a child, but Janee admitted in the quietness of her thoughts and dreams this would never happen. Yet, every time she held a lonely or frightened child her heart pleaded it might be so.

Speaking engagements at churches were scheduled. They both testified of the cleansing power of the blood of Jesus Christ. They began to witness souls being saved and churches encouraged. Janee's fame garnered many television and radio appearances, as well as newspaper write-ups. She used the opportunity to not only witness for Christ, but to bring about a greater awareness of the devastation of AIDS. Third world hospitals they visited were filled with AIDS' patients. Most were infected because of their lifestyles or abusive decisions; however, some were innocent victims.

"If I trust Jesus, will He heal me?" asked a young mother. Janee could see the woman was very ill, so she held her hand and gently stroked her hair.

"I don't know," Janee murmured. "I know He can."

"I don't want to die; my baby needs me," the woman cried.

"How did you - contact -?"

"From my husband - when I married him. Neither of us knew. We had a baby boy, and he has it too."

"How is your husband?"

"He died last year. My sister has the baby."

"What is your name? I'm Janee."

"I know; I saw you in a movie, once. I'm Tonya."

"Tonya, the important thing is that you believe on Jesus Christ, the Son of God," Janee admonished.

"But I don't know who He is?" Tonya was reaching out.

Janee explained as simply as she could, concerning the death, burial and resurrection of the Messiah. The young woman gripped Janee's hands tightly. Tonya begged Jesus to come live in her heart and was gloriously saved before Janee's eyes.

"Did Jesus heal you?" she later asked Janee after a time of rejoicing.

"My doctor says no," she laughed, "but what does he know? Even if I'm not, Tonya, I know we will be - when Jesus gives us our new bodies."

Tonya was at peace and soon drifted off to sleep. Janee couldn't wait to tell Bernard, who was visiting in the men's ward.

"Wow! Praise God, Janee! That's great!" He was excited. "I had some meaningful encounters myself. I witnessed to several men, but I don't know whether they responded or not. One coughed up blood on me."

"Oh, dear God!" Janee gasped. "I don't want you catching this hideous disease!"

"I washed good. I'm not afraid. By the way, I called home. Everyone is well and sends their love. I found out you've been invited onto the Theon Dice Show, when we get back to the States."

"You're kidding!" Janee was thrilled. The Dice Show was the ultimate talk show to be on, boasting high viewer numbers. "What about you?"

"Husbands of Academy Award winners aren't that interesting. Being a former agent doesn't energize an audience either," Bernard teased.

"I won't go without you."

"Don't be ridiculous, Janee. I'd only be a dead log out there. Besides, I'll be right behind you."

The invitation was accepted, and the day of the taping found Janee as nervous as a hunted cat, pacing back and forth behind the stage. Theon Dice had the reputation of ripping up his guests. That's what got him the huge ratings.

"I'll be praying for you, honey," Bernard smiled.

Janee stopped to give Bernard a quick kiss.

"Mr. Dice is making your introduction Mrs. Swift," a crewmember spoke low. He held up five fingers indicating a countdown - four, three, two, one - he pointed her to the opening in the curtains.

Her heart was pounding as she stepped into the bright lights she was so familiar with. Applause rose from a sizable live audience, but Janee was more aware that behind the three cameras that focused on her waited millions of viewers.

Janee waved to the audience and threw kisses before taking her seat. Silence fell on the stage, as Janee faced her host.

"Welcome to the Theon Dice Show; I am delighted to have you. Tell me, how are you?"

"Well, that depends on which part of me you are referring to, Mr. Dice."

"Please, let us not be so formal, Janee. I almost called you Stemper. I grew up on your movies, you know. I was your greatest fan, no joke!" Theon turned to his audience.

"I didn't know you were that old, Theon," Janee replied with a smile. The audience laughed, and Dice laughed with them.

"To answer your question, 'How am I?' Physically, I'm dying, but aren't we all. Emotionally, I'm the happiest I have ever been. Spiritually, I feel clean - inside."

The audience was unsure of how to take the actress' statement, and gave a mixed response. Theon made a quick comeback.

"Of all the people I have known or heard of, you, undoubtedly, are the most diverse in experiences, Janee. Would you say your life has been full?"

"I would say my life has been wasted, Theon."

"Wasted? You won an Oscar. You've starred in many, many wonderful movies. You are noted among the rich and famous."

"I'd give it all - all - to have my health back."

"Of course, and who wouldn't, but to say your life was wasted - look at this. Camera - zoom in on this."

Theon held up a picture of Janee in Viet Nam dragging the rifle.

"Do you recognize this picture, Mrs. Swift?"

"I would have hoped you could have found a photo where I, at least, had some makeup on," Janee attempted a laugh.

"The whole world saw this picture, Janee. You were a hero!"

The audience applauded. Janee nodded to them, before growing serious.

"I'm no hero. Just before that picture was taken, I had killed over twenty human beings. Most were men, but I think some were women - maybe even children. I fired that rifle like an insane person until I ran out of ammunition. Nothing heroic about that! The rifle belonged to a young soldier who died in my arms. He was the hero."

"I lived a lie. People saw the glamorous movie star who seemed to have it all. In reality I was empty. You want to know what happened after that picture?"

Theon encouraged her on. He was loving this exclusive!

"I was forced into a barracks by seven dopers – cowards – rats and viciously raped. Not by the enemy – but by our own soldiers. I passed out from the pain and woke up battered, with a splitting headache, a bruised and torn body and no clothes. I was full of anger and shame."

Theon and the audience gave a nervous laugh, some looked sick and disgusted.

"I trust your husband - knows about this?" he remarked dryly.

"Bernard knew long before he married me! The truth is I was empty, and I tried to fill a vacuum in my life with things - fame, wealth, power, drinking, drugs, relationships - no, I must be brutally honest - sex. I did it all, but nothing filled the void. My indulgences only filled me with - AIDS. I got it from one of the many men I slept with or from a dirty needle.

God forbid; I may have even passed the disease on to others. God only knows!"

"Let me tell you, Theon, who a hero is. It's Bernard standing back behind the curtains. He believed in me; he loved me; he never gave up on me. He found the answer, and he shared a mystery with me. Things don't fill the emptiness inside us, not even a spouse, or family or friends. It's a spiritual emptiness that only the Son of God, Jesus Christ, can fill. Bernard took me to church to hear about Jesus. I believed, and Christ not only filled me with peace and joy, He changed me! In that instant I came alive and was set free!"

Theon stopped her and went to commercial break. Noise flowed from the audience as Janee's words were dissected and reviewed. Theon leaned over with what struck Janee as a fake smile. He spoke low so the crew couldn't hear. The mics were dead.

"I have to ask you to keep religion out of our interview, Janee, otherwise I may have to ask some embarrassing questions."

"I'm not religious, Mr. Dice, just a Christian woman, and I can't keep that out of our interview. It's a predominant part of my life," Janee smiled back. "I doubt you can embarrass me farther than I have already exposed myself. Let me warn you, however, Theon, if you edit any of this out of your program, I will cry to every tabloid and news network how you infringed upon my freedom of speech."

Theon Dice stiffened and sat back up. "Have you declared war?" he snarled.

Janee ignored her host and turned to charm the cameras and audience.

"Welcome back to the Theon Dice Show. We are speaking with our guest, actress Janee Stemper Swift. What a revelation you have given us, Janee, but I'm wondering about your newfound faith. For so long you were anti-religion. It seems you have vacillated back and forth so much in your life. You were active in church as a little girl, and then seemed to - hate it. A war hero on tour for the USO, then you defected to the anti-war camp. You did drugs, now you are against that. Seems like when you got into health problems you found God. What in this world do you believe? I have trouble figuring out what you actually stand for. How can you claim a loving God who allows war and lets you die?"

"Well," Janee started off slow as she prayed for wisdom and words. "You brought up a lot of points, Theon, and some that are hard to answer. I will say this, I have not been a Christian long, so there is an infinite number of things I don't yet under- stand. I'm like a baby learning to walk, but I can tell you this, I've never been happier in my life. When I received what Christ did for me on the cross, He came in and washed away the guilt and shame. I could never have said this a few years ago. I was wrong in turning my back on God, but you see, I didn't find Him, He found me, and you can receive Him too. Would you pray with me to receive Christ as your own Savior?"

"What?" Theon was unsettled.

"I'll lead the prayer. You can do it, Theon, right now."

"This is neither a good time or place!"

"What better time? What better place? Now is the time! Jesus is knocking at your heart's door. Please, Theon, do it! Now!"

Not a sound came from the audience. A shout pierced the deafening silence.

"Yes! Do it, Theon!" a woman encouraged.

"Listen to her," a man cried in agreement.

"Shut up," an angry voice erupted, and other shouts could be heard. The audience was nearing mob level.

"Please, Theon, pray now - before it's too late. You're dying too; it just may take longer."

"We're in break," the floor producer informed them. Theon was furious, but also elated. He knew the show's ratings had just gone through the roof.

"Too many years of drugs have warped your mind, Janee, but you always were a fanatic for whatever cause you clung to. Thank you for coming; please exit off the stage. Good night!"

Janee blindly made her way through the curtain into Bernard's waiting arms. She had stood her ground courageously, but was now visibly shaken.

"You were magnificent!" Bernard consoled.

"I wasn't!" Janee sobbed as she fell apart.

"This was your moment of destiny, Janee. You know the place in history you were created for - your whole life preparing for this one appointed task and encounter, everything you've ever said or felt or done, moving to culminate at this precise time! Janee, you just invited millions of people to accept Christ!"

"Not if they edit it out!" Janee wailed.

"Don't you believe it. No one has ever gotten to Theon Dice like you did. A show that hot - they'll air it!"

Chapter 52

Approaching the End

Death is an event waiting somewhere on a far distant shore. Without being conscious about the matter that is how one's passing is viewed. This is, until we come face to face with the grim reaper. Suddenly armed with the knowledge that the end is near, there is an abrupt realization that is lethal in itself.

'How cruel,' Janee thought. 'It would be so much more merciful to just have death come unexpected, like grandpa! He didn't have time to even think about it, but I must face my death everyday, never knowing which sickness I contact will prove the fatal one.'

Janee and Bernard had wonderful, carefree days living life to the fullest and loving each other with burning passion. Amid the joy, the nagging truth of Janee's shortness of time constantly hung over both their hearts.

Symptoms of opportunistic infections were increasing in frequency and severity. Her mind at times was not clear, and her vision diminished to where she had to wear glasses all the time. Some days she was so tired she couldn't get out of bed, and she experienced substantial weight loss. But the most aggravating was her constant cough, accompanied by a difficulty in breathing.

"Do I still have TB?" she asked Doctor Davis.

"No, we knocked that out Janee, but you have been so many places the last two years, around so many people - I'm afraid you may have a combination of bacteria and viruses - possibly some fungi or parasites; however, tests haven't shown those. I can't protect you when you expose your -"

Janee took the old man's hand.

"It's alright," she murmured. "You have been - a wonderful doctor to me. I know you have done your best, and I haven't helped you much, but it's alright…"

Concerned family and friends bombarded Janee with countless suggestions - some medical and some spiritual.

"If you have faith, God will heal you," one of her Christian friends admonished. "You only need to believe, and it will be done!"

Janee prayed with all her might, believing her Lord for a miracle. She became depressed when tests revealed her positive T-cell count remained critically low.

"I don't have enough faith for God to heal me!" she confessed to her pastor. She sobbed out her disappointment to him. "Why doesn't He just do it and make this awful sickness go away! Is He punishing me? I don't know how to have more faith - I've tried, really tried - I don't know how to have - strong enough faith!"

The pastor thought for a moment. He answered with kind understanding.

"I can't answer why God doesn't just take care of it. I have asked the same question - like why did He take our second child in crib death. He gave me no answer except in the heartbroken cry of a king when David lost his child. He said, 'I cannot bring him back to me, but someday I will go to him.' I think that God wants us to see a bigger view of life than just the here and now. I do know concerning your faith, it's not about you or me - it's about Him, and His healing is not based on just your faith. I've seen the Lord do miracles when my faith was weak, and not when even the greatest men and women of faith prayed. But you can know He loves you, Janee, and you are precious in His sight."

Bernard took Janee to various clinics and even some treatment centers in foreign countries. She felt a tinge of guilt when she tried different treatments, as though she was displaying a lack of faith in Her Lord, but she was desperate to get well and live!

With each new treatment administered, with every experimental drug taken, a bevy of suggested diets eaten, Janee's hopes would grow and her spirits lifted, only to be dashed into the ground by dismal test results.

The last two years of her life was rich with meaning. She had not really lived before that. She was like the walking dead! She had made peace with God, and discovered true love with Bernard. She found something special in living and wanted more than anything to hold on to it. She bravely fought on, but in November of 1987, she had to be hospitalized again. She told no one, not even her beloved Bernard, but in her spirit she sensed she would not come back this time. She seemed to give up, as her body grew weaker. Pain now began to make its throbbing invasion in full force. She was thankful for the relief morphine afforded, but the drug made her mind fuzzy!

She could hardly recall when her mother told her that her grandma's sister, Susan had passed away in Texas. She was 89.

She cried in gasps when the family told her three weeks before Christmas that Uncle Walter was flying his plane in a storm and crashed in the mountains. He had three other people with him and they all died in the tragedy. Grief of unknown depths hit Janee as her mother held her, and Bernard patted her hand. They all left that night for the funeral to be held in Douglas Landing. Walter had wished to be laid to rest there. Only Bernard stayed behind to be with Janee.

'How hard this must be on my family,' Janee thought as she prayed for them. 'Grandpa used to say death comes in threes. I know I'll be the third!'

One morning after breakfast before the family returned from Walter's funeral, Janee was stirred from sleep by a familiar voice. She struggled to open her eyes and clear the fog from her head. She recognized Jason. He was cheerful and set some flowers down that seemed lost amid all the others that had collected.

"Jason," she whispered and held out a shaking hand.

"Molly and I brought you flowers," he went on as he took her hand.

"Where?" Janee searched the room.

"Oh, she couldn't come, but she sends her love and best wishes that you will get well soon."

Janee could tell he was trying to be sincere, but doubt clouded his face.

"Bernard?" she tried to get up.

"I didn't see him, Janee. You just be still. I'm sure he won't be gone long. How are you, anyway? You look as lovely as ever."

"Jason, you are - a horrid - liar!" she gasped and managed a weak smile.

"How am I? Don't know. Haven't watched the news this morning. Media - was - planning my funeral - yesterday." Janee laughed, but mostly ended up coughing.

They spoke of times gone by.

"We sure wowed the troops in Viet Nam. Especially you, Janee. You stole every show!"

"'Cause I - had pretty - legs -" Janee did a coughing laugh.

"We gave them hell at Khe Sanh, didn't we?"

"That it was," Janee agreed, "and they still won."

"Our best work still was 'A Bowl Of Dust.' I'll never forget our times together, Janee."

"Nor I," Janee whispered as tears rolled down her cheeks.

"We both made it to the top!" Jason squeezed her hand.

"I'd give it - all - away - just - to be - well - again," Janee coughed.

"You'll beat this, Janee; you're a fighter!"

"Not this time, Jason; it's too big!"

Jason put his head down on her hand and wept.

"I'm so sorry I judged you, Janee; please forgive me!"

"You know I do, Jason. I did - before you - asked. I am -thankful - we both have - wonderful - mates. Jason, when I'm gone - Bernard will need – help, please, if you are my friend - be there for him."

Jason raised his head to look deeply into her eyes.

"I swear, Janee. You have my promise."

Janee was heavily sedated when Paige came for a visit. Her friend had been crying. Janee reached out to her.

"Paige, you look like crap!" Janee wheezed.

"You're no pretty picture yourself, girl," Paige forced a smile.

"Out - with it! What's up?"

Paige began to cry.

"Oh, Janee, you are so sick, I can't burden you with my problems. It's nothing."

"That's - bull! No - it's Billy! What's he done - now?"

Janee had a coughing fit. She could make out Paige was pouring out her heart. She fought to clear her mind! She thought and moved in slow motion, all she could do was hold onto Paige.

"Billy left me. He wants a divorce! He's in love with - some - young - Barbie!" Paige's words were soaked in raw emotion - brokenness over a marriage disintegrating - fury over a trust violated was tearing her apart.

"Oh, Paige!" Janee groaned. "If I had the strength and a - gun - I'd shoot him!" Janee was aghast at her own thought. She couldn't mean that!

Paige laughed amongst her tears.

Next thing Janee remembered was her dad sitting next to her. She heard him speak. She wasn't sure if he was addressing her or God.

"Isn't right, me outliving my daughter!"

"I don't want to die, Daddy, not yet!"

Most of her time was spent sleeping, when the pain would allow. She was having great difficulty breathing. Once she heard singing and wondered if she had died. She struggled for consciousness. When she opened her eyes, she saw her mother sitting on the edge of the bed and felt her hand smoothing her hair. She was singing a little melody Janee remembered from her childhood.

"I'm here," she said softly, when she saw Janee's eyes open. "I'm here - like I've always been."

"I love you, Momma," and Janee drifted away.

In bits of conversation Janee surmised that Christmas was a few days away. She could hear the family talking and understood even though they thought she was knocked out.

"If she can just make it 'til Christmas," she heard Bernard say. From that moment she fought with all her might to stay alive! It was a goal set to look forward to - to stretch toward - to live for!

"We'll have a little tree and decorate it," they joyfully told Janee when she was awake. "What would you like for Christmas?"

Janee managed a childish giggle.

"What - could - you - possibly give - me? That - I need - or - could use?"

"A jogging outfit," someone in the room joked.

"A new Bible for church!" she heard Bernard say.

'He was always ripe to come up with harebrained ideas,' she thought.

"Some movie videos? Those are hot Christmas gift items," someone else suggested.

"Ridiculous! All of you!" Janee waved them away with her hand.

Three nights before Christmas Eve, Janee stirred. Her mind was more alert than it had been for many weeks. Janee struggled to sit up. The hospital room was barely lit, so it must be the middle of the night. She thought she saw a young man standing in the shadows. The sight of him startled her, and she gasped in fright, but when she blinked her eyes the figure was gone. She must have imagined seeing someone; then she saw Bernard asleep in a chair. She called out to him with a hoarse voice.

"Bernard."

Instantly, he was up and by her side. "Are you - alright?" He felt her forehead and smoothed her hair.

"I - must - look - ghastly," she could barely speak.

"You are the most beautiful woman in the world, Janee Swift."

Janee smiled. She still thrilled at the sound of his voice, even as sick as she was.

"You'll be up in no time and home in your own bed," he went on. Janee knew he was putting on the cheerful encouragement.

"I'll be home soon," Janee labored to speak, "but not here."

"Please don't leave me, Janee, please don't leave me! I love you so much - I feel I'm dying with you! I can't - picture life - without you!"

Bernard buried his face in the pillow next to Janee's cheek. She managed to get an arm up around her husband's neck and caressed his hair.

"Bernard, you must - promise."

"Yes," Bernard sat up.

"When I'm gone - promise - you'll - find someone - else."

Bernard looked like he was just shot in the chest.

"Promise, my love! The - Bible - says - 'til death." Janee was gasping for air!

"I don't want - you - to - be - alone. You don't - have - to wait - like - grandma."

Bernard covered his face in his hands shaking his head in protest. He turned and ran from the room.

A little Christmas tree appeared with some presents under it the day before Christmas Eve. The room filled with visitors. Coming in and out of consciousness, she recognized her pastor and some church members. Her mother and father were there constantly, as was Bernard.

Sometime that day, she was surprised to see her Uncle Clifton and Aunt Rachel. She recognized cousins David and Morgan. They both were with their spouses and children. She remembered Morgan's son, Caleb, talking or praying - she wasn't sure which. She saw David's wife, Cynthia, and Morgan's husband, Joseph, standing beside a far wall in the room. She tried to recall their names, but felt she was drifting away. She saw again the young man in the shadows, and wondered who he was.

She woke with a start. She couldn't seem to get enough air. She coughed and tried to speak. Her pain was unbearable!

"When - Christmas?" she whispered into Bernard's eager ear.

"She wants to know when Christmas is." Bernard relayed her message.

"Tomorrow is Christmas Eve," they all said in unison.

Janee must have passed out from the pain. She was so weak it was a tremendous effort just to breathe. When she came to, all she saw were faces of her family and felt loving hands holding her. She thought they were singing hymns. Her mind formed the words, 'I love - all of you - so much. Goodbye - goodbye, Momma and Daddy - goodbye my sweet Bernard - goodbye - ' but no sound came from a voice that was now quiet.

Chapter 53

The Battle is Over

Janee sat up on the edge of her hospital bed. Her family was sad and weeping. They appeared so upset, and Janee couldn't understand why. She had not felt this good in months - years! The pain was gone; her mind was sharp and clear.

"I think I've been healed!" she blurted out, but no one paid her any attention.

A nurse came running in and stepped around Bernard who was on his knees beside Janee. She followed his arms with her eyes to see he was holding a hand - her hand?

"Dear God!" Janee gulped in shock when she saw herself - her body lying in bed. The nurse was feeling her neck for a pulse.

"She's gone," she exclaimed quietly to the family.

Bernard threw himself across Janee's still body, sobbing in convulsions.

"Oh, Janee! Oh, Janee! Janee, my love! My honey!" he cried.

"Hey!" Janee shouted loudly. "I'm not dead. I'm still here! Look!"

"They can't hear you." She turned toward the sound of the voice. It was the mysterious man she had seen before. He motioned for her to come to him.

"It's your appointed time. We must go."

"Can't we stay - just for a - little while?"

"The Master waits. We have a journey we must make. Come with me, and I will lead you."

Janee took one last look at the ones in the room. She said, "This is not goodbye - only so long for awhile. We will be together - again." She blew them kisses, as she turned to follow the stranger.

They went out the door of her room and down the hall. Nurses, doctors, visitors made their way past the two, oblivious of their presence. It dawned upon Janee there was no color. It was like evening when darkness sets in, and everything is light and dark shades of grey.

"How dismal. I thought Heaven would be beautiful," Janee commented.

"We are entering the shadow of death," the young man answered.

"Who are you? Why are you here?" she questioned, but sensed in her spirit she already knew the answer to her own question.

"I am your guardian angel, Miglia."

"Well, Mr. Guardian Angel, Miglia; I guess you are out of a job now, huh?"

"No, a fallen angel waits outside this building."

Janee, who had tried to tease, was instantly snapped back to the gravity of the moment.

"Why is - it - outside?" Janee choked.

"The King has strong prayer warriors in this place. Their prayer covering makes it impossible for evil ones to enter in."

Janee was amazed they didn't open doors but passed through them. Outside the hospital was dark, and as they began down a street the shadows blackened, and the mortal world was no longer visible. A man was walking several feet in front of them accompanied by his guardian angel. He also had come out of the hospital. Suddenly, a creature from the shadows appeared. It was so hideous it made Janee scream out in fear. The creature pounced on the man who yelled out in terror. He struggled like a weak animal trying to free itself from the deadly grip of a venomous snake!

"I came to claim what is mine," the foul creature snarled. It had sunk sharp claws into the man who now clung tightly onto his guardian angel's garment.

"Save me!" the man screamed.

"I cannot," the angel replied with great sorrow. It was as though the guardian was helpless.

"But I worshipped God!" the man pleaded. Janee could see vividly the fear and agony in the man's face and hear it in his pitiful screams. The more he struggled, the deeper the demon's claws dug. He grew motionless in the monster's clutches!

A foul stench belched from the creature's mouth and nostrils. He laughed a long and loud mocking snarl that reverberated off the building walls.

"Yes, you did - that's the god I'm taking you to. He tore the man loose from his grip on his guardian angel.

"Save me!" the man screamed again. His terror was raw.

"Only Jesus Christ could have saved you," the angel replied.

"Jesus! I accept You. Please! Come into my heart and save me!"

Again the demon belched out his hideous mocking laughter.

"You fool! It's too late for that. You belong to me."

Janee watched in horror as the demon slowly sucked the man down into the earth. She thought she would faint and wavered greatly in her own faith. What if she had made a mistake - or hadn't truly been saved. Might what she just witnessed be her own fate? She clung tightly to Miglia. She appealed to him to help the man. He sadly shook his head that he could not intervene.

"Once a human passes from life into death, their destiny is sealed."

Watching the man disappear into the earth far surpassed any horror movie Janee had ever seen. It was like sinking in quicksand. The more the man struggled and fought, only hastened the end. The look on his face revealed he recognized his doom. Soon the ground swallowed him and the demon.

The guardian angel cried out in sorrow, then vanished.

"Come, we must hurry!" Miglia urged her. They passed by dark-shadowed alleyways. Janee was certain she detected eyes and movement, which caused her to hold tight to her guardian.

A few feet beyond one of the alleys she heard a scurrying noise behind her. She was too frightened to look. She felt Miglia stiffen as he stopped and turned. She gasped when she saw a cockroach the size of a football. Her voice was frozen! That was the one creature she had feared in life. No matter how tough and strong she tried to be, upon encountering this insect that lived in the filth, she would make a hasty retreat and get Bernard to take over its disposal. Bernard was not here but Miglia was. She tried to climb upon his back. He firmly put her off with a stern, "Stand! Do not be afraid."

Janee felt weak and wanted to run and hide, but she obeyed her angel.

"You disguised your form Pucka, but not your smell," Miglia addressed the roach.

As Janee watched, the cockroach began to take a different shape. It grew and molded into a woman. The demon had so much makeup - especially lipstick - that it looked grotesque. Its body was distorted having a narrow waist that widened greatly at the hips. Her legs were large and muscular - like a dinosaur's. She walked toward Miglia with a sluttish slide, circling the angel and his ward several times. She took a swipe at Janee with a scaly, long-nailed hand. Janee jumped and cried out! Pucka got in Miglia's face as if she would run her hands over his body, yet she was careful not to touch. She was panting, and her breath made Janee gag. She wanted to throw up but could not.

"Come, Miglia, with me. I will show you pleasures you never knew possible. Remember how we played?"

"That was before your fall, Pucka."

"Before my eyes were open. Let me give you pleasure, Miglia," Pucka began a seductive little dance.

"Stop! Be gone. My pleasure comes from serving the Lord Most High!"

"How droll, Miglia, but anyway, I have come to take - Janee." The demon turned her attention to the frightened woman cringing behind her guardian angel. She moved near Janee and reached out to take hold of her, but Miglia blocked her move placing himself between the demon and Janee.

"Leave me alone!" Janee managed in trembling voice. She had never in life known such terror as she was feeling now.

Pucka smirked a fiendish response.

"Oh, come now, my little friend. We have been together for so long and had such good times, how could you leave me now?"

"No!" Janee cried out. She was in panic.

"She is the Lord's redeemed," Miglia stated boldly. "She has the Spirit's mark!"

"You lie!"

"I believed in Jesus!" Janee exclaimed.

"Don't speak that name!" Pucka shrieked. "You were afraid to die. Like so many you made a hasty decision without meaning - like you did when you were a child."

Janee was so beside herself her screams came out in guttural squeaks.

"No! She is the Lord's redeemed!" Miglia stood firmly in the demon's face.

"I could out fight you before the fall; I still am the stronger!"

Pucka leaped at Miglia trying to claw him with her powerful feet. Miglia nimbly stepped aside allowing the demon to crash onto the ground. He drew a glistening sword, which shone in the grey. Janee ran to a wall. Pucka lashed out at Miglia with her long fingernails. He struck at her with his sword! As the battle raged between these two angelic beings they began to grow taller - reaching above the buildings.

"She's full of pride," Pucka accused, "full of the stain of sin. She's mine!" The demon struck a building, a blow intended for Miglia. Rubble showered the street below. Janee covered her head as she huddled against a wall.

"She has the mark of the Holy Spirit," Miglia shouted, his sword finding a mark on the demon's leg. Pucka roared in pain - then spewed profanities from her mouth.

"I will have the bastard child!" the demon raged, renewing the battle.

A quiet confidence began to build in Janee. Where was her faith? If her faith was good enough to die by - it must be good enough to live by. What was it that would save her - what? She felt a song well up in her heart, a song she had not sung since she was a little girl, yet the words were clear - it filled her heart and soul, dancing in her spirit. She stood up and with a quivering voice began to sing.

"Would you be free from the burden of sin?"

Pucka stopped as if waiting for the answer. Miglia stepped aside and sheathed his sword.

"There's power in the blood."

Pucka screamed in disgust and agony!

"Would you o'er evil a victory win? There's wonderful power in the blood."

Pucka shrieked again! She shrank in size.

"Would you be free from your passion and pride? There's power in the blood-power in the blood. Come for a cleansing to Calvary's tide, there's power in the blood of the Lamb."

Pucka drew close to Janee - searching her face - her forehead. Something of great power hurled her backwards against a wall. She groaned and reverted back into the form of a cockroach. She scurried into the darkness of an alley.

"The battle is over, Janee," Miglia reassured the shaking woman. "It was over at the cross of Calvary. Over when you believed in what Jesus Christ did there."

Chapter 54

Transition

The way grew so dark the buildings were swallowed up in blackness. Miglia's robe-like garment had a resplendent belt on which his sword's sheath was attached. The whole being of her angel glowed and was the only light in this dark place. She followed Miglia closely picking her way along. She had a million questions, but dare she ask? What if the sound of her voice brought about a renewed pursuit of that hideous creature – or other demons, which might attack? Finally, her curiosity overcame her fears.

"I suppose I made you earn your keep?"

Miglia remained expressionless for all Janee could tell looking up at the back of his head.

"I feared I would lose you," her guardian replied.

"I was pretty bad?"

"Were I human I would have applied a rod - at least once a day."

Janee smiled at her angel's humor.

"Your rebellion nearly cost you eternal life, but the Master never gave up in His desire to reach you. He loves you greatly!"

"I know - I think -. I am afraid! I'm afraid to face Him. I wasted my life!"

Janee was hoping for some reassuring word from Miglia that Jesus wasn't greatly disappointed with her. She imagined the Lord as thoroughly disgusted with the mess she had made of her life. Miglia did not remark.

"I must have been horrid to guard," Janee went on.

"Yes."

Janee waited for Miglia to elaborate. When he did not, she continued her pursuit of information.

"Did you keep me - from death?"

"Yes."

Janee waited for more as the two walked.

"When?" she demanded.

Miglia's wings snapped open as though in battle. He turned to face her. She cowered back from him.

"I'm sorry," she dropped her eyes and then looked up at him. She saw no anger in his face. His wings folded again.

"Once when you were riding your grandfather's horse. I stood in the way so Dusty couldn't run under a branch."

"Another time I grabbed the steering wheel of your car when you had a near-miss of a fatal accident."

"Strange, I remember that. It was - like someone took the wheel away from me," Janee murmured.

"I protected you numerous times in Viet Nam. Death was near you! Another time when you were high with drugs, I knocked a syringe from your hand. You would have died."

"I was so stupid, Miglia, say I was!"

"I cannot accuse you."

Janee walked in silence for a long while deep in thought. She picked up the conversation with another question.

"You knew - that demon - before?"

"Pucka? Yes, before the fall. She was a beautiful angel."

"Are there - boy angels and girl angels?"

Miglia smiled.

"In Heaven there is no male or female. We only take on the appearance of one or the other."

"Do you know my grandparents?"

"I saw them when you visited."

"Have you seen them - in Heaven?"

"No, Janee. I have been with you. I was sent the day you were conceived. For that purpose I was created - I have been by your side since - I will be forever."

Janee was overwhelmed and speechless. She walked behind Miglia rolling over and over in her mind what her guardian had said. As she looked down, she realized her feet were not touching what appeared to be a street. Her legs were moving - she was walking on air - or nothing.

"We are getting close," Miglia pointed ahead. Janee could perceive a light far off in the distance. It was but a speck, and grew larger and brighter the closer they got.

"What is that?" she was inquisitive.

"It is the veil. You must pass through it."

"Is it the bright light I've heard some who died and came back to life describe?"

"The Son has given a vision to some, but only a vision. Very few who have crossed the veil ever came back."

"Will it hurt?" Janee asked, and instantly saw the absurdity of her question. She was dead! How could it hurt?

Miglia gave her a knowing look as though he read her thoughts.

On and on she trailed behind her angel. The blackness was so thick it would seem to suffocate even life itself, but Janee wasn't afraid any longer. They kept moving closer to the light. As they walked, Miglia made his way carefully along. Janee wondered why they didn't fly. Maybe he was in unfamiliar territory - perhaps he couldn't see in the dark. How long had she been dead - when would they get to the veil? And what about a bathroom - wait, she didn't need to go! Did that mean she never would again?

'I am so like a woman,' she mused.

"Yes, you are!" Miglia answered. Janee was stunned. Now she wanted to hide her thoughts, but how can one do that?

The light that once was only a tiny glimmer in the darkness had grown enormous in size. As they came close, Janee could see that the light came from the other side of the veil. She had to tilt her head back to look to the top, and it stretched a great distance on either side. She caught sight of people and angels entering into the veil and knew she and Miglia were not alone.

Janee walked up to the veil fascinated. It held the appearance of millions upon millions of crystal beads shimmering in the light coming from behind. The movements of the beads in the light made the veil look like a huge waterfall - but the base was dry. She reached out to touch it, but Miglia stopped her.

"The veil is not something you can test," he was most serious, and Janee knew she better get serious too. She took a deep breath.

"I'm ready," she announced bravely.

She stepped into the veil. To her surprise it felt like fine sand pouring all over her body. The sight of an incredible land on the other side took her breath.

"Oh!" she cried in surprised delight.

Chapter 55

Meeting the Master

🌹

Janee gazed upon a land of enormous proportion and beauty. It was a wondrous land that both captured her imagination and fascination - an unbelievable land of enchantment that defied description. She saw why the God of creation had prevented the Bible writers from telling about it. If every word in the entire universe enjoined they would expire in their attempts to describe this place Janee now beheld.

"Heaven!" she shouted, holding up her hands, running into a patch of flowers.

"What brilliant vivid colors! What fragrances! I am thrilled! I love it here! What ever possessed us to think we could depict Heaven in movies? We weren't even close!" Janee began gathering flowers.

"This is Paradise," Miglia corrected. "It is near Heaven which surrounds the Throne of the Most High."

"Oh!" Janee laughed as she ran into the trees with her bouquet of flowers. "It looks like Heaven to me. I want to see everything!"

Miglia followed her, watching with curiosity as she examined trees, and bushes and flowering plants. She was startled when a handsome pair of deer stepped from the trees into the clearing where she had run.

"Hello," she called out to them. She was not afraid, and they held no fear of her. They came closer. The stag was a magnificent animal with an impressive set of antlers. The doe stepped gracefully by the stag's side. She offered them her flowers. They gave what Janee took to be an appreciative glance after they sniffed the lovely bouquet, but did not eat.

"I once told attendees at my grandma's funeral that my grandparents were deer in a beautiful, peaceful forest."

She gave a questioning look to Miglia. Had she actually been right? She shook her head.

"But my pastor told me that wouldn't happen. We don't come back in some other form," Janee murmured. The deer muzzled the new arrival in Paradise before walking on.

"Your pastor was wise in the Word. Only the fallen of Heaven's host take other forms. That is only because they possess whatever they enter into. Pucka entered a cockroach."

Janee shuddered!

"I don't want to talk about that," she ran on and discovered a pathway hidden from view by the plants and trees. It sparkled in the light and evolved in different colors. Janee knelt down to examine it.

"These are crystals - or jewels!" she shouted to Miglia. She looked up to see him, but was startled to see a man and his guardian angel approaching her on the path. She jumped back and started to offer her apologies. Miglia silenced her.

The angel was strong and impressive, commanding her attention; the man was dressed in a royal robe. His stride was slow and stately. He looked neither to the right or left, but straight forward only. His eyes were clear, and he held his head high. Janee was awestruck! She turned to Miglia who hovered behind her.

"Is it the Lord Jesus?" she asked, not taking her eyes off the man who appeared to be a king.

"No," Miglia answered. "He was a ruler among men."

When the king reached the place where Janee stood, he stopped, turned his head slightly to face her and appeared as if ready to speak. His angel touched his mouth to prevent any words. The two proceeded down the path.

"Why didn't his guardian let him speak to me?" Janee was puzzled.

"Because when you pass through the veil, the Son of God will be the first person you speak with."

"But I'm talking to you!" Janee retorted.

"I'm not a person, I'm an angel," Miglia answered calmly. "Come, we must go. We can follow them."

The path wound its way down a steep slope covered with all manner of plants - some Janee recognized, others she had no idea what they were. She did know she had never been in a forest like this one. The trees presented a deep green lushness unsurpassed. She realized there were no weeds - no thorny growth. It was perfect - it *was* paradise!

Something else about the vegetation suddenly burst in on her thoughts. It was an exciting new revelation. There were no dead leaves, no turning of colors as it was in the fall on earth. Color? There was no absence of color. She looked at the flowers in her hand, which should have started to droop - no; they were as fresh as when she picked them. No dying - no death in this place! There was only life and a sense of the joy of doing just that. She skipped on the jeweled path - free - like a child.

Animals made their presence known, and Janee observed species that weren't even in textbooks. Miglia heard her thoughts.

"The Creator made some of them for earth and some for paradise. The kind that just came out to you were with Adam and Eve. Others did not survive man's fall.

"Are there horses here? I loved - " Janee choked up.

"Yes, many kinds of horses."

323

The king who preceded Janee appeared briefly in open patches of the trees. She strained to get a glimpse of him. She was curious about this man and figured she must have heard his name mentioned on the news. He had already crossed a stream by the time Janee emerged from the trees onto its banks.

On the other side of the stream was a gentle slope. It looked like a wild flower garden covering a hillside. Thick luxurious grass carpeted the whole hill. Flowers and other plants grew amongst the grass and dazzled her eyes, but one who was fairer stood at the top of the hill. Her heart began to pound for she knew this was Jesus! She had to tear her thoughts away to concentrate on what Miglia was saying.

"You must cross the stream of living water before you meet the Master."

Janee shook her head - dazed. She refocused on the river before her. It was running deep, passing swiftly by her. She looked again toward Jesus. The king was walking up the hill to meet the King of Kings.

"Come, Janee," Miglia urged.

"No! Please! I must see!"

It was an unforgettable sight! The king walked his slow stately pace, head held high, while Jesus walked in normal fashion down the slope - hardly the look of a King, but Janee knew He was. His garment seemed - casual - almost - like a fisherman. Closer and closer the two came until they were face to face.

The king dropped to his knees, bowing his face to the ground, an act of total surrender. Suddenly Jesus' countenance shown with a brilliant light, and when Janee blinked, her Lord was dressed in a robe of greatest splendor! The King lifted the man up off the ground. He collapsed into the Master's arms.

Janee sat hard onto the path with a groan. She was gripped in fear and wanted to run away. The king who seemed so mighty had fallen apart when he faced Jesus. What would happen to her? The king was dressed in a royal robe – she was in a ghastly hospital robe.

"The Master waits," Miglia encouraged her again to cross the stream of living water.

"No, He isn't. He's talking to that - king - guy."

"He will be ready. Come."

"Miglia, I can't meet Him - like this! I'm in my hospital gown - the back is all open for gosh sakes. My hair's a mess; I look horrid."

"He loves you as you are, Janee."

"Love? How can He love me? I squandered my life! I have nothing to offer, if only I had my Oscar - I'd give Him that!"

"He is your Redeemer. Your love is a precious gift."

"Miglia, I'm afraid!"

"Come, you must cross the river of living water."

"Will you hold me?"

"This is one time in all of eternity I cannot be with you. I will be by your side after you meet the Master."

"Miglia, I'm not a good swimmer," Janee tried to delay. The water appeared over her head.

"You cannot stay here, and it's impossible to go back. You must cross the stream," Miglia was firm.

"Should I take - my gown - off? I have nothing - underneath."

"You may go as you are," Miglia took her hand and led her to the water's edge. She stepped in. The water felt cool, not cold, it was refreshing. She waded out further until she was up to her neck. She looked for Miglia. He was standing on the bank with folded arms.

"You don't have to guard - just be my guardian - angel!" she sputtered. She tried to swim but promptly sank to the bottom of the stream. She desperately tried to surface against the force of the running water, but to no avail. She bounced along the bottom; she held her breath as long as she could!

"Dear God, I'm going to drown!" she gasped for air, then discovered - it made no difference. She was breathing in the water, and living! In fact, a transformation was taking place. Life and energy filled her very being. There was no pain, no hunger or thirst, no weariness. She felt whole and well! She wasn't sure what the transformation was exactly, or what it meant. When she climbed out of the water on the other side, her hospital gown had become a white garment - clean and new - like she felt inside.

"Shoes! I've got shoes!" she exclaimed, and started up the hill, but with each step, the dread and fear in her mounted, like stone heaped upon stone, until she thought she would surely flee in panic or be crushed. She gave in to the impulse to hide and dropped flat in a sea of swimming, swaying flowers. She hid her face and lay shaking, fearing the reproach of the Master. She hoped He had left! Then came a familiar voice. It was strong and gentle - One she had heard many times - in her heart, and ignored.

"Janee, my daughter, why are you afraid?"

"I'm ashamed!" Words began to spill out, coming from the depths of her soul and spirit!

"I was angry because you took my grandpa. I tried to punish you. I even denied you existed! I sinned - I wasted my whole life. You spoke of the prodigal son - I was a prodigal daughter!"

Jesus sat down in the flowers beside her.

"Janee - Janee - what am I to do with you?"

"Please have mercy! Please forgive me, Lord - I am so sorry!" Janee sobbed. She dared not even lift her face.

"Child, when I died for your sins, how many of them did I die for?"

"I don't know, Jesus, I had so many!"

"I don't remember any of your sins," the Lord said, lifting her face up with His hand. She looked into the face of her Redeemer - the One who had taken all of her sins, not in part, but the whole, and nailed them to a cross. His face spoke of kindness. She dare not look on him, but couldn't keep herself from His gaze!

"There is therefore now no condemnation to them which are in me," Jesus said gently.

Wave after wave of God's love flowed over Janee like water, washing away her painful past. Tears began to spill down her face as Jesus lifted her up into his arms. He held her as she wept.

"I can't stop!" Janee cried uncontrollably. She went on for what seemed hours until she was totally emptied of fears, doubts and condemnation. "I'm sorry, my Savior," she sobbed. "This is so unlike me."

"You held back your tears your whole earthly life, it is time for them to freely flow," Jesus began wiping them away.

"I didn't think there would be - tears here," Janee murmured. She felt so safe and secure in the arms of the Good Shepherd.

"Remember my Word where I said I would wipe away their tears. That meant there would be tears. When all things pass away and are made new - then there will be no more tears."

As Jesus spoke his love continued to flood her soul. They stood to their feet.

"My life was useless, profitless and barren. I threw it all away. I buried the talents you gave me! To my sorrow I come to you empty-handed, - I have nothing. I'd give you my Oscar, if I had it." Janee hung her head.

"Are those for me?" Jesus asked, looking at her hand.

To her horror, Janee realized she still clutched the flowers she picked on the other side of the river.

"Thank you for your gift," Jesus smiled and held out His hand.

Janee placed the flowers in the Master's hand.

"I feel so foolish. You made - these. I picked your flowers - without even asking - to give - to you. This is no gift!"

"It is indeed, child. I have looked inside your inner-most thoughts, and I know you. I saw your love for me that came from a tender heart. Even when you tried to smother it with hate and anger, I still saw who you really were, Janee Stemper. My hand was upon you, and I knew you would not forsake what you learned as a little one. Welcome home. Enjoy the rewards of your labor."

As they walked to the top of the hillside, Janee was ablaze with an eagerness to learn. She bombarded the Savior with questions! He patiently explained that the gift of eternal life is the same for all - whether they served the Lord faithfully from their youth, or came trusting from their deathbed.

"But I'll have no reward," Janee remarked with sadness and regret.

"Your reward is living here - for eternity, but that's not all. I took the little you gave me and grew it into great things. You cannot understand fully now, but in due time all will be revealed."

"But you let me get sick! I prayed to be healed, and you could have granted me more time to serve you - but you didn't heal me. You are right - I don't understand!" Janee blurted out.

"Your sickness was a consequence of your choices. I didn't make you sick, but I allowed the disease to turn your life and heart back to me. Your life in sickness glorified me, and your death was precious in my sight. Your healing will be complete in the resurrection. Because of the decision you made that day on the beach, you will inherit eternal life and share my Kingdom as joint heir."

Jesus' Words burned deep into her heart and set her aflame! The magnitude of what the Savior just said sunk in. She saw Him now as the Lamb who was slain. He was the Lion of Judah, the Rose of Sharon, the Bright and Morning Star; He was her Gate, her Door into Heaven. When He gathered her into His arms He was her Shepherd, Counselor, Prince of Peace, the Mighty God, King of Kings and Lord of Lords all rolled into one. The joy and excitement she felt had to be expressed. She knew what David meant when he said, "Thou hast turned for me my mourning into dancing: thou hast put off my sackcloth, and girded me with gladness. To the end that my glory may sing praise to thee, and not be silent. O Lord my God, I will give thanks unto thee forever."

"I am so happy! My cup runneth over!" she burst out. "I love you, Jesus!" She wanted to sing. "Thank you for the cross, thank you for the cross, thank you for the cross," she repeated the simple refrain that sprung from inside until she fell on her face before Him in worship and adoration. She remembered the terror of the soul drug into a devil's hell and grasped what she had been saved from. She thanked Jesus over and over for paying the price of her salvation. She was content to remain there at the Savior's feet forever, but Jesus lifted her up. She kissed Him sweetly on the cheek and waited for His instructions. He spread His hand in a wide sweeping motion revealing a beautiful valley spread out before them, displaying the stream of living water, making curves through groves of trees. Janee felt a light breeze brush her face, and became aware of gentle movement of the grass and flowers. It was then her gaze stopped on a group of people gathered by the river.

"Oh, dear Lord!" She had been so thrilled with meeting the Master, she had completely forgotten about who else would be - in Paradise! Her heart began to race!

"Are they?"

"Yes. Your family is anxious to greet you!"
"Can I?"
"Yes - go."

Chapter 56

Homecoming

It was like Janee remembered, running into her Grandpa Farmer's arms when she was a little girl. He was the first one she saw standing just like she remembered him - arms stretched wide to swoop her in and hug her tight.

"Papa! Papa! Papa!" she cried. "I've missed you so much."

"We be powerful glad to see you, Janee!" He spoke in that familiar Texas drawl. She held onto him as though she feared losing him again. She buried her face against his shoulder.

"Janee, we were all terribly afraid you wouldn't trust Jesus and be lost forever."

Janee looked up.

"Grandma!" she held out her hand to Emile who eagerly embraced her granddaughter. Janee began to cry.

"I was horrid the way I treated you, grandma. I hope you can find it in your heart to forgive me. You were right - I was a hateful fool."

"I forgave you while I yet lived, Janee."

"Reckon, we jus' be mighty happy thet ya be here with us in this beautiful place," Farmer added.

"I'm so thankful you never gave up on me, grandma. All the messages you sent..." Janee laughed. "I hated you for it - but loved you later!"

"Walter told us ya got powerful sick," Farmer was anxious to hear news.

"Uncle Walter? Where is he?"

"Right here, Janee, waitin' fer a hug. Thet ol' AIDS get ya?"

"Yes, a horrid disease. I died a slow and agonizing death. You crashed your plane. What a tragedy!"

"Not as bad as you, Janee. Mine was over on impact."

Janee stepped back to take it all in - the family and their angels. What a sight! She cried out with delight, and the sheer joy of the reunion brought her hand to her bosom. She recognized Great Grandfathers Franklin and Hirum from pictures - but they looked so young! And there was Great Grandmothers Allison Trevor and Vivian Holt. She saw Grandma Emile's sister Susan, who waved and wrinkled her nose in a smile meant just for Janee. Her husband Andrew stood by her, and there were grandpa's brothers and their wives.

"Oh! This is too much!" Janee cried with glee as she clapped her hands in pure excitement.

"You all are so beautiful - and young!"

"You look a pretty sight yourself, darling," grandma smoothed Janee's ash blond hair.

"I want to see! I want to see!" Janee bubbled over. She ran to the river to look in, but there was no reflection. She turned back to her family. She was puzzled.

Grandpa joined her, put his arm around her and led her back to the family.

"Paradise holds no mirrors or images. I reckon the good Lord didn't want our attention on ourselves - just on others."

"I'm sorry, Papa, I didn't know." Janee was embarrassed.

"Ya found out jus' like the rest o' us," Farmer chuckled.

The family members moved to step aside revealing a handsome young man. He hesitantly approached Janee. He acted shy and uncertain. His face displayed a longing sadness which Janee had seen on earth, but couldn't recall the time or circumstances. She looked to her grandparents for an indication of who this young man was. They simply nodded toward the lad.

"Hello, Mother," the boy haltingly held out his hand to her - then hastily withdrew it when she didn't respond.

Janee was dumbfounded!

"I don't understand," she stammered. "I don't have a - Oh! Dear, God! Don't tell me - oh, no!" Janee covered her mouth with her hand. She couldn't believe her eyes.

"My son! I had a son!" she gasped.

"I love you, Momma!" the boy's face contorted as the sorrow and regret surfaced. He tried to keep from crying.

Janee ran to him and held him!

"I'm so sorry! I'm so sorry! How cruel and selfish of me! I was a fool! Please forgive me! Oh, dear, Lord, child. I didn't even give you a name!"

"Name's Seth. Jesus gave it to me," the boy blubbered.

"I never knew - I never knew - I didn't think of you - a child - yet. What a fool I was! I was only worried about myself - my stupid reputation - my dumb career - I listened to - your father - Oh, Seth, how could I have been so blind - how can I ever right this wrong?"

"Tell me everything!" Seth stepped back to look her in the eye. "Tell me everything! I have no history. There are no life pictures on my walls. I don't even know you or my father!"

Janee began to sob! She hadn't even considered her aborted child would be here. She was ashamed, and her heart broke.

"I want to know - about you - about my father. Tell me how it would have been - the house where you lived - the school I would have gone to - would I have been in movies like you? Great grandma told me about that. Would I have had friends - where would we have gone? What places on earth would we have visited? What would it have been like to fall in love - get married - to have children of my own? I want to know everything!"

Janee was completely shaken! "I murdered my own son," she confessed. "How can you ever forgive me, Seth?"

Now it was his turn to hold his grieving mother. "I love you, Momma," he repeated. "You can know I forgive you. Please, let me stay near you - at least for a million years!"

Janee had to laugh through her tears.

"I'll never let you go. I lost you once - never again!" Janee whispered.

"What a homecoming!" Farmer shouted, as the family surrounded Janee and her son, Seth, to embrace and encourage them with love. Everyone wanted to talk at once - there was so much to share!

Chapter 57

Concert

How can one know the passage of time when the light of day is eternal with no transition into night? There are no clocks to glance upon, no hunger pangs to remind it is suppertime, no weariness to claim bedtime. Had five minutes passed, five hours, five days or five years? Or did anyone in Paradise even concern themselves with it? Probably, the only consideration of time would be in reference to the arrival of friends and loved ones - or the events of prophesy lived out in the Bible, which were still to come. Janee's pastor had taught about a rapture of the church, the ruthless rule of the antichrist, the return of the Lord Jesus and His thousand-year reign upon the earth.

Somewhere in that chain of events, time would again be relevant - Janee instinctively knew that - but for now, time passage was lost on her and her family. As everyone talked and shared, there wasn't any sense of urgency to conclude the reunion. It reminded Janee of certain Sunday Services where the presence of the Spirit was strong and sweet, and the mood and bond of the members so warm that after the singing and pastor's message was over - no one wanted to go home.

"Where is my home?" she spoke her thoughts out loud, "not that I'm in a hurry to go anywhere - this has all been so wonderful! I could stay right here - forever!" she gushed, laughing.

"Stay with me!" Seth spoke up happily.

"You are always welcome at our place," grandma smiled.

"Now I reckon that ain't where Jesus wants us ta take her," Farmer drawled.

"Where am I to go?" Janee's curiosity was ignited. "Oh, I want to see! Will you take me, please? Is it far?"

"Depends on how fast ya wish ta go," grandpa teased.

"I'm ready! I can hardly wait!"

Farmer gave out a whistle and hollered with a loud yell. His actions reached far back into her memory, back to summers past when she was a very young girl standing on the back porch of her grandparents' Douglas Landing house. She listened for the answering snort and neighs of the horses, and was delighted to catch sight of Dusty racing to the back fence to see her.

But this is Paradise! What is grandpa doing?

Farmer yelled out again, and to Janee's girlish delight she heard the answering whistle of a horse.

"Dusty?" she questioned.

"Don't reckon ta know thet Janee, but the Lord knows how much ya loved ta ride, so's He gave - me - instructions just now - I heard His voice - what ta do…" Farmer's voice trailed off as a superb white stallion trotted up to the gathering. The horse came directly to Janee as if it knew exactly who to approach. She ran her hand over its neck and felt its long mane. The animal eyed her and nodded its head up and down.

"What are you saying to me?" Janee smiled.

"Mount up, Janee, he's ready ta take ya ta yer place," Great Grandpa Franklin offered.

"He'll fly like Wind use ta!" Farmer added.

"I don't know where to go!" Janee cried out as she jumped on the horse's back.

"Horse sense, girl," Great Grandpa Hirum laughed with his gravelly voice.

"We'll be right behind you," Emile called after her as the horse bolted into a run.

Janee ducked her head low and clung to the horse's mane like she had learned to do when she was little. The ride was as thrilling as she ever remembered. She was flying, and Miglia was right beside her! She glanced over her shoulder to catch sight of her family running behind along with their guardian angels. This seemed a dream - still, so very real. It was glorious!

Janee's steed followed the stream of living water dashing in and out of groves of trees. They were making their way across the valley toward a range of small mountains in the distance. As they neared the mountains, Janee could make out a canyon passage from which the river emerged.

Janee glanced back again and was amazed the whole family was keeping pace with her horse. How could that be? On earth no mortal could run as fast as a horse - but this wasn't - earth. It was Paradise! It appeared they could go slow - or fast - not even touching the ground - by perhaps just the thought or will to do it. Janee hadn't tested this yet, but would as soon as the opportunity afforded itself.

Janee was fascinated! The horse's mane blew in the wind, but was this air? She could feel it on her face - she seemed to be breathing - yet, did she need to? She didn't when crossing the stream of living water. Was that her heart pounding in her chest - or just a memory of what once was? It was amazing!

The river changed its appearance in the canyon. The water that flowed smooth and deep in the valley now tumbled over rocks in rapids. Some places displayed small water-falls. Janee loved the sound of the rushing, cascading river and wished she could stop and wade a spell, but her horse galloped on through the canyon.

When they neared the head of the canyon the stallion slowed to a walk. It shook its head and neighed. It was then they stepped out into the open where the canyon began. Her horse stopped and stood gazing out into an immense spellbinding valley.

"Oh, my!" Janee gasped.

"Ain't it a perdy sight?" Farmer exclaimed as the family caught up to her.

"This is Paradise," Emile added.

"Unbelievable!" Janee whispered, shaking her head in disbelief. Her mind reeled trying to take the enormity and beauty of it all in. The size of the valley was massive reaching to far distant peaks. The valley floor was rolling hills and full of life!

"Did earth have anything like this?" Seth asked.

"Not like this…" Janee murmured. "I could never have imagined."

"Hirum being the lawyer questioned the Lord one day. He wanted to know the correlation between Heaven and earth," Great Grandma Vivian spoke up brightly.

"He told me straight," Hirum growled; "said earth was a mirrored image, only vaguely, of what Heaven is. He said Paradise was on earth 'til sin entered. Said Paradise was in the earth 'til He brought it and those who was in it here. I couldn't understand how Paradise could be in the earth being so hot and all. He simply told me, 'With God, all things are possible,' but for the life of me, I can't figure it!"

"Oh, Hirum," Vivian laughed, "Give it up!"

There was so much to see! There were herds of animals, and flocks of birds. Plants and animals and colors blended together in perfect harmony. The sky itself changed from one hue to another. It wasn't just sky, but seemed like a huge dome covering all of Paradise - and where was the light coming from?

Miglia read her thoughts.

"The Holy One on His Throne is our Light. That is Heaven."

"Will I ever - see it?" she wondered.

"One day," he answered.

Her gaze took in people. Some were close enough to see, but as her eyes swept the huge valley, she saw countless cities and villages of indescribable splendor. No human mind had designed or planned these communities! No human hands had built them, but God in His love and kindness had molded and shaped these cities for His children to live in. Janee's eagerness got the best of her. She urged her horse on, but he just stood still.

"Reckon this be as far as ya ride, Janee," grandpa laughed. "We's a gonna walk from here. Lord Jesus jus' tol' me where ta take ya."

Janee dismounted and followed her grandparents. She had not seen the Lord but figured He was speaking in the spirit. Soon they stepped onto a golden roadway. "This looks like the yellow brick road," Janee joked.

"I remember that movie," Auntie Susan injected, catching on to what Janee was meaning, "Except these bricks are pure gold."

Janee became so excited she began to skip and sing a song that glorified the Father in Heaven. The family joyfully joined in, Farmer and Emile leading the way deep into the valley. After some time, Janee's skip slowed to a walk, and her singing drifted into serious conversations with different family members. She was full of questions, and so were they. She felt there was so much to tell - so much to learn.

The gathering climbed its way up a sizable hill that was situated far into Paradise Valley.

"There it be!" Grandfather Farmer announced when he topped the hill. The golden road had wandered through a forest, and now they walked into the open. The sight of a large glistening city left the group speechless. There were tall buildings clustered in the center, rising high above the dwellings spread out around them. The city sparkled in brilliant colors as the light shone on it.

"Oh, dear!" Grandma Emile cried out. She put her hand to her mouth.

"Is - this - for -?" Janee could barely speak.

"Reckon it be," Farmer smiled as he watched his granddaughter's surprised expression.

"Oh! Let's hurry!" Janee exploded into excitement.

"Just wish and think it, Janee!" her Great Grandma Allison Jane implored, jumping up and down, clapping her hands.

Janee blinked and looked at her Great Grandma Trevor. She so reminded her of herself and remembered her mother telling her Janee's name came from Allison Jane. She was determined to get to know the great grandma she was named after. She followed her instructions to wish and think it! Instantly, she was at the entrance to the massive city. Two angelic beings were there to greet the arriving party.

"Welcome, Janee Stemper, to the city which is called, 'Concert'," one of the angels spoke, bowing to her.

Chapter 58

Janee's Place

She stood in amazement! There lay before her a city of exquisite charm and design. Somewhere inside was the dwelling, which Jesus had prepared for her. The sight of it dazzled her! The walls of the buildings appeared alive and moving just from the glistening light that was reflected from each surface - hues of soft shades of colors taking in the whole spectrum of the rainbow. The shades blended and turned in a slow rhythm that was both pleasing to the eye and captive to the soul.

Janee wondered about the name. It must have meaning as the Lord did nothing without a plan and purpose, but what could it be? Was this a city of music and musicians? Janee was a singer; however, never considered that one of her best talents. She would wait. She knew the answer would be forthcoming. 'Jesus Christ is an awesome God,' she thought, 'to create such a place of wonder - and to tend to such detail.'

'When I was alive on earth, my prayers were only one in millions - millions that were praying at the same instant - day and night - twenty-four hours a day - year after year - yet, He answered prayers. What a great God who could do that! And of all the people coming to Heaven - He has prepared a place with me in mind!'

"Yes, My child, it is because I love you," the gentle voice of the Savior filled her mind.

Janee was shocked! She spun around - looking!

"I heard Jesus speak to me! Is He here?"

Grandma Emile took her hand with a knowing smile.

"He does that often, Janee. He hears every conversation. He knows every thought. Remember how He told your grandpa where to bring you when we were at the mouth of the canyon."

"Yes, I remember…"

Janee snapped out of her thoughts. She had been gaping at the magnificent city in awe. She looked at the two angels who were waiting to lead her into the City of Concert.

"Come," they said in unison, and Janee started after them.

"When I first arrived ta my place - well, my temporary house," grandpa was explaining, "I was greeted by some folks I hed known along the way in my life."

"Me too!" Grandma added.

"There was Ruth Riggs, Margaret Hatchet an' her -."

"Did Jesus tell you I was coming?" Janee interrupted her grandfather with a question, which popped into her head, "like He spoke to you about where to take me?"

Farmer hesitated a moment, then answered with a smile. He realized the importance of her question based on future arrivals.

"No, Janee. We never know who's a comin' I reckon the Lord delights in surprises - an' thet's how He makes it - a surprise. I'm a thinkin' it pleases Him to see how happy we be. I know I was when my Emile got here. I behaved like a kid turned loose in a toy store." Farmer spoke with loving humor, but even greater insight. He hugged Emile whose eyes danced with delight!

Janee pondered what grandpa had said. People he had known in life greeted him. There wouldn't be anyone to greet her. The people she had known mostly in her life wouldn't be in this place. Her greeters were already with her. It was okay! She was just glad to be in Paradise at all!

The splendor of the city recaptured her consciousness. It dawned upon her that the glitter and sparkle of the buildings were small diamonds embedded in the walls.

"Diamonds!" Janee stammered.

"They sure ain't glass fakes," Uncle Walter quipped, and the family laughed.

Upon entering the city, the golden road had given way to streets that resembled frozen ice. The whole family was curious about the streets, as no one was quite sure what they were made of.

"Maybe crystal," Hirum growled.

They all felt the material. It was cool and smooth.

"Anyone got ice skates?" Walter joked again.

"This is Paradise, not Central Park!" Andrew came back, and everyone laughed as they walked on.

Moving deeper into the city a crowd of well-wishers began joining the family. Residents along the way shouted hellos and welcomes. Amidst the din of voices and city sounds of happy people, strains of music could be heard. It was soft and peaceful. It brought from inside the soul the feelings of harmony and unity. In her spirit, Janee knew there was no distrust, cheating, gossip or hate in this city. It was void of anything that would divide people. Sin with all of its ugly sub-plots would never gain foothold here. It truly was a place of tranquility.

"I love it here!" Janee shouted. "Yes!"

The procession became a parade as the family walked through streets lined with beautiful sparkling houses. Some were single dwellings while others were larger, resembling what Janee had known as apartments. They appeared to have more than one person residing inside these larger units. Janee was curious about the whole city wondering about the people who lived in it. And what about the huge buildings in the center rising high into the sky - or whatever it was! Who lived there - and why?

Turning a corner, Janee heard someone call her name.

"Wait! Stop!" she yelled. "Someone called my name." She peered into the crowd, searching for a familiar face. A timid woman stepped out and took Janee's hand.

"I'm Tonya. Do you remember me?"

Janee searched her memory, but couldn't recall where or when she had known this woman. Her puzzled look prompted the woman to continue.

"You visited a hospital in Kenata. I was dying of AIDS, and you visited me."

"Kenata? Oh, dear Lord! Tonya!"

The two women grabbed each other in a warm embrace. Both were crying - laughing! A silent respect fell on the crowd as they watched this scene unfold.

"I wished to thank you from the spaces of my heart for coming that day - for introducing me - to Jesus Christ."

"Oh, Tonya, I'm so excited to see you here! It seemed such a brief - insignificant meeting we had - but here you are!"

"I am here because of what our Savior did upon the cross - you were His messenger. Thank you a million times - for telling me about Jesus!"

"Your husband?"

"He is not here. He had not heard - the story."

The crowd began to grieve for this woman's mate.

"You had a son, I think."

"He was also ill - yet he lives upon the earth. I hope the letters I left him will convince him to trust Jesus also!"

"Reckon I tol' ya, Janee, ya would have someone greet ya. The Lord does His work in mysterious and wondrous ways," grandpa chimed in as he also gave Tonya a hug. "Welcome ta our family," he beamed.

"Oh, do come with me!" Janee took Tonya's hand. "Is your house in this city as well?"

"No, I am in the village of Partitioned. My house looks like it is in a storybook. You must come see! It's most wonderful!"

Deep in the heart of Concert the family arrived at Janee's place. It truly resembled a mansion as Jesus had spoken of in His Word, but it struck her as odd that it was obviously three homes in one. In fact, the whole family was stunned. Grandpa scratched his head, and Uncle Walter twisted his mouth up trying to figure it out.

"Well," grandpa drawled at long last, "it done seems the good Lord sure hands out some powerful surprises. Reckon ya hev some close neighbors."

"Oh, my!" gasped grandma.

"This will do just fine," Janee said brightly. "Lord knew I always had close neighbors in California."

"But these be livin' in the same house!" Great Grandpa sputtered.

"Not so, Franklin," Great Grandma Allison hit his arm playfully. "They be separated by a wall."

"Hope they don't play no loud music!" Uncle Walter teased.

"Hush! Remember we are in Paradise," Great Grandma Vivian laughed. "We don't need radios or -."

"Come - see your place." the two angels called and disappeared through the door which looked like a large emerald. It had a solid gold doorknob and her name, Janee Stemper, written also in gold, above the door. She hesitated, before reaching for the knob.

"Jus' pass on through it, dear," Emile chuckled. Her sister Susan giggled. The family watched her.

"Go on - you can," Grandma Emile encouraged again.

345

She started to walk through the door, but something stopped her. She turned to look in the sad face of her son. She held her hand out to him.

"Come with me, Seth, my son. My place is your place."

A broad smile graced the lad as he eagerly took his mother's hand. Together they walked through the emerald door into a sensational home.

"Oh!" Janee had to catch her breath. "My home."

"Wow!" Seth was amazed. "I learned that word from Uncle Walter," he added.

The two angels made a sweeping gesture of the large living room before they bowed to her. Janee was flabbergasted. If she had all the money in the world and renowned designers and architects, she could not have built a house like this. The changing hues of color from outside lit the inside of her house. The walls were translucent, allowing light to pass through. Furnishings inside the room were plush and cozy looking. Janee plopped down in one of the sofas to test it.

"In your words, Seth, wow!" Janee snickered. She couldn't believe this was hers!

In one part of the room was a low table with bright-colored pillows on the floor surrounding it.

"Master Jesus told me this was the way they had the last supper," Seth explained.

"Yes," Janee agreed and breathed a 'Thank You' to her Lord.

On the table were golden bowls filled with the most luscious fruit she had ever seen. She somehow knew that in Heaven one didn't eat because they were hungry, but for the simple joy of eating and sharing a meal with others.

"I learned from the Bible that one day, Seth, there will be a marriage feast with Jesus. What a meal that will be!"

"When?" Seth questioned.

"Perhaps - soon…it will happen," Janee, murmured. She was looking at some pictures on her walls. Rich-looking frames magnified them. To her amazement each one was a picture of someone she had known and situations she was in - others were of people who were total strangers to her.

"They are called life pictures. You don't have very many - not like my great grandma and Pa - they have lots in their place..."

Seth saw the shame in his mother's face, so he was quick to add, "'Course, I don't have any - on my walls."

Janee turned toward Seth; she was deeply moved by her son's words.

"I'm so sorry, Seth," she whispered. "I eliminated your whole life! I'm so sorry!"

"Oh, Mom, I didn't mean to make you sad!"

She hugged him and walked to some pictures on another wall.

"Bernard!" she cried. In all the rush, so much happening at once, she had forgotten her sweetheart. How could she? She felt ashamed!

"Oh, Bernard," she whimpered as she looked at his picture. She raised her hand to touch his face. "I miss you terribly!"

The love she had for Bernard was magnified in that moment. Inside her heart grew an ache and longing for the one she had loved on earth. It grew and grew until weeping soaked her face.

"Be strong - for me - Bernard - be strong," she whispered as she kissed her fingers and placed them on Bernard.

Seth, who had been watching her, asked, "Is he my Father?"

"No," Janee sniffled. "It was - another man."

"Will I see him?"

"I don't know. I'll explain later - come, let's look at the rest of my house," Janee wanted to cheer things up.

The side room was large, complete with furnishings and a large bed.

"Hum, no kitchen or bathroom. What do you make of that, Miglia?" she addressed her guardian angel. He smiled but said nothing.

"Reckon you won't need 'em, 'cause if you did, Jesus woulda made 'em," Seth offered.

"Oh, silly, you sound like your Great Grandpa Farmer."

"Your guests await you," the two angels who had led her into her home reminded her.

"Yes! Of course! How rude and thoughtless of me."

She opened the door to the crowd of family and new friends waiting patiently outside.

"Welcome to My Place! Do come in, all of you, and rejoice with me!"

Chapter 59

Seeing Other's Places

Janee had attended socials all of her earthly life. She had experienced the spectrum, ranging from Hollywood bashes to simple family gatherings. None surpassed the church fellowships she partook of, whether in America or abroad. All had a unique warmth and closeness that made them distinct but unnoticed by a hungry and searching world. Undoubtedly, some of the most meaningful and endearing socials she was ever a part of were held in her early days as a Christian at the Church on the Beach. However, as great as those times were, they didn't even come close to what was happening now.

There was no sense of closure, no hurried glance at the watch to make aware the lateness of the hour. Gone were the idle, pointless, shallow conversations. Absent was the need to make an impression, or a contact, or to be the center of attention. Gone were the boorish people who frequented the 'invitation-only' gatherings. Absent was any need for alcohol or drugs to have fun or to be liked by others. Here was a sense of total love and acceptance. Each family member was held in high esteem. What each person had to say held value and was eagerly received and listened to. An unbridled bond of oneness flowed amongst every person in Paradise. Honesty and openness pervaded throughout.

As soon as her guests entered her house, ministering angels appeared and began serving food and drink. Janee was awestruck by the sight of it. Humans and angels mingling together in a party, the likes of which had never been seen on the earth - at least not that Janee was aware of.

At one point, all eyes turned on Janee. Not a word had been spoken; everyone just knew it was time.

"I'm a dyin' to hear your story, Janee," Phyllis Trevor blurted out. Everyone laughed at her pun.

"I told some of it at the river," Janee commented.

"We want to know everything, child," Great Grandma Vivian was also anxious to learn of Janee's life.

"Recount to the minute," Hirum added to his wife's request, with his gruff humor.

"We don't mind hearing parts again," Emile encouraged Janee to reiterate her life.

"Okay..." she began. She relished the things of her childhood - her entry into the world of movies, days of school with a private tutor. With deep sorrow she told of her anguish over her grandpa's death, and her flagrant anger at God over it.

The room grew solemn as she relived her Viet Nam War experiences, the anti-war years, her degeneration into drugs and alcohol.

Everyone cheered when she shared her victory over her addictions and the winning of an Oscar. Praises to God were lifted when she testified of how Bernard took her to church where she trusted Christ as her Savior. The gathering's voices swelled into a praise meeting. Even the angels joined in the rejoicing.

How long the fellowship lasted was anyone's guess, nor did anyone care. Janee only knew she was indescribably happy, and that no one from earth had joined them. Maybe the guests spent a year at her house, maybe two, she didn't mind how long they stayed - she was having a blessed time of it all.

Slowly, family finally began to depart to their own places until only Seth remained, and Tonya who had lingered behind.

"Please, please, come to my place," Tonya pleaded with Janee. "It is most beautiful and special. I want you to meet my neighbor."

Janee agreed so she and Seth went with Tonya. They followed along the banks of the river to what truly resembled a storybook city.

"What did you say the name of your city was, Tonya?"

"It is called, Partitioned."

The name of the city puzzled Janee; however, she said nothing. Soon they stood in front of Tonya's place.

"How lovely and quaint!" Janee cried out in childish glee. She could have been envious of such a cute little house, were it on earth instead of Paradise. Envy and jealousy found no fertile soil here in which to take root! She was happy for her sister's blessing and eagerly went inside.

"Wow!" Seth exclaimed again.

"Outa sight, Tonya, this is fabulous!" Janee squealed.

Inside of Tonya's house, the furnishings were muted colors, making them warm and inviting. One was compelled to sit and stay awhile. Janee was ready to plunk down in one of the chairs, when her attention was directed to three pictures on the living room wall. Janee walked over for a closer examination.

One was she and Tonya holding hands in the Kenata hospital. The next was of Tonya writing letters and the last of her sick in her hospital bed speaking to a doctor and nurse.

"She only has three pictures;" Seth observed and then quickly added, "I don't have any on my walls."

Before Tonya or Janee could comment, a woman appeared through the door.

"I saw you come home, Tonya. I just had to come over!" the woman exclaimed in greeting.

"Oh, yes, welcome, I want you to meet the woman who told me about Jesus, my Savior. Janee, this is my neighbor, Betty Jean, and Janee's son, Seth."

"Do you live in Partitioned?" the woman asked of Janee after greetings were shared.

"No, I live in the City of Concert, and I'm not sure yet where Seth lives. I've not been there. I just arrived."

"I live in a place they call 'The Heart of the Father'," Seth spoke up brightly. It has - well, you'll see it Mom...I'll take you there."

Betty Jean eyed Seth a moment, then Janee. Her gaze was penetrating as though she was looking inside. Her gaze grew gentle and her voice kind.

"I hear it told, that is a huge city close to the Father's Heart. They say it is filled with murdered, unwanted babies."

Janee instantly burst into tears!

"True - true - murdered - yes! Unwanted? No! I just - didn't - know!" Janee sobbed. Betty Jean put her arm around Janee to console her. Tonya patted the distraught Janee's hand.

"It's alright, Mom," Seth searched for words. He felt badly for his mother. "You're here now, and we have - forever - together."

"I neither condemn or judge you, Janee. Jesus washed your sin away as He did mine. I have only love and acceptance for you," Betty Jean spoke with sincere kindness.

"It seems each city is occupied by certain groups which the name denotes," she continued. "You live in Concert; I'm not sure of its meaning."

"That's right!" Seth injected with enthusiasm. "Great grandpa and grandma both stayed in a town called Passage. That was because they were moving to their own place together!"

"They live together?" Janee was surprised.

"Sure do. You have to see it!"

"I don't understand. What does Partitioned mean?" Tonya spoke her thoughts.

"I didn't either, Tonya, so one day in my grief for my husband, the Lord came and told me. He explained there is a partition between Heaven and hell-a great gulf fixed and no one can cross it."

"I still don't understand," Tonya shook her head.

"Is my husband here? Is yours? The brother on the corner - is his wife here? The woman next to him - is she seeing her husband?"

Betty broke down and began to weep.

"We are common in that," Tonya was hit with the revelation. "We are all - here - our mates - there! Oh! What can we do? We must pray for them!"

"Too late! Too late! Praying is past!" Betty Jean wailed. "I have wished to God a thousand times ten thousand I knew when I was alive - what I know now! I would have gone to every couple I could find that was in love and married. 'Why?' I would ask, 'would you love each other and live a lifetime together - and be separated forever! Why? Please,' I would plead with them, 'give your hearts and lives to Jesus! Do it now before it's too late!' My poor Benjamin, my love - lost - forever!"

Betty Jean was crying uncontrollably. Her emotion and the truth of Heaven and hell spilled over onto Tonya, who mourned for her husband. Janee and Seth tried in vain to quiet them. Even their guardian angels folded their wings and bowed their heads in solemn reverence. The women's despair shook Janee's confidence and faith giving doubts about Bernard's decision for Christ. What if it was unreal? What if he only thought he was saved? Janee buried her face in her hands - she couldn't bear the thought. She shuddered in dread as she saw again the horror on the face of the man sucked into hell. The Master's loving voice broke into her troubled thoughts! "All those who are mine hear my voice. I know them, and they know me." His words eased her mind.

She looked up into the faces of the other two women and immediately sensed the Lord was also speaking to them and comforting them.

"Janee," Miglia interrupted their thoughts. "Your Grandpa Farmer and Grandma Emile wish for you to join them in their place."

"Farmer - do you mean Farmer and Emile Trevor?" Betty Jean cried out in amazement.

"Yes!" Janee answered.

"Bless God; Farmer was my man, Benjamin's, best friend. God only knows your grandpa tried his best to win his childhood friend over, but Benjamin was a darn proud and stubborn blind - man - and I loved him terribly. Oh, Benjamin…" Betty moaned, then grabbing Janee's arms she stepped back to look at her.

"Well, well, Farmer and Emile's granddaughter. They told me all about you - I just didn't have the sense to make the connection. I love you!"

With that Betty Jean gave Janee a strong hug.

"Go see your grandparents!" Tonya urged. "We have forever to visit."

The next instant Janee and Seth along with their angels were standing in a thick forest, which covered a distant mountain range. Through a clearing in the trees Janee could make out a house. She and Seth and their angels picked their way to the house.

"Dear Lord! They have a log house!" Janee exclaimed when they emerged into the open and captured a full view. "I can't believe my grandparents live in a log house! This is just too much! Look at it, Seth! It is huge! It's a mansion - it's perfect!"

Everywhere you went in Paradise the eyes were dazzled with sights so rare and diverse, all your senses were energized. The extent of the Lord's creativity was totally awesome. The variety overwhelmed your capacity to absorb. Every turn you made - each city or village was unique and different - all displaying the Master's divine touch: now to behold her grandparents log mansion.

The Trevor house was situated in a rustic mountain setting. The forest was thick and a lush deep green, far surpassing the pine and fir-covered mountains of Douglas Landing. A clear mountain stream gurgled pleasantly past the log house. A log home in Paradise - how fascinating! Janee couldn't wait to see inside!

She walked up onto the long porch that surrounded two sides of the building. She smiled at the rocking chairs sitting still on each side of a table. She ran her hand along the logs of the house. The grain was rich and flawless. It looked like a thick layer of clear resin had been poured over the whole house - so thick Janee caught herself trying to finger into it. She laughed at herself as memories of playing on her grandparents' back porch came flooding back from her earthly past.

"Great grandpa says these logs fit so perfect there's no need to chink them. He tol' me thet was fillin' mud in the cracks," Seth spoke brightly. "Ain't it a sight to see?"

Janee nodded her agreement and smiled at how much her son sounded like her grandfather. She was grateful for Papa teaching her son and being there for him. The sting of regret passed swiftly over her - then vanished. She raised her hand to knock on the door when it flew open.

"Come on in, child, ya don't never need knock in Heaven. Ya be welcome anywhere ya visit," Farmer pulled her into the house with a warm laugh.

Emile came to hug her. She saw a couple in the room she didn't recognize at first.

"I reckon ya remember Joe and Sally Baltman?" Farmer introduced them.

"Auntie Rachel's mother and father - of course." Janee was glad to see them but surprised.

"You were still alive, Mrs. Baltman, when I came to..." Janee hesitated to say it.

"Your grandma's funeral - yes, and just barely alive. I was called home not long after that."

"I didn't - know," Janee murmured as she dropped her eyes, "Mrs. Baltman, but as my grandpa would say - 'I'm right proud ta see ya here - as well!'"

Farmer roared in jovial laughter, and Joe joined him. They both knew Janee had snuck one in on them.

"I see you inherited your grandpa's sense o' humor, Janee, and you can call me Sally. We just are casual and easy here-bouts - all the same. Just me, Sally! An' speakin' o' makin' it here - I'm happy and relieved to see you made it! Emile and me had our moments of doubt mingled with lots of tears and prayers. She gave me a message to give you, but I was just too frail to deliver it."

Janee looked at Sally with a smile.

"Sounds like they were a gangin' up on you," Joe Baltman joked.

Janee laughed!

"If I would have received one more message that day of the funeral - I would have screamed - and - bit somebody!" Janee laughed, growing serious. "Later, I was grateful - for every one of those messengers. Your words never left me. Sally, did you tell about the Indian woman who traveled to be at grandma's funeral?" Janee asked.

"No, I was too sick to remember much. She spoke, but I didn't know her - only yer grandparents helped the family."

"Walter tol' us," Farmer injected into the conversation. "Thet was somethin' - little Omney Wild Eagle all growed up."

"That was precious - her coming to my funeral. She has not arrived here yet, though her family is here - waiting," Emile added.

Janee was off exploring her grandparents' home. It boasted of finished wood on a grand scale. The wood tones were varied and beautifully polished to bring out the grain. The furnishings displayed a rugged western style that was perfectly suited for the house. Cushions and pillows were splashed with colors that reminded her of dawns and sunsets in Douglas Landing. There was a large table with chairs around it - just like she remembered. She spun around to face the others.

"Next you'll tell me you have - cattle? Don't tell me you have cattle!"

The two men looked at each other with a knowing wink.

"Well, Janee, I reckon the good Lord knew how much we missed havin' 'em, so - He gave us a few -."

"Us? You and grandma?"

Farmer and Joe tried to keep a straight face.

"I reckon all o' us," Farmer drawled.

"We got some too," Joe piped up.

Janee was incredulous.

"Next you'll tell me you herd them on horses!"

"Don't need no herdin' either; cows all do what we tell 'em," Joe added.

"You men are teases!" Emile hit playfully at Farmer.

Janee was exploring again. The living room was gigantic with seating to accommodate a large number of people. Knowing her grandparents she guessed it was full often. She looked inside the bedroom with childlike curiosity.

"Does anyone - ever use - these?" she asked timidly when she came out of the bedchamber.

"Reckon it ta be a nice place fer thinkin'," Farmer remarked.

"Don't need sleep or rest, but we like to talk there," Emile added to what Farmer said.

Janee was amazed at the number of life pictures that graced the walls of the log house.

"Tol' ya so," Seth chuckled to his mom.

"Yes, you did, son," Janee hugged his neck. She began looking at the pictures in more detail. A few had people in them she knew - most were of individuals and families she had never seen. Her eyes searched the pictures until she came upon some of her - most were of her and Grandmother Emile. She knew without being told those pictures were there because Emile was trying to witness to her about Jesus. It saddened Janee to see how many times she rejected her grandmother's tearful pleadings. She turned to the group.

"I died in a hospital," she began. "When I came out into - the shadows - on a street of some sort - I was with Miglia. We followed a man with his angel. We watched helpless, as the man was drug into the ground - to hell. His own angel couldn't guard or help him. I stood petrified!"

"Then this hideous monster tried to attack me. I have never been so scared in my life. I came to the understanding in that instant, were I not covered by the blood of the Lamb and marked with the seal of the Holy Spirit, I would have been…"

Janee shivered at the thought of it.

"I can't thank you enough for the prayers you prayed for me and the witness you lived out. I know now what I was saved from, and - and - I can never thank Jesus enough - for His sacrifice. It frightens me to think I almost lost - this - forever…"

"But you didn't," Emile held her granddaughter as the others gathered around her and loved her. They praised and thanked the One who had saved them all from hell.

After some time Janee went back to the life pictures - the ones she had seen of her and her grandma only brought back sad memories filled with anger, defiance and stubborn rejection. Then she came upon one when she was little. It was of her and her grandpa. He read her thoughts.

"Do ya remember thet?" he asked.

"I'm not sure," she responded. "We were talking - I think - about, Jesus?"

"I reckon we were. I tol' ya about the cross, and trustin' an' invitin' Him inta yer heart."

"Yes - oh, yes! I remember! I wanted to sing you a song I learned."

Precious memories swept over Janee's soul in a sweet and peaceful song. The words came back to her, and she so wanted to sing - just like she had done when she was a little girl.

"Can I sing it again - to you - now?" she asked ecstatically!

There was no permission needed. They found places to sit on sofas and chairs and waited, watching Janee, ready to hear her sing. It was exactly like Janee remembered.

She opened her mouth and the words and melody flowed like refreshing rain. Seth was boyish with his eager anticipation while tears streamed down the other's cheeks. It was a difficult song for a child to learn, and she had labored long to master it that summer. At the time, she didn't fully understand its meaning, she just memorized the words. But its richness filled her now impacting her with its message. Suddenly she was not just singing to her family, but to the One who had purchased her with a great price! The melody welled up freely transfixing all present into a response of praise and worship.

"Be Thou my vision, O Lord of my heart; naught be all else to me, save that Thou art: Thou my best thought, by day or by night, waking or sleeping, Thy presence my light."

The group sat spellbound! Janee continued.

"Riches I need not, or man's empty praise; Thou mine inheritance, now and always: Thou and Thou only, first in my heart, High King of Heaven, my Treasure Thou art."

She saw all the money she had accumulated, the fame, the Oscar, all of it, fading away.

"High King of Heaven, my victory won; may I reach Heaven's joys, O bright Heaven's Sun! Heart of my own heart, whatever befall, still be Thou my vision, O Ruler of all."

Chapter 60

The Heart of the Father

🌹

The stay at her grandparents was shortened by Seth's eagerness to show his mother where he lived. Janee had noted how her son acted more like a lad of seven than a man in his thirties. She would discover that the residence of Seth's city displayed similar childlike characteristics. Her grandparents warned her of this before she left their house.

The Heart of the Father was a massive, breathtaking city. Everywhere were high cliffs jutting up from a velvet green covered floor. Water spilled down the cliffs splashing off rocks making a mist that glistened in streaks of rainbow colors. The waterfalls fell onto the floor forming streams and ponds. Janee could make out doors dotted all across the faces of the cliffs marking where the residences were located.

Janee was appalled there were so many people living here, but she remembered that abortions were legalized, which increased the population of this city by several million a year - just coming from America.

"God, have mercy!" she breathed a prayer.

"Here's my place!" Seth announced - pointing to an elaborate gem-studded door. Light seemed to make the gems glow. On the door was a gold knob and the letters, "Seth," written in gold as well!

Upon entering Seth's abode, Janee was strangely surprised that the décor was more appropriate for a boy than a man. The chairs and sofas were filled with pillows. All these were simple fashion, but somehow tantalized Janee's imagination. A table was near a wall, and filled with golden baskets of scrumptious-looking food.

Seth walked to the abundantly loaded table, picking up what appeared an apple.

"Want one?" Seth asked as he threw it to her.

Janee accepted the fruit and took a crunchy bite out of it. She had already learned in Heaven that no one ate anything because they were hungry. They ate for the pure joy of it - and it was always connected with fellowship. She had so far never observed anyone eating alone.

Seth joined her as she looked around. It was smaller than her place and way smaller than Farmer and Emile's log mansion. Seth had been truthful - no life pictures were attached to the walls, which were made of rough grey rock. Upon closer examination, Janee discovered dainty little flowers growing in the walls. These flowers were of orchid-like appearance, which gave Seth's walls a subtle hint of color. It was a genius idea that only a Master designer could have thought of!

"I love your place, Seth!" Janee went on over what she saw. She deeply felt happy for the blessings her son enjoyed.

"You do?" Seth displayed his pleasure upon having his mother's approval. They found a comfortable, stuffed sofa to sink into. The two sat in silence for some time, enjoying the fruit and each other's company. Janee saw Seth's countenance take a strange turn. He acted as though he was struggling with something. Janee was about to ask him about it when he turned to face her squarely.

"Tell me - about - my - father," he choked the words out.

Janee was taken aback. She had not anticipated this question now - here - but knew she should have. Seth wanted to know - and she must tell him.

"Seth," she began slowly. "I don't expect you to understand all I am about to tell you, nor will I try to justify what I did - to you."

"I was doing well as an actress in the movies. I was very young."

"Great grandma and pa told me what movies were - I think."

"What you need to know, Seth, is that I wanted to do more - and better. There was a famous director of movies that a starlet like myself would do anything to be in his movies. His name is Aaron Mocknour, and I was invited to his home one night. I went after the lead role in his film and got it – without any indiscretions. But, while we were shooting I fell in love with him. One night he drove me to a romantic place by the ocean where he confessed his love. Like a fool, I believed him. Later, I gave myself to him. Aaron Mocknour is your father Seth. When I look in your face and eyes, I see so much of him."

Seth sat quietly, deep in thought for a long time before he spoke.

"Then why - did..." he didn't know how to ask the question that continued to haunt him.

Janee so needed wisdom to answer and a special measure of God's grace and love.

"Aaron had a doctor - he sent me to see - he - er - performed - the operation. Aaron, your father, paid for - it," Janee's words felt empty and cruel. She so wanted to talk about something else.

"It was my father . . . who didn't want me?"

Janee threw her head back, looking up at the ceiling. How could she answer this? It was not the fault of one or the other - both she and Aaron were guilty. She couldn't tell Seth that he was murdered because his father was afraid of tainting his reputation and didn't have time or interest in having a family. She couldn't tell her son that her career came ahead of him. What to say! She took his hands in hers.

"We both are at fault. I can't speak for him, but, Seth, believe me, if I could do it over - I would have given you a life. I would have carried you - given you birth - held you in my arms - been the mother to you that you deserved. I would have been there to kiss your knee where you skinned it. Your first day of school would have found me at your school, not on a set somewhere. I would have rivaled to watch you play ball - cheered at your victories - sang you to sleep at night. Jesus would have been on my lips to be sure you knew Him - we would have been in church together. I would have been so proud at your graduation, and cried at your wedding as you took your place beside your bride! I would have thrilled to see your children. Regrets? Yes, all three of us lost so much. If only I could do it …!"

Seth pulled his hands free and threw his arms around her neck, burying his face into her shoulder. She could say no more, and he could not bear to hear anymore.

"Shhh, Mom," he quieted her, and the look he gave her, and the expression on his face and his actions told Janee her son understood, and she was forgiven.

A commotion outside that had been growing now commanded their attention. They listened a moment.

"What is that?" Janee frowned.

"Let's see," Seth jumped up and flew through the door. Janee joined him outside. He was looking below.

"Oh! It's Mother Mary."

"Who?" Janee looked on a pathway carved along the side of the cliff. She could see a woman compressed on all sides by a sizeable group of people.

"Mother Mary - the Master's Mother. She comes here often. Would you like to meet her?"

"I - don't know - she seems so - busy," Janee answered with an excuse.

"She won't mind. I'll ask Niko to invite her to visit."

"How will he do that? They never leave us."

Niko, Seth's guardian angel, began to raise his voice in beautiful sounds. As the song swelled, the angel lifted up from the pathway in front of Seth's place.

"Can Mary understand that?" Janee wondered, since the angel's song made no sense to her. Maybe it was in a different language. No, everyone seemed to understand one another.

"My angel talked to her angel," Seth replied.

Niko settled back on the path with folded wings. "She accepts," he informed Seth.

Janee watched the woman below her as she made her way through the throng of people. She felt herself grow nervous. How should she act? What could she say - to the mother of Jesus? From habit, she looked at her robe and felt her hair.

Seth smiled at her but made no comment.

"Let's wait inside," he offered, and they went back into Seth's home. The angels positioned themselves in the room.

Janee walked around the table. She contemplated flying to her house, but considered how ill mannered that would be. She must wait.

Seth watched her fretful actions.

"She's nice - you'll like her," he finally spoke up.

Janee turned toward Seth with a glance that said you don't know what you're talking about. Our lives were two thousand years apart! She spun around and was startled to be face to face with the woman she had seen on the pathway below.

"Oh!" Janee cried out. She looked into eyes that reached down into her soul. Her face shone with a lovely beauty that spoke of simple kindness. Janee was humbled and flustered. She was taken unaware by such an abrupt entrance. Mary's angel was magnificent and shone with a bright light. She was aware that Miglia and Niko bowed their heads before this creature. Janee felt she should show reverence also to Mary and dropped to her knees before this woman who was called blessed among women. She felt a tug on her arm.

"Get up! I am only a woman as you," she said with a gentle authority in her voice. Janee stood up.

"Greetings, Seth," Mary hugged the young man. "What a lovely home the Lord has blessed you with - and is this - your mother?" Mary motioned toward Janee, who just wanted to disappear.

"Yes, it is, Mother Mary! Seth beamed proudly. "Her name is Janee Stemper."

"Greetings in the Name of the Christ, Janee Stemper."

"Uh, hello," Janee felt tongue-tied and foolish.

"In earth years, when did you see death?"

"It - was - the day before Christmas Eve in 1987," Janee stammered, trying to gain her composure.

Mary studied her a moment in thought.

"One thousand nine-hundred eighty-seven years - almost two thousand," she spoke thoughtfully.

"And how did you die?"

"Of AIDS."

"I have heard of it - a disgusting disease of sin."

Janee dropped her head. She could not look this woman in the eye. Mary stepped closer to her and lifted Janee's chin.

"Your sins were paid for by the Son of God. Fear not! Tell me, Janee, in your days on earth, did many still think of me as - perfect?"

"Yes. They pray to you."

"Did you?"

"No," Janee confessed. "I didn't - think to."

"Good. If only they could have seen how imperfect I was. Yes, I was blessed above all women to bear the Son of God.

He was God in the flesh - and I His mother. But - I needed a Savior, and I trusted Him as the Christ who died - for me - His own mother - I accepted his gift and invited Him into my heart - just as you did."

"It saddens and perplexes me that any would elevate me to a position where they would pray to me. I can't hear those prayers. Do you hear any earthly prayers? Of course not! Only prayers offered to God in the Name of Jesus are heard in Heaven."

Janee didn't know what to say, but she was warmed by Mary's smile and loving spirit. She felt no condemning attitude in Mary's words or demeanor.

"I had a good husband in Joseph. In fact he's in another part of this city. We come here together often. I gave birth to Jesus - He came from the Holy Ghost – then Joseph and I had other children. We loved them all."

"Now Jesus - He was the perfect child - but not James!"

Mary stopped to laugh putting Janee at ease. It felt like she was visiting with her next-door neighbor.

"That James," Mary shook her head. "He was a wild one. I nearly beat him to death with a rod at times. I feared for their growing up years that he would reject his half-brother, Jesus. He didn't believe and was insanely jealous of Jesus 'til he saw the Resurrected Lord in His Glory - we all saw Him!"

Mary seemed to gather her thoughts and went on.

"Speaking of wild, you should have seen my cousin Elizabeth's son, John? He drove me out of my mind when he was a youngster," Mary had to laugh as she recalled some incident.

"But look how he turned out."

Mary got a far-away look on her face.

"Joseph died, leaving me to raise the children, and they crucified Jesus and killed James - still we made it alright – we turned the world upside down, it was glorious…but hard! So, you see, I know loss, and the pain that goes with it."

Mary sat down in silent thought. Janee wanted to hug her but dared not. Mary came back to where they were with a jolt.

"You understand, Janee, those who live in the Heart of the Father don't know their parents."

"Yes," Janee murmured. "Will they ever - know them?"

"They will either face them here - as you have Seth - or at the White Throne Judgment!"

Janee shuddered at the thought. Mary grew serious.

"Will you help me be a mother to these children?"

Chapter 61

Unexpected Visitors

Immediately, Janee kept her promise to Mary. She began by singing to those who would come to Seth's house. Word of Janee's presence and what she was doing spread quickly throughout The Heart of the Father. Seth's home expanded to accommodate the young men and women until Janee feared the walls would collapse. She moved to the grassy valley floor below and positioned herself on the banks of a small lake. The crowds swelled even more during the times she would describe the conditions and ways on earth. They clapped and got excited when she drew them a verbal picture of playgrounds and children laughing and playing. They grew misty-eyed when she told them of mommas and daddies and the tucking in at night and bedtime stories. She felt like Wendy in "Peter Pan" surrounded by lost boys.

Once, she was relating how she visited her grandparents and rode their horse, Dusty.

"There are horses here!" one shouted. "Can we not ride?" The crowd grew noisy, and some took off, no doubt to find a horse. Janee wondered if she had caused trouble. She heard her Master's whisper.

"Heaven is a place of joy and freedom. Mistakes and trouble do not enter. With you I am well pleased."

Her audience grew to thousands. They filled the valley, many stood in their doorways above, hungry to hear every word that Janee spoke. They wanted to know all about the stories she did in the movies, and they were full of questions, yet they mostly responded to the telling of her home and family when she was a little girl.

Mary joined them on one occasion and asked Janee to testify how and where she trusted Jesus. She knew her telling of the Church on the Beach brought back memories of when Jesus and His followers walked the shores of Galilee. Mary didn't have to say a word. Janee knew she was pleased with what was happening. She smiled lovingly and kissed Janee's cheek before she left.

Janee did meet Joseph and was impacted by the man's strength and insight. She had questions she wanted to ask, but nearly as soon as he came, he was gone.

Another time Mary Magdalene, Joanna and Peter's mother-in-law joined her. There were others who came and Janee made many new friends. In all of this, Seth remained by her side, and often her grandparents came just to be grandma and grandpa to many.

She was surprised later on to see a couple walking on the water's edge approaching her. They seemed vaguely familiar, but Janee wasn't for certain how she might have known them. A happy smile spilled across their faces when they reached her. The man held out his hands.

"Janee, we're so overjoyed you heeded the messages, and made it here."

The throng around Janee fell silent as they sensed this was an important meeting. Janee sat blankly. The couple was young; the man was handsome; the woman displayed a beautiful charm. They were happy with a kind of sadness hidden behind the smiles. Janee stood up and grasped the man's hands.

"Who are you?" she asked bluntly.

"Don't you remember? I delivered a message from your grandma, just before the funeral."

"Oh, merciful Father, of course! I remember! Gordon and Ella May Brooks from Douglas Landing."

"You heeded your grandma's message."

"Yes, but I fought so hard and stupidly. It was despicable the way I treated you that night Mr. Brooks; please forgive me. You were right; I was wrong, bullheaded and angry!"

"Of course, we forgive you," both Gordon and Ella May spoke in unison. "We just rejoice you trusted Jesus - our Gordie didn't."

"We searched Heaven. He's not here. Farmer told us he searched too when he first got to Paradise. He just didn't make it!" Gordon elaborated.

"Dear God!" Janee gasped. A vision of the man being dragged into hell resurfaced in Janee's thoughts - she dare not share that with this grieving couple.

"We truly are devastated," Ella May began to cry. "If only I could have - taken his place!"

The three held each other and wept.

Ella May began to laugh through her tears.

"We cannot be sad in such a happy place," she said. Gordon and Janee agreed.

"I never got over Little Gordie's death in the war, and not to find him here seemed such a heartless second blow, but Jesus gave me strength and comfort. Since our son is not here, we have come to be - a mom and - dad - to these," indicating the young people clustered around them.

And a mother and father to the unwanted, they were. Janee had not seen such love in any person for the inhabitants of The Heart of the Father, as was demonstrated by Gordon and Ella May Brooks.

Months, perhaps years, of loving, telling stories, just giving of herself to the masses left Janee with the desire to return to her own place. She wasn't tired or weary - no - tiredness and sleep were absent in Heaven, but for the first time she gained an understanding of why the houses contained a bed. It was to think, to review what had transpired - to let the Lord speak.

Seth remained with Gordon and Ella May, and Janee was thankful to be alone a spell, although she wasn't quite sure of her own feelings. It just felt nice for a change, although she wasn't really alone. Her faithful guardian angel Miglia was stationed in a corner of the room.

"Do you understand me, Miglia?" Janee asked a silly question.

"No, but the Master does - completely," came the simple answer.

Janee reviewed events she had experienced since the time of her death. She thought of the magnificent sights seen in Paradise. She wondered what Heaven and the Throne Room of the Most High looked like. Would they ever go there - when - who else besides God and Jesus were there now?

She was thrilled to see family and friends, and she realized she was just getting started. Remembering the Brooks' son was in a devil's hell hit her hard! Now her thoughts turned to countless friends and acquaintances she had made who would not be given the gift of eternal life if they failed in life to believe. She began to grieve over them and wished with all her might she could see them one more time to tell them about her Savior - her Jesus - but she knew in her heart - those opportunities were over - forever!

Miglia interrupted her thoughts.

"You have visitors."

"Where are they?"

"Even now at your door."

Janee flew into the living room and threw open the door. She faced five men.

"Hello," she hesitated.

"Miss Janee Stemper?" one asked.

"Yes, I am. Won't you please come in?"

The men filed in. Immediately ministering angels were present to serve food and refreshing drink. While this was taking place, the men introduced themselves.

"One thing I've learned about this place, Paradise," the one who appeared to be the spokesman for the group began, "is that we have a time of thanking and making some wrongs right."

"Yes, but I'm not sure I – understand."

"You hardly knew me, but you were my angel."

Janee tried to remember.

"You had your own angel," she responded.

"Yes, I saw my angel just before I died – but you were my angel too. You remember the battle of Khe Sanh? I'm Preacher Man who died in your arms."

"Oh!" Janee gasped, "Oh, dear! It is you!"

"I kept checkin' Paradise to see if you were here. I was overjoyed to find you did make it by the Grace of God. I wanted to thank you for not letting me die alone. I saw you hold me and stroke my face. I tried to tell you, but you couldn't hear me."

Janee didn't know what to say! She was surprised at what came out!

"Did Jesus answer the questions you were asking?"

"He did - to my peaceful satisfaction. It was my appointed time, and since I never had a wife, He sent me to comfort those in Partitioned."

"Have you met Tonya - or Betty Jean? I know them!" Janee was excited.

"No, but I'll look them up," he replied in a loving manner that told her Preacher wasn't moved by lust or a need to find a mate. Heaven was void of that - He just wanted to be a friend.

"It's because of him that I'm here," the man next to Preacher spoke up. "I'm Shot-Gun. I was wounded with Preacher."

"I'm so glad - you both lived - and trusted..." Janee spoke warmly.

"Thank you - me too - but I need ask your forgiveness. I should never have let you take that rifle and - go - fight!"

"You couldn't have stopped me!" Janee laughed. "I was mad as a hornet! But I do forgive you."

"I also need to ask forgiveness," one of the other men held up his hand like a boy asking permission in school.

Janee gave him a puzzled nod.

"I wasn't passed out! I was pretending," the man began to weep.

"What? Who are you?"

"I'm Gater. In the room that night - I was scared outa my gourd! I was scared of the war - of dying - of what I had become – of what they were going to do to you but paralyzed with fear- so I played dumb and pretended that I had passed out. I coulda stood up for you that night. I'm so sorry for what we did to you - that night."

"Did you -?"

"Didn't touch you - but didn't fight for you, neither. I couldn't live with myself! I became a drunk! I found Jesus, thank God, in a Rescue Mission. He set me free!"

"But I touched you, Janee. I'm Alabama. I wasn't raised that way. I went to Sunday school and church. I was a Christian but sank so deep in sin; I doubted there was ever any more forgiveness; I used up all my chances. Guilt and shame drove me back to the Lord – and - Thank God, there was forgiveness and another chance. I lived the rest of my life longing for this moment when I could beg your forgiveness for what I did to you. Please!"

Janee looked into Alabama's pleading eyes. Gone was any anger toward these men. She felt only love for them. She reached out her hands to pat the faces of Gater and Alabama.

The last man dropped to his knees before Janee. He took her hands in his and began to kiss them as he wept out his confession.

"I'm the worst of the lot. I'm Bally Hu. I prevented your leaving, I tore your clothing, I was the first to – to – have you! I was a sick, perverted, selfish, lustful dog. Thank God, I married a good Christian woman who led me to Jesus. I never told her of you, but I bragged to friends…an' remembered."

Bally Hu buried his face in Janee's knees. She removed her hand from his and stroked his hair to solace him. He wept like a baby for a long time.

"I attempted to kill you the next morning, Bally Hu, and would have succeeded had it not been for Gater. I wanted to send you straight to hell! I won't deny your brutal rape left scars on my life. The pain, anger, shame – allowed for bitterness to take deep root in my soul. That bitter seed produced briars with nasty thorns for much of my life. What you men did that night pushed me to ruin – still that is no excuse for the life I lived, because you weren't the sole reason I messed myself up. But thank God, when the love and forgiveness of Christ filled my heart – I too forgave each of you.

Chapter 62

Arrivals

ς<u>ℚ</u>

One thing Janee observed in Paradise, because it grew
strongly in her own soul and spirit, was the anticipation everyone had for arrivals from earth. Even people,
whose family ties or friendships were not that strong or deep,
displayed an eager hope for ones they were acquainted with
on earth to be with them in this wonderful place.

With that hope was also a growing, sickening sense that
some they knew would be condemned to a devil's hell. The
reality of the horror, terror and torment of that dreaded place
was now crystal clear. No more was hell a thoughtless or
joking matter. Even the angels mourned with humans when
news of someone's death was learned and frantic searches
failed to produce that person. Sometimes the grief was so
unbearable that Jesus Himself came to comfort.

Thus, arrivals became of utmost importance to everyone.
It was not only a grand and glorious reunion, it was a time of
receiving news - even of establishing what month and year
it was on earth.

Janee eagerly accepted her grandparents invite to come
meet some new arrivals at their home.

'Who could it be?' Janee wondered as she and Miglia
flew to her grandparents' log house in the great forest. When
her feet hit the porch she bolted right on through the door.

"Here you are, child!" her Grandma Emile turned to greet her.

"I reckon ya ta be a mite interested ta see these two," Grandfather Farmer drawled with a grin.

Janee saw a man and a woman. The man seemed vaguely familiar, but not the woman. The man left the couch and approached her. He extended his hand warmly, and his smile was sincere.

"Can't tell you how tickled I was to hear you trusted the Lord - and to find you here makes me happy as a bear findin' a honey tree." Then a teasing smile filled the man's face. "I'm still a wondering about them deer?" he asked with a laugh.

"Donald Parrigan - how could I not recognize you - and I was a pigheaded fool, a hard-headed, opinionated, dumb blonde. I had to eat every word I spoke to you that day."

"I heard you got that terrible disease AIDS. Me and my missus prayed for you everyday - for the healing of your spirit and body - and to throw a little extra on your personality for good measure."

Janee laughed. Gone was the contempt, and in its place was the love of the Savior.

"He answered your prayers," Emile said thankfully.

"How did - you die?" Janee asked of Donald.

"Was feelin' poorly - no energy - like a fella tryin' to cut down a Redwood with a pocket knife. Just couldn't get the job done and was all out of figuring, so I went to the doctor. He told me I had an empty head an' a cold heart, but he had medicine for that. Must not a worked 'less he was wantin' to send me here to this wonderful place - and Farmer, this sure ain't the way I pictured Heaven - not at all!"

"Anyway, I went to sleep one night and woke up in bed with my angel talkin' to me. I sure wanted to wake Beth - least say goodbye to her - but too late - she couldn't hear nothin I said."

Janee saw this tough old lumberjack's eyes water up. 'She had heard stories of Donald's drunken brawls when she was a little girl. His manner had frightened her at times; now she marveled at the work the Lord had wrought in this man's life.

Farmer directed her attention to the woman.

"You never met this lady," his face shone. "She be Miss Omney Wild Eagle. We all came together in the Arizona desert on our great travel west."

"Yes," Janee interrupted her grandpa and went to hug the woman. After the embrace, Janee looked Omney in the eyes.

"You were at grandmother's funeral and made such tender remarks - after my horrid deer - fantasy. You traveled far - I never thanked you - I only hated you - for speaking of Jesus Christ. I was blind. Please tell me of your life – your family."

The conversation became animated and happy. Love flowed among them as they laughed and encouraged one another.

Omney told of teaching poor Indian children. Not only did she teach reading and writing to the children, but of Jesus and the cross. Her school home caught fire one night. Her guardian angel tried to warn her, but she succumbed to the smoke and perished in the fire. She felt sure it was arson. She described her journey to the veil, her washing in the River of Living Water, meeting the Master, and her grand reunion with her family.

Donald wept over missing his wife, Beth, and how he longed to see her. He voiced concerns for their daughter, Beverly Ann, and hoped she was saved. Listening to him made Janee realize how she loved Bernard beyond any feelings she ever had on earth, and how so very much she missed him. As the conversation chattered on, her thoughts drifted to little things she remembered about him - his mussed hair

- his crooked glasses - watching him shave or sip his coffee. She would never forget his face the night she confessed her love for him - seeing him waiting for her on the beach the day she became Mrs. Bernard Swift. A thousand thoughts passed through her mind all the way to the end. The grief and agony, which pained his face the hours before her passing - what she saw in him when she died - made her cry!

A gathering angel interrupted the conversation and Janee's memories. He summoned Farmer, Emile and Janee to gather at the river.

"Who could it be?" Emile wondered as the trio quickly made its way to the banks of the Living Water.

'Must be family, I reckon,' Farmer was thinking. 'Can't remember a summons fer friends.'

"This is my first," Janee spoke up. "Do you think it could be Bernard?"

"Reckon so." Farmer answered.

Walter, then her great-grandparents and her great uncles and cousin Sidney Dean, soon joined them. They spoke in excited tones as they waited anxiously to see who would top the hill with their Lord Jesus. To their utter surprise they saw a man and two women.

"Who is it?" Emile cried. She shaded her eyes - an old habit - to see better.

No one recognized the three because of the distance. The Lord seemed to take an extra long time. He held each one as He tenderly talked to them. He indeed appeared to be the Wonderful Counselor at this moment. Farmer began to pace back and forth.

"Musta been somethin' powerful bad happen!" he muttered.

"Why do you say that?" Allison Jane questioned.

"Cause they all died at once!"

"Wasn't natural for sure," Hirum agreed.

Finally, Jesus sent the three to the family.

Walter was the first to attempt recognition as the three came down the hill.

"It looks like - David!"

"Merciful God! It is!" Emile screamed. "It's David - and Cynthia - and -!"

"Little Mary!" Janee finished the sentence. She recognized her cousin's daughter.

The three ran into the waiting arms of their family. David, Cynthia and Mary were weeping in agonized grief. It was a long time before they could speak.

"Tell us what happened?" Farmer ventured the question when he thought the arrivals had calmed enough to answer. David started.

"We were driving Mary's fiancé from Anchorage back to his home in Fairbanks."

"Mary met him at college, and it was spring break," Cynthia explained. "The weather forecast was clear, so we drove."

"We got caught in a freak storm - the likes of which I had never seen," David continued. "Slid off the road!"

"It was so cold, and Kasha wrapped me in his coat," Mary sobbed.

"I tried to ward off the cold - it was bitter - let me tell you. I would run the engine in short spells, but I had to watch the fuel. We were so drifted in - impossible to get out." David stopped to reflect before he told more. Janee was struck by the sadness in their faces.

"We kept hoping, praying, believing a car or truck - a snow plow would come by. It wasn't long until the snow buried us," Cynthia added.

"I tried to push it away until my hands and feet froze!" David went on.

"Oh, Kasha! My love - my life," Mary was repeating over and over as the family attempted in vain to comfort her.

"Our fuel ran low and with it our hope. I let the engine run and we fell asleep. We died from Carbon Monoxide - or froze to death - not sure which," David shook his head. "We sure didn't leave our house that day planning to die ..." David's voice trailed off. His wife picked up after him.

"Next thing we knew we had these angels gathered 'round about us."

She motioned with her hand pointing out their guardians.

"We asked Jesus why He let us die. He said all would be revealed. I don't understand!" Cynthia spoke her heart.

"He told me the same thing," Janee injected.

"He will do as He says - you'll see," Farmer could speak from experience.

Mary broke down again.

"Kasha isn't here!" she wailed.

"Maybe he's meeting his family. We can ask the angels to search -" Farmer wanted to be helpful, but Mary cut him off.

"You - don't - understand!" she belted out the words between sobs. She couldn't speak - holding her head she shook an emphatic, "Noo!"

"What she means - we saw - it was horrible!" Cynthia covered her mouth and also shook her head. The family's eyes turned toward David. With downcast eyes he sadly finished the story.

"We saw with our own eyes - so awful, I can hardly tell it. A monster - so fierce and terrible - I went numb - and not from the cold - this devil grabbed poor Kasha and dragged him under the snow. Kasha fought and screamed - like I've never heard a man scream, and none to help him - not even his angel."

David at that point also broke and began to weep.

"It hit me like an avalanche, we talked about Jesus around Kasha, but never thought - took the matter serious enough to ask about his salvation. We just assumed because we loved him and - and - he was a nice kid - he was - one of us," David could not go on. He appeared spent. Not tired, but drained.

"Dear God!" Janee exclaimed as she put her arms around the grieving Mary. "I saw that happen too- but it wasn't anyone I knew - that would have been even worse. It was horrid to watch and scared the hell - me to death - humph - none of those work here. I just know it was horrid, and I was shaking!"

David found humor in Janee's spontaneity. He had to laugh.

"Janee, you are too - much!"

It was Emile who brought the family back from its mourning for Kasha. Their hearts ached for David, Cynthia and especially for Mary. However, there was another serious matter that needed to be considered, and it was Emile who brought it forth.

"Poor Clifton and Rachel. These unexpected, untimely deaths of their children and grandchild will no doubt break their hearts. I'm afraid this accident will prove to be the death of them."

It was 1995 in earth years. Emile seemed to indeed speak words of prophecy. Clifton soon came home followed three months later by his lifelong friend, love and mate, Rachel.

Chapter 63

A Friend and an Enemy

Janee could never have anticipated what happened next. An encounter took place in a gorgeous garden in the City of Passage, which her grandpa had revealed to her. She delighted in walking through pathways that perked her imagination and she basked in the light and quietness of the place.

The paths were lined with perfectly manicured rows of rich colored roses. Smaller flowers whose colors complimented the roses highlighted these. Lovely trees filled the garden. The scent filled her whole being. She was enjoying a walk and communing with the Lord, when a man and his angel rounded a corner and strolled directly toward her. He began waving and calling her name. Her heart stopped! Could it possibly be?

"Jason?" she cried with joy.

"Janee!" he answered, and they ran to each other.

"We have so much to catch up on, Janee, but first there is something I must tell you. I didn't see it until I met Jesus, and He opened my eyes. I don't know how I could have been so dense!"

"Is it even important now?"

"It is to me - and I think you. I have to tell you what the Lord revealed."

"I'm listening, Jason," Janee spoke lovingly as she sat on a low garden wall. He joined her and held her hand.

"You remember the day - on the Freedom Bird?"

"Oh, Jason, please, let's not remember that!"

"We must - that's where I went off course."

"You mean we both went off course"

"No - Master explained the Father's perfect will - and His permissive will."

"What do you mean?"

"God's will for me was to forgive you and lead you to trust Jesus."

"You knew Jesus?" Janee was shocked.

Jason bowed his head in shame. He did not answer immediately as he was struggling with the shame of what he was on earth.

"I hid my faith. I was the light hidden under a basket!"

Janee could see tears trickle down her friend's cheeks. She wanted to kiss them away.

"I had so fallen in love with you, and I wanted to tell you of my faith in Christ - but - I - just couldn't, I was afraid – afraid of so much. I was the only one on the USO team who was a Christian. I should have spoken out - could have - but a strange sort of fear gripped me. Isn't that ridiculous, Janee - Jason Finn, the actor, Academy Award Winner, guest speaker in dozens upon dozens of functions - afraid to speak."

"I - can - understand - that," Janee's voice was gentle and displayed her understanding as she squeezed his hand.

"I too was afraid to speak, Jason. I wanted to tell you the truth, to start our love on an honest plain for I loved you too. I couldn't tell you I was a virgin because I wasn't. I loved and had an affair with Aaron Mocknour. I found out I was pregnant, but Aaron rejected my love and his child. He insisted I have an abortion, and threatened my life if I told. I was afraid to tell you. And those dopers in Khe Sahn! They gang raped me, Jason! I wanted to tell you about it – tried to tell you, but my pride and anger got in the way, I was so foolish and dumb."

By now both Jason and Janee were crying. Janee kissed his tears.

They both sat in silent thought for a long time. Janee started to say something numerous times, and there was so much she wanted to talk about, but something inside - perhaps the Lord - told her just to listen. She did. Finally, Jason began to speak.

"I should have let you explain, but I was too angry and hurt. I formed my own opinion of what I wanted to believe. I never knew about the rape until I read what you said on the Dice Show. God's will for us was to fall in love; I was to introduce you to my Savior; then we would marry and have a beautiful family. But did I listen to him? No! My ego was smashed; I was devastated! All I could see were you being - by other men - not one - but - who knows how many. I viewed you as soiled and – untouchable."

"Janee, I know now, in your way you were trying to tell me of your love. If I would have forgiven and forgotten about what I thought happened in Khe Sanh, if only I had listened. I know I could have led you out of that lifestyle into a life with me."

"I wish to God you had," Janee responded with sadness. "I would have followed you to the ends of the earth!"

"I'm so sorry, Janee," and Jason held her. She melted into his arms. It was not a man-woman thing - not even hinting of husband-wife now. This was different and precious! Janee wasn't sure what it was. All she knew was that it brought healing. It was pure and right. Janee drew back to look at him.

"What about Molly?"

"What about Bernard? That's what Jesus explained as the Father's permissive will, Janee, and I'm so afraid I repeated my mistake."

"How?" she didn't understand.

"Molly was of another faith and a division came between us. For the sake of peace and our marriage, we just grew silent on the matter. I realize now the mistake and how I failed you both. We must pray for the Lord to send a witness to her - to open her eyes and heart!"

Jason had a look of desperation on his face. Janee touched his face gently to quiet his fretting.

"Shhh," she said softly. "It's too late for us to pray - but we must trust Jesus to do everything possible to win her, and He won't give up as long as she yet breathes."

"I have fleeting thoughts – fears – at times that Bernard didn't really find the Lord – until I remember little things. Indications that told me he knew the Savior. I saw fruit in his life and I know I will see him one day. You can and must hope for Molly."

Jason buried his face in his folded arms and nothing further was spoken until Jason raised his head.

"Have you seen Aaron Mocknour?" he asked.

"No why?" Janee was surprised at Jason's question.

"Because he died in a flaming car crash over three years ago."

"What?" Janee was shocked. She immediately turned to Miglia.

"Is he here?" she hurriedly inquired.

Miglia and Jason's angel raised their voices in melodic search as they lifted above the garden trees. When they silently settled, their countenances were deeply downcast.

"He is not here," Miglia answered with great sorrow.

Later, Janee would break the disheartening news to Seth.

"Your father has died on earth, but he won't be coming to live in Heaven."

Chapter 64

Questions

In life on earth, Janee was always an inquisitive person. This part of her nature came out again at a large gathering of family and friends held at Farmer and Emile's place. It struck her while listening to Gordon Brooks talk that she remembered something he said that night in her grandma's house in Douglas Landing. She turned to Emile.

"People who found you said you were lying at the foot of your bed - like you were seeing something or someone - and reaching out. Did you see your angel Froton?"

Emile thought for a moment, moved by Janee's question.

"Yes, I saw him, but I wasn't reaching for him."

Farmer looked puzzled and curious. He had not heard this story.

"When we made our trip from Texas I began a journal. I wrote of our travel and life in a new land." She looked at Farmer and smiled.

"I never shared it with anyone. It was to be a gift to our children and grandchildren. I decided before I died I wanted to leave a last goodbye message, hoping to make sure you all knew Jesus, but time slipped away from me and when I caught glimpses of Froton I knew my time was at hand, but I had unfinished business with my journal. I was trying to get to it, my Bible and a pen. I never made it to the dresser. But the Lord answered my prayers and here you all are – around me." Emile smiled.

The group was silent.

"Leah and Harold, Morgan, Joseph and little Caleb still live on earth. I worry over them." Emile murmured, glancing at Farmer. He nodded his agreement.

"Caleb ain't so little no more. He's ready for college," Clifton laughed.

This sparked another question in Janee.

"Uncle Clifton, what did you hear of Bernard? How is he?"

"Not a lot, Janee. Been awhile since I've spoken with your Ma and Pa, but last I heard Bernard was representing another actor."

"A woman?"

"No, a man, but he seemed to be gettin' along okay."

"Tell me of my parents."

"After you passed on, they bought a cabin at a lake named Arrowhead. They spend part of the year up there. Both of them took your death mighty hard. Your ma broke down at your funeral. Two weeks before your passing we buried Walter. It was too much for her – too soon."

"I asked Bernard for a small quiet farewell. I thought that would be easier on the family," Janee commented.

"Bernard tried," Clifton went on, but Rachel interrupted.

"It was a frenzy, Janee. Fans came from around the world. They lined the streets weeping and waving. Police had to escort us into the church - the media was everywhere - around - overhead! It became a nightmare for us all."

"I'm sorry," Janee shook her head in disbelief.

"Bernard was upset! It was out of his control."

"Janee, you were loved and adored by many people," Cynthia said, reflecting, "young and old alike. They came great distances to be there."

"They waved from the overpasses on the section of freeway the Hearst traveled. You were their star, Janee," David spoke to encourage her as he put his arm around her shoulder and gave her a hug.

"I'm nothing - Jesus is the Bright and Morning Star," she whispered.

The conversation went on to other topics, but Janee could not get a release from the feelings of sad regrets that filled her soul. She finally excused herself from the fellowship and went to her place to be alone. She was full of questions, which she had no answers.

"This is Paradise, Lord; I didn't think I would still have all these feelings. I look on all the wasted years of my life. Crowds came to my funeral - to see what? - A mythical character they watched on a screen - someone who wasn't even real to them."

"Did I make life better for them? Was my parting message of salvation for the crowds, an hour and a half of relief from their hum-drum lives - a few laughs here, some tears there. I lived a famous life that held no substance for them. My message was fame, fortune, drink, sex, and drugs, live for the day, be free, die young. I fear I pointed more people toward hell than Heaven! Lord, I am so ashamed!"

Janee's grief overwhelmed her. When compared to those around her she was a dismal failure. Janee threw herself across her bed - she could not stop crying from a breaking heart - until she felt a gentle touch on her shoulder. She looked up into the face of Him who loved her with a great love. She fell on her face on the floor holding His feet. She poured out her heart to Him, the one who had poured out His Blood for her!

"I did so little for you, Master!" she sobbed. "If only I had listened to You when I was little. I regret the worthless life I lived for you - I came to - Heaven - empty-handed."

Jesus tenderly reached down and lifted a sad and broken spirit to her feet. He led her into the living room.

"Look at your life pictures - behold!" as Jesus spoke, waves of love and strength began to fill Janee.

He took the picture of her and Tonya in the hospital off the wall.

"You led this one to Me," He showed her the picture.

"That's only one!" she cried.

"Child, what is the worth of a soul snatched from hell fire?"

Janee could not answer.

"Souls come into My Kingdom one at a time, and each is precious beyond price," the Savior went on. He pointed to a picture of a group of people, but did not remove it from the wall.

"This one is still unfolding and changing," Jesus commented. "All will be revealed in due time."

"Lord, I don't understand! Many of my pictures are people I don't know!"

"See this one, Janee?"

"Yes, it is a group of people in the church with my pastor."

"These have come to trust me."

"But, I didn't lead them. I don't even know most of them."

"Did you not provide the building for my people to meet in where My Word is taught?"

"Yes - but - that was - nothing."

The Lord smiled at Janee, and she knew in her heart the Master was pleased.

"Look upon these whom you loved and encouraged in your travels, my child."

Janee looked at the set of pictures Jesus was referring to. She saw men, women and children. Places and faces came to her in flashes - ones she had visited, others she helped financially, many she had witnessed to of the saving, healing power of the Savior. She was speechless!

"This one is mine because you were my faithful witness," Jesus pointed to a picture she had looked at often. She recognized her long-time friend, Paige.

"And all of these," Jesus took a picture from her wall and handed it to her. She studied it carefully.

"Lord," she discovered something. "What is this? This fellow, right here, used to be in that other picture. I'm sure of it! He changed pictures!"

"That is true, Janee, for he is now here," Jesus laughed. He was impressed with her eye for detail.

"You mean - these are dead - those over there - still living?"

"Yes," the Lord answered, "or you could say those are dying, and these are now alive."

Janee studied the picture she held, more closely but could make no connection with the large number of people contained in it.

"Lord, these are strangers to me."

"They know you," Jesus assured her.

"How? I never met them!"

"Shall we let them tell you?"

"What?"

"Behold, Janee, the joy of your labor!"

Jesus led her to the door, which He opened wide, revealing the very people in the picture standing - waiting in front of her home. The Savior motioned for her to go out into their midst. One after another they reached out to her with warm hands, hugs, pats and words of thanks from grateful hearts.

"I was in a hospital and heard of your faith on the news," one spoke through tears.

Others testified of articles in magazines they had run across or someone had sent them that told of her faith - and they trusted her Savior as their own!

"I heard your invitation on the Theon Dice Show and believed," many shared.

"I too watched that show with great interest," a voice boomed.

Janee immediately recognized the king who preceded her into Paradise.

"I am monarch king of the small nation of Krydostan. My Queen wife laughed at you and called you ill informed, but I listened not to your words but to your heart. I saw a love and passion there that drove me to seek a copy of your Bible and discover for myself what you had found. I embraced your Savior, but sadly my wife did not. We were both assassinated in a violent car bombing, but not before I gave Christian missionaries time to enter our country with the Gospel message. I am here to thank you for speaking out that day in the face of opposition and ridicule." Tears trailed down the proud king's face as he bowed to her and kissed her hand.

Janee was humbled and did an eloquent curtsy in return.

Radio and television interviews around the world had made Janee a true fisher of men and women. Her campaign to heighten AIDS awareness had netted hundreds - maybe thousands of HIV patients into God's Kingdom. The streets of Concert became filled with people pressing to meet Janee to tell her how she had in some small way set them on a path to find the Christ. Janee's heart overflowed for this multitude she had never known on earth, yet was a part of the reason they now enjoyed eternal life. Jesus looked on with a divine pleasure. Finally, the crowd dropped to their knees before Jesus Christ, giving Him the praise and glory for His great plan and sacrifice. They truly could sing of His love forever, and Janee remembered the words her Lord and Savior had spoken to her.

"I took the little you gave me and brought it to great things."

Chapter 65

It's a Wrap

When a day of shooting a movie was concluded, the director usually would call out, "It's a wrap." That meant work for the day was over. Janee heard that term used many times in her earthly life.

Janee felt death was a wrap on her earthly life. But for some reason, which Janee didn't understand, some phase of her Heavenly life was coming to a wrap. She knew it had nothing to do with Heaven because that was eternal, so she sensed it must be tied to earthly life.

'Perhaps it will be revealed at this time,' she thought when a gathering angel called her to the River of Living Water. She hoped it was Bernard; however, she wasn't quite sure enough time had elapsed for him to meet death.

She was thrilled, but not surprised to welcome her daddy into Paradise. Harold Stemper was overjoyed to see the family, saddened to discover his own mother and father were not there. He thought surely his father, who gave his life to save another, would be in Heaven.

"Only by grace through faith can one be saved. It is a gift of God, not of works," the Lord had explained, but that did little to ease the ache in Harold's heart.

Janee could hardly wait to ask her dad concerning Bernard's state. As soon as she saw an appropriate time she posed her question. Harold studied his daughter's face before he answered.

"You haven't heard?" he questioned.

"Heard what? All I know is that he took on another actor - a man."

Harold looked away, the telltale sign he was pressed to talk about something he wasn't sure he wanted to discuss.

Janee knew that look - she had seen it countless times.

"What is it, Daddy?"

"Paige divorced Billy," Harold spoke slow and in a low voice.

He nervously looked her in the eye to conclude.

"She married Bernard."

Janee was flabbergasted. She shouldn't have been, but this news came as a shock and knocked the props out from under her.

She was still struggling with it two years later in earth time when the family gathered to greet Leah. When the opportunity came, Janee sought out some alone time with her mother.

"Mother, I was shocked to find out Bernard married Paige - my best friend!"

"Are you jealous?" Leah asked.

"Of course not! There is none of that here."

"Bernard did not do well alone. He loved you deeply, but I think the loneliness overcame him," Janee's mother spoke with wisdom and insight.

"If he loved me so much, how could he marry Paige?"

"He said you told him you wanted him to remarry."

Janee threw her hands up with a short laugh, "I didn't really think he would!"

"Marriage vows say until death do we part."

"I know, Mother, I know! I'm happy for them! I'm sure Bernard is good for Paige - and she is - for him!"

"What's really on your heart, Janee? I know when you aren't saying everything."

"It's just - I pictured - Bernard waiting - like grandma did for grandpa - and Bernard and I would live in the same mansion - like them. Now it's all messed up. How is this going to work?"

"Well, Janee, I haven't been in Paradise long, but if I recall, the Bible says there is no marriage in Heaven."

"Yes, yes, but I wanted to be like papa and grandma. Look at how they are. If Bernard and I are like them - where does that leave Paige?"

"I can't answer that question Janee. You will have to ask the one who created and blessed marriage."

Janee did ask Jesus - many times she called her questions out to him, but for reasons only the Master understood, he was silent on the matter. Finally, Janee put it aside, trusting the Lord to work it all out His way. Much time seemed to drift by before a gathering angel called the family to the river.

Janee had a growing sense of excitement this time as deep in her soul she had the feeling this would be her husband, Bernard's, arrival. She recognized his gestures, his hair and hands, even from a distance.

"Oh! It is Bernard!" she cried for joy. Of all the family she had welcomed into Paradise, none compared to Bernard. As soon as Jesus pointed him to the family, Janee ran up the hill, her heart pounding. She was as breathless as a schoolgirl!

"Bernard! Bernard!" she screamed. "It's me - Janee!"

"Janee! Janee! I'm here!"

The two fell into each other's arms, falling to the ground - laughing and crying at once – excited to be re-united in Paradise.

Chapter 66

Epilogue

🌹

Janee was curious as to where Bernard's place would be. She was surprised, and very pleased to find out his home was next to hers.

Janee was quick to ask Jesus how this could work. She wanted her and Bernard to be like her grandparents.

"Only certain couples live together in their own place," Jesus graciously explained.

"Ones who love each other and are faithful to each other for a lifetime have the privilege that they truly became one! Like Farmer and Emile. But even so, love here in Paradise, in eternity is different from that of your fleshly life. It is not shallow, but is of a deeper kind that comes from the Father. No longer will you question who loves more or less for here love is equal in its perfect, purest form."

"Do you recall my Word, when the Sadducees questioned me to discount the resurrection? They made up a story of seven brothers. The first took a wife and he died so the second brother married her and died and eventually she was wife to all seven and she also died. They asked the question, 'whose wife shall she be in the resurrection?' Do you remember my answer? 'Do ye not therefore err, because ye know not the scriptures, neither the power of God? For when they shall rise from the dead, they neither marry, nor are given in marriage; but are as the angels which are in heaven."

"Concert is a city of people who have been married more than once. Some live in clusters in the tall inner buildings, others in houses, but all in harmony – like many musicians playing the same song on different instruments to make a beautiful melody. The third home here belongs to Paige."

Janee was concerned about that living situation. When she was alive on earth she would have pulled Paige's hair and clawed her eyes when she found out Bernard was in love with her – best friend. Then she remembered what Jesus had said. Love was from God and was equal. The love she now felt was just that. It matched exactly what Jesus had described!

Janee and Bernard sat in amazement after Jesus departed.

"His ways are so awesome," she murmured.

"They surly are." he answered deep in thought.

"Perhaps Paige will come soon. I will be glad to see her – my best friend."

Bernard was silent a long time. When he spoke, his voice was coarse with emotion.

"Janee, we lived ten lifetimes all crowded into one."

"Yes we did Bernard."

"I loved you as much as any man could have loved a woman. Our few married years were the best of my life."

"Yes they were, Bernard. Mine too!"

"I loved Paige also – but differently. I too look forward to Paige's arrival. I fear for her because conditions on earth were becoming more and more difficult and dangerous. But, I've been thinking Janee. Paige may not experience death. There was increasing talk among Christians worldwide that believe the rapture of the church is very near! Janee, our loved ones taken in the rapture will never know the sting of death."

Printed in the United States
200209BV00003B/73/A

9 781604 772173